First, everyone thou
thought he was crazy
er...

Four loud bangs on the front door interrupted them. "Open up, Jax. It's Captain Martinez."

Jax went to the front door and opened it. Two uniformed deputies brushed past him into his living room. One held up his hand and stopped Alex at the kitchen archway. The other stood beside Jax and put a hand on his arm holding him there.

Captain Martinez strode in with Jeremy close behind. Jeremy stepped behind Jax and slipped handcuffs onto his wrists. "Nothing personal, Jax." Then he tightened the cuffs one ratchet too far. "Not much."

Martinez walked up to Jax. "I'm sorry. I have no choice."

"Where did you find her, Cap? I want to know it all."

Christie stared bullets at him. "She was shot point blank, Jax, in an abandoned trailer down along the Potomac."

Jax had to turn his head. "Jesus, no."

"She had your engagement ring clutched in her hand," Martinez said, giving Jeremy a chin. "It was a forty-five, Jax. I'm betting yours."

"You thought the forty-five was my imagination," Jax said, but Jeremy jerked the cuffs and sent pain stabbing his shoulder.

"Richard Jax," Jeremy said, pushing him toward the door. "You're under arrest for the murders of Leo Carraba and Kathleen Cullen."

Murder, like history, often repeats itself. And, when it does, it's the worst kind of murder.

Detective Richard Jax was never good at history—but, after years as a cop, he is about to get the lesson of his life. Ambushed and dying on a stakeout, he's saved by Captain Patrick "Trick" McCall—the ghost of a World War II OSS agent. Trick has been waiting since 1944 for a chance to solve his own murder. Soon Jax is a suspect in a string of murders—murders linked to smuggling refugees out of the Middle East—a plot similar to the World War II OSS operation that brought scientists out of war-torn Europe. With the aid of a beautiful and intelligent historian, Dr. Alex Vouros, Jax and Trick unravel a seventy-year-old plot that began with Trick's murder in 1944. Could the World War II mastermind, code named *Harriet*, be alive and up to old games? Is history repeating itself?

Together, Jax and Trick hunt for the link between their pasts—confronted by some of Washington's elite and one provocative, alluring French Underground agent, Abrielle Chanoux. Somewhere in Trick's memories is a traitor. That traitor killed him. That traitor is killing again. Who framed Jax and who wants Trick's secret to remain secret? The answer may be, who doesn't?

KUDOS for Tj O'Connor

"O'Connor's debut in the increasingly crowded ghost-detective genre provides plenty of suspects and an eclectic mix of motives among the living." ~ *Kirkus Reviews*

"Tj O'Connor's debut novel, he gives readers an interesting premise and great characters…overall, a great start to a new series." ~ *Mystery Scene Magazine*

"…the murder mystery itself is a real puzzler, both for Tuck and the reader. A strong start to this series with more to come. As the mysterious Doc Gilley—who appears now and then to help Tuck stay the course—says at the end, "Do you think you can solve one or two little murders and poof, you're home free." ~ *Omnimystery Reviews*

"A spirited, suspenseful, and sensational new read, *Dying to Know* sizzles from page one. Brimming with humor, a mesmerizing historical subplot, and true-to-life (and death) characters, Dying to Know is a clever and captivating tale. With its to-die-for plot, inventive and imaginative storyline, and unforgettable protagonist, Oliver Tucker, the determined departed detective, *Dying to Know* is a dynamic debut from a fantastic new voice in the world of mystery." ~ *New Book Journal*

"It's got all of the elements you expect in any good mystery, betrayal, intrigue and murder along with family feuds, bitter rivalries, mob bosses, hired hit men and villainous industrialists. All that and a historical twist, another ancient mystery that unfolds concurrently with the main storyline. I found *Dying To Know* to be highly entertaining and completely addictive. It's a great debut into a competitive section of the crime genre and hopefully the first of many in this 'Gumshoe Ghost Mystery' series." ~ *Crimesquad.com*

"*Dying to Know* is a first endeavor for TJ O'Connor—a successful one. His interpretation of the life—or non-life—after life ends is worth reading. I don't plan on being murdered, so I probably won't be able to test his fantasizing. But it sure makes a good read. I look forward to book number two..." ~ *BookLoons*

"O'Connor does a wonderful job of conveying the feeling of urgency about the case as well as the frustration of Tuck adjusting to his new "life" on the other side. The story is so good that readers may tend to momentarily forget that Tuck is a ghost..." ~ *BookPleasures.com*

"*Dying to Know* is a fast-paced, humorous exploration of the netherworld and how life goes on after death. Inevitably crimes will be committed and, fortunately, Tuck will be on the job ready to investigate through the Gumshoe Ghost series." ~ *Mystery Maven Blog*

"Well, this book was definitely a surprise...Just when I thought the book couldn't get any more interesting, I was delightfully surprised. I say that because I am a huge Civil War devotee, and intermingling with not only Tuck's murder, but others', is finding out that the dig at the farm has to do with the Civil War and brings elements of that into the story. Yet when you dig deeper into Tuck's murder, you will find that things are not always as they appear, and what does appear may not be what you see after all. Read the book." ~ *Open Book Society.com*

ACKNOWLEDGMENTS

Being an author is a lifelong dream come true. While the stories, characters, and the countless hours bringing them to life is a solo endeavor, there are still many people to thank.

So, many thanks to Dave for the cover and guidance in all things artsy. For my daughter Jean for all her support, interest, and love. Thanks to the rest of my beta team—Gina, Nicki, Natalia, and the freeloaders, Laurie and Lindsay. A special shout-out to Terri, too. While she didn't play a role in this novel, her support and friendship has meant so much to me and my work. Big thanks to LP, Lauri, Faith, and everyone at Black Opal Books. Not just for publishing *New Sins for Old Scores*, but for the support, guidance, and interest along the way. My biggest homage has to go to Kimberley Cameron, my amazing and talented agent. She is a friend, a mentor, and a champion to me. You have no idea how much it means that you are in my corner.

When *New Sins for Old Scores* was first drafted, I had my pals Mosby and Maggie Mae to keep me company in the early hours and late at night. They are gone now, but never out of my heart.

New Sins
for
Old Scores

Tj O'Connor

A Black Opal Books Publication

GENRE: PARANROMAL THRILLER/MYSTERY-DETECTIVE/CRIME
THRILLER/POLICE PROCEDURAL

This is a work of fiction. Names, places, characters and incidents are either
the product of the author's imagination or are used fictitiously, and any re-
semblance to any actual persons, living or dead, businesses, organizations,
events or locales is entirely coincidental. All trademarks, service marks,
registered trademarks, and registered service marks are the property of their
respective owners and are used herein for identification purposes only. The
publisher does not have any control over or assume any responsibility for
author or third-party websites or their contents.

NEW SINS FOR OLD SCORES
Copyright © 2017 by Tj O'Connor
Cover Design by David Gesell
All cover art copyright © 2017
All Rights Reserved
Print ISBN: 978-1-626946-75-0

First Publication: MAY 2017

Published by Black Opal Books **http://www.blackopalbooks.com**

DEDICATION

For

McKayla, Kira, Jaiden, Rylee, Railyn, and Jack...

So far.

And for David—
if only your brush was as fast as your wit.
Thanks for everything!

Chapter 1

October, 2011, Loudoun County, Virginia:

*M*urder, like history, often repeats itself. When it does, that kind of murder isn't the byproduct of some psychotic break or an unintended emotional frenzy. That kind of murder is conscious and considered. It is deliberate.

History is full of that kind of murder.

Richard Jax was never a good student of history—but he knew murder well. He was more pragmatic than philosophical, and except for watching the History Channel and old movies, the past occupied little of his time. His time was reserved for murder and violence. Yet, history taught him a very important lesson—an axiom of parents with teenagers—that nothing good ever happens after midnight.

Jax wasn't married and had no children. But it was after midnight and he was alone.

He sat in the darkness, huddling behind his steering wheel, wishing for another cup of coffee. The book he'd brought along to read sat beside him half-read—biographies bored him even if they were about military heroes. He checked his watch—twelve thirty-nine a.m.—and then tapped the number three on his cell. And just as he had the last five times, he got voicemail. "You've reached Leo Carraba. Leave a message."

"Dammit."

It was mid-October and the night air was crisp with the musky-scent of fallen leaves. He was chilled and tried to brush his brown hair over his ears to keep them warm but it wasn't quite long enough. On a good day, he was one-ninety after a hardy meal—sturdy and strong. This was not a good day, or night, and he hadn't eaten since breakfast. His stomach growled and he considered driving to the convenience store three miles up the road for a slice of pizza and a coffee.

No, that would have to wait.

A vehicle turned off County Route 15, heading east toward him. It slowed near the entrance to the inn, turned off its headlights, and rolled down the long drive. Crunching gravel and the occasional glare of starlight off its windshield betrayed its path until it disappeared behind the two-story stone carriage house beside the inn.

Jax pulled his Glock-22 out and took a long breath, listening. His stomach growled again—this time from nerves.

"Who said, 'If strength were all, tiger would not fear scorpion,'" he said to no one. "*Charlie Chan's Secret*, 1935. Warner Oland played Chan."

Movie trivia calmed his nerves.

Slipping out of his car, he maneuvered through the darkness to the rear of the carriage house. The cold night air and half-empty trees would allow sound to travel and give him away if he were careless. At the corner of the building, he stopped and caught his breath before he inched to the corner and peered out.

There was a dark cargo van thirty yards away.

He froze.

Someone was heading toward him. He didn't see the threat but the footsteps grew louder with each gravel-footfall.

He flattened himself into the carriage house's shadows and didn't move. He tried to calm his breathing and hide the billowy clouds of breath.

What detective was murdered in the opening of The Maltese Falcon?

He took a step into the darkness.

The first shot took him by surprise. It seared fire and pain into his shoulder. He stumbled sideways, off balance. The second shot slapped his head sideways. He careened into the carriage house's stone wall. The ground rose and took him. Warm dampness spread over him, the ooze poured life onto the damp ground. He tried to rise but his legs wouldn't obey. He was unmoving but still falling— spinning away.

Footsteps stopped as someone hovered overhead, waiting, perhaps contemplating a third shot, perhaps waiting for him to bleed out.

A voice exploded in his head. "Get up. Fight back. It's not over. It can't be—fight."

Jax looked across the driveway. Someone lay on the gravel a dozen feet away. The figure stared wide-eyed back at him. Then, in strange, freeze-frame movements, the man stood. He looked around and brushed himself off. He gave Jax a nod, picked something up off the ground, and placed it on his head.

"Come on, Mac, fight. Don't quit. You can't."

Jax tried to focus but knew he was already done.

"Come on, Ricky. You have to do this yourself. Until you do, I can't help."

Jax watched the man across the parking lot as warmth pooled beneath his cheek. His vision blurred, and he wasn't sure what he saw was right—a cone of light engulfed the man—just him. Everything surrounding the light was black and murky. The man was tall and lanky. He wore a hat—a fedora—and a dark, double-breasted suit. Behind him was a 1940s Plymouth with wide, squared fenders and a dark green, four-door body.

Was he dead and Heaven was playing a film noir festival for his arrival?

"Shoot 'em, Ricky. Shoot or he'll kill you."

Jax looked up at the silhouette standing over him. The warmth that flowed from him minutes ago now left him cold and spent.

The silhouette raised his gun for the final shot.

"No," Jax grunted. "No—"

A flash of light. A deafening crack.

Silence.

"Miles Archer, Ricky," the fedora-man said, leaning over him. "Bogart's partner was Miles Archer—ya know, in *The Maltese Falcon*. I saw it open in '42 at the Capitol Theatre in DC. You did good, Ricky—real good."

Darkness.

Chapter 2

He's gone, Captain," one of the uniformed deputies said, lowering his radio. "Jax flatlined. EMTs said they rushed him into surgery but there's not much hope."

The words hit Captain Mike Martinez in the gut like a punch in a title fight. "Jesus, one night, two down."

Martinez had been a Virginia State Policeman his entire professional life and a Bureau of Criminal Investigations— BCI, Virginia's version of the FBI—commander for ten years. He couldn't recall the last agent killed in the line. He swallowed hard and walked toward the medical examiner kneeling in the middle of the inn parking lot beside the second body.

"Doc, talk to me."

The examiner didn't look up as he jotted notes on his iPad. "Single gunshot to the chest. I'd say it was close but not point blank—no burns or stippling. I'm guessing forty-caliber but I won't know for sure until I get to the lab."

Martinez knelt down and looked into the face of Agent Leo Carraba. "Good God, Leo, what happened out here?" He looked at his watch—it was closing on three a.m. "Jesus."

A female agent with short, dirty-blonde hair and wearing a blue and gray raid jacket waved at him from across the parking lot. She was in her mid-thirties but could pass for twenty-five. She walked to Martinez and held up an evidence bag. Her pretty face was tear-stained and her large, blue eyes were red and flowing.

"Cap," Agent Christie Krein said, choking on broken words. "This cannot be what it looks like."

Martinez jerked a chin at her. "We'll see. But until then, you have to get a grip. There's no time for emotions, Christie. Not even yours." He looked away. It damn well couldn't be what it appeared. If it were, he had a rogue agent and that meant his long career might be over.

"Jax fired one shot from his Glock—a forty-cal. I think I have his casing here." She held up the evidence bag. "Doc says Leo was hit just once."

"Yeah, I know. Looks like a forty. Tell me again how you found them?"

She took a long breath. "Jax was out of radio contact and not answering his cell. Leo called me for backup. By the time I got here, this is all I found." She looked down at Leo's corpse. "Leo got off two rounds. We bagged the casings."

Martinez threw a thumb over his shoulder at a team of crime scene technicians scouring the area for evidence. "And them? Have they found anything?"

"Not yet. But it's dark and, even with the floodlights, it's a hard search. We're going to need better light to find the two slugs that hit Jax. Both went clean through." Christie tucked the evidence bag in her pocket. She looked down at Carraba. She coughed and wiped her eyes. "Jax's car is parked up the hill there over behind those trees. From the trampled grass it looks like he was there a while. At some point, he worked his way down through the scrub trees and brush to here. No sign of more tracks so he came down alone."

Martinez turned and looked at the Explorer parked at the front of the inn. "And Leo pulled up there?"

Christie shrugged.

"Jax was waiting up there. Leo drove in here. Leo got off two shots before he got popped."

She nodded. "Looks like."

"Jax was hit twice."

Her face fell. "He took one through the soft tissue in the shoulder and one grazed the side of his neck. If we'd found him right away, he'd be okay. The wounds weren't all that bad. But, he'd been out here a while. EMTs said he went into shock. Guess he bled too much and—"

"Yeah, too much." Martinez turned to the medical examiner and jabbed a finger toward Leo. "Get some facts on the ballistics, Doc. Fast."

"Cap," Christie said. "There have to be more casing and slugs. No way Jax and Leo shot it out. I'll have the techs go over every inch of this place with metal detectors until we find them. There has to be more."

"I didn't know what these two were working on here. Did you?"

She shrugged again. "No. I asked and no one knew why they were here. They were off last night and today. Then Leo called me, all frantic. He told me to meet him here. He didn't say why. We all have a lot of cases. Could be any one of them brought them here."

"Did Jax say anything in the ambulance? Did the hospital get anything?"

"Yes, Cap, something weird." Christie flipped open her notepad and scanned through several pages. "He mumbled a name, 'Miles Archer.'"

"Who the hell is Miles Archer?"

"I've checked with everyone. Nobody knows the name. Nobody ever heard it. But I'll look through all their files myself."

"Dammit." Martinez's cell phone rang and he looked at the screen. "It's the colonel, just what I need. Christie, you take charge of the scene. Find me something. Find me anything. Internal Affairs is coming and all I have is, 'I don't know.'"

"Yes, sir." She watched as Martinez opened his phone. "Cap, I don't believe this. No way. You don't, do you?"

Martinez turned away. "Yes, sir, Colonel, I'm afraid that's correct. Carraba and Jax. But it's too soon to know what—"

Silence.

Yes, he knew his career was hanging in the balance until he caught the shooter. Yes, he understood no one could recall the last BCI agent killed, let alone like *this*. And yes, he understood the media would crucify him for any missteps.

"I understand. Yes, sir. It's possible, I'm afraid, that Agent Jax killed Agent Carraba."

Chapter 3

W ho played the leading dame in *Casablanca*?"
The overhead lights became too intense, and Jax forced himself to sit up and look around. His eyes wouldn't adjust and confusion whipped his thoughts into a tornado. He heard a familiar voice but couldn't find its source. His mouth was dry and his chest sore, but he managed to croak, "Ing—Ingrid—Bergman."

"Give the man a kewpie doll. That was easy, Mac. I figured you needed a warm-up. Hey, Ricky, you look like shit."

That voice was familiar but Jax couldn't place it. He struggled to clear his thoughts, and when he did, he knew the voice didn't belong. A strange euphoria gripped him and he wanted to get up and move around. He sat upright in a room—a stark, white room—void of anything except a constant high-pitched whine. The overhead lights were glaring down and their brightness hurt his eyes. When he tried to shield them with his hands, his arms wouldn't budge.

"Who—who are you? Where am I?"

"Right here with me," the voice said. "You gotta concentrate. If you don't, somebody might get the wrong idea and bury you. Come on, you got a lot to do."

Jax squinted until his vision gelled. Across the room, sitting with his long legs stretched out and his hands behind his head, was the fedora-man in a double-breasted suit.

"Ricky? You hear me, pal? How are you feeling?"

Jax shrugged. "Do I know you? And no one calls me Ricky. Where am I?"

"Some fancy-smancy hospital. I've never seen anything like this place before."

Jax blinked several times and tried to take in everything around him. The room was coming into focus and, for the first time, the hospital equipment and furniture surrounding him emerged. His chest hurt as though he'd gone twenty-rounds without blocking a punch. Bandages covered over his neck and shoulder and wires were attached to him everywhere.

"Hospital? Yeah, right. I got shot. Who are you? FBI?"

"Nope, not even close." The fedora-man laughed. "OSS, Ricky, I'm OSS."

Jax stared as his brain sorted the words. "OSS? Like from World War II?"

"One and the same."

As the precursor to the CIA, the Office of Strategic Services was founded by the colorful and bold World War I hero, Wild-Bill Donovan. The OSS began in 1942 to carry out espionage, sabotage, and general mayhem against the Axis Powers. Its operatives came from the military, civilian workforces, and even academia—the best and the brightest—and above all, the most daring.

None of that made any sense to Jax.

"Come again? OSS? That's not possible."

"And yet I'm here." The fedora-man stood and ambled over to his bed, extended a hand, but then winked and retracted it. "Sorry, right, you can't move, can you?"

Jax shook his head.

"Call me Trick."

"Trick? What kind of a name is Trick?"

"Irish." Trick bent over and peered into Jax's eyes as though examining him. Then he stood upright and saluted. "Captain Patrick McCall, OSS, at your service. You'll make it, Ricky. Trust me. But, listen, you have to keep me under your hat. Ya know, loose lips sink ships."

"Loose lips?" Jax looked around as the furniture and hospital machines faded. The room breathed in and out, and each time it exhaled, less clarity returned. "What's happening to me?"

"Easy, now. You have to focus." Trick stepped back. "You gotta follow the alarm. We have a lot to do, you and me, and I've been waiting a long time."

"Waiting for what?"

"Later. Just listen for the alarm. Listen and follow it. And remember—loose lips, Ricky."

"Trick? Trick—" A violent jolt sent Jax arching above the bed. He quivered and his chest ached. "Trick—"

The high-pitched whine returned, piercing him everywhere. He tried to push the noise away but Trick's voice called out. "Hurry, up, Ricky. They're giving up."

The whine became shrill and, although it hurt, Jax ran to find it.

&∽&∽

"Again—Clear."

Jax's body arched above the bed again as the gray-haired doctor pressed the defibrillator paddles against his chest for the fourth time. The cardiac monitor's alarm quieted and a steady, rhythmic *beep-beep-beep* replaced it. Seconds ticked by as man and machine waited for another false hope.

The rhythm held strong.

"He's back. Son-of-a-bitch he's back. That's the fourth time." The doctor wiped a pool of sweat from his brow and studied the data pouring from the menagerie of respirators, electrocardiograms, and other monitors half-circling Jax's bed. "I wouldn't have bet on him."

A tall, heavy-set nurse laid Jax's arm back down beside

him on the bed and rechecked the monitors, scribbling numbers and notes on a chart. "Doctor Chekov, his heart rate is stable. His pulse is growing steady. Blood pressure is returning and even his respirations are normalized. Will he make it?"

Doctor Chekov sat down on the chair beside Jax's bed. He looked at the nurse then at Jax and shook his head. "Kate, God knows he lost a lot of blood and he suffered from shock."

"I can't believe he's lasted this long, Doctor."

Doctor Chekov stood up and studied the electrocardiogram readout. "His physical trauma was not that severe. It was the blood loss. He was dead. Four minutes the last time, and two minutes both times before that. We brought him back. Something brought him back. I've never seen anything like this."

The nurse smiled. "He's a very lucky man."

"Lucky? He died four times, Kate. God knows what the lack of oxygen has done to his brain."

Chapter 4

The sun finished burning off the dew and warmed the mid-morning air. Leaves covered the ground and the remaining canvas was beautiful—a stark contrast to the grim mood settling over the Grey Coat Inn.

The Grey Coat Inn had been the center of violence before. It was built two years before the Civil War began when Leesburg was a small farming community. It sat along the Carolina Road, now State Route 15 and was often believed to have been a secret meeting place for the American Colonization Society—a movement of Quakers, Presbyterians, and Methodists trying to send freed slaves back to Africa. In the mid-1800s, it hid runaway slaves as part of the Underground Railroad.

During the Civil War, Leesburg changed hands more than 150 times, had seen its people divided, and felt destruction everywhere. The inn had not been spared—five times it was hit with cannon fire and twice had to be rebuilt. Now, after more than one-hundred forty years, the inn had claimed more casualties.

All around, teams of sheriff's deputies and BCI agents combed the grounds. A team of crime scene technicians reentered the Grey Coat Inn for the fifth time, carrying cameras and evidence kits. Near the carriage house entrance, they had set up a large metal table for staging evidence. Some technicians inched along the gravel parking lot and driveway while others searched the woods and field behind the inn with metal detectors.

"Dammit," Martinez said when Christie emerged from the inn's rear kitchen door. "We've got two BCI agents down—three gunshot wounds fired from two guns. Do we have anything inside? Casings, blood, anything? It cannot be just the two of them."

"Not yet," she said. "There's been activity inside, but that could be anything. It's hard to tell what's what."

"Who owns this place? It's been vacant for as long as I've lived up here."

"Quinton Properties Group."

Martinez watched two technicians working the tall grass behind the inn and one of them stopped, motioned to the ground, and stripped off his metal detector's earphones. The second technician dropped into the grass, searching. "They have something, Christie. Go check."

Before Christie took a step, the second technician stood, shaking his head.

"Damn." She turned away to hide the frustration sliding down her cheeks. "Cap, we've been over this place for hours. I hoped daylight would help, but so far, we don't have any slugs or more casings. It looks bad for Jax."

"The poor bastard just beat death only to face this. What's his motive? Why kill Leo?"

Christie turned away again.

"Agent?"

"Nothing, Cap. Jax doesn't—didn't—have a motive. He didn't kill Leo."

"That's not what the evidence says. Not so far."

"It's wrong."

Christie scribbled in her notebook. Martinez wasn't buying it. He'd known Christie Krein for years, and she was good at playing her cards close—very close. If his BCI unit had a chameleon, it was her. He'd sent her undercover a dozen times, and she'd always made the collar. Each time, her targets had been seduced by her deception. She was a tomboy one moment and a sassy vixen the next—fire and ice, leather and lace.

This time, though, Christie had a tell.

"Out with it, Agent."

"Cap, it's a rumor—that's all."

Martinez lifted his chin, watching her with eyes that could turn sand into glass.

"Jax wouldn't kill him over her, for Christ's sake. They weren't even married."

"Agent, I've got a dead officer." Martinez stepped close to Christie—uncomfortably close. "And another on the short list for the murder—if he survives. Cut the bullshit."

"It was Leo. I think he was, you know, seeing Jax's fiancée, Kathleen."

"What?"

She bit her lip. "For a month or so. I've seen Leo over there several times myself—Cap. I never caught them doing anything, though. Jax wasn't there. I heard a couple deputies commenting on it. I guess people knew—suspected I mean."

"Did Jax?"

"No, not as far as I know. Cap, it's just a rumor."

"Rumor my ass. You get to her and find out." Martinez noted the way she looked away whenever she mentioned Jax's name. "Agent, you haul her ass in as a material witness if she doesn't bleed the truth."

Christie nodded and turned to go.

"And Christie, keep this between you and me. Got it?"

Martinez watched her leave and spit on the ground. Just what he needed now—a motive—a bad, terrible motive. He spit again and watched a dark sedan parking behind the crime scene tape at the front of the inn. He walked over to the car as the driver's door opened.

A big man in an expensive suit got out of the sedan. He was six-four and two-hundred sixty pounds. He had sophisticated, intelligent African-American features framed with a touch of gray and round, wire-rimmed glasses. His suit was immaculate and his shoes shined like he'd bought them that morning. His glasses seemed small on his square, hard cheekbones. But unlike many big, powerful men, his movements were smooth and relaxed as he showed something to the deputy guarding the entrance to the crime scene and approached Martinez.

"Captain Martinez?"

Martinez tried sizing him up. "Who are you and what are you doing at my crime scene?" He wasn't in the mood for reporters or town councilmen trying to wiggle information from him. "You'll have to wait for a statement. I'm busy."

"I'm sure you are. And so am I." The big man extended his hand, not for a customary handshake, but with his FBI credentials. "Special Agent H. P. MacTavish—WFO."

"What's the Washington Field Office doing out here?"

"Can we talk? In private?"

Martinez waved a hand in the air. "We are in private."

"All right." MacTavish took a step closer. "You have a big problem."

"No shit."

"No, Captain, a *bigger* problem." MacTavish took a folded letter from his suit coat pocket and handed it to him. "Take a moment, please."

"If this isn't the lottery numbers or tickets to the Skins game, you're wasting my time." Martinez took it. "What does the FBI have to do with my crime scene, MacTav—"

"*Special Agent* MacTavish. Read."

Martinez read the letter and looked up when he noted the signature. "You gotta be kidding me? You feds show up now—right now—and drop this crap on me? This is pure bullshit."

"We didn't create this situation, Captain."

"Situation? Are you're sure about this?"

The big man nodded and retrieved the letter, folded and secured it back in his breast pocket. "No doubts."

Martinez turned away and watched his crime scene

teams digging in the field behind the carriage house. "I suppose the governor has been informed? And my chain of command?"

MacTavish looked at his watch. "The governor is being briefed right about now. But you will have no communication with him or your chain of command. It all goes through me."

"You're taking over?"

"On the contrary." MacTavish slipped off his glasses. "I'm at your disposal. The FBI will support whatever you need. I'm your new best friend."

"Wonderful."

Fifteen minutes later, Martinez finished briefing MacTavish. When he was through, he stood waiting for him to reciprocate. He didn't.

"Now, how about a little information from the FBI, Agent MacTavish?'

"Sorry, it's all I can share at this time."

"More bullshit."

MacTavish looked toward the inn. "Captain, I'm going to have a look around the inn myself. Maybe another pair of eyes..."

"Go ahead. I'm sure the Bureau taught you about crime scenes, so sign in and use gloves."

When MacTavish entered the inn, Martinez followed him to where the chief of the crime team—Chief Reggie Rogers—was on his knees examining the sidewalk. He excavated gravel and tiny spoonfuls of earth into evidence bags and he looked...*happy.*

"What do you have, Rogers?"

"I think it's bleach." Rogers handed a small paper cup of gravel to him. "And it's fresh—within the last twenty four hours, maybe less."

Martinez waved the cup below his nose. The pungent sting bit his senses. "Okay, it's bleach. What are you thinking?"

"This inn's been under construction, so maybe bleach isn't a big deal."

"It's blood," Martinez said, taking a second whiff of the stones. "It's sometimes used to clean blood from crime scenes. Perps have been known to use it, too."

Rogers hefted the shovel and nodded. "I'm going to take bigger samples. If there is blood here, we're thirty feet from where Leo was found. Nowhere close to Jax. Maybe we have another vic or maybe a shooter who got winged."

"Great find, Chief." Martinez returned the cup of stones to Rogers. "Listen close—very close. You run your tests and do what you do. But no one—not one other person—gets the results before I do. And then no one I don't authorize. You got that? No one."

"Sure, Cap. Sure. But you better change your search for the slugs."

Martinez turned and looked back at the crime technicians searching the field. "You're right. We lined up Leo and Jax's bodies. If either of them shot at or were shot from this direction where the bleach is, the trajectory is all wrong." He pointed to the north side of the carriage house wall. "The bullet's path would be over there."

"That's about right. There's a wood pile beside the stone wall that aligns Jax's body with this spot. The way the ground slopes, it makes sense the round impacted in that area."

"Good work, Rogers. I'll check that area myself."

Chapter 5

The creak of the apartment door's doorknob sent alarms rumbling through Antonio's body. The short, thin, Salvadoran jumped to his feet and yanked on his jeans. He dug under his bedcovers for a dirty sweatshirt and stuffed his naked feet into his cowboy boots. The last things he grabbed were the short-barreled .38 revolver and his cell phone from the cardboard box turned nightstand.

He punched cell keys and listened. "You've reached Leo Carraba. Leave a message."

"*Madre de Dios.*"

Antonio listened at his bedroom door. The doorknob creaked again. He rooted through his jean's pockets until he found a fast food receipt and dialed the number he'd scratched on the back. "*Por favor…*"

The call failed. His hands were shaking. He closed his eyes to think—he failed to add one number to each of the last four digits of the emergency telephone number. He adjusted for the code and dialed again.

"This is Jax. Leave a message or call back. You pick."

Something moved outside his apartment. Then silence. A long pause and the lock jiggled. Seconds later, the door creaked open and closed.

"No, no." Antonio started into the hallway but a figure passed by at the end of the hallway in the living room and stopped him cold. "Get out. Get out of my house." He raised his gun, backed into his room again, and slammed his door.

Light footsteps—almost unheard—stopped at the hall entrance. A metallic snap of a weapon being charged sent tingles up his spine. Another few steps and Antonio jerked two shots off through his door into the hall.

"Go man, go away. I didn't do nothing. Leave me be." He looked around his bedroom—nowhere to run. "*Por favor*. I do nothing. I say nothing. Leave me be."

A five-round burst from a submachine gun rattled through his doorway, splintering wood and sending splinters flying everywhere—yet the sound was more the destruction than the weapon itself. The assassin had come prepared, with a silencer, to kill with stealth.

Antonio dove for cover beneath his bed even as several pieces of splintered wood cut his face.

Silence.

A second burst began shredding the door until a jagged hole was formed in the door's center.

The sound terrified Antonio as much as the bullets—the metallic clacking and the dull, muffled shots.

Another burst.

"Go. You go." Antonio kept his .38 pointed at the doorway and rolled to the window. He was on the third floor with nothing to break his fall but concrete and the short, scrubby fir trees beneath his window.

Another burst from the submachine gun made Antonio's decision.

He fired twice into the hall and twisted himself out the window. He would rather chance a few bones than to rely on the assassin running out of ammunition.

For the first time in many months, Antonio Cavallo made the right choice.

Chapter 6

Martinez tossed another rotting log onto the pile he'd created beside the carriage house. He worked with slow, deliberate care, examining each piece of wood for any sign of injury. Earlier, he'd searched the carriage house wall and found no signs of bullet holes, ricochets, or blood splatter. Now, he worked the woodpile Rogers suggested.

Rogers was a smart man.

A gnarled log, stained brown and black by rot and age, had a piece of bark scraped away, showing a clean, new score. He examined it. It wasn't a gouge at all but an entrance hole with a corresponding exit hole on the other side where something penetrated the log and landed in the earth behind the log pile.

A bullet hole.

Martinez looked around to ensure the team of technicians was still traversing their search grids. The second team worked the parking lot and driveway and they were focused on their work. He calculated where the bullet holes aligned themselves and pulled out his pocketknife to excavate earth. It took him fifteen minutes and an eighteen-inch cavity of dirt before he found it.

A bullet.

"I'll be damned," he said to himself. "A nine-millimeter."

He stood and slipped the slug into his pocket.

"You find something, Cap?"

Martinez looked up to see a young agent standing behind him near the corner of the carriage house. The agent had tight, black curls and heavy, thick eyebrows. He was thin and wiry, and his arms looked too long for his body. "Jeremy, are you finished inside?"

"Yeah, Cap." Jeremy Levin looked down at the woodpile and nodded. "Techs are checking again, though. What you find?"

"Dirt." Martinez closed his pocket knife. "I thought I had a bullet hole in a log, but it was dry rot."

"I'll get a shovel and help."

"No, I have a better assignment for you." Martinez pulled out his billfold and handed him several twenties. "Go find some coffee and sandwiches for everyone. We've been out here for hours. We need to give everyone a break."

"Come on, Cap, me?"

"I'm hungry, Levin."

Jeremy looked at the tall, heavy-set detective watching them from the inn's second floor window. "I'll send Finch. Deputy sheriffs are expert at coffee runs, even old crusty farts like him."

"Fine, just make it fast. And Levin," Martinez said, looking at him square in the eyes. "Don't get into another pissing contest with Finch. He might be old and grumpy, but he's a marine and can kick your skinny ass."

"Like to see that." Jeremy laughed but Martinez didn't join him. He added, "I get it, Cap. Team work."

As Jeremy ambled down the driveway toward the row of cars, Martinez slipped the 9-mm slug from his pocket and wiped it off with his handkerchief. The bullet was in fair shape and its ballistics might be able to be matched to a source. "Evidence," he said to himself as he wrapped the slug in the handkerchief, pocketed it again, and walked past the table where the few pieces of processed evidence were laying.

He never stopped.

Chapter 7

Jax woke feeling foreign in his surroundings. His room was dark. The normal *beep-beep-beep* from his monitors was silent and the bank of lights and LED readouts was gone. Sitting upright, he found he was no longer tethered to the cardio equipment and felt good enough to slide his feet over the bed and stand.

A wave of nausea came and went before he dared take a few steps. On his third one, he faltered and dropped to his hands and knees, trying to keep from retching his gelatin and chicken soup lunch. His head spun as he eased his way to the bathroom and splashed cold water on his face.

When he stepped back into his room, he wasn't in Kansas anymore.

❧❧❧

Allied Airstrip Somewhere North of London, 1943:

Jax bed was gone and, in its place, sat a green Willy's Jeep. There was the pungent smell of aircraft fuel in the air. The coughing of a prop aircraft trying to start its engines reached him and it wasn't startling or unusual. He turned and followed the sound into the darkness where men worked on an old military cargo plane.

A few yards away, just outside what should have been

the ICU nurses station, stood a shack with two men sitting inside the open door. One of the men was in an olive drab Army uniform he recognized from the scores of World War II movies he owned. The other wore civilian clothes and he held a radio headset against his ear, dictating something as the soldier took notes. The two worked in tandem for several minutes until the civilian put the headset down. The soldier handed him a page of notes and waited.

Whatever they'd heard, they were in agreement with because the civilian slapped the soldier's back and strode out of the radio hut. Oddly enough, he walked straight to Jax and lit a cigarette, offering him a puff when he stopped.

"The order came from Pettington just now. It's on for tonight. Are you ready?"

"Do I have a choice?" Jax said, but as the words came out, he didn't know where they came from or what they meant. It wasn't his voice and his thoughts were foreign, too. He was a bystander, perhaps a player someone else controlled. "Give me the details, Johnny. And let's get a cup of joe before I go. Maybe some doughnuts."

"Oh, boy, are you taking the plunge." Johnny lifted the notepaper up to catch more light from the radio shack. "You're on a '47 in two hours, out of our secondary strip. You're taking the long way south to throw off the Jerrie spies watching the main strips. Then it's across the channel around Morlaix. They'll drop you south of Châteauroux. Our Resistance friends will be there."

The Resistance? None of this could be happening, and yet it was all very real. "Can you make my contact a blonde with Greta Garbo's legs?"

Johnny laughed. "I think I can, pal. Your contact is Abrielle. She'll be waiting at the drop. If you're not there by oh-three-hundred, you're on your own until tomorrow night. The code is—and pay attention, the Resistance will shoot if you louse this up—'It is too dark to be out walking.' Her response is, 'Yes, but the moonlight is enough to see. It is beautiful.' Got it, Captain?"

"Roger, Mac." Jax's problem was that he *did* get it. He just didn't understand how. "Johnny, when I get back, you better knock off all the 'captain' malarkey. You're givin' me a bad reputation."

"Sure, but you come back first. We've lost two agents on this mission already. So, no sightseein' on this one, okay, Trick?"

ⲉⲝⲉⲝ

Beep-beep-beep.

The lights flashed on and someone took his arm. He tried to rise but the spider's web of wires and tubes once again had him confined. The nurse was changing his IV bag and looked down at him.

"Agent Jax, did you have another nightmare?"

He nodded but couldn't get the images out of his mind. For a second, he still smelled Johnny's cigarette and aircraft fuel.

The nurse touched his arm. "My, my, you look like you've seen a ghost."

Chapter 8

O kay, folks. It's been over a week. We're no closer to solving this than we were that night. Let's think fresh." Martinez sipped his coffee and leaned back in the conference room chair at the end of the table. He looked around the small room and at the three tired, frustrated faces. Jeremy sat at the far corner of the table. Christie had her back to the wall, away from the table, sipping tea.

Then there was Deputy Dylan Finch, the lone Loudoun County Sheriff's detective assigned to the unit. He sat opposite Jeremy in the corner of the room. Martinez didn't like having an outsider around, even another cop. But the Loudoun Sheriff had insisted on Finch's assignment to the BCI major crimes unit eight months prior. If they were in his county, he wanted a seat at the table.

"Come on, come on." Martinez waved toward the two chairs. "It is what it is, people. Jax came out of the coma two days ago and IAD interviewed him last night. He can't remember much except he claims Leo had an informant who sent them to the inn. Until we have more, this is an undetermined shooting. He'll be out of the hospital soon. The search warrant on Leo's place turned up nothing except dirty laundry. We've waited on Jax's place until now. I was hoping for more evidence one way or the other but we can't wait any longer."

Everyone exchanged glances.

Christie spoke first. "Cap, will internal affairs give us any leeway? Or are they gonna jam it to him while he's still in the hospital?"

Martinez nodded. "For now, they're letting us work the case. I called in a favor from the commander. But it'll run out soon. He's the one who knows what happened and the doc says he's got some kind of memory loss."

Christie had been on the team since Captain Martinez took over the BCI Task Force three years earlier. She was tenacious and smart, and above all, she was tough. The look on her face now, though, was anything but tough. "Cap, I've got nothing new on Kathleen and Leo."

"What's that?" Finch tipped back his ever-present Marine field cap, hiding his gray hair. "Kathleen and Leo? What's that about, Christie?"

"Christie, tell them what you told me," Martinez said,

Christie looked around the room. "Kathleen and Leo were involved. She didn't deny anything. She planned on telling Jax and was gonna give his ring back. That's where Leo was before he was killed at the inn."

"Did Jax know?" Finch asked.

Christie shrugged. "Kathleen thought so. She said Jax was acting odd."

"There's a motive," Jeremy said. "He and Leo got into it."

"Screw you, Levin," Christie snapped. "Jax didn't murder Leo."

"Maybe not murder, but he shot him. Ballistics proves that," Jeremy snapped but then he eased his tone. "How long have you known?"

She looked down. "A few weeks. Anyway, I've got her statement and she's devastated. She left out of town for a couple weeks. She promised to call me, and I have her cell."

Martinez watched Finch fold his arms and grunt. "Something to add, Finch?"

"Nope." Finch was an outsider and the oldest cop in the

room by a decade or more. Some resented him for being a local. Some resented him for being older. "That's okay, Cap."

Captain Martinez just resented him. "Out with it."

"Well, Captain, it's not my place, but you asked. This Kathleen was way outta Jax's league and everyone knew it. She comes from family money and made four times his paycheck in DC, right?"

"What's your point?" Jeremy said.

"Just sayin', it was a crazy match anyway. Not as crazy as Leo and her. Screwin' and marrying are two different things."

"You're being an ass, Finchy," Christie said. "But you're not wrong."

Martinez held up a hand. "I don't care what—"

"It seems to me, Cap," Finch continued, boring his eyes into Martinez's, "that if you knew Jax was being screwed over by his partner and rich girlfriend, someone should have said something. She wasn't worth it, and we're supposed to cover each other's back, right?"

Touché. "I didn't know. Not before, anyway."

Christie looked at Finch. "You're right, Finchy. I went to see Jax when he came out of the coma. He isn't sure what happened. IAD came in so I didn't push anything. The nurse says he has nightmares and calls for someone named 'Trick.'"

"Trick?" Martinez asked. "Any idea about that?"

Christie shook her head. "No, Cap. But look, while I was there, he was spaced-out on the meds. While I was talking to the nurse outside his room, I heard him talking to someone. Nurse said he does that a lot."

Martinez thought for a long time with all eyes locked on him. "I'll talk to IAD. Let's keep running whatever leads we can. I'll go see Jax later and see what else he can tell us."

Christie smiled and leaned back. "Thanks, Cap. I'll tag along if that's okay."

"Ah, boss, there's not much else to chase without more from Jax," Jeremy said. "Except maybe the scene. What did Rogers get? He told me he found something by the back door of the inn. The reports should have been here days ago."

Martinez opened the large folder on the desk in front of him. He scanned over several pages before closing it. "As you know, we've not recovered the two slugs that went through Jax. So, we can't match anything to Leo's gun. Jax's gun fired the shot that killed Leo. That you all know. Jax shot Leo."

Jeremy started to speak, but when he saw Christie glaring, he leaned back, silent.

"I'm running down a couple leads from Quinton Properties who owns the inn and has for a decade or more," Finch said. "I hit a dead end on them last week. The number from the corporate records is an answering service, and no one is returning my calls."

Christie turned to Jeremy. "Tell 'em about Archer."

"Oh, that." Jeremy laughed. "Miles Archer. You know, Jax mumbled that to the EMTs. There's no reference in any case files we have. But it is a name from an old 1940s movie. "

"Miles Archer?"

"Come on, Cap," Finch said, cracking a grin that drew everyone's attention, "it's from *The Maltese Falcon*. Jax loves all those old movies and trivia."

"Trivia?" Martinez's scowl told the others he wasn't amused. "Jesus, you'd think he might give us some evidence instead of that bullshit. Glad you think it's funny, Finch."

"You staties don't like to have any fun, do you?"

"All right," Martinez said. "Let's go back over everything we've done and see what we missed."

"We're chasing our tails," Finch said.

"Chase them again. And remember, everything comes through me before it goes anywhere. And I mean anywhere.

I'm trying to keep this tight because the commander is giving us some time to sort it out ourselves and I don't want a mess."

Everyone nodded but Jeremy. He sat with arms folded, watching Martinez.

Christie asked, "What about the feds?"

Martinez frowned. "Yeah, Agent MacTavish will be back around. He's sticking his nose in deep. No one talks to him without my permission. Got it?"

Grunts and grumbles answered him.

"All right everyone," Martinez said, standing. "We're done. Christie, you're with me later. I'm going to talk to Jax and see if there's anything he remembered since IAD."

"Yes, sir."

Everyone stood.

"A word before you go," Martinez said to Finch.

Jeremy and Christie filed out the door.

Martinez didn't mince words. "Finch, you know it's nothing personal, but the sheriff and I don't quite see eye-to-eye about your assignment here. I'm sure you're a good cop, and—"

"I'll tell him you said so. Thanks, Cap."

"You do that." Martinez tapped the table. "Look, I don't want to hear about Agent Carraba and Kathleen in the rumor mill around the sheriff's department. Got it? A dead agent is bad enough without—"

"Got it, Cap." Finch walked to the door and turned around on his arrival. "A dead cop is bad enough without the rest of us knowing you staties stood by while his pal screwed him over. Yes, sir, Cap, I got it loud and clear." He left the room.

Martinez stared after his wake. Finch was right, of course, and that irritated him more than his insolence. Martinez was not a simple-minded man, nor an intellect or sophisticated man. But he had been a careful man all his life. The business before him now worried him. He cursed and opened the case folder in his hand. The top page made his teeth clench and for a moment, he thought about ripping the folder to shreds. It was a memo from Chief Rogers. If any of his people learned too soon what he knew, it would make him a liar and raise the alarm.

He couldn't afford either.

He slipped the memo out of the folder and scanned it again.

> *Captain Martinez, please call soonest. Chemical analysis of crime scene debris outside rear door revealed the presence of sodium hypochlorite or common household bleach. Further examination pending. Should have final results by end of day.*

"Dammit, Jax." He crumpled the memo, stuffed it in his suit coat pocket, and slammed the folder closed. "What the hell have you gotten me into?"

Chapter 9

I cannot believe Leo's dead." Jax lay back on his bed, still entangled in a plethora of wires and monitors. He looked at Martinez. "What happened, Cap? Do you know anything yet?"

"Not much, Agent. We're hoping you can fill in some more blanks. IAD said you were pretty out of it yesterday and couldn't recall much. How about today? Take us through what you do remember."

"Leo was supposed to meet me that night at nine-thirty. He never showed. A bit before one I think when a cargo van drove up. I went down to check it out and some bastard shot me—*twice*. Somehow, I got a shot off before I passed out. At least I think I did."

"You did," Christie said. "Jax, you shot Leo. Do you remember that?"

"What? No. No. I didn't shoot Leo. He wasn't there. He never showed up." Jax's eyes darted from Christie to Martinez and back. "What the hell are you saying, Christie? You guys think I killed Leo?"

"Yes," Martinez said. "Maybe by accident, but you shot him, Agent. Try and remember. Tell us what happened. Dammit, Jax, give us something."

Jax closed his eyes as tears welled and spilled down the sides of his face. He stared at the ceiling, shaking his head in slow, painful denials. "No, Cap. No. This guy came out of the dark and popped me. He came right up on me. I saw someone. I think there was a witness. I saw him there. He was lying on the ground and got up, yelling at me to shoot."

"Who, Jax? Who was there with you? Was it Leo?" Christie slid her chair in closer to him. "Try to remember. Can you describe him?"

"I don't know. Wait, yes." He closed his eyes and concentrated. "He was a tall guy in a suit, an old suit—and I mean *old*. And he wore an old hat, a fedora I think."

"A fedora?" Martinez asked. "Like a gangster hat?"

"Yeah, I guess."

The room lights flickered and that voice jingled in his head again. This time, he didn't hear the voice as much as he *thought* it. *Hey, Mac, we talked about this. You gotta keep this under your hat, Ricky. I warned you.*

Jax looked around but didn't see Trick anywhere in the room.

Christie took his hand, following his freeze-frame glances. "What's wrong? What are you looking for?"

"Trick."

"Trick? What Trick?" she asked. "What are you talking about?"

Jax closed his eyes. "Oh, no. It's happening again."

"Cap?" Christie looked back at Martinez and shrugged. "Maybe we should—"

"No. Jax, there was no sign of any witness. Leo was killed with your gun. Think, man. Was it an accident? Did Leo shoot you and you defended yourself?"

Jax tried to sit up but the bullet graze across the left side of his neck sent spikes of pain stabbing through his muscles. He winced. "Leo didn't shoot me, Cap. The perp did. He tried to end me and I got him first. That's it. That's all there was."

"Why were you there at all, Agent?" Martinez asked. "Why did you call Leo there that night?"

"I didn't. It was Leo's plan. He had a snitch who said something big was going down there. He told me to meet

him. Look, I already went through this. I have no idea what
it was. Leo said meet him. I went. Leo didn't show. That's
it."

Martinez looked at him and frowned. "What about Kathleen, Agent? Tell us about Leo and Kathleen."

"I haven't seen her yet and I'm worried. In fact, the
nurse said she hasn't been to see me. What the hell is going
on, Cap? What are you saying?"

"Jax," Christie said in a low, hushed voice. "Leo and
Kathleen—did you know they were...well, involved?"

"Involved?"

"That's why he was late that night."

"No. No way."

"Yes. I'm sorry. She admitted it to me." Christie gave
him a few moments. "Did you shoot Leo because of her?"

"I didn't shoot Leo. Why won't you listen?" Jax snapped
his head around and winced from the pain. The faint image
of a man walking toward him in the darkness stabbed into
Jax's mind. The gunman shot him twice and moved in for
the kill. That voice had prodded him, demanding he fight
back. He got off one shot and defended himself. But he
hadn't seen the face. He hadn't heard a voice. Not the gunman's anyway. Had it been Leo? "No, it couldn't have been
Leo. It couldn't."

"Jax, I spoke with Kathleen the morning after you were
shot," Christie said. "She confessed to me. Everything. She
said you knew. Jesus, she threw your ring in the trash and
asked if you killed Leo because of her. She said you called
Leo to the inn that night. Meeting there was your idea."

"No. She's wrong. You're all wrong." Jax leaned back
and stared at the ceiling. "You have to be."

The nurse stood in the doorway and barked at Christie
and Martinez. "Enough. He cannot take any more right now.
Out."

Christie ignored the nurse. "Kathleen told me Leo was
with her that night He left after midnight. He called me to

meet him at the inn. By the time I got there, he was dead
and you were down. He shot you twice and you defended
yourself. That's how it went down, Jax. Right?"

Jax closed his eyes. "No, not Leo."

"It was self-defense, Jax," Martinez said, tapping the bed
frame again. "Tell me that. Tell me it was self-defense."

Tears poured down his face and the row of monitors and
readouts began complaining. "No, I didn't kill Leo."

"Stop this," the nurse commanded. "Everyone out.
Now."

Christie stood and leaned over Jax, whispering, "Hold
on, Jax. That bastard was screwin' Kathleen. I get it. I'm
here if you need to talk." Then she stood and went to the
door.

"Why would Kathleen tell us the meeting was your
idea?" Martinez asked. "Why would she lie?"

"I don't know. But I didn't kill Leo." Jax didn't know
why. He remembered little and saw less that night. But he
knew he didn't kill Leo. Even if he'd caught them together—his best friend and fiancé—he didn't think he could.
"Cap, I'm gonna talk to Kathleen as soon as I'm outta
here."

"No, you're not." Martinez stood up. "She's a witness
and you're not seeing her. If she has anything more to add
to her statement, Christie will get it. You stay away from
her."

"No, Cap, I can't. I gotta find out what's going on. I—"

"Enough, Agent." Martinez went to the door beside
Christie. "You're suspended, pending the investigation.
Your gun and badge will stay in my safe. I'm sorry, Jax. I
really am. Be thankful you're not under arrest. And Jax,
stay away from Kathleen."

"And if I don't?"

"Then you're through."

∽∾∽

The moment the room door closed behind Martinez and Christie, Trick walked from out of the bathroom to the side of his bed. "Hey, sport, you don't look so good. Can I do anything?"

Jax closed his eyes twice. Each time he opened them, Trick was still there. "It's you. I was hoping it was all the meds I'm on. Who are you? What do you want?"

"Gee, thanks a lot, pal. I saved your life a couple times." Trick tipped his fedora onto the back of his head and dropped down in the chair Christie had moved beside the bed. "And that's the thanks I get?"

Jax just stared.

"Look, Ricky, I don't want anything. Not much, anyway. I'm here to help you. And you are back here to help me. It's one and the same thing."

Jax's eyes narrowed on him. He tried piecing together the hazy memories that had accumulated over the past week. "You're trying to make me believe you're an OSS agent from the '40s? What could you do to help me?"

"It's simple," Trick said, winking as he faded. "But get better first. Some knucklehead killed your pal and almost killed you, too. Another knucklehead killed me. It just so happens that was in 1944."

"If you're not a dream or the painkillers, then maybe I *am* nuts."

Trick slipped into nothingness. "You're not nuts, Ricky. You're alive. And that's what's important. I know stuff and you can do stuff. That's what it's all about."

Chapter 10

Memory loss and confusion is natural," Doctor Chekov said as Martinez jotted in his notebook. "Agent Jax had serious blood loss, trauma, and of course, he was revived four times."

Christie looked back at Jax through his observation window. "Is he in any danger?"

"No," Doctor Chekov said. "His body is recovering well. The shoulder wound was clean and, in a week or so, he can go home. He's on the mend."

"His body?" Martinez looked up. "What aren't you saying, Doc?"

Doctor Chekov followed Christie's gaze into Jax's room. "We don't know what to expect from him. His brain underwent serious challenges during his trauma. He could have more challenges ahead. Or, he could be just fine. I've seen it both ways."

Christie frowned. "Like what challenges?"

"He could have memory loss that does not recover. It would not be unusual for him to have anxiety or adjustment issues. The brain is very complex. His emotions could deal with Agent Carraba's death in many ways. He could choose to repress those memories, or he could react in different ways."

"Delusions?" Martinez said. "Like this fedora-wearing witness or him hearing things?"

Chekov nodded. "Yes, that is possible. People deal with trauma in many ways. The extremes are that he could face the reality and adjust well, or he could change his memories to make it more palatable to his mind. The brain is capable of many self-defense mechanisms."

"So, he could be lying and not even know it." Martinez made a note. "Wonderful."

"It's too soon to know, Captain Martinez. Give him time to adjust. But I warn you, his behavior may not return to normal right away."

As a nurse drew the curtain closed on Jax observation window, Christie looked at Chekov. "How are we gonna know what he remembers is real or not?"

"Ah, now that's your line of work, Agent Krein. But I can provide you with a psychiatrist if that helps. Agent Jax will, perhaps, require some degree of counseling."

Martinez closed his notebook. "Terrific, Doc. Agent Jax could a killer who doesn't remember killing, or he might be nuts. I don't like either possibility."

Chapter 11

There was a witness, Ricky."

Jax sat up in his hospital bed and eased his legs around off the side. He looked across the room as Trick appeared by the window. "I wish you'd knock or something. You've been scaring the shit out of me for two weeks, popping in and out of my room all the time."

"Sorry, sport. I'll keep that in mind."

It had been two weeks since the shooting and Jax was ready to go home. The first week was a blur of dreams and blank spots. He was in and out of consciousness and a coma after blood loss and shock took their toll on his body. For the past week, Jax had been poked and prodded, had undergone every manner of test, and had been confined to his room for bad meals and few visitors. Among those was Christie, who visited each evening without fail. Between nightmares plaguing him, forcing him to relive his final memories from the inn, and Trick's constant visits, Jax was less and less sure what Trick was at all. Was he imagination or apparition?

Over the past two days, the hospital began weaning him off the meds. Slowly, he'd become clear and steady. He slept more, focused better, and was coming to terms with his situation. At least, being a suspect in his partner's murder. Still, he was no clearer about the existence of Trick McCall.

"Tell me about this witness, Trick, if you're real. If you're bullet holes and painkillers, leave me the hell alone."

"That's not very nice. I got something for you. Something good, too."

"Oh?" Jax went to his room door, peeked outside to see if anyone had been close enough to hear, and shut the door. "What is it?"

"In there," Trick pointed to the hospital-white nightstand. "Inside the drawer."

Jax pulled out a manila envelope that contained his wallet, some coins, house keys, a pocket knife, cell phone, and a string of amber beads that Jax didn't recognize. "What's this?"

"That skirt dropped it off when you were sleeping."

"Christie?"

Trick smiled. "Yeah, Christie. They didn't make coppers like that when I was around."

"I'll bet." Jax dumped the bag's contents on his bed and picked up the beads. The beads, about thirty of them, were strung on a leather tie. Each bead was a half-inch in diameter. The leather tie formed a loop. One end was fastened together by a flat piece of decorative amber—the other end had no amber.

"What's this?"

Trick winked. "They're called worry beads."

"Worry beads?"

"Yeah, sport." Trick moved beside him. "The Greeks invented them, but they're all over that part of the world. They're like a rosary, sort of."

Jax picked up the string of beads and spun them with his left hand. "What am I doing with them?"

"I told you I had something for you. Let me show you."

As Jax held the string of beads out, Trick gripped one end.

Lightning.

A jolt of electricity stung Jax. His breath caught deep in

his chest. The room lights flickered and he felt cold and damp. For a moment, lethargy gripped him and he tried to lie down on this bed. He never made it. The room folded and was gone. Darkness and silence filled its space…

☙❧☙

A second later, a breeze dusted him with the musty smell of fall leaves and he saw his breath billowing from his lips. He turned to get his bearings and found himself standing in the dark beside the old green Plymouth at the Grey Coat Inn

"Trick, what's happening?"

"Just wait. You're a detective. Watch and detect."

Jax looked at the car and recognized the Plymouth from the night he was shot. The carriage house was behind him and the inn just ahead. He understood where he was. It was nighttime—nearing one o'clock. The dark cargo van was parked near the inn's rear door. He turned back around. Someone was there, just beside the carriage house. The figure moved in the shadows, coming around the corner of the stone building.

It was him—Special Agent Richard Jax—moments before he was shot.

"Trick, what the devil?"

"Just watch."

Jax watched as the other him—the Richard Jax from two weeks ago—took his last step before the first gunshot punched into his shoulder and sent him staggering backward. The second spun him sideways and put him down.

"No," Jax yelled. He tried to run forward to his own defense but he was frozen. "Stop. No."

Trick grabbed his arm and held him fast. "You can't stop it. It already happened. You're here to learn, not change things."

"I don't understand, Trick. Why are we here?"

Trick pointed to the Richard Jax lying on his side, staring back at them. "Watch."

The gunman appeared from behind the van and approached the fallen Richard Jax. He moved in slow, deliberate steps. His hands were out in front of him. His gun at the ready. The gunman stopped just a few feet away and waited.

The fallen Jax stared at Trick and nodded. When the gunman raised his weapon to finish him, the fallen Jax fired one shot and was spent.

The gunman reeled and staggered back to the van, falling onto the van's front fender and sliding to the ground just feet from the inn's rear kitchen door. He coughed and called out but his words were mangled. The inn's rear door banged open and two figures emerged. They knelt down by the gunman and spoke in hushed, urgent tones. One ran back inside and the other picked up the gunman's weapon and eased across the parking lot toward the fallen Jax.

"Help me, please, help me." Jax's voice was faint and fading. "Please, I'm a cop."

The figure stopped and looked down at Jax, waving the gun as though it was awkward and unfamiliar. Then, in an unexpected move, the figure knelt down and pulled Jax's gun away, tossing it back onto the ground.

"Father—father. Come, it is policeman." The voice was a woman—a young woman—more a teenager. "Father, come now."

The girl leaned over Jax and pulled something from her pocket, stuffing it beneath Jax's shirt and pressing hard into the gushing wound. "Still. Still. Do not move."

Jax tried to resist but the girl persisted, pushing his hands away while she tried to stop the bleeding. On the fourth attempt to calm him, she took something from her pocket and placed it in Jax's hand, cupping it in his fingers and whispering something that soothed him.

There was a flurry of movement from the inn and two men ran to the girl's side. One of the men, a stocky, muscular man, snatched the young girl's arm and yanked her backward. As he did, the van's lights snapped on, and Jax saw a dark image on his forearm. It was a scar or a tattoo. A crude blemish that resembled a dagger.

"Jesus," Jax said to Trick. "Who are these guys?"

The man dragged the young girl away from Jax's body and retreated to the van. She resisted, but was no match for the scarred man as he forced her into the vehicle. A second before they closed the door, she turned and looked away from the bleeding man on the ground and right at Trick and Jax.

More people emerged from the inn, boarded the van, and sped off toward Route 15.

The kitchen door opened again and another figure emerged, standing above the gunman but all the time looking across the parking lot at the fallen Jax.

"Son of a bitch," Jax whispered. "The girl tried to save me."

"She did save you," Trick said. "She slowed the bleeding. Without her, you would have died. Well, died for good that is."

Jax took a step toward his fallen avatar but still could not move. "There were others there that night. And someone stayed behind."

Trick placed his hand on Jax's shoulder. "Time to go."

The lights burst on and the hospital room walls emerged. The October scents were replaced by the smell of forced air and disinfectant.

"Who was it?" Jax asked steadying himself. "I didn't see who stayed behind."

"That's the point."

Jax looked around the room. "I'm getting out of here, Trick. I have things to do."

"Yes, we do. What's our first move?"

"I have to find a killer and prove myself innocent. But first, I have to go see a few people."

Trick shook a finger at him. "Good idea. Except the doctor won't like that, Mac. You ain't ready to leave. They think you're traumatized and seeing things."

"They're right," Jax said, finding his pants behind the door. "And maybe those things will help solve my case."

Chapter 12

W hat the hell is it with Martinez?"
Christie was sitting with her back to the interview room door when Jeremy barged in. She
spun around and slapped her phone closed. "Jesus, Levin,
don't you knock?"

"Sorry." Jeremy walked in and stood over her. "Who
was that?"

"An informant. I'm trying to find a lead on Leo's informant. I have some contacts inside the Latino community."

"What makes you think Leo's snitch is Latino?"

Christie lowered her voice. "Never mind. Now, what
were you saying about Captain Martinez?"

"Jesus, he just chewed Finch and me out for asking about
the forensic report from Chief Rogers."

"What?"

Jeremy leaned on her desk. "All Finch did was ask if
Rogers was done with his report, and the captain went off.
We aren't allowed to make a call or interview anyone without his approval these days. Since when? He always tells us
to work together. You know, smarter as a team, and all that
crap."

She laughed. "We are. He—"

"No, you don't get it. Listen, there's a lot wrong going
on here. I haven't said anything, but at the scene that morn-

ing after Leo was killed, I heard Rogers telling him he found bleach near the rear door at the kitchen. Bleach is used—"

"I know. Bleach is used to clean up blood."

Jeremy nodded. "Yeah, right. That made both of them think someone else might have been there."

"That would mean someone else was hit. The number of shots and wounds wouldn't match up anymore. What else?"

"Ever since that FBI guy showed up, Martinez is not himself. What's going on? Since when does the cap bow to the feds? These past two weeks have been weird."

Christie leaned back in her chair and watched Jeremy. He was a rookie agent with little more than five years on patrol when he made the BCI cut. Why he wanted to be a cop mystified her.

He'd earned his law degree from Princeton when he was twenty-three. He spoke Spanish, Arabic, and Hebrew. He could have walked into any law office in any city and demanded six-figures without a blush. Yet, he rode empty stretches of Virginia highways until the BCI called him up. One day, she would ask him why.

"Jeremy, the cap has his reasons. Don't question him."

"He's lying, too." Jeremy's face hardened. "He got Rogers's lab report last week. Rogers found something, and he's been keeping it from us."

"Did you read it?"

"No."

"Then how do you know?"

"Because when I asked the cap last week about the report, he said, 'nothing yet.' But before I asked, I called Rogers. He told me to go to the captain and that he wasn't allowed to discuss his findings. *His findings*."

She watched Jeremy settle back in the chair. "So? Cap said he was the focal point. Everything has to go through him."

"Dammit, Christie. If there wasn't anything in Rogers's

report, then why be so damn secretive about it? And why keep it hush-hush so long?"

The rookie had a point. "Yeah, well, the cap has his reasons. After all, a cop is down and another may be responsible."

"Yeah, I get it. But I figured with the captain acting so weird and all, hiding the report would piss you off. You know, with the way you feel about Jax."

Christie glared at Jeremy. "What's that supposed to mean?"

"Come on, Christie. You gotta be upset."

"I'm pissed off, Jeremy. That's why I'm doing things my way." Christie ran her fingers through her hair and let a pinky open another button on her white silk blouse. Then she winked, transforming her round, blue eyes into a flirtatious trap. "How do I look?"

"Hot as always." Jeremy's eyes followed her finger. "What are you doing?"

She stood up and dialed a number on her cell phone.

"Hello, Chief, it's Christie Krein. I was calling to see if you still wanted to buy me lunch? Maybe dinner?" A few moments later, she smiled. "Sure, that would be fine. Call me when you're through."

She hung up.

"Are you sure about this?" Jeremy asked.

"Rogers has been after me to have dinner with him for months. I think tonight is good. But he said he had a meeting with some doctor who wants to interview him. He got his name in the papers on this case and now he's a forensic-celebrity. So maybe afterward, I'll get a peek at that report."

Chapter 13

It was nine-thirty at night when Jax arrived home. Since leaving the hospital, he'd learned the hard way that being a right-hander in his new left-hand world was going to be difficult. His right arm was in a sling and, even after two weeks of healing, some pain meds were still necessary. Until his shooting, the dexterity in his left hand was limited to cutting a good steak and clutching his motorcycle. Now, zipping his pants, buttoning his shirt, and driving were skills he'd have to relearn. He smiled to himself as he manipulated his front door lock and deadbolt without dropping his keys.

The success vanished the moment his front door opened and the silence greeted him.

There was a problem.

His alarm system was off. The window blinds were closed. The room lights didn't switch on as he entered his house.

Someone had been inside.

He stood in the middle of the living room and turned in a slow circle. He hated closed blinds and loved the natural light and fresh air. Someone had turned the room lights off at the switch, disengaging the motion sensor when they did.

In his den, he found his French doors open. They should be closed. Several photographs and knickknacks were misaligned on his bookshelves instead of spaced side-to-side with even intervals. A stack of old bills and mail was scattered in his wooden filing tray, not aligned and stacked and grounded to one corner of the tray. Even more obvious was his ten volume American History collection with three volumes out of order. A volume of Mark Twain sat upside down.

Jax was not an obsessive compulsive, but Phyllis, his housekeeper, was. She spent extraordinary time on details and Jax had given up trying to curtail her a year ago. If she had been the last one in his home, no open doors, misaligned bric-a-brac, and misplaced books would exist. Her compulsion would forbid it.

But Phyllis's OCD was not the real reason he knew his home had been violated. Raymond Chandler and Agatha Christie tipped him off. Jax's leather collection of the American crime novelist's work sat beside his collection of Christie. Chandler occupied the top right corner of his bookshelves, Christie the left. Behind the mystery writers hid his Smith and Wesson Model 1911.

The .45-automatic was gone.

Whatever and whoever had happened to his home hit him hard.

He stood in the middle of the room with a vacant, disbelieving shadow ebbing into his thoughts. In the past two weeks, he'd strayed within inches of death, become a suspect in his best friend's murder, and had lost his fiancé. Perhaps worse, he was visited by a phantom who was either a product of his shooting or his personal guide to a rubber room.

He fought back tears. "Damn you, Martinez. Cut me some slack."

Jax retrieved a bottle of expensive Tennessee bourbon from the living room bar and poured himself a very tall, very straight glass. Halfway through it, he fumbled with his jacket pocket and retrieved his cell phone.

He dialed and listened for Martinez to pick up.

"Captain Martinez."

"You son of a bitch. I want my forty-five back."

There was silence for a long time. Then, "Agent Jax, watch who you're speaking to. I am still your commanding officer."

"Screw you."

"Where the hell have you been? Doctor Chekov called me in a fit. He wasn't going to release you until next week. You belong in the hospital. He—we are worried about you. Where have you been for three hours?"

"Early release program for future cons." Jax sat his drink down. "Where's my forty-five?"

"Enough, Agent. You listen to me. We searched your house a week ago. We didn't seize any guns."

"You left my alarm off." Jax slumped onto a straight chair at the dining table and pushed his bourbon away. "Are you being straight with me about the gun?"

"Your alarm was not activated when we got there. Levin made a note in his search report." Martinez mumbled something to someone at the other end before continuing. "You stay right there, Jax. I'm sending Christie over. Don't touch anything. This may be another crime scene."

"Maybe? My whole house is a crime scene."

"Christie's on her way. Anything missing?"

"They took the Smith but left my big screen, my computer, and my sound system. So forget calling it a routine break-in. The place was searched and with great care to hide it. If it wasn't you, then who?"

"Jax, listen to me. Stay put and don't touch anything else. Do you get me?"

"Fine. Just tell Christie to hurry."

While he waited, he fixed a pot of coffee and sat at the table. For two weeks, Leo's loss had eaten away at him. Jax's friends and colleagues seemed unsure if he'd killed Leo over some affair with Kathleen. An affair he neither knew about then, nor believed in now. Yet despite his near-death experience and the loss of his best friend, her absence from his hospital room—and her leaving town—said it all.

"Time to grow a pair, Jax," he said to himself. "She's gone."

Deep down, Jax knew losing her did little damage to him. In the time they'd known each other, including their torrid engagement, she never quite fit. He loved her. At least he told himself he did. But theirs was not a soft, comfortable romance. It was, in words he'd hidden from her, a *convenient one*.

"Hard luck, Mac. She's a louse. Good riddance, I say."

Jax looked up and found Trick sitting across the table. "Yeah, maybe. But who asked you? You're not real. You're—"

"Dead." Trick tossed his fedora on the table between them. "Yeah, yeah, I know. I'm your drugs and all that malarkey. I've heard all that, sport, and I'm telling you, I'm not any of that. I'm here."

Jax closed his eyes and wished the fedora-man away.

"Nope, still here, Ricky."

"But you can't be. You can't."

"Well, 'can't' is one thing, but 'am' is another. And I *am*."

Jax retrieved another cup of coffee but wanted the bourbon on the bar.

"Stick with the joe," Trick said. "You're gonna kill yourself mixing booze and the pills. And trust me, dying isn't for the meek at heart."

"Stop." Jax held up a hand. "You're telling me you're a ghost?"

"What did you think I was? I told you, Captain Patrick McCall, OSS. I was born October 1, 1916. Died on October 22, 1944."

Jax stared at the man—the image—sitting at his dining room table. He was young, perhaps thirty-something, but doing the math told him Trick was twenty-eight. His fedora and dark, three-piece suit didn't look right either, the fit and wide lapels belonged in an old late show Bogart movie.

"Okay, Captain McCall, how'd you die?"

"It was war, Ricky. People died."

"What battle?"

Trick watched Jax get up and wander the room, glancing back at him now and then but trying hard to avoid eye contact. "Look, Ricky, OSS guys like me didn't often do battlefield stuff, you know? We were here and there and worked in small teams behind the lines. Let's just say I was killed in 'The Battle of the Paperclips.'"

"Paperclips?" Jax laughed. "What is that supposed to mean?"

"Never mind. That'll all come out in the wash. Right now, though, we have to focus on you. You have to let that dame go. She's yesterday's news. Let's find out who killed Leo. Maybe we start with the witness."

"Witness? That wasn't just a dream?" Jax went to the window and peered out into the darkness. "Christ, I'm standing here talking to a ghost. Maybe they're right. Either I killed my partner, or I'm nuts."

Trick picked up his fedora and slipped it on the back of his head. "Then I guess you're nuts, Ricky."

"Thanks. Coming from my imagination that makes me feel better."

"It should. 'Cause I was there and saw it all. You didn't murder your partner."

"Not killing him makes me nuts?"

"No, but you only gave me two choices." Trick winked. "Either you killed your partner or you're nuts. I'm giving you the benefit of the doubt."

Chapter 14

Shortly before eleven p.m., MacTavish found the crime lab annex in the basement of the old Loudoun Hospital annex a few blocks from downtown Leesburg. Everyone was gone but the night security officer and a few doctors working late hours. The basement level was dim with the occasional overhead bank of fluorescent lights on at hallway intersections.

The cheap plastic name plate beside the heavy wood door read, "Virginia Bureau of Criminal Investigation (BCI) Crime Scene Unit."

The door was locked and MacTavish knocked three times.

No one answered.

He knocked again, this time his colossal fist pounded so hard the name plate vibrated beside the door.

Still no one came.

The big man took out his cell phone and hit redial. He'd called Chief CSI Rogers three hours earlier and made an appointment to meet him. Rogers had insisted on waiting until the late hour and MacTavish had agreed. Now the cell phone rang twice and a faint rendition of The Who's "Who are You?" reached him from inside the door.

Rogers was inside.

MacTavish looked around. No one was about. He unzipped a small, leather case from his jacket and went to work on the lock. Forty-five seconds later, the door opened.

There were no lights on inside. No noise.

MacTavish tugged his Sig Sauer out and pushed open the door, careful to stay behind the door frame until he saw the room open before him. As a rookie agent in New York, he'd failed to follow that procedure six months out of Quantico. The result landed him in the hospital with three pellets from a twelve-gauge shotgun in his hip.

Still no one.

"Rogers? It's Agent MacTavish. Are you here?"

No Rogers.

MacTavish hit redial and a second later, followed The Who farther into the office, passed the lobby and waiting room, down the tiled hall to the rear offices. Inside, he answered The Who's question. It was Chief CSI Reggie Rogers.

Rogers lay face down behind his desk. There were no outward signs of trauma No bruises, no ligature marks, no gunshot wounds. He had a pencil still in his right hand. The papers and folders on his desk were disheveled and strewn across the desktop and floor. To the untrained eye, Chief Rogers might have had a massive heart attack and fallen from his chair while working. The angina pills spilled on his desk blotter would confirm a pre-existing condition and an autopsy would no doubt draw the same conclusion.

MacTavish examined the corpse, taking his time under the fingernails, inside his nose, and beneath the hairline. Just inside Rogers's left ear, he found a small white corner of tissue paper and used a pen to retrieve it. There was a tiny, almost unnoticeable trace of blood on the corner and MacTavish knew how Roger's died.

Chief Rogers was murdered.

MacTavish examined everything within reach of the desk—drawers, file cabinets, and a dozen files on Rogers's desk. When he turned on the computer and was greeted by the blue screen of death.

He was too late. Someone had wiped the computer and destroyed all its files.

He tried to rebuild the scattered pages from the last file Rogers worked on. It was the Grey Coat Inn file. After ten minutes sorting the scattered pages, MacTavish determined the inch-thick file was complete except for the two things he wanted most to see—Rogers's chemical analysis of the gravel and dirt samples and whatever else Martinez secreted from the crime scene. If he had read the BCI commander right, and he wasn't wrong often, Captain Martinez was keeping secrets from the scene. Those secrets, and perhaps more, might be in Rogers's files.

MacTavish flipped open his cell phone and tapped the number two. It rang once.

"You have something for me?"

"Yes, sir, I do. Rogers has been eliminated. The files are gone—all of them, including the computer records."

"There is no evidence? How about backup files or other records?"

"I cannot confirm that yet," MacTavish said, scanning the room again. "But considering what I see here, there won't be any trace."

"Do you need assistance?"

"Yes, sir. I need a team. We need to handle this before Martinez finds out."

Silence. Then a grunt. "They're on their way. Thoughts?"

"None. It might be any of them—or none of them. But I think the former."

"Well, not any of them. Agent Jax is in the hospital. I don't see how—"

"No, sir. Jax has made a remarkable recovery. He checked out of the hospital a couple hours ago."

Silence.

"Sir?"

"Your backup team will be there within the hour. Secure the office and, if necessary, seize it as the FBI would do.

But secure it one way or the other."

"Yes, sir."

"And understand, Mr. MacTavish, I expect you to do your job well. I don't want anything, or anyone, from the Grey Coat coming back to haunt us."

Chapter 15

L ove what you've done with the place," Christie said, walking around the pile of couch cushions and broken bric-a-brac scattered throughout the living room. "I thought the captain said it was just your gun?"

"No, no," Jax said, waving his hand around the room. "I did this. The house wasn't touched. Someone got my forty-five out of my office, and that's all I know right now."

"You did this?"

"I lost it, Christie." Jax's mouth tightened and he looked down, surveying the remnants of his tantrum. "Just for a few minutes. I'm fine now. This was all the stuff Kathleen gave me."

"Well, better it's her stuff." Christie gave him a thin smile. Then she came to him and gave him a long, warm embrace. "It's gonna work out, Jax. I promise."

He looked at her and was thankful to have someone *real* to talk with. Someone flesh and blood who wasn't the ghost of a World War II spy.

"Thanks, Christie. We've been friends a long time and I know I've never opened up to you."

She smiled. "That was Leo's job. He was your partner."

"Yeah, well, thanks for being here. It's good to have someone to talk to."

"Good." She straightened a chair up and sat down. "I've got techs on the way to look for prints. We can't contact

Rogers. He's probably buried in the lab. Are you thinking a break-in?"

Jax pointed to the alarm panel on the wall. "I didn't see any signs of one."

"Are you sure you alarmed your system?"

"Yes, of course I did. I always do." When Christie looked at Jax, he knew she was unsure. "Check for yourself."

"All right, let's see."

Jax watched her start with the alarm panel mounted on the wall around the corner from the front door. It took her a moment to cycle through the various buttons and codes, but she found the menu of reports. Three entries later she had what she needed. Next, she went to the front door and examined the door lock and frame. They were both intact with no more wear and tear than expected. There was no splintered wood or gouged metal. There were no signs of a forced entry.

Jax snorted but she ignored him.

He followed her outside where she found the same. Nothing. She took a small penlight from her pocket and checked each of the windows and the crawlspace access panel. It took her twenty minutes to circle the house before she returned to the living room and flipped her penlight off.

While Jax retrieved coffee for them, she disappeared into his office at the rear of his house. He called out, "Satisfied? No break-in, right?"

Christie returned to the living room and slumped into a tall-backed chair. "Nothing. You're right. No signs of forced entry. Someone came in the front door with an alarm code and house key."

"And you're surprised?" Jax knew she doubted him. Her eyes were fixed on his and she was trying to hide a frown with a fake, pasty-smile. "Someone came into my house while I was at the inn that night."

Christie leaned forward. "Are you saying someone knew

you were out of the house on a stakeout or working late that night and broke in?"

"Is there another explanation?"

Christie looked down.

"What? Go ahead, Christie, say it."

"Jax, Doctor Chekov is worried about you."

"So I've been told. I'm fine."

"Jax, listen to me. Your alarm code was activated that night at six thirty-three p.m. A couple hours later at about eight forty-five, it was deactivated using your code." She moved close and put a hand on his arm. "No one broke in."

He knew what she was trying to get at. "So you think I came back in."

"I didn't say that."

"You might as well have."

Christie squeezed his arm. "Where have you been all afternoon? You checked out this afternoon. Where did you go?"

"I went to the library. Look." He pointed to a stack of books on the entranceway table. "I checked out some books on the inn."

Christie went to the table and sorted through a dozen books. They were histories of Leesburg and two on the Grey Coat Inn and other landmarks. "Okay, where else?"

"Nowhere. Here. Why?"

She waved a hand in the air. "Nothing. So, you say you were at the inn all night, Leo was, well, elsewhere, and someone came through your front door. Maybe it was Leo or Kathleen."

"I *say* I was there? Is that a question?" Jax looked at her and tears welled in his eyes. He wasn't an emotional man, by any means, but events were crushing him. He went to her and embraced her long and close—something he couldn't recall ever doing before.

"Jax, look." She watched his eyes. "The captain is worried. The doctor says you could be...you know...traumatized by all this. Maybe have memory issues."

"I am traumatized, Christie. What's that got to do with anything?"

She hesitated. "I checked the firearms records. There's no record of you owning a forty-five."

"What?" He thought about that. "Oh, yeah. I bought it at a gun show when they didn't have to do all that paperwork or anything. It was a private buy. Why?"

"And your alarm. Come on, Jax." She looked at the alarm panel and then back to him. "The alarm was turned off four hours before you were shot."

"Right. And someone must have gotten in and stolen my gun."

"Jax, you can't account for your whereabouts, remember? No witnesses. You could have turned off that alarm, right?"

"I didn't."

"But your memories are unclear." She looked at him and patted his arm again, this time taking his hand. "I believe you, Jax. I do. Whatever happened on your stakeout went bad. I believe you."

He stepped back. "Christie, you're the first one to believe I was on a stakeout and not ambushing Leo. Do you believe me? Do you?"

"I do." Her voice was a whisper as she leaned in, kissing him soft and long on the cheek. "You're a handful sometimes, but I don't think you murdered Leo. Not that I could blame you."

Jax had often wondered about Christie—about her interest in him. When they'd met five years ago, he was alone and might have welcomed it. But their timing never gelled. She was too busy trying to prove her right to be in the BCI when word she had friends in high places reached the team. Sometimes, good looks, brains, and a non-male anatomy were a tough sell. As their friendship grew, she paid him more attention and often met him for drinks or lunch. But, when Leo introduced him to Kathleen, Jax stopped noticing

Christie. Soon after, Christie made her dislike of the fiery-redhead well known to anyone who would listen. Twice when she and Jax were alone on stakeout, Christie had suggested he dump her and move on.

Now, Jax wished he'd listened to her. "Thanks. I need someone to believe me right now. Drink?"

She cocked an eyebrow. "No, and you shouldn't either. Meds and booze don't play well."

"Yeah, I know, I'll be seeing ghosts. I'm having coffee."

She smiled and brushed his cheek with a slow, lingering finger. "Like your new friend, Trick?"

"Don't get me started."

She changed the subject. "Who has your house key?"

"My housekeeper, but she would never leave it un-locked, and Kathleen and Leo. They all have the alarm code, too. Leo crashed here a lot, and Kathleen...well, you know."

"Very convenient for everyone."

"You never did like Kathleen, did you, Christie?"

"No." Her face softened when Jax turned away. "Jeez, I didn't hide it. I'm sorry anyway. And about Leo, too."

Four crime scene technicians appeared on Jax's lawn, and he called them into the house. Christie took over and began barking her orders and sending them scurrying throughout the house. In minutes, they were dusting for prints and examining each room for evidence. Two of them began on the front door and alarm key pad. The other two began in Jax's office.

"Sit tight, Jax. I have to make a call, okay?" She headed for the front door.

Ten minutes later, while the crime techs were dusting and examining his bookshelf, Christie came back into the living room and spoke with the crime scene technicians.

"Anything, Christie?" Jax asked.

"No. Too many prints, but no signs of forced entry or anything. So far, we have nothing."

Jax's spirits fell. "Great. Now I look even more nuts for Martinez."

She tipped her head toward the kitchen where he followed her. There, she turned around and folded her arms. "Jax, I have to ask a few things, okay?"

He dropped into a wooden chair beside the small breakfast nook table. "Go ahead."

"And, Jax, you've gotta be straight with me." She slid her chair in close. "And you have to forgive me for it, too."

"Forgive you? Oh." He rose but she grasped his hand and guided him back down. His eyes met hers. "I didn't murder Leo. I love—loved—Kathleen. But I wouldn't kill anyone because of her. I'm a cop, dammit. You should understand that, Christie."

"Good." She shrugged. "But that's not the question I was going to ask. Is anything—any little thing—you're into that might have caused all this?"

"Into?"

"That night, Leo doesn't show on time, and you shoot someone trying to kill you. It's Leo. About the same time, someone broke into your house. No one knows anything about Leo's snitch. Then, poof, he's vanished. These events are not random, and they are not coincidence."

Jax looked down at their intertwined hands. He didn't pull away. "I'm not involved in anything, little or big. If you're asking if I did anything to piss off the wrong people, that's the job. If you're asking if I'm *involved* with the wrong people, you already know the answer, or you should. The answer is no."

Christie sat back watching him. She had an uncanny ability to read people—an ability better than any cop he knew. Professionals called it body language or kinesics. Christie called it being a woman.

Jax called it being a witch.

"Okay, Jax. I'm gonna tell you something that stays right here, okay?"

He nodded.

"I got a little juice here and there. You know that. Anyway, I found out the FBI is watching our every move. And it's not just this case, either."

Jax mouth dropped. "What for?"

"No one knows and the Bureau isn't sharing. I'm trying to find out but every time I ask, or my friends ask, we get our fingers slapped. Something's up."

"I don't know, Christie. Every time the Bureau sees headlines, they show up. Then if something goes wrong, they pin it on us locals. Maybe they're snooping around because of Leo."

"Maybe Leo's murder is connected to the Bureau's investigation." She looked away. "Maybe Leo was—"

"Don't go there, Christie. He was my best friend. He was my partner."

"Don't go there?" Christie jumped up. "Are you kidding me? He sent you on a stakeout so he could go screw your fiancée. He was late—very late—and you got shot. Was he setting you up? Did he come in here for something? You were supposed to die. He got wacked and you're holding the bag."

"No. That's not how it was. You're saying Leo went bad? You're saying he was into something that I didn't know about. That none of us knew about. No way. Not Leo."

"Maybe. Right now, all this makes you look like you're 'into something.' So if not you, maybe him."

"Bullshit."

Christie went to him and grabbed the front of his shirt. "Face it. Leo went bad one way or the other. He was screwing you over, right? And then there's someone coming in here looking for something of Leo's they thought you had? Or was it Leo that night before he went to the inn? You tell me you're clean. Maybe Leo wasn't. Maybe someone figured you were involved with him. So you had to go, too."

"Are you done?" Jax looked down into her eyes and the blue was cold as arctic ice. "That's a lot of maybes."

"If you have a better theory, I'm listening."

He didn't. "Has anyone been to Leo's house?"

"Yes, the morning of the killing. First me and then the cap and Rogers's team searched his place."

"Anything?"

She shook her head. "Dirty laundry and old take-out."

"There's one person who knows why Leo was going to the inn." Jax tapped his head. "We have to find his informant. He could be in danger, too."

Chapter 16

Chief Rogers died from a heart attack?"

Martinez stopped sipping his coffee and looked over the paper cup at the big FBI man sitting across the desk. Since returning from the Crime Lab Annex, Mac-Tavish had been unspoken and brooding. He was a hard man to figure out, but then again, the feds played that game too much—silent, mysterious, sneaky. "Yes, he had a heart problem for years," Martinez said.

MacTavish emptied his coffee. "Interesting."

"Interesting, why?"

"Quid pro quo."

Martinez laughed. He'd seen the same movie. "Sure, you first."

"I don't think Rogers died of any heart attack. And neither do you." The words got Martinez to his feet but Mac-Tavish patted the air and waited for him to sit back down. "Relax. What about his files? The crime scene evidence? Have you accounted for it?"

"We're working on that. So far, there are no discrepancies. But we had to bring in another crime team. They won't know for sure for a while."

"It's a homicide, Captain. We both know that." Mac-Tavish stood up and retrieved the coffee pot across the room, holding it up to offer Martinez a refill. "That just added to your problems."

"How the hell do you know Rogers was killed? Do you know something you're not saying?"

"I don't know any more than you've told me. Well, except for my imagination. But Rogers's dying is connected to what I'm working on."

Martinez slid back in his office chair. "You want to explain that to me?"

"No, I don't. I told you, Captain. I have my own investigation. I'm not screwing around with your ego or jurisdiction. Now, tell me about Agent Levin."

"What?"

"Levin. He's some hotshot lawyer working as a state cop. Why?"

"Screw you." Martinez glared at the FBI man and folded his arms. "He likes being a cop. What of it?"

"And Finch? A retired marine pushing a second retirement? He's on your team. Why?"

Martinez's face went red. "Because Sheriff Michaels wanted him on the team. He's a good detective and local. That works for me."

"Krein? Does she work for you the same way?"

"You son-of-a-bitch. If you're implying—"

"I don't imply things, Martinez." MacTavish took a long sip of his coffee. "Tell me about the ballistics on Carraba's hit."

"Hit? I wouldn't call it a hit. There's no evidence of that."

"Fine. Give me the ballistics on his *murder*."

"No." Martinez stood up. "I've had about enough of this shit from you."

MacTavish framed a cold smile. "Remember the letter I gave you two weeks ago, Captain. I can make that call if you like."

"Screw you. Fine." Martinez sat down and opened the case file on his desk. He wasn't rechecking the facts behind Leo's killing. He wanted to stall while he decided how much to reveal. "Carraba was killed with a forty-caliber round. Forty-caliber jacketed hollow points. Standard issue. The kill-round was matched to Jax's duty weapon. Jax was hit twice, we're guessing a 40-cal, too, but the rounds were not found. We did find all three bullet casings. All 40s, all from Leo and Jax's duty weapons."

"How do you know Jax fired the gun?"

"How do we know *what*?" Martinez looked at the FBI man with narrow eyes. "Who the hell else would have fired it? We found Leo in one spot, dead, gun in hand with two rounds fired. We found Jax in another spot, almost dead, gun in hand with one round fired. You do the math."

"I can count to three but that doesn't make me a mathematician." MacTavish sipped his coffee again. "What about Jax's magazines?"

"What about them?"

"I assume you inspected them. All rounds were accounted for?"

"Of course."

"And?"

"And what?"

"Jesus, Martinez, can we cut the games?" MacTavish set his coffee cup down on the Captain's desk and stood up. "Were all the rounds matched or not? Were they all the same manufacturer? All in the same condition? No strays? Could anyone have replaced any of the rounds in either gun?"

"There were no discrepancies." Martinez closed the case folder without another glance. The big man was pissing him off. MacTavish arrived at the Grey Coat Inn without notice and had concealed Rogers's death for three hours. He seemed oblivious to Martinez's rank and command and spoke as if crime scenes, jurisdiction, and chain of command were a bother.

"Then good night, Captain." MacTavish turned when Martinez beckoned him back.

"Whoa there. What about the quid pro quo?"

MacTavish turned and looked at him.

"You have something, I can tell. I want it, MacTavish."

MacTavish turned to the door and opened it. "My name is Horatio P. MacTavish the Third. My friends call me Mac. You can call me *Special Agent* MacTavish."

ꞔꞔꞔ

Twenty minutes later, Martinez finished rereading the Grey Coat Inn's crime scene report that Rogers had copied for him days before. It was an unofficial draft but Martinez had insisted on having it even before Rogers finished. The report confirmed that Rogers had inspected and inventoried Leo and Jax's service weapons himself. The inventory matched his recollection. Leo had forty-three rounds accounted for among three magazines plus two empty shell casings located near his body. Jax had forty-four rounds among his three magazines and one empty casing collected.

All rounds were accounted for.

Martinez flipped the inventory page and cursed, hammering his fist on the desk so hard it toppled his half-full cup of coffee over his desk. Rogers didn't note anything further about the ammunition—not their manufacturer or the conditions of the rounds. He scoured the report a second time and came to the same conclusion.

"Damn you, *Special Agent* MacTavish. Damn you."

Chapter 17

D o you think she'll help you?" Christie watched the rear of the restaurant through her driver's window. She turned to Jax beside her. "What makes you so sure she'll know who Leo worked with?"

Casa de Amigos sat on the outskirts of Leesburg in the corner of a rundown strip mall. Christie drove into the parking lot through the rear entrance and parked back among a long row of industrial dumpsters where no one would notice them. Two short, Hispanic men came out of the restaurant's rear door carrying boxes of trash. After emptying them, they lit cigarettes and laughed and joked for several minutes, sitting at a wood picnic table at the far end of the restaurant.

Jax sighed. "The last case Leo worked was about the Salvadorian Muchachos moving guns and drugs up from the south. We hit a dead end and couldn't find a way inside the gang to get any leads. Leo said he was going to keep digging even after Martinez put us on another case."

Christie nodded. "Yeah, that makes sense. You mumbled something to me in the hospital about that. I told Jeremy I thought his informant was Latino."

"It's the one lead I have. Lydia has helped us before. Several times. Her parents own the restaurant and she works there. The Muchachos have taken it over and hang their hats there. She hates it but it's all they have. If Leo was looking for a way in, it might have been her."

The two restaurant men finished their break and returned to the restaurant. As soon as the door opened, a Mexican girl emerged and took a seat at the picnic table.

"That's her," Jax said. "I'll call her over."

"I better split. She might be nervous around someone she doesn't know. Go easy, Jax. You're not a cop right now." And with that, Christie slipped from the car and jogged off into the darkness.

"Hey, sport," Trick said, appearing in the rear seat. "I'm going with Christie. You know...so she won't get lonely."

"Are you going to appear to her or something?"

"No, just keep her company."

Jax laughed. "I guess if it were Finch or Jeremy Levin, you'd be keeping them company, too?"

"Oh no, guys don't need company." Trick vanished into just a voice. "Remember, Ricky, I'm a fortyies man. Chivalry was okay with us."

Jax rolled down his window and called out for Lydia. It took him several attempts before she heard him. She was reluctant at first, but after peeking back inside the restaurant door, she slipped through the darkness and into the rear seat of Jax's car.

"Lydia, I need your help." He explained what he wanted. "What can you tell me? Were you working with Carraba?"

The young girl shook her head and kept her eyes glued on the restaurant. "No, no, Senor Jax. Not me. He ask me many times but I say no. My papa would not be happy. It scary enough with Hector 'round all the time."

Hector Lupino was the chief-gang-banger in Loudoun County and four surrounding counties. He had used violence and arrogance to fight his way to the top of the Salvadorian Muchachos—a lethal criminal gang who dealt in drugs, guns, human trafficking, and extortion.

"But you know who worked for him." Jax smiled his best "trust me" smile. "It's important, Lydia. Leo's dead and someone tried to kill me."

"*Si, si*, I so sorry for Senor Carraba. But I dunno nothing. Please, Senor Jax, the *federales* already talk to me and my papa. Please."

Jax turned more in the seat to look at her. "The FBI was here? What did they want?"

"What you ask. Same thing. They say we must help them find Antonio."

"Antonio?" Jax had her. "Lydia, out with it. How do you know Antonio?"

Lydia's face fell and she slumped back in the seat. Her expression was a mixture of anger and fear. "Antonio Cavallo. He is my cousin, Senor Jax. He is a good man. But he so afraid and someone trying to kill him."

"Where is he?"

She shrugged. "He gone for two weeks now. He call my papa but we don't know where he stayin'. He's so afraid, and now *federales* want him, too."

"Lydia, I'll protect him." Jax jotted a number on a piece of plain paper from the glove box. "This is my cell number. Add one number to each of the last seven digits. Do you understand? Add one number to each one."

It was a simple trick to concealing his number should anyone find it. He'd read it in some spy novel he'd read years ago and had taught Leo to use the code, too.

She read it back to him. "*Si*, I understand. Antonio have somethin' the same."

"He does? Do you know what it was? Was it a code?"

Lydia checked out the window for any eyes watching. "No. He say to me they send him funny messages. Strange things they say. He say he gave them to Senor Carraba."

"Gave Leo what, Lydia?"

She shrugged. "I am not sure. He gave Senor Carraba the messages."

Whatever Antonio gave Leo, it was important. "All right, Lydia. That'll help. Find Antonio and tell him to call me. I'll protect him."

She nodded and glanced out the window again. "*Si,* okay. But he very afraid."

"Who is trying to kill Antonio?"

Lydia tucked the paper into her jeans pocket. "Antonio say he saw someone. He know something very dangerous."

Jax nodded. "Do you know who's trying to kill him?"

Her answer sent chills down Jax's spine. "He think the *federales,* or maybe *la policia.*"

Chapter 18

Ameera woke when the shouting became too loud to sleep. She sat up beside her younger brother, Khaled, on the old mattress tucked against a similarly worn and dirty one he slept on. He was already awake and crying. The fighting in the grand room outside their door woke him and he couldn't contain his young tears.

"Shsssh," she said to Khaled and opened her arms. "Shush."

Khaled peeled back the dusty bedcovering and crawled across his mattress, jumping the short distance to hers and scurrying to her. He clutched her and laid his head on her shoulder, sobbing and shaking.

"Shsssh," she repeated. In Arabic, she said, "Ameera is here now. It is all right, Khaled. Be brave for me."

She looked around in the darkness. The small storage room had chairs and tables stacked on one side, and her family's belongings—what few suitcases and duffels they were allowed to bring—sat on top of them. Beside Khaled's mattress were two others where their mother and father should have been sleeping.

The shouts in the main room outside told her where they had gone.

She laid Khaled down on her bedding, bade him to stay quiet, and headed for the large, empty room outside her door.

Ameera was small and thin, still maturing in her thir-
teenth year. Her hair was rich and black and it was pulled
back and tied for sleeping. She was dressed in a long, mod-
est cotton evening dress that was too big and dragged the
floor. She took handfuls of the fabric, lifted it off the floor,
ventured to the doorway, and stepped out.

Scant moonlight fluttered through the side windows and
glittered off the grand chandelier's few remaining glass
stars and tassels dangling overhead. Earlier, she'd admired
the fixture. She'd never seen one before and Manuel, one of
their keepers, was kind and explained what it was.

Now, the shouting grew louder, and she looked beyond
the pretty dancing reflections to the top of the grand stairs
across the room.

Her mother and father were there. Her mother held tight
to her father's arm, pulling him back, trying to restrain his
ferocious temper. Her father's free hand chopped the air
with every angry word. He motioned back toward
Ameera—not noticing her presence—and shouted in broken
English and Arabic. He was angry about his family sleeping
on hard floors and eating cold food. His anger was not from
the many abandoned buildings and dirty hotel rooms they'd
shared, but at the thousands of American dollars he'd paid
for better treatment.

Ameera took a few steps and recognized the man called
Lobo.

Lobo's Salvadorian features were lean and hard, with a
chiseled face and a greasy, long ponytail. He jabbed a steel
finger into her father's chest and backed the Arab two steps.
When he did, Ameera could see the strange scar etched into
his flesh. That scar scared her more than anything the man
had ever said to her, and she knew its image of a sharp
Janbiya—dagger—could only mean his position as guard
and enforcer.

Lobo backed her father up another step. "English, asshole. I dunno no Arab words. And I said, you money don't

get you no first class digs. Now, go back to bed."

Her father stepped forward again, pressing himself into Lobo's finger until the Hispanic grabbed his shirt and shoved him backward and down onto the hardwood floor.

"Don't do that, asshole. Don't touch me again." Lobo looked up and saw Ameera watching. "And get you damn brat outta here. Now."

Ameera's mother turned, saw her, too, and ran back to her. She clutched her and whispered to return to the storeroom and back to bed.

As Ameera backed toward the room, Lobo's cell phone hummed and he stepped away from her father. She watched him tap the keyboard, wait, enter several more taps, and wait again. His face tightened and he shut off the phone, pocketed it, and returned to her father.

"Change in plans. Get you family up early. We leavin' again tomorrow. Be ready to go. Manuel come to get you before dark. Understand? *Comprende?*"

Her father stayed down on the floor, kneeling on one knee. His eyes were on fire and his chin high and pointed. He was not a violent man. He was just a man escaping the violence of his homeland torn by decades of war. "*Na'am—* yes. Understand. Yes."

Lobo laughed and looked back at Ameera. He thrust his scarred arm out and pointed at her. "And I told you, none of them Arab clothes. You gotta look American. Don't make me tell you 'gain."

Ameera ran from the ballroom and slid herself back beneath her bedcovers in beside Khaled. He was asleep again and she rolled him away to give herself more room. She listened for more fighting but it did not reach her ears. Comforted, she lit a small candle beside her bed and slipped a small cardboard box from behind her pile of clothes. Inside, she took out the cloth sack of amber beads and a short ball of leather ties. She poured out a dozen beads and began threading them on an eight-inch tie, forming a short, crude strand of worry beads in just a few moments.

These would be for the old man. He had lived in this strange place first, before they arrived. Lobo had sent him away but Manuel—kind Manuel—helped him settle his belongings in the workshop next door. The old man was kind to her and, when Lobo was not around, he showed her the strange, broken sticks he'd called "clubs." One morning, while her mother made tea for breakfast, the old man found a small, hard ball and taught her to hit it in the field behind their building. The American sport she knew was golf and she had only seen pictures of it in her village.

Perhaps one day, when it was safe, she, too, would learn to play golf. Until then, Ameera knew they would go on hiding.

Chapter 19

"If Martinez catches me here, he won't be happy." Jax followed Christie through the side door into the BCI office. "He thinks I murdered Leo."

"Don't worry about Martinez," Christie said, flipping on the lights above Leo's desk. "It's after midnight and we're alone. And besides, he told me to keep track of you. I had to come to the office, and you're along so I can keep track of you."

"That works for me." Jax stood over Leo's desk and couldn't help but notice his files and computer were missing. He pulled open two of his desk drawers and found them empty. "You guys took it all as evidence?"

Christie nodded.

"Then what are we looking around for?"

"Anything we missed or something that might lead us to Cavallo. I'll get Leo's personal items." She disappeared down the hall where the evidence property room was located.

"Ricky, are you sure you want to do this?" Trick asked from where he was perched in Jax's desk chair across from Leo's desk. "I mean, you might find things you don't want to find. Not all clues should be found. You know that, right?"

"What's that supposed to mean? If there's a lead here, I have to find it. I need to prove my innocence and find out who killed Leo."

Trick spun around in the chair. He tipped his fedora over his eyes and propped his feet up on Jax's desk. "Okay, but don't say I didn't warn you. And remember, not everything is as it seems."

"Are you trying to tell me something, Trick? Just say it."

"Say what?" Christie reappeared with a cardboard box labeled with Leo's name, date of his death, and the BCI investigative case number. "Who are you talking to?"

"No one." Jax shook his head at his empty desk chair. "I was just thinking out loud. What do you have?"

"Leo's personal stuff that we didn't book into evidence. I stored it in lockup just to be sure you had a chance to see it."

The air stuck in Jax's chest when she laid the box on the desk and opened it. It was half-empty. Sitting on top was a framed picture of Leo and him receiving commendations from the governor three years ago. They'd taken down a major drug kingpin and during the final days of the investigation, stopped the assassination of two informants who had been instrumental in toppling the drug gang. The good guys won that round. Now, however, the photograph was a painful reminder that the good guys didn't always win. In fact, the good guys weren't always so good, either.

"What can I find that you guys missed?" Jax couldn't wade into the box. "I'm no help."

"Just try. You knew Leo better than all of us combined. What meant nothing to us might solve his case if you see it. Just look, all right? Take your time."

As Jax reached into the box, the dull pain of angst and anticipation struck him like a gut-punch. The room closed in around him. A baseball, signed by two dozen minor league players, brought the smell of spring grass and the taste of cold beer and popcorn. A slingshot put the scent of gunpowder in his nostrils. It was Leo's award for coming in last place in a county pistol contest two years ago. The dog-eared deck of playing cards, all jokers, for Leo's favorite poker game—five-card draw, joker's wild.

Jax trembled with a mixture of laughter and sadness. The box contained the best and the last of Leo Carraba.

It took him twenty minutes to sift through the years of memorabilia and accumulated desk-fodder. Some of the items brought Jax to tears and others to laughter. None of them brought a motive for murder.

"Is this it? Where are his keys, Christie?"

She put a manila envelope beside the box on the desk. "I have a copy of his house key from the search."

Jax picked up the envelope and examined the ring of six keys hung on a miniature set of handcuffs. "Nothing here. His handcuff key, car key, house key, locker, and gun safe key, and another I don't recognize. Nothing jumps out."

"Did he keep your house key on his key ring?"

Jax shook his head. "No. It's on a hook on his frig at home, along with my alarm code. I don't know what this other key is."

"That extra key is…um…well, it's something else. I've already checked it out."

Jax picked up the bag. "What is it?"

"I verified it the day after he was killed. No worries."

"What is it?" Christie looked away and Jax knew the answer. "Oh, it's Kathleen's."

"Yes. Sorry." Christie moved around the desk and put a hand on his shoulder. "She confirmed it. I've got his vehicle records to check next."

Jax wasn't listening. He couldn't take his eyes off the keys. He wasn't sure how to feel, He wasn't sure if he was angry or sad. When he dropped the bag onto the desk, he was neither. It didn't bother him at all. But how could that be? His best friend and fiancé betrayed him. They played him for a fool and now he was a murder suspect because of it. Yet, staring at a key Kathleen never offered him, he didn't seem to care.

Leo's death hurt. Kathleen hurt, too. Yet, that hurt was not from her betrayal but from her willingness to believe he could be responsible for Leo's murder. When he looked up at Christie, he felt...*relief.*

"I didn't know he had one. I don't. I guess I found out the hard way, right?"

"We'll go to his place next." She picked up the deck of playing cards and tossed them back into the box. "I went through his computer. He didn't have any appointments or notes on his desktop calendar. No unusual files either."

"No, he wouldn't." Jax refilled the box. "He hated computers. He kept notes and appointments on his desk calendar and in his notebook. He said if the power grid went down, no one would know how to do police work."

"He was right, you know."

Jax replaced the box lid and moved it off Leo's desk. He sat in the chair and scanned the desk blotter and calendar sitting in the center of the desk. It was covered in scribbles and hieroglyphics and it took Christie's help to decipher several of Leo's notes. Most were lunch appointments, notes on dry cleaning, and references to Jax's schedule, too. How many of those were openings for him to use Kathleen's house key made Jax wonder about how well he had actually known Leo Carraba or Kathleen Cullen.

"Oh," Christie said, heading for her desk. "I have a printout of his BCI car's GPS tracker and black box."

Each Virginia State Police car, as many law enforcement vehicles around the country, were fitted with their own "black box" that records its geographic movements, engine conditions, speed, and other vehicle performance metrics. Not unlike airplane black boxes, the data recorded could be critical in identifying the cause and effect should an officer be involved in any accident or vehicle incident.

"He was home, here at the office, and at the inn twice. He made a few stops I identified as a gas station, convenience store, and in and out of home twice more." Christie handed the printout to Jax. "There are visit to Kathleen's and a couple addresses I don't recognize, but they're residential areas. I'll have to check his call logs to see what's there."

Jax studied the list. "Maybe it's where AC met him."

"Antonio Cavallo?"

Jax pointed to a scribbled notation on Leo's calendar for the afternoon before his murder. "That's my guess. It says 'AC one-thirty.' Maybe one of those addresses is AC for Antonio Cavallo."

Christie moved beside Jax to examine the notation closer. "He was at the inn earlier that day at about one-twenty until near two o'clock. He was at the same residential address before and after. One of them has to be Cavallo's."

"So he met Cavallo at the inn and either before or after. Assuming the entries are related." Jax took a notepad from Leo's desk and made copied the addresses. "Let's go to Leo's place. I want to get my house key back and have a look around."

"We can check the other addresses in the morning."

Jax stuffed the note in his pocket. "If it was Cavallo he met at the inn, then Martinez should give me a break. That proves I wasn't lying about him setting up the meeting."

"Well, it proves *he* was at the inn," Christie said. "That's all. We have to find Cavallo to make that case."

"Whose side are you on?"

"Your side, Jax. But I'm still a cop, remember?"

"How could I forget?"

Her smile put him on notice. "If you give me a chance, I'll show you."

Chapter 20

Jax was silent as Christie turned into the cul-de-sac and parked close to the row of townhouses facing the entrance. She got out of the unmarked cruiser and waited for him in front of the car.

He sat in the front seat, looking around with a dull, empty face.

The neighborhood was still. It was near one in the morning and only one house had lights on inside. The cul-de-sac was lit with decorative, nineteenth-century streetlamps that lighted the few trees on the circle. The neighborhood trees were bare and Leo's yard was ankle-deep. Yellow crime scene tape and a BCI police seal were fastened to the front door.

Jax took a hard swallow and climbed out of the cruiser. How many times had he climbed those from steps with an armload of pizza and beer? How many times had he been unable to return down them and slept off a long night of five-card, joker's wild tournaments?

"Come on, sport," Trick said as Christie unlocked the front door and disappeared inside. "You gotta do this. I can't help. Go on, it'll be okay."

"Dammit, Trick, you're not real. Let me do this my way."

Trick pulled his collar up against his ears and held his fedora against a sudden chilly breeze. He didn't need to, but old habits died harder than him. "Sure, Ricky. I get it. I'll sit this one out. Yell if you need me."

Trick vanished.

"Ah, shit." Jax looked around and saw Christie watching him from inside the front door. "I'm coming."

Inside, Christie studied him. "You know, Jax, you keep talking to yourself and you won't have to worry about murder charges. They'll be packing you off somewhere else for a long stay."

"Yeah, yeah. Look, this is hard on me, okay?"

She lowered her eyes and closed the door behind him. "Sure, I know. But we gotta do this, right? Don't let whoever you're talking to convince you to cut corners."

"Yeah. So let's do it."

The townhouse was as he had last seen it—cluttered and unremarkable. The stereotypical bachelor house. Leo's furniture was a mixture of warehouse-overstocks and garage-sale hand-me-downs. His walls were adorned with framed sports posters and game-day photographs. Jax never knew who took the shots since Leo couldn't operate an automatic camera. The dining room table was littered with newspapers, paperback books, and weeks of junk mail. Any mail of value was already in the evidence room back at the BCI office.

Jax went to the fireplace mantel. Leo displayed some sports memorabilia—a couple signed baseballs, framed tickets to the 2009 playoffs, and an autographed picture of some pitcher Jax never heard of lined up. In the center of the mantel was a picture of Leo, Kathleen, and Jax at last year's sheriff's Labor Day barbecue. Kathleen stood between them, an arm around both but her head on Leo's shoulder. Leo had brought a date to the picnic. If Jax remembered right, she had taken the photograph, but her name and face escaped him.

Regret tasted bitter in his mouth.

"You okay?" Christie asked, breaking his stare at the photograph. "I remember that bash. Wow, you two were the life of the party. Didn't you do a duet or something?"

"I'd rather forget that." Jax put the photo back on the mantel, face down. "I never noticed this shot before. In fact, in all the photos from last year we're all together. I should have seen this coming, Christie. I was always chasing the beer and he was always keeping her company."

Christie pulled him from the mantel. "Look, Jax. Get over this one, will you? You two weren't destined to be married. Hell, when you got back from the Poconos that time, you didn't tell anyone you were engaged for two weeks. Doesn't that tell you something?"

She was right. Their engagement had also been rushed and unsteady. A rare weekend in the Poconos at Kathleen's demand. He hadn't taken a day off in weeks and she wanted some adventure. The weekend was a blur, now—too much wine and too little sleep. On their return to Leesburg, they bought her ring. It had been Kathleen's idea and more than half her money. A decision born from wine, romance, and fancy. Jax had been tepid about it all, but he felt the prospects of a cop in a small town would never be better than Kathleen Cullen. Still, he never quite felt safe, never felt secure or confident with her. He didn't know if it was the disparity in their lives, or something deeper, hidden from view and their touch.

"Jax?"

"Oh, sorry." He looked around the living room. "I was just thinking. I'm embarrassed to say that I'm not sad she called off the engagement. Of course, I'd rather it not be because of all this. But you're right. We weren't right."

Christie's face lit up. "Good for you. She doesn't deserve you and you didn't deserve Leo."

Jax's face hardened and he looked to the floor.

She crushed into him. "I'm sorry, that's not what I meant."

"I know, Christie. I know what you meant." He gave her a squeeze and headed for the kitchen. "Let me get my house key and we're out of here. I can look the place over another time."

"Good."

Jax found the key rack attached to the side of Leo's refrigerator. On the rack was a spare key to Leo's car, and one for his backyard gate. Jax's house key and alarm code were missing.

"Shit, Leo. What did you do with it?" He rummaged through the kitchen drawers and cabinets for ten minutes but didn't find his key. When he returned to the refrigerator door, he found Leo's macramé of sticky-notes and business cards from lawn services to veterinarians. The veterinarians surprised him since Leo had no pets. On the countertop, tucked under a coffee mug, was a business card from a Washington DC military defense consultant that Jax recognized.

The card was from John S. Singleton, president and chairman of the board. On the back of the card was a string of nine numbers separated into four groups by a dash. Without any more thought, he tucked the card in his pocket and returned to the living room.

Christie admired a row of wine bottles in a rack in the corner of the room. "My key and alarm code are gone. But I found something else—"

"Jax, wait," Christie said, drawing her automatic from behind her back. "Stay put." She yanked open the rear door off the living room and peered out, gun first. Then, waving him back, she bolted outside.

"Christie, wait."

She was gone.

Jax went to the door and looked out. The backyard was dark and the neighbor's dim patio floodlight shed a broken glow through the five-foot fence, casting an eerie, jagged montage of shadows.

Christie was nowhere to be seen and the rear gate was ajar.

"Shit, Christie. Where the hell did you go?" He looked

around the yard again and went back inside. "Trick? You around? Trick?"

Nothing.

"Jesus, I get a ghost and he's unreliable."

"I'm not unreliable." Trick walked in from the hallway with his hands tucked into his pockets. "You didn't want me in here, remember?"

Jax waved in the air. "Ignore me next time. Can you find Christie? She could be in trouble."

"No, it doesn't work like that."

"Huh?"

Trick went to the back door and looked out. "Why didn't you go with her?"

"I don't have a gun."

"Neither do I."

"Yeah, but you're already dead." Jax frowned and rubbed his eyes. "I cannot believe I just said that. Look, she heard something outside and ran out. I don't know where she went."

Trick turned to him. "And you didn't hear anything?"

"No."

"You sure?"

"Yes, I'm sure. Why?"

Trick shrugged. "Interesting. But, hey, I can't just 'go find her.' It doesn't work like that. I have to have a connection, you know, something to zero in on. Like radar."

Jax pulled out his cell phone and hit a speed dial. "I'll see if she picks up." A few seconds later, he closed the phone. "Shit, she's not answering."

"Hey, sport," Trick said, walking up and tapping his phone. "What's this thing everyone's always talking into? A radio?"

"Cellular telephone."

"You don't say?" Trick tipped his fedora onto the back of his head. "A telephone? What's cellular?"

Jax tried explaining but gave up after a minute. "It's sort of like a tiny radio that works like a telephone. Just think of it that way. It's global. You can get your calls anywhere. Well, almost anywhere. And there are ones that work off a satellite, too."

"No kidding. What's a satellite?"

"Later. We have to find Christie."

Trick faded until he was just a voice. "No you don't. She's back."

Christie appeared through the rear door. Her face was flushed and blood trickled down the side of her temple. When she came in, she dropped onto Leo's couch and lowered her head into her hands.

"Bastard clobbered me."

"Christie, are you all right?"

"I'll live."

Jax went to the kitchen and found a clean washcloth and a bowl of hot water. He returned and sat beside her on the couch. "Let me clean you up. Do you need a doctor?"

"No." She took the wet cloth and dabbing her head. "I ran around the corner of the building just down the street. Someone was waiting and clocked me."

"Did you see anything?"

"Stars for a little while. Nothing to ID him."

Jax inspected her head and found a short gash just above her left ear. "You might want to have a doctor look at this. It doesn't look bad, but you never know."

She wiped the side of her face and dropped the cloth into the bowl of water. "Nope, I'm good."

"Christie, I'm sorry. I should have gone with you. But I didn't see or hear anything before you ran out."

She shook her head. "No worries, Jax. You would have slowed me down. After just being released from the hospital, that's all I would need is for you to get clobbered. Martinez would have my ass."

"Still, I'm sorry. I guess we didn't learn much tonight."

Christie winked. "Sure we did. We learned that you and

Kathleen were never gonna get married. We learned Leo has lousy taste in women—"

Jax shook his head. "Christie, don't do that."

"—we learned that someone has your house key and alarm code." She took his arm in hers and headed for the front door. "And we learned that someone was watching this house. Someone who's fast and strong."

"Boy, we learned a lot, didn't we? Anything else?"

"Sure," she said, flipping off the lights. "You like talking to yourself way too much."

Chapter 21

Are you sure you're all right?" Jax asked as Christie pulled into his drive. "I can take you to the hospital. They know me there."

"I'm fine. No worries." She put the car into park. "You know, I was thinking about Lydia and Cavallo. They think the feds are trying to kill him? I'm not buying that, are you?"

"That's what she said, Christie. Antonio Cavallo thinks the feds or the cops are trying to kill him. That's why he went to ground. Maybe that's why Leo was hit—and me."

Christie shifted in the seat to face Jax. "Maybe that's why this MacTavish FBI guy is hanging around, too. But come on, are we saying cops or feds did Leo?"

"It's happened before."

"I know you're pissed off at the world, but no cop is going to do that around here. I don't believe it. No."

Jax looked away. "Someone killed Leo. Someone tried to kill me. It could be anyone. And tonight, someone was watching Leo's place and almost took your head off."

"But a cop? Do you know what you're implying?"

"Why is it okay for all of you to think I killed Leo, but not okay for me to suggest another cop or a fed did it?" Jax opened his door. "We have to get to Cavallo before someone else does. Can you check those addresses in the morning?"

"Done. And I'll get Jeremy working it, too. That little shit has a big mouth, but he also has a notebook full of snitches like you've never seen."

Jax slid the business card out of his pocket and held it up. "I found this at Leo's place. It's got odd numbers on the back. I'll check into those and see what I find."

"What about what Lydia said to you? Something about strange words or messages?"

He nodded. "I think it's some kind of code, but I'm not sure. Antonio Cavallo may be the key to that, too." He started to get out of the car but he turned back to her. "Thanks, Christie. I appreciate all this. I couldn't do this alone."

"Jax," she said, reaching across the seat to take his hand. "I'm here for you, just like always. Do you want me to tuck you in tonight?"

"What? No, not tonight. I'm still woozy from the hospital. But let's talk about it another time."

"Okay, rain check. Come up sometime and see me," she said with a smile that set him back in his seat. "You know?"

Jax stared at her until it hit him. "Mae West from, *She Done Him Wrong*, 1933, right?"

"Yeah, Mae West." Christie leaned over and kissed his cheek. "Get some sleep, I'll see you tomorrow."

As Jax stood on his front stoop watching Christie drive off, Trick appeared beside him.

"Ricky, you better keep an eye on her. She's a dish and she's ready to cook you breakfast."

Jax jumped a bit and turned to him. "You heard all that?"

"Sure, I did. And I think Lydia might have a point, you know. You gotta watch everyone involved in this case. It only takes one bad apple to spoil the bunch."

Jax looked at him. "Just what is that supposed to mean?"

"For a time, I was in Morocco and Algeria looking for spies. We were hunting double agents, more to the point."

"Double agents?" Jax unlocked his front door and led them inside. "What are you talking about?"

"Double agents, sport. You know, good-guy spies pretending to work against the bad guys, but they're working for the bad-guys, spying on the good-guys."

"What?" Jax shook his head. "No, no. That's not what I meant."

"Anyway, maybe you got a double agent." Trick lay down on the couch and propped his feet up, slipping his fedora over his eyes. "Or at least someone who isn't who they say they are."

Jax headed for his bedroom. "And maybe you saw too many movies at the Capitol Theater."

"Boyo, I *was* one of those movies at the Capitol Theater."

Jax flipped the lights off. "Good night, Trick."

"Good night. Oh, and Ricky?"

Jax turned around. "What?"

"Christie's a real dish." Trick faded. "Pay attention. When you meet the right dame, you'll know. I sure did. And when you do, don't fool around. Close the deal quick."

"Okay, Trick. Okay."

Trick was just a voice now. "I mean it, don't dawdle, Ricky. Life can be short."

Chapter 22

The wind rushed against him like a tornado approaching. He was off balance, disoriented, terrified—falling into the darkness as it swallowed him. He wanted to cry out but knew no one would hear him. A flurry of brush and foliage ripped against his body a second before he jerked upward and twisted back and forth like a yoyo. For an instant, he struggled with an unfamiliar binding until it loosened, and he dropped to the ground, hitting hard and rolling away.

It took a moment to catch his breath before he dared kneel and look around. When he did, his breath came fast and his thoughts were all colliding, competing for a turn at deciphering his surroundings. Nothing looked familiar. Nothing seemed unexpected.

He looked up. The stars poked through the tree canopy overhead. His parachute was knotted and tangled and he knew he'd never pull it free from the trees. He'd have to abandon it and move quickly to escape the area.

From around his neck, he lifted a strange, L-shaped Sten submachine gun, snapped back the bolt, and hurried into nearby bushes for cover. Then he took out a small metal compass and searched the darkness for a bearing, without success. He decided to head north.

As he moved along the trees, Jax's body was on autopilot. Nothing seemed right. He wasn't in command of his own thoughts or movements. He wore tattered, old leather boots and baggy, cotton trousers. His shirt was dark and worn thin, and he smelled of perspiration and fear. When he stroked his face, there was a week's growth of stubble and a heavy mustache.

There was nothing familiar about himself, nothing he recalled, nothing he understood. Yet there he was, walking in the darkness, listening and preparing for any sudden threat to emerge, knowing he was ready. He didn't know where he was going or what his intent was. No, that was not true, there was one, of that he was sure, but it escaped him and that thought was hard to grasp.

But he had a purpose. He had a mission.

A shout ahead—perhaps fifty yards—stopped him cold, and he lowered himself to the ground. Movement. Someone running. Another shout.

"Halten Sie an! Kommen Sie hier!" More movement. *"Halten Sie an, oder ich werde schießen."*

Jax knew—but didn't understand how—every word the man yelled in German. With his Sten ready, he moved closer and stopped in the dark recess of a bushy clump of trees. A man stood there with his back to him. There was a second figure, just in front of the man, but smaller and silent. Both were difficult to see in the darkness, and it struck him that he felt no need to. The small was still unknown to him but he knew the man with his back to him was a German soldier.

"Was tun Sie hier?" The German reached out and grabbed the smaller figure, lashing out with a savage blow to the head. The German lashed out again and the figure crumpled to the ground.

"Non, s'il vous plaît. Je me seulement promène." It was a woman and she tried to explain that she was out walking by herself. She cried out and repeated her answer.

Jax slid his Sten across his back and withdrew a length

of wire with two wooden handles affixed—a garrote. He waited.

The German soldier grabbed the woman and yanked her to her feet. He shook her like a marionette. "*Geben Sie mir Ihre Identifizierung,*" he growled, demanding her identification.

The woman tried to speak but was struck again. This time, he followed her to the ground and onto one knee, striking her again and again. The German grabbed her hair and yanked her head backward, his other holding a knife to her throat. Its blade glinted in the moonlight, taunting her.

Jax sprung from the brush and, in three long strides, looped the garrote around the soldier's throat and jerked him backward, off balance. He thrust a knee hard into his back, bracing the kill with strength and leverage. They struggled. The soldier tried calling out but found no voice, no air. His hands flailed to his neck, desperate to strike but without a target.

It was over in seconds.

The woman jumped to her feet and wiped a smear of blood from her cheek. "*Merci, monsieur, merci. Comment vous appelez-vous?*"

Panic. He couldn't recall the code response and Jax didn't know why he knew there was one at all. The words came to him and for the first time in his life, he spoke French.

"*Je m'appelle Patrick. Il fait trop sombre pour faire la promenade.*" I am Patrick. It is too dark to be out walking.

The woman grabbed the soldier's feet and motioned for Jax to help her. "*Oui, mais on peut voir au clair de la belle lune.*" Her code response was correct. Yes, but the moonlight is enough to see. It is beautiful.

The woman nodded. "Quick, into the trees," she said in accented English. "My men will take care of him soon. Come."

Jax didn't struggle much under the weight. His body was

more fit and steady then he'd felt in years. They carried the dead soldier into the brush and hid him beneath an outcropping of heavy bushes.

The woman searched the German. "I am Abrielle."

Jax caught the occasional glint of starlight on her. She was about twenty and beautiful with black hair and deep, dark eyes. Her heavy leather coat couldn't conceal her feminine charms that filled her blouse and rounded curves.

"Right, I'm late, sorry. My plane had to double back twice. Jerries were heavy with *ack ack* tonight."

"*Oui*, we were about to leave here. But you came in time. We must hurry."

And without another word, he stood and followed Abrielle deeper into the trees until they disappeared into the nothingness.

٭٭٭

Jax bolted upright in bed. He shivered with sweat and angst. His night terror had sent his blankets into a pile on the floor. The darkness around him was now somehow familiar and safe. The dim images of his dresser and nightstand were now a comfort. There was no German soldier. No sentry to stalk and garrote. No Abrielle.

He was home. He was safe.

But he wasn't alone.

Trick stood at the foot of his bed. He folded his arms and smiled a thin, wry smile.

"Welcome back, Ricky. The French countryside is lovely in April, isn't it?"

Chapter 23

Jax fidgeted behind his desk at the BCI office, not sure whether to check his mail or leave the files unopened in the wire basket. It had been two weeks since he'd been a member of the team and he was already an interloper. It started when Ms. Leweski, the office administrator, demanded he enter through the security doors and magnetometer since Martinez had taken his security badge when he seized his gun and shield.

Now, she kept a beady-eye on him from across the room.

When Jax looked up, Dylan Finch stood over his desk with two cups of coffee. He sat one down between them and continued stirring his own. "Hey, Jax, you look great considering the hole in your head."

"It's the hole in my shoulder that hurts. My head is solid stone."

Finch laughed. "I knew that. Honest, I did." He got serious. "You're gonna find out from the captain, but Chief Rogers died last night. They're saying it was a heart attack."

"No kidding?" Jax looked up to the ceiling. "He was young. Are they sure?"

Finch shrugged.

"I heard he had heart problems, but right in the middle of this case sounds odd to me."

Finch leaned forward. "Yeah, me too. But that's the scoop."

Jax just nodded and looked at him. Finch, not one for office politics, leaned forward and lowered his voice. "How are you doin', man? This has been a shitty couple weeks, huh?"

"Healing pretty good"

"No, I mean, you know, everything else."

Jax sat back in his chair and looked around the squad room. There were two uniformed sheriff's deputies across the room talking, and two administrators working silently on their computers. Other than Finch, only Ms. Leweski seemed to notice he was present.

"Lousy, I guess. I'm not sure what's worse—everyone thinking I murdered my partner or getting shot. I can heal. I'm not sure how I my reputation back."

"One day at a time."

"Easier said." Jax tried to smile but it didn't work. He liked Finch and had the instant Sheriff Michaels gave him a detective's shield and assigned him to the Task Force. Finch retired from the marines after twenty years and the sheriff was smart enough to hire him ten days after returning to Loudoun County. "Thanks anyway."

"For what it's worth, Jax, I don't buy any of this crap. I don't know if you shot Leo or not, but if you did, there was a reason. And I don't think him banging your girl was it. I'm not looking for an explanation, Jax, I'm just saying."

"Thanks, Finchy." Jax forced a smile. "I appreciate that. Fact is I didn't shoot him. Something's all wrong with the crime scene. All wrong. Can you help me out? Can you get me a copy of the crime scene notes?"

"No, he can't." Martinez came around the corner of his office doorway and stopped at Jax's desk. He looked over at Finch. "Don't you have work, Detective?"

"No, not at the moment, Captain. I'm waiting on Christie to get in. We're heading out to soon as she does."

Martinez looked around the office. "It's eight. Where the hell is she?"

"We had a busy night," Jax said, then explained about what he'd found on Leo's calendar and Christie's chase through Leo's neighborhood. "She got hit pretty good, but she seemed okay when she dropped me off."

"She should have called me. I told everyone no action without my permission."

Jax glanced at Finch, who shrugged and looked back at Martinez. "So, Cap, I found Leo's notations about meeting someone the day before his murder," Jax said. "And we're looking for his snitch, Cavallo. How about letting me back to work?"

"You're suspended, Jax. You shouldn't even be here. I'll have Christie's ass for taking you to Leo's last night. I don't want you anywhere near this thing. You got that?"

"What the hell is wrong with you, Cap? I'm not the enemy."

"Well, not with me you aren't," Finch said.

Martinez shot a death-ray at Finch and tipped his head toward his office. "Come in, Jax, and we'll talk." To Finch he said, "Find Christie and get moving."

"Right, Cap. I'm on it." He didn't move.

Jax followed Martinez into his office and sat on the sofa against the wall. "Cap, look, I—"

"No, you look, Agent." Martinez stabbed a finger at him. "You cannot hang around here. Suspended is suspended. Chief Rogers is dead, and I've got an FBI agent running around."

"Rogers died of a heart attack. Do you believe that?"

"Doctor says heart attack, so it's a heart attack."

"Bullshit." Jax rubbed his right shoulder and winced a little. "How many weird coincidences do you need before you know this is a frame? I didn't kill Leo. You have to believe that."

"I want to. Trust me, I don't want any more heat around here." Martinez held Jax's eyes. "If you want to stop by, call and get it cleared through me first. Understand?"

"No, I don't understand. If you won't let Finch help me, will you show me Rogers's report? I have a right to defend myself, don't I?"

"You're not a cop right now, Jax. You get that, right?"

Jax's face tightened. "You guys haven't read me my rights. Internal Affairs hasn't arrested me, and the FBI is running around doing whatever. Why? It's my life and my career. How about a little quid pro quo?"

"Jesus," Martinez snorted. "You sound like the FBI. No, I haven't read you your rights, and no, I convinced the commander to give me some time. You were supposed to be in the hospital another week. He was holding IAD back until after you got released. I haven't told them you're out yet. Be thankful."

"So I have a couple days before you guys fry me."

"It won't be that way."

"Sure, it will." Jax leaned forward and dropped his head into his good hand, staring at the floor. He knew the moment IAD showed back up, they'd bury him in paperwork and doubletalk. If he was lucky, they'd give him a polygraph. Not that a polygraph would help. How would he explain Trick and the vision he had? What he saw that night—cold and shot twice—was less and less clear.

Martinez's phone buzzed and he scooped it up. "What do you want, Finch?" He cast his eyes at the ceiling. "Okay, okay. Let me come out there, I don't want to talk here."

"Something wrong, Cap?" Jax asked.

"No." Martinez dropped the thick crime scene file on the corner of his desk and went to his office door. "Wait here, Jax. I'll be right back."

The moment the door shut, Martinez's desk chair spun around with Trick sitting in it. "Hey, Ricky, I can save you a lot of time with that."

Jax ignored him, staring at the report folder.

"What gives? You want to know about that report or not?"

"Trick, if anyone hears me talking to you I'm done. So, knock it off."

Trick shrugged and changed the subject. "Last night was interesting, right? Wasn't Abrielle a real dish? And hey, if we hadn't taken that Kraut out, she could'a done it herself. She's got a great pair of legs and she's good with a knife, too."

Jax didn't know what to say.

"Suit yourself, Ricky. But all you're going to find is nothing. Your captain is holding out. He already got rid of the good stuff. You don't think he's going to make it easy on you, do you?"

Jax glanced out Martinez's door. In the bullpen, Martinez was debating with Finch. Finch handed Martinez a file and gave Jax a quick nod. Jax took the cue, grabbed the crime scene folder from Martinez's desk, and flipped it open.

Ten minutes later, Jax knew Trick was right. The crime scene report was sparse and missing too much information. He noted the small tear of paper stuck in the binder clips and knew Martinez had removed pages from the file.

Trick spun around in the chair like a schoolboy. "I hate to say I told you so."

"Shut up, Trick."

"What you need is credibility, Ricky. Your old pals will believe in you again."

"What's that mean?"

"Let's give 'em a body. Right there at the inn. Then they'll listen to you again."

"A body? You know where the guy's body is?"

"Give 'em a body and that'll buy you some time, right?" Trick walked to the couch and sat down beside Jax. "I mean, a little anyway."

"It should. It might prove my innocence, too. Where is it?"

"Tell Martinez you can deliver one. But get something for it first."

Jax heard Finch call out, "Thanks, Cap," and he knew his time was up. He put the file back.

Seconds later, Martinez walked in. "I don't know why I let that damn sheriff stick me with Finch. He's the biggest pain in the ass I've ever seen."

"Finch is okay, Cap." Jax stood up to leave. "Do I have any credit left in the bank, Cap?"

Martinez raised his chin. "I'm not sure, Jax. What do you want to buy?"

"A little time."

Chapter 24

J

ax, there isn't a body out here. We've been over this scene for two weeks."

Martinez watched Finch and Sheriff's Deputy Mike Gerard unloading a spunky, tail-wagging bloodhound named Sam from the rear of the deputy's patrol car. Sam was a specialized cadaver dog used for search and recovery. He could find corpses buried under tons of concrete and earth in the worst conditions imaginable.

"You have to trust me, Captain." As the words came out, Jax wasn't sure he trusted himself.

The fifteen-minute drive from the BCI office to the Grey Coat Inn had unnerved him. The Captain wanted an explanation how he knew where a body was after two weeks of silence and denials. Further, he wanted to know whose body they were looking for.

"Cap, I told you while I was lying there I was in and out. I heard someone talking about moving 'the body.' I didn't remember it until last night. I think the entire night is coming back. You know, in little flashes here and there. I've been cutting back on the pain meds and that's helped."

"Bullshit." Martinez waved for Finch and the canine team to join them. "You're holding something back and I want it out, now."

"Yeah, there's a lot of that going around, eh, Cap?"

"What the hell does that mean, Jax?" When he received

no response, he frowned. "You watch yourself, Agent. The colonel is giving me some leeway with you, but that doesn't mean I have to take it. I can slam you in a holding cell and no one will give a shit."

Finch approached them with Deputy Gerard and Sam. "Where to?"

Jax had no idea. He closed his eyes and concentrated on that night. He searched his thoughts, hoping to find a message swirling around with Trick's name on it.

Nothing.

"I gotta walk around a little, Cap. I'm feeling a little queasy. Let me get my bearings."

Martinez waved a hand toward the inn. "You're wasting my time, Jax. This is all bull. Finch, you and Deputy Gerard run the dog around the inn. Let me know if you get any hits. And it better not be a dead squirrel."

"Just give me a few minutes, Cap." Jax rubbed his shoulder. He was about to follow Finch when something caught his eye in the carriage house's downstairs window. It was Trick tipping his hat. "Come on, this way."

Inside the carriage house, Jax stood in the center hall and looked around. The stone and timber house was stark and empty. It smelled musty and aged. The yellow "POLICE DO NOT CROSS" tape on the outer door and fingerprint powder speckled on the window frames were the few hints of recent life left by crime scene team from their search days before.

"It's here, somewhere."

Finch watched Sam sniffing the floors and doorframes. "Mike, take him around. Jax, tell me what you remember. Think man, think. Martinez is about to go nuts."

Jax went back through his memories but nothing new broke through. They began walking the rooms and halls. After five minutes wandering the first floor, all he succeeded in doing was aggravating Martinez and increasing the pain pounding in his shoulder. They ended up in the stone-hearth kitchen when Jax heard a voice through the heavy wood plank door in the kitchen hall. He didn't hear the words. He *felt* them.

"Cap, in the basement." At the top of the narrow, timber stairs, Jax explained. "The reason Rogers's people didn't find anything was they didn't know where to look. This place used to be a stopover for the Underground Railroad. The innkeeper hid slaves moving through Virginia to the North. We just have to find the hiding place. There should be a root cellar or something down there."

Martinez peered down into the darkness. "Are you kidding me? You heard all that when you were unconscious? I don't know what you're up to, but this is insanity. Finch, let's go."

"Just a few more minutes, Cap, please."

At the foot of the stairs, Finch flipped on a powerful flashlight, bathing the large stonewalled cellar in dim light. "Nothing here, Jax. The same thing we found that morning. Nothing."

The cellar occupied the entire footprint of the carriage house with a wall dividing it into two halves. There was old furniture and boxes of junk stacked up along the walls. In the second half were the remnants of empty storage racks that covered the walls with broken pieces littering here and there. A few odd pieces of broken furniture were stacked in the far corner.

There was no body.

Jax walked the two rooms three times, searching every crevice with his penlight before stopping in the doorway separating the two rooms. "I don't get it, Cap. There should be an entrance to a root cellar. It has to be here."

"We're through," Martinez said, heading for the stairs. "Finch, take Gerard and Sam out and call it a morning. Jax, come back to the office with me."

He made it halfway up the stairs.

"Cap, Sam has something," Finch called.

Deputy Gerard followed Sam back through the doorway

into the second half of the basement. There he dropped the dog's long leash and waved his flashlight around the walls. Sam left the cone of light and headed straight to the rear wall of storage racks. When he got halfway, he barked and lifted a paw. Then he barked again and lifted both paws held up, paddling the air. He woofed again and moaned a long, playful moan.

"Finch, do you see this?" Gerard said. "Sam, back. Back, boy."

Sam sat, then cocked his head back and forth as he threw his paws out to shake hands with no one. Twice. Sam gave a short, stout bay and then sat back on his haunches with his front paws raised and begging. He moaned again.

Gerard turned to the others. "I don't know what the hell he's doing. He has something, but I've never seen him respond like this. It's like he's playing with something."

"Playing with something?" Jax brushed past them and went to Sam. "Good boy, Sam. Show us, boy."

"Find, Sam. Find," Gerard commanded.

Sam did. He lunged off his haunches and thrust his front paws onto the center rack against the wall. He howled twice and jammed his nose beneath a shelf, drawing it across the rugged seam of fieldstones. Each time he completed a pass along the rock seam he sat down and waited for Gerard to command him to search again. He continued the probe until Gerard ordered him back.

Sam retreated. This time, he stayed beside Gerard and awaited his reward.

"Captain," Jax said, watching Finch and Gerard exchange nods. "There's something behind that wall."

Chapter 25

The remains were wrapped in a piece of rotting canvas tarpaulin that was rolled like a rug destined for the trash. There was no flesh, no muscle contour or remnants of a body remaining. There was just the frail skeleton of a figure still wearing a tattered, decaying suit. A faint smell of death, more stale air and dust than actual flesh, hung in the heavy cold air. The skeleton's hands were crossed over his chest. He still wore a wristwatch on his right wrist whose hands had stopped decades before. A dilapidated bundle of material rolled behind the skull when they unfolded the tarpaulin.

Gerard stooped and picked up the bundle, trying to reshape it. "It's a hat."

"A fedora," Jax corrected, and at that moment, he understood.

It took them two hours to remove enough timbers and fieldstone from the basement wall to find the century-old timber door that led to the root cellar's antechamber. Once the wall was excavated and the door breached with strong arms and sledgehammers, Sam's were the first feet to cross the threshold in more than six decades. Jax's were the first human ones.

The others followed with flashlights and intrepid nerves.

It was Finch who had yanked the corner of tarpaulin aside and discovered the remains. When Jax's flashlight beam swept over what tumbled onto the stone floor, they knew they'd found not what they were after, but something more incredible.

All eyes fixed on Jax when the first dull, dusty hand bone escaped from beneath the canvas.

Martinez was the first to speak. "All right, Jax, you better explain."

"I can't."

"Try."

"I told you, I heard someone talking that night after I was shot. Someone said there was a body here." Jax knew no one believed the lie. "That's all I remember, Cap. And it must be true, right? I mean, here it is—a body."

"No, it's not a body, Jax. It's a hundred year-old skeleton."

Jax knelt down and examined the remains. He was drawn to them as the hollow eye sockets stared through him. When he moved a piece of canvas, the skeleton shifted and the skull slipped sideways. A dirt-crusted, jagged hole shown in his flashlight beam at the rear of the skull. He moved the skull to the side and there was no exit hole.

"He's been shot through the back of the head." Jax stood up but didn't take his eyes off the remains. "In October 1944."

"1944?" Finch repeated. "What are you talking about?"

"Jax," Martinez turned his flashlight to his face. "What *are* you talking about?"

"His name is Captain Patrick McCall," Jax said as Trick walked into the root cellar, fedora in hand. Jax nodded to him. "But he liked to be called 'Trick.'"

Trick winked as he stopped between Finch and Martinez, looking down at his own remains. "You did good, Ricky. Real good."

"But Jax," Finch began, "I thought we were looking for the perp you shot that night. How did you know this guy was here?"

"Trick was in the OSS during the war. He lived through

hell sneaking in and out of France. He worked with the French underground and some bastard murdered him and hid his body down here."

Finch looked at him. "How do you know all that?"

"Come on, Jax." Martinez took Jax's arm and tried to ease him toward the doorway. "Let's get you some rest."

"Get your paws off him, Mac," Trick said, putting a hand on Jax's shoulder. "He's with me. We're going to prove Ricky's innocent and find out who did kill that sap Leo."

No one heard him except Jax, who took the fedora from Finch and laid it back over Trick's skull, covering his empty eye sockets and giving him some lost dignity.

"That's right, Trick, and we're gonna find out who killed you, too."

Chapter 26

You're doing what?"

MacTavish stood in front of the carriage house entrance and pulled Martinez to the side, allowing a team of FBI agents to descend upon the stone house. When his team was inside, he guided Martinez to his sedan parked close by.

"I'm taking over this scene, Captain. It is now under federal jurisdiction."

"Just how do you figure decades-old homicide—if that is what this was—as federal jurisdiction?" Martinez stared daggers at the big man. "Besides, this is part of our investigation into *my* agent's murder."

"Maybe you don't get it yet. I'm taking over that case, too." MacTavish didn't mince words. "If these remains are in fact Captain Patrick McCall, then he was an American intelligence officer. He's been listed as missing since May 1944. There are national security considerations here."

"National security?" Martinez's face lit up and he laughed. "Come on, MacTavish, national security considerations after almost seventy years?"

MacTavish said nothing.

"No way."

"Captain, it doesn't matter what you say. I'm taking the case. Besides, if you want to go see the judge, you'll have a harder time proving a sixty-seven-year-old murder has anything to do with your dead cop. It's done. Over. I'm taking this scene and I want every report and every piece of evidence turned over to me. Remove your men. Now, Captain."

"First, you were here to help with our investigation of Carraba's killing. Then you play games with me about Chief Rogers's death. Now, it's national security. What's going on, MacTavish? And don't give me that national security crap."

"Captain, I suggest you comply with my instructions and withdraw your team." MacTavish's face was stone and his voice flat. "I don't think the governor would want to know about the missing lab reports and mysterious vanishing bullets, do you? I'm sure he might not take well to his BCI field commander obstructing justice."

Martinez's face turned red and tight. "I don't know what you're talking about, MacTavish."

"That's Agent MacTavish."

"Fuck you."

"Good, then we understand one another. You and your people are not to involve yourselves with this case or anything connected to it in any manner. That means Carraba, Jax, or this inn." And with that, MacTavish turned and disappeared through the carriage house door, slamming it in his wake.

Martinez watched the big man leave. He didn't know what was happening around him, but he knew he didn't like it. He also knew there was something about Agent MacTavish that was not in the FBI playbook. What that was, he wasn't sure, but he was sure it was a new set of rules he hadn't encountered before. He cursed again and headed across the parking lot where Finch, Christie, and Jeremy were waiting. From the looks on their faces, Finch had filled them in on finding the long-dead OSS agent.

"Cap, what's the deal?" Christie asked. "Are we going in or not?"

Martinez ignored her. "Where's Jax?"

"I sent him home with a unit," Finch said. "Crazy bastard may be talking to himself and all, but he sure pulled a rabbit out of his ass this time. He'll give us a full statement later. He needed some pain meds or something."

"Christie, go check on him," Martinez said. "I have no idea how he knew about this, but he did."

Christie looked around the group. "Well, maybe I do, boss." She explained about the library books. "Maybe he found something in the history of this inn that gave him an idea where to find the body. He had a few books on WWII and the OSS from the library, too."

"Meaning what, Christie?"

She looked from Finch to Martinez. Her mouth tightened a little as she looked away. "When I was with him last night, I went through his office a little."

"And?" Jeremy said with a huff. "What did you find?"

She slipped a folded piece of notepaper out of her pocket and handed it to Martinez. On it were a dozen book titles and their authors. "Three histories and biographies of OSS during the war. Two books of Leesburg and the surrounding area. One book on the Grey Coat Inn that included a detailed architectural review done by some history-group twenty years ago."

Finch looked over Martinez's shoulder and read the list. "So what? He took a bunch of library books out."

Jeremy huffed again. "Finch, maybe he found the old cellar and the pile of bones with these books. Maybe he's been researching this McCall character all along and somehow he's got all this twisted in his brain."

"Come on, Levin," Finch said. "Jax is as okay as us."

Christie shrugged and that got Finch's attention.

"What's that mean?"

She reminded them about Jax's alleged break-in. "He could have returned to the house himself. He's adamant he didn't. And those books and all didn't make any sense to me until just now."

"Terrific." Martinez threw a thumb toward her car. "Get back to him. We can't afford him having another 'break in' or a gun stolen that no one ever knew he owned."

"Okay, boss," she said. "But I still believe him."

"For what it's worth, he still found this body, Captain," Finch said.

"Yes, I know," Martinez said, watching an FBI crime scene team descend on the carriage house. "All the books in the library can't explain how he found McCall's remains. Can they?"

Chapter 27

Jax slammed his front door and looked around the house.

"Trick? Where are you? Trick?"

"I'm not a dog, Ricky. I'm right here."

Trick was lying in his now-usual place on the sofa, stretched out with his arms behind his head. His fedora was slipped forward, shading his eyes like some Hollywood movie scene. The one thing missing was Ingrid Bergman.

"I'm sorry, Trick." Jax sat down across from him. "All this time I thought, well, that you were all in my head."

"I get it. No need to apologize." Trick sat up. "I figured my bones would get your attention. We square?"

"Yeah, you bet."

"Now what, Ricky? We have to beat the pavement and find Leo-boy's killer, right?"

"Right. First we clear me so I can get my badge back and go to work. Then we can concentrate on you." He went to the bar and poured a tall bourbon. "I cannot believe what we found. I mean, what you that is."

Trick stood nearby. "Boy, Ricky, you are a lucky guy. Good bourbon was my drink. It was hard to find sometimes with the war and all. Brother, I sure miss it now. Although it is a bit early."

"To your health." Jax tipped back a long mouthful. "You don't know what you're missing. If I can help you, I will."

"Maybe you can." Trick eyed Jax's drink. Then he stepped so close to him he was almost touching him. "Hold your water for a second. Okay, sport?"

"What?"

Without another word, Trick took a short, slow step into Jax, evaporating into him like fog burning off.

Jax sucked in air. His eyes snapped shut as a vibrant warmth filled him. Trick soaked into him. At first, he was a warm mist toughing his skin, then he was a shutter of electricity that spread through him, his nerves sizzling as if every synapse in his body singed from the heat. A wave of energy spread through him. His thoughts raced and twisted, churning as though some strange brew fermented. When he opened his eyes, light and images vibrated around him, then...elation.

"Here's to you, Ricky," Jax said and lifted his drink, draining the bourbon in one long, slow pull. He sloshed another into the glass and drained it again.

"I missed that. You're the best. Thanks, pal."

A flash of light. Nausea. Faintness.

Jax collapsed against the bar and slid down onto the floor. He wanted to spit up the liquor but held it down. His right arm tingled beneath the bandages and for the first time in days, he wiggled his fingers without igniting the stabbing pain in his shoulder. Even his neck was unstrained and loose. His wounds tingled as though they were waking from a deep sleep. As he tried to stand, the room ebbed and flowed around him, forcing him to stay seated until the walls and furnishings fell back to normalcy.

When he finally looked around for Trick. "What did you do to me, Trick?"

Nothing.

"Trick?"

Jax rose on unsteady legs and made his way to the sofa where he sat down and lay his head back. It took him several moments sitting there, laying against the pillows, concentrating on keeping the bourbon down. He felt as though he'd just ridden a wild rollercoaster backward, upside down, and blindfolded. When it passed, he sat up and looked around again.

"Trick, where are you? What happened?"

A faint image coalesced across the room like a fine mist. Then, after what seemed an eternity, Trick's image gelled and he sat staring at Jax on the sofa.

"Holy mackerel, I pushed it that time."

"What happened? What did you do to me?"

Trick grinned. "To us, Ricky. Not just you."

"Huh?"

"You offered. I took you up on it. I sort-a joined you, you might say. You know, shared you for a drink."

"You possessed me?"

Trick shrugged. "Possessed is a pretty strong word. Let's call it *shared*, okay? I gave you back, didn't I? If I possessed you…well, that sounds like I stole you or something. I'm no Mata Hari."

"You scared me to death. I felt you take me over but I couldn't do anything. It was like the other night in my dream."

"Yeah?" Trick winked. "That was interesting, wasn't it? You never told me, did you like Abrielle? She was a sweetie. I called her Socks when no one was around. She liked that."

Jax stared. Had Trick possessed him? *Shared him* in his dream? Was it Trick who killed the German soldier after parachuting into France? How had he been there, with him, that night decades before? Did Trick have that power to take him over and propel him to other places and times?

"How did you do that?" he asked Truck, rubbing his eyes.

"I don't know. I just can. It takes a lot out of me, but in time I get it back. I never did it before I met you. I just knew how. Look, Ricky, don't ask a lot of questions, okay? I don't have the answers. There's no instruction book. No training. I'm dead, and sometimes, I just know things."

Jax looked down at the floor and tried to absorb it all. He was forty and had been a cop for twenty years. He made a living of facts and evidence, right and wrong. He wasn't sure what he believed about the afterlife or religion and had struggled with anything close to either. Life for him had been simple in those matters. He believed what he touched, what he proved, and what he could understand. Belief wasn't a product of wishes or faith, but of understanding. Facts. Evidence. Now, however, everything he thought he understood just emptied with his glass of bourbon.

"Show me, Trick."

"Show you what?"

"I want to see what happened to you." Jax motioned him to sit on the sofa beside him. "Take me there, like you did with Abrielle. Show me what happened to you."

Trick crossed the room and stood looking down at him. "You sure, sport? It isn't as easy as drinking bourbon. And it wasn't my finest mission. I'm not sure you'll understand."

"Then explain it later." Jax sat up and reached out for Trick's arm. "I think you possessing me for seventy-five-year-old bourbon ought to get me something, don't you? Show me."

"Okay, Ricky." Trick sat beside him and took hold of his shoulders melting into him again. "Don't say I didn't warn you."

A storm.

Chapter 28

Leesburg, Virginia, 1944:

The descent was rough and turbulent as the small Beechcraft dropped through the clouds, shaking and stuttering with each crash of thunder. The plane rose and pitched, yawing left and right as it fought the thunderstorm that consumed Leesburg with no warning. The pilot made a desperate dive through the clouds. He banked and nosed down in time to catch a small opening in the storm's wake, enough to guide the aircraft below the violence and toward the ground.

As the plane fluttered and fought for landing, the sickening ball in Jax's stomach told him he was there—with Trick—*somewhere*. He held onto the canvas strap over his head. Twice his head slammed into the fuselage and the pain told him it was all real. He was there, in the darkness with Trick on some mission that he didn't understand.

A few minutes later, the wheels clambered and the passengers braced themselves while the plane caught earth and bounced along the dirt landing strip known as George's Field.

Trick was the first to climb out of the small observation plane. He pulled his trench coat tight against the rain and took his time surveying the area.

Jax knew he was a passenger with no control, no voice—

nothing more than a spectator, watching a movie playing around him.

A second man climbed down from the aircraft. He was a strong man in his young twenties with a hard, serious face. He stopped outside the hatch and called back to the pilot. "As soon as the storm breaks, turn her around and be ready to evacuate. You have my instructions. Follow them."

"Johnny, did you set the backup team in place?" Trick called into the wind.

"Yes, all set. One on the north side, one on the south." Johnny hefted a rucksack and started leading the way to the only building in sight. "Let's check gear in the hanger."

Inside, Trick watched Johnny rummage in the rucksack. "Are we set?"

"Set." Johnny pulled a standard issue .45 automatic from the rucksack and handed it to Trick. "Take spare magazines. I've packed a Tommy gun just in case. Our radio is in this kit. If something goes wrong, you can Morse the plane to be ready for us. Each backup team has a radio and can move in when we're ready."

Trick hefted the .45 and loaded it. "Silencer?"

Johnny tossed him a stubby, cylindrical device.

"The team is set up around the inn. Kirkman, Fuchs, and Schiller should be there by now. They were taken from a remote airstrip in Maryland yesterday. Harriet is staying on script."

"How many men should Harriet have tonight?" Johnny asked.

"One escorting Schiller's bunch and just Harriet." Trick picked up the rucksack. "That's it. No word on who Harriet is?"

"No. Pierre's last message gave me this drop point and the time. We'll know after tonight."

"Let's hope he shows tonight. I'm not looking forward to flying back in this storm empty handed."

Johnny winked. "I bet old Donovan will shit sauerkraut when he finds out what we uncovered."

"Are we ready?"

"Yes. I'll drop you half-mile from the inn behind the carriage house. I'll come in from the north. I'll give the signal when I'm set. Flash once back. At oh-one-hundred we move in."

Trick swallowed as his stomach knotted. "Let's go get Harriet."

Thirty minutes later, Trick knelt behind a bushy outcropping of small evergreens fifty yards behind the Grey Coat Inn. He crept through the grass and angled in behind the carriage house for cover. There, he concealed the rucksack against the building's foundation. He didn't want the extra bulk to be a hindrance as he moved in. Inching along, he rounded the northeast corner and knelt close to the wall.

Jax was still there—still with him—still part of the action yet not a participant. The cold October night chilled his face as it was two weeks ago, yet sixty-five years from that moment. His movements had been almost identical, almost practiced like a dance choreographed over time between them. Was that the bond they shared?

Footsteps bristled through the tall weeds somewhere behind him. Trick turned, raised his .45, and retraced his steps around the rear of the carriage house. As soon as he turned the corner, he came face-to-face with a man.

"Hold it, pal, or I shoot."

"*Ich bin Professor Claud Schiller.*" He was an older man in his fifties with gray hair and beard. He wore round eyeglasses and carried a small duffle. "*Bitte, nicht schießen.*"

Trick nudged the old man farther back into the safety of the shadows. "English, *Herr* Schiller."

"Yeah, you understand me. Good. Please. Take me from here. Something wrong. I am afraid."

"Tell me. Hurry."

Schiller tightened his leather coat against the rain. "You are him? You are da man I must pay? Herr Smith?"

"No. And the arrangements have changed."

"What?" The old man's eyes went wide. "How can this be? I paid so much."

Trick stepped in close and let the .45 touch the Schiller's stomach. "Herr Smith has betrayed you. He betrayed us all. I'm here for him, not you."

"Not me? Yeah, yeah." Schiller looked around into the darkness. "I knew there was something not right. The money I pay. The others pay nothing."

"Yes, we'll talk later."

Car lights made a wide, slow arch across the field beside the carriage house and Trick pushed Schiller down onto his knees. Two doors opened and closed.

"Herr Smith is here I think. It is too late for me."

"No, we'll handle Smith."

Schiller held out a bulky leather pouch from his pocket. "*Bitte,* take this. It is payment. Take it and let me go without Herr Smith. It is all I have."

"No, stay here. You'll be safe. I have help coming."

Schiller tried to stand but stopped when Trick raised his gun. "Please. It is more than five-thousand in your dollars. Let me go."

"Listen, Mac, I have someone you can trust. I don't want your money. Go back to the woods." Trick pointed the way he had come. "You wait back there. Someone will find you. Tell them...ah...tell them Trick sent you. Trick. Understand?"

The old man stared at him. "What is 'trick?'"

"Just do it. Remember, Trick sent you."

The old man stuffed the pouch into his jacket, nodded, and started to turn. Then he stopped and faced Trick again, handing him something from his pants pocket.

It was a gold watch.

"*Bitte,* take this young man."

"No, I cannot."

Schiller forced it into Trick's hand. "*Bitte*, it was my papa's watch. It was good luck to bring me here to America. It bring you good luck, too. Return it to me when we are safe. *Bitte* be safe." The old man slipped away from the carriage house and disappeared into the darkness toward the trees.

Trick examined the watch, shrugged, and slipped it into his jacket pocket. Then he moved around the side of the carriage house to watch the parking lot. He checked his wrist-watch. It was 0045 hours. Johnny should be moving, too, ready for the signal. When Trick peered around the wall again, a green Plymouth sat idle in the parking lot. No one was inside. He crawled around the corner and waited in the shadows for Johnny's signal.

Twenty minutes passed. Thirty. No signal.

The plan failed.

Trick edged back toward the corner of the carriage house, crawling toward the Tommy Gun and radio in his rucksack.

Two gunshots split the air. Someone called out.

He broke from the shadows and angled toward the rear of the Plymouth. A flash of light sparked the darkness somewhere at the inn's rear entrance. The bullet whistled past his head. He fired two rapid shots back as he dove beside the car.

Another shot dug into the ground beside him.

Trick fired at the muzzle flash, pivoted, and readied to fire again.

A bullet slammed into his back. The pain seared through him like a hot poker. He collapsed face down against the car's fender. He reached for the hood to steady himself and lifted his gun.

Another shot punched into his back. This one put him down. He rolled off the Plymouth facedown onto the wet earth. The pain and haze consumed him, stealing his breath and focus and turning movement into screaming assaults of pain.

Jax felt the attack just as he had two weeks ago. He shared Trick's pain and fear, and fought with him for control. They were losing ground, losing the battle to fight back. Losing.

Trick stayed immobile. Footsteps approached him and a boot nudged his back. He lay motionless. The foot prodded him again. He continued to feign death.

The final gunshot startled Jax an instant before he felt Trick's face crush into the gravel driveway. He was released but before he left his host, he thanked God that Trick McCall was already dead.

The storm passed.

Chapter 29

I told you it wasn't pretty, Ricky." Trick stood in front of the sofa looking down at Jax. "I've been over it a hundred times and I can't find a clue."

Jax sat up and waited until the nausea passed. His fingers were still tingling and his body trembling. "Who is Harriet, Trick? And Schiller?"

"Harriet was a traitor." Trick had a faraway look on his face—eyes glassy and his lips tight. "He was one of us. OSS. We were sure. A traitor smuggling Germans into the country using OSS operations."

"Didn't we do that during the war?"

He nodded and his eyes turned cold. "Yeah, Ricky, we did. But not for money. Harriet was selling the service for profit."

"Nice guy. Very enterprising."

"Sure, until he killed me."

Jax sat forward and rubbed his eyes, trying to recall what he'd witnessed just then. "And the others?

"Schiller, Fuchs, and Kirkman were a group Harriet was smuggling in. We got onto him and set a trap. I guess he was the one who got onto us and ambushed us."

Jax watched Trick begin to pace until stopping across the room and keeping his back to him. "I didn't see much. I was hoping I'd find something to help. I'm just not sure what that is."

"Simple," Trick said. "You and me, Mac, we're connected."

"Connected?"

"Sure. I saw this movie once down at the Capitol Theater."

"You saw a lot of movies."

"Yeah, I did. Anyway, this movie was about a ghost who comes back to get help from this banker to solve her murder. See, he could do what she couldn't do and vice versa."

Jax rubbed his eyes. "I don't see the connection."

"Well, okay then, I saw this other flick—"

"Forget it. I get it. You were killed there and I was almost killed in the exact spot. Have you ever haunted anyone else?"

"Haunted? Well, I'm not haunting you, Ricky." Trick folded his arms. "This is my very first opening. You should be flattered. But I know this. You and I are connected. Two people don't die the way we did at the very same place and not be. You made it back alive and well, me, I just made it back."

"When I first saw you in the hospital, you said to me, 'I've been waiting a long time.' What did you mean?"

"Nineteen forty-four is a long time ago. I've been waiting for someone to help me. I figured it was you. And before you ask, I don't know where I've been, I just know I've been waiting. Time isn't the same as it is for you. What matters is I came back just when you were in trouble."

"Right. It must be to help me solve Leo's murder. Yours, too. Whoever killed Leo has to be connected to whoever killed you. Solve one, solve both. Let's start with what we know."

Trick tipped his hat back. "You got clipped five feet from where I did, sixty-seven years later to the day. That would make my killer almost ninety, or dead. I don't think some old codger in a wheelchair killed your pal. Do you?"

"Maybe not. But you might be surprised these days,

Trick." Jax stood up and stretched. "I heard Christie say no one had used the inn since the war. Your war, that is. Maybe your murder is why."

"Does that make me famous?"

"No, just old." Jax allowed a smile. "But it might make finding your body a problem for someone."

Trick took a chair at the breakfast table and watched Jax making coffee and a sandwich. "Man, I sure miss a good cup of joe. You got any doughnuts?"

"Forget it, Trick. I'm still seasick from the last time."

"Sure, sure, I get it. Maybe later?"

"Maybe." Jax sat at the table across from him. "Martinez won't give me the time of day, so chasing Leo's case is going to be tough. Maybe we go at this starting with your case. Let's track down any of your old OSS pals still around. We'll start with your partner Johnny."

"You're forgetting one thing, Ricky."

"What?"

Trick frowned. "That was sixty-seven years ago. I don't even know if any of them made it out of the war."

"If they're dead, wouldn't you know?"

Trick grinned. "Being dead isn't like a reunion party. And you think *I* watched too many movies."

"Sorry." Jax sat his sandwich down. "Well, maybe they are dead and maybe they aren't. Let's start with Johnny."

"Singleton."

"John Singleton?"

"Yeah, John H. Singleton." Trick leaned forward and ogled Jax's sandwich. "He was some kind of descendant of John Singleton Mosby, the Civil War Confederate raider. Boy, Mosby would have made a great OSS agent. In fact, he sorta was. At least that's the story Johnny told. We were pals. Best friends, Johnny and me. In fact, we went into France and Africa a few times together, and I tell you, we made a great team."

"I'm sure. And I already heard of him." Jax went into his office in the rear of the house and turned on his computer.

Then he dug around his desk and retrieved the business card he'd found on Leo Carraba's kitchen counter. "I think John Singleton is alive. And Leo was in contact with him, too."

"Oh, yeah?" Trick stood looking the computer over and sizing it up from all angles. "What is that thing, Ricky? I've been meaning to ask you about it."

"A computer."

"A what?" Trick moved behind him to look at the screen. "I never saw one before, what's it do?"

While the desktop started up, Jax tried to explain computers. Wireless radios and radar were the new technology in Trick's day, and computers were decades away.

"Yeah? Social networking?" Trick listened with arms folded and head shaking. "Holy smokes, in my day, social networking was sweet-talking girls at a bar on Friday night while dancing to Glenn Miller. What's a giga-thing?"

Jax tried to explain. "That's how much you can copy and store on your computer memory. It's like a filing cabinet. Except my small computer can store a few million pieces of paper. More even. And then you can access it, read it, print it out, whatever. You can even watch movies, get the news, and talk to people. You can even send mail to people with the click of a button."

"Mail?" Trick looked around the keyboard and monitor. "Where do the letters go in?"

"No, no, never mind. It's like a telegraph but don't get me started."

"Holy smokes, Mac." Trick watched Jax click on several media websites and other sites to show him some of the information searchable. Then he brought up a website about the OSS created by a Washington-based historical group. Trick was amazed and read through several pages.

"This computer is dangerous, real dangerous, Ricky. It's a spy's dream. Heck, if you can get all this information anytime you want, why would you have to parachute anywhere? Who needs spies now?"

Jax laughed. "You'd be surprised, Trick. Spies are still important, don't worry."

"If you say so."

Jax typed on the keyboard and scrolled through several searches onscreen, choosing the second one on the results list. "How about this guy?"

"Hey, he looks familiar." Trick scrutinized the photograph. "Yeah, real familiar. Older but close."

It was an aged man speaking behind a podium. He had a full head of white hair, combed back with meticulous care. He wore an expensive gray suit and thick, round eyeglasses. Even with decades of age, he still had a hard, serious face. The placard on the podium read, "chairman."

"He should look familiar, Trick." Jax sent the article to the printer. "That's John H. Singleton. He's the Chairman and CEO of the Singleton Group."

"Chairman and CEO, huh? Johnny looks like he's doing all right. What's the Singleton Group?"

Jax retrieved the printout. He laid it on the desk for Trick to read. "The Singleton Group, as is your old spy-pal, Johnny, is the most powerful defense consultant in the country."

Trick read over the printout. "I think we should go see him, don't you?"

"Well, it's not that easy. I doubt we'd get within a mile of him." Jax looked down at the business card lying face down on the desk. He saw the strange sequence of numbers on the back and picked it up. "I almost forgot about these."

Trick looked at them. "Is that some kind of telephone number these days?"

"No, I don't know what it is."

"Well, this computer will know, right?"

Jax's eyebrows rose. "Yeah, maybe it will." He typed the numbers into the search program. A litany of wild-card results popped up on the screen and after reading page after page, none of them made any sense. "No luck. Any more ideas?"

"Try putting them in backward."

Jax did and the computer netted a similar jumble of odd results. "Nothing that makes sense. Unless..."

A smile etched his lips. He typed the numbers into the internet browser but replaced the dash between the numbers with a period.

An instant later, a new screen appeared with a log-in box in the center. A user name and passcode was required. He had neither. They were at a dead end.

"What the heck does that mean?" Trick asked. "This some secret place?"

Jax nodded. "Yes, I think it is. The numbers are an IP address. That's internet protocol, a sort of address just like you said. The question is to what?"

"What now? Do you know the password and user name?" Trick asked. "Whatever a 'user name' is."

"No, but we're going to find out somehow."

Trick snapped his fingers. "Hey, we used to work with codes all the time. Once, Johnny and I were in Algeria. I told you we were hunting these double agents in Tangier, and they had this secret code for contacting their network."

"Trick, you might be onto something. All this does sound very OSS, doesn't it?"

"Yeah, I think it does, too. If I get what this website stuff is all about, it's like us sending messages to the Frenchies."

Jax checked his watch. "This will have to wait. I have to go see Kathleen."

"Oh, boy." Trick pointed a scolding finger at him. "Now, Ricky, having it out with your girl isn't going to solve anything."

"Sure it is," Jax said, heading for the front door. "Martinez thinks I set up that meeting with Leo to kill him. There are two people who know the truth. One is Antonio Cavallo and I don't know how to find him. The other is Kathleen. She told Christie the stakeout was all my idea."

"So?"

"It wasn't." Jax stopped at the front door and looked at

Trick. His face fell. "So either Kathleen is lying or Leo was."

Trick frowned. "Or Christie is."

Chapter 30

Kathleen Cullen lived in a gated community that Jax often called "posh." Kathleen always feigned resentment and preferred, "upscale." Upscale meant you needed a referral from a board member for property ownership, a sizeable six-figure income, and an occasional garden party with A-list guests.

The property sat a half-mile off State Route 15 and was surrounded by a tall, brick wall with a decorative wrought iron gate and a security entrance gate. Inside the wall was a small community of luxury townhouses and condominiums designed for well-paid, well-heeled professionals. Most of the residents considered this their country homes and worked in and around Washington DC during the week, escaping to Loudoun County's historic, rural life each weekend.

Kathleen was one of them. She came from old money and not her parent's but her rich cousin Frank. For decades Frank had been a Washington insider and had no time for children.

When he died of cancer fifteen years prior, Kathleen inherited his small but viable fortune. His influence and her legal credentials landed her a high-powered office among Washington's elite.

"So this is a Jeep, eh?" Trick asked as he played with the electric window and door locks. "I used to drive Jeeps. They sure looked different. I should have invested in Jeeps in my day."

"Yeah, yeah, I know. Be quiet. I have to speak to the security guard." Jax pulled up to the intercom in front of the ten feet high iron gate. He pushed the call button and waited.

"What guard?"

"It's a remote control gate. The guard's in a security office somewhere else. He's watching us on cameras. This is all controlled over the internet."

Trick rolled his eyes. "The internet-thing again. I sure hope that never breaks because no one will be able to find their ass."

"Quiet."

The intercom clicked on. In the top corner of the gate wall, a closed circuit television camera rotated down to fix on Jax.

"This is Officer Koontz. Can I help you?"

Jax leaned out the window. "Richard Jax to see Kathleen Cullen."

"Is she expecting you? I don't have you on the list."

"No, but it's important."

"Oh, Agent Jax, I didn't recognize you. Wait a moment I'll ring her."

A few moments later, Officer Koontz returned. "I'm sorry sir, she's not answering. I can buzz you in if you'd like to check. She might be outside or on the courts."

"Sure, that would be great."

The giant gate opened, and Jax drove through. He followed the street around to the right, passed an empty tennis court and to the third set of townhouses. There, he parked in front of a brick and wood end unit.

Trick waited on the sidewalk. "Fancy, Ricky. How come you don't have a place like this?"

Jax ignored him and climbed the steps to the front door.

No one answered repeated rings.

"Stay put," Trick said. "Let me do my thing."

"Your thing?"

Trick vanished. A few moments later, the front door unlocked and Jax heard him say, "You better get in here, Ricky. It isn't good."

Inside, Jax found Trick standing in the middle of the high-ceilinged living room amid piles of strewn books, pieces of furniture, and broken bric-a-brac.

Trick waved his hand around. "You two have the same decorator."

"Is Kathleen here?"

Trick shook his head. "No. And whoever was here last checked every nook and cranny. And they didn't leave the crannies in one piece."

Jax searched the house, room by room, floor by floor. He even checked the garage beneath the house. He found more of the same carnage. When he returned to the living room, Trick stood by the front door looking worried as he kept waving for Jax to follow him.

"Hey, Ricky, maybe we should exit stage left. You can't be found here."

"No, I'm calling Christie. Kathleen's in danger."

"Ricky, I think it's too late for her. I'm sorry. Your cop pals are going to think—"

"Too late?" Jax dropped a stack of books he was sorting on the floor. "Can you see that for sure? I mean, do you know when people die?"

"It's not like that, Ricky." Trick frowned. "I'm not some kind of fortune teller. I don't need to be. Look around. You don't need a crystal ball to know your girl's in a jam. Somebody was looking for something. If Kathleen was here when they were, they weren't in the mood to ask nice."

"I know. I know." Jax pulled out his cell phone. "I have to call Christie or Martinez. I'm still a cop. I have to call this in."

"Oh, boy, you learn the hard way," Trick said. "Loose lips, pal. Loose lips sink ships."

Jax spoke with Christie for several minutes then rejoined Trick in the living room. "They're on their way. I can't believe all this. First Leo and now Kathleen. This isn't good."

"No, it isn't. But it could be worse, pal."

"No, it can't be. Kathleen's car is in the garage." Jax lifted a toppled chair in the corner of the room and looked down at the floor. "And there's dried blood on the carpet over here."

Chapter 31

W hat do you think I did, Captain, break in, ransack the place, and then call you?"

Martinez stood in the parking lot beside his cruiser. He had been grilling Jax for thirty minutes while the uniformed deputies set up the crime scene and began their work. The neighborhood was alive with on-lookers and everyone's attention was on Jax.

Christie stood beside them taking notes. She hadn't spoken a word since they arrived. Martinez hadn't allowed her to.

"Jax, what am I supposed to do with you? I ordered you to stay away from Kathleen."

"As you can see, I haven't disobeyed that order, Captain." Jax leaned against his Jeep. "She's not here. I called you when I found her place trashed. There's dried blood on the floor, and I'm afraid she's in trouble."

"You know what I mean—"

"Jax, see it from our side," Christie interrupted. "With Leo, and McCall's body yesterday, things look bad. The captain is trying to protect you. Why don't you listen?"

Martinez threw up a hand. "Agent, I'll handle this. Thank you."

"Listen to you?" Jax snapped. "The other night, you were on my side, remember, Christie? Do you think I left

the hospital and ran around town killing and tearing up everything I found?"

Martinez jabbed a finger into his chest. "Settle down,
Agent. You listen to me. Go home. Stay there. Let us do our
jobs and maybe—just maybe—you won't get arrested today."

Someone called out for Martinez and they all turned.

Jeremy Levin walked up with a young security guard in
tow. "Cap, this is Officer Koontz. I have his statement but I
thought you'd want to chat with him."

Koontz was a short, pudgy man who didn't look old
enough to shave and carry the revolver and badge he did
now. He was dressed in dark gray slacks and a white epilat-
ed shirt with a red and blue tie. There was an obvious bulge
of a handgun beneath his blue blazer and the jacket was ill-
fitting enough without it.

"Officer Koontz, who was the last visitor to see Ms. Cullen?" Martinez eyed him like a teacher waiting for the
chalkboard answer.

"Well, like I told Agent Levin," Koontz said, gesturing
at Jax. "He came night before last sometime after seven-
thirty. Maybe eight o'clock."

Martinez looked at Jax. "Agent Jax came here? You're
sure?"

"Yes. He's here a lot of nights."

Jax pushed himself off the Jeep fender and took a step
toward Koontz, but Christie grabbed his arm and pulled him
back. "You're a liar, Koontz. I wasn't anywhere near here."

"Ah, excuse me, sir, but you were." Koontz faded beside
Finch. "You rolled up and asked for her, and I let you right
in."

"You lying weasel!"

"Shut up, Agent," Martinez barked. "You saw him?"

Koontz threw a thumb over his shoulder. "In the CCTV.
I was watching a movie and he buzzed me."

"What was I driving?"

Koontz shrugged. "I don't know. But you buzzed the intercom and said, "I'm Agent Jax for Kathleen Cullen. I recognized you. You been here often enough so I let you in."

Christie stepped forward and confronted Koontz. "So you never called Kathleen?"

"Ah, well, no. Most times, if I recognize who it is, I don't bother. Is that a problem?"

"It's okay," Christie said, flashing her sweetest fake-smile. "Tell me, when did she get back?"

Koontz gave her a dumb look. "Back?"

"Yeah, when I was here a couple weeks ago, Ms. Cullen was leaving town for a while right after Agent Carraba was killed. When did she return?"

Koontz shrugged. "Sorry, ma'am. I didn't know she was gone. Guests have keycards to come and go. I don't know when she got back."

"All right, thanks."

"I'm sorry I didn't pay that much attention. People are in and out all the time." Koontz looked between Jax and Martinez. "Agent Carraba was that cop that was killed, right? Too bad, too. Ms. Cullen saw a lot of him."

Jax lunged at him but Christie stepped forward and intercepted him. "Easy."

"Go home," Martinez said, pointing at Jax. "Christie, take him. I'll call you. But get him out of here."

"Yes, sir." Christie took Jax's arm again and led him back to the Jeep, opened his door and motioned him in.

"This is all wrong, Christie," he muttered. "I wasn't here."

"I want to believe you, Jax. I do. We'll talk about it on the way home."

೭ා೭ා

As Christie pulled away, Martinez looked at Koontz. "Let me get this straight. Mr. Jax was the last person to come see Ms. Cullen two nights ago, is that right?"

"According to the log book, yes. I been working my normal shift and I haven't seen her around for days, but I guess so."

"Do the cameras record anything?" Martinez asked.

"Nope."

"And no one else saw her since?" Jeremy read over his notes. "You said that earlier."

"Nope. I don't think so, sir."

Jeremy looked at him and cocked his head. "You're sure of that?"

Koontz looked from Jeremy to Martinez and back. He shrugged. "Okay, well, maybe I'm not all that sure. But I'm here in the mornings when she goes to work. About that time I walk the residence gate area. I haven't seen her for a while, I guess."

"And you didn't see her or speak with her that night, right?" Jeremy caught Koontz's eyes. "Right?"

"No, sir."

"How about when he left? Any idea what time?"

Koontz held up his hand, shaking his head. "Sir, we don't record that. You roll up to the gate, push the exit button, and the gate opens. We don't pay any attention to departures, so I can't be sure."

"Terrific." Martinez's face tightened. "Did you hear anything or see anything suspicious that night?"

"No." Koontz frowned. "And if any of the other officers did, it would be logged in. There ain't any notes about Ms. Cullen."

"Agent Levin," Martinez said stepping so close that Koontz began to sweat. "Take Officer Koontz somewhere and see if his memory can be motivated a little better. I want proof, not, 'I'm not sure, sir.'"

"Come with me, Koontz," Jeremy said. "We're gonna go have a nice long chat again. This time, we're gonna find out what else you forgot to tell us."

"Ah, sure, sir." Koontz looked back at Martinez. "I'm

real sorry, sir. It gets lonely out here at night. I must have not been paying attention. I should have called Ms. Cullen. I'll apologize to her soon as she comes back."

"I doubt that," Martinez said in a cold, shallow voice. "I don't think Kathleen Cullen is coming back."

Chapter 32

Antonio Cavallo checked the parking lot one more time and, when he was sure no one was outside, retreated to his bed and picked up his cell phone off the nightstand. Three times he dialed the number and three times he hung up before it rang. The decision to make a deal was daunting. If he chose the wrong partner to parlay with, he was dead.

He dialed again and this time, let it ring.

"Yes?"

"Ah, ah—" Antonio's voice was strained and he failed to maintain any falsity of calm. "This is a friend of Hector Lupino. I—I—"

"You have the wrong number. I don't know any Hector Lupino."

Fear turned to anger. "Don't fuck with me, man. The Grey Coat Inn…you know…where da cop was killed."

Silence. Then a sigh. "What do you think you have?"

"I know who was there, *amigo*." Antonio's hand shook. "I got pictures. Ones with all the people in 'em. Everybody being pals."

"I see. And what do you want from me?"

"Money and a place to go. I want outta here, man. Now. I don't want none of this."

The silence made Antonio sick to his stomach. Then, the voice on the line said, "I think we can arrange that. Where are you, Mr. Cavallo?" Antonio tensed. "You listen to me, *muchacho*." The voice on the phone was cold. "You give me those photographs or you're dead. And don't play with *me*, Cavallo."

Antonio clapped the phone closed, dropped it, and ran to the window.

Three was still no sign of anyone waiting outside.

He turned around and looked back at the phone sitting on his hotel bed. "*Madre de Dios.*" He grabbed the phone again and tried to steady his nerves. This time, he searched the called-numbers list until he found the number he'd dialed days before but never completed. He redialed it and waited.

"Jax."

Chapter 33

That was Antonio Cavallo." Jax looked across the breakfast table at Christie. A pot of coffee and two cups sat between them. "He wants a deal."

"Is he coming in?" Christie asked.

"I think so. I never met him, but Leo gave him my number. Leo was strange about this one. Secretive and such. I'm not sure why, and he told Cavallo to call me if something happened. He has something for me."

Christie spooned sugar into her cup. "What?"

"He didn't say. But he wants to meet this afternoon."

"Where? Do you think you can trust him?"

"No. I told him he had to give me something. Something that would prove he was working with Leo and had information worth my interest."

Christie lifted her cup halfway to her lips and stopped. "And?"

"I'll show you." Jax led her back to his computer in the office at the rear of the house. "He gave me el toro and oso102311."

"And you know what this means?" she asked, looking at the notes he had on a pad. "The code?"

"Yes, I think I do."

Jax typed in the IP address he'd found on the back of John Singleton's business card. A second later, he reached the secure log-in page he'd found earlier. Then he typed *el toro* into the user name and "OSO102311" into the password block.

The screen went blank.

"Ah, crap."

Suddenly, the screen flashed from white to black twice and then went to a screen with the word, "DELETED" centered at the top.

"A dead end. Whatever was here is already gone," Jax said. Then he explained how he'd discovered the website to Christie. He'd left out Trick's role. "Any ideas?"

Christie shrugged. "I think the 'OSO102311' is a date. That's the day before you were shot, right? Try changing the date to yesterday and see what happens."

"A date? Yes, good idea. Let's see."

A moment later, the screen went black again and stayed dark for several seconds. But when Jax started to hit the 'back' button, the keyboard locked. "Damn."

Christie touched his hand. "Wait, this could be a dummy window to throw off anyone not supposed to be here."

She was right. Thirty seconds later, the black screen turned white and a page full of printed messages were displayed. Each was a simple sentence, several words long. Each one had a number at the beginning.

The first read *4—Alice chases the rabbit from hole to hole on Friday nights.* The second was *9—John will call at eight o'clock.* And the last one at the end of the page was *2—The pine trees are stacked into firewood for the winter.*

Christie read through the list, mouthing the phrases as she did. Jax tried printing them but the keyboard was disabled. Instead, he grabbed a pen and transcribed them onto a yellow legal pad as fast as he could. Halfway through, the screen went black again.

Seconds later, the website closed and sent them to the national atomic clock website. He rushed to jot down the last few codes he could recall.

"What the hell is this all about?" Christie asked, reading

the list Jax was writing. "Do you know what this all means?"

He kept scribbling what he could remember and ended up just a few phrases short. As he read them over, flashbacks of a dark April night in France came to him. He thought back to what he'd said to the lovely French Resistance fighter and what she'd said in return—*Oui, mais on peut voir au clair de la belle lune.*

He knew what he was writing on the pad now. "I understand. I know what this is."

"What?"

"It's an old code system. Each number refers to a person or a group. The phrase means something particular. We have to have the clear texts for the coded texts to know what they mean and who they are meant for."

Christie's eyes narrowed and she sat on the corner of his desk. She took the yellow pad from him and read it over several more times. "And just how do you know all this?"

"It's called a Jargon code. It was a code system the Allies used by Radio London to send messages to the Resistance and the OSS and SOE operating in France," Trick said. "I think a Frenchy devised it. Pretty neat, too."

Jax threw his chin at the stack of books sitting on a small table near the window. "I told you I went to the library. It's a code system used during World War Two."

"World War Two?" She handed him back the pad. "You mean the OSS."

He nodded.

"And who has the code's clear text for these?"

"I don't know." He stood up and went to the stack of books. "When we find both halves of the codes, we'll know more than just who's involved. We'll know who killed Leo Carraba and who sent them to do it."

Chapter 34

This proves that Antonio Cavallo is on the level? You're going to trust him?"

Jax looked at Christie across the room. They'd been trying to sort out the codes from the website for thirty minutes without any success. "Yes. I'm going to meet him. If he had that much, he has the decoded messages, too."

"Where are you meeting him? What's the plan?"

Jax considered that, knowing she was planning on going along. "No, Christie. I'm doing this alone. If the captain ever found out you have been helping me, you'll be on suspension next. If Cavallo has something that'll help my case, I'll call you and you can take him into protective custody."

"This could be a setup."

"By who?"

Christie stood and crossed the room, stopping in front of him. "I don't know, Jax. But I don't like it at all."

"If you have any other way for me to get traction on this case, now's a good time to tell me."

"I don't." She took his hand. "You know, I'm on your side. Even if you did shoot Leo, it was self-defense or something. But I'm in this with you."

"Thanks, Christie, but I didn't kill anyone. I think this website and Cavallo's codes are going to help prove it." Jax squeezed her hand. "I didn't shoot Leo. There were others there."

She let go of his hand and stepped back to look into his eyes. "Did you remember more? Tell me."

Trick tapped the office door to announce his presence. "Whoa there, Ricky. Think about this. Who is gonna believe what I showed you? Be careful what you say."

"I remembered more last night." Jax began a spin about what Trick had shown him. "I had a dream and when I woke up, I remembered more."

"Oh, brother." Trick took a seat at the table. "You still don't understand 'loose lips,' do you?"

"Tell me everything." Christie took out her cell phone, turned on the digital recorder application, and set it between them beside the coffee carafe. "And go slow. I want to get it all."

He did. He explained the vision of his shooting that Trick shared with him in as much detail as he dared. He went through the night twice, struggling to tell it as though he saw the events while lying on the gravel drive and not standing aside as a witness to his own attack. Playing with words was trying. He ended with, "It wasn't a dream. I know what I saw, Christie. You have to believe me."

"I'm not sure," she said. "It's so odd. You think there was a van loaded with people there? One of them shot you. You shot him, and some foreign kid saved you?"

He nodded. "I know how it sounds. But the doc said my memory would come back in pieces. The girl gave me those worry beads you returned to me at the hospital."

Christie considered this and slowly nodded her head. "Okay, maybe."

"Ricky, let this go, pal," Trick said. "Please."

"No," Jax said before realizing he was speaking to Trick. "I mean, no, I think whoever shot me was someone different than the people in the van. The others were frightened. The shooter didn't flinch. He just shot me. The young girl called for someone. Her father, I think. But some thug with a scar grabbed her and dragged her off."

"A scar?"

"I think it was a scar or a tattoo." Jax grabbed the yellow pad and sketched out a crude dagger. "It looked like this on his forearm all the way to his wrist."

"It could be all in your head, Jax. You know that, right?"

"Like Trick?" Jax dared a look at him. "Trick is real, too. I mean, we found his body, right?"

Christie folded her arms. "I have to hand that one to you. But we're investigating Leo's death, not McCall's."

Jax sighed and walked to the kitchen where he began making another pot of coffee.

Christie followed him. "Jax, don't be mad at me."

"Look, I'm investigating Trick McCall's murder, too. Martinez won't let me work my own case. So, if I can work Trick's and help myself, all the better."

"What do you mean?"

Jax saw Trick sitting at the table. When Trick shrugged, Jax decided to tell her. "Christie, don't you see there has to be a connection? Are you telling me that two murders, almost three, at the exact same spot separated by sixty-seven years is a coincidence? Leo said he was onto something big and to meet him at the inn. There's something about that place that connects all this together."

Christie sat at the table and lowered her eyes. She turned off the recorder application on her phone. "Jax, you don't know that McCall was killed at the inn. He could have been killed anywhere and dumped there. Someone might have dumped the body in the forties and it was never found. The inn has been empty all this time. Coincidence is what it is, Jax, just coincidence."

"Ricky, she doesn't buy it," Trick said. "Let it go. If you tell her the rest of what you saw, she'll be packing your bags for the funny farm."

"Okay, okay," Jax said. "Tell me what you found about Trick McCall."

Christie picked up her coffee and took a long sip. "Not much, I'm afraid. You were right, although I don't know where you got all this. He *was* OSS. The FBI swooped in after you left and seized the crime scene."

Jax smiled. "But I detect there is more to the story."

"Yes." She sighed. "Jeremy checked with some of his contacts. In 1944, McCall went rogue. He disappeared one night during his last mission moving some German scientists into the country. He disappeared with a fortune in stolen diamonds."

Jax leaned back and threw a glance at Trick. "Stolen diamonds?"

"That's not how it was, Ricky."

Christie nodded. "Yes. He was extorting money from the scientists apparently The OSS was onto a traitor and it was him. That's where the story ends. Jeremy has a friend who has a friend and he has a friend."

"I get it. The OSS thought Trick McCall was a traitor?"

"Lying bastards." Trick jumped up from his chair. "I never had the diamonds. I didn't even know about them until that night. Schiller tried to get me to take his money, remember, Ricky? It was the Harriet, not me."

"I know, I know." Jax patted the air and when Christie narrowed her eyes on him, he said, "I know what they think of McCall."

She eyed him for a long time. "Jeremy said that CIA has been looking for him since 1944. Traitors in the OSS were almost unheard of. They called him 'Trick' because he pulled off dangerous missions and pulled unconventional tricks doing it. Then, after he disappeared—"

"Dirty Trick." Trick stood across the room, head down, with his hands in his pockets. "Bastards. Every one of them. Whoever set Johnny and me up put the whole ambush on me."

Jax felt for him. Dead or not, having to hear himself maligned as a traitor. Jax understood that feeling all too well. It was how he felt with his own team thinking he murdered Leo Carraba.

"Trick McCall wasn't a traitor, Christie. I'm going to prove it."

She aimed a finger at him "It doesn't matter, Jax. What matters is that you're the one being called a traitor now. *You.* We have to prove them wrong."

Jax took her hand in both of his. He caressed her fingers with a gentle, familiar touch. When he caught himself, he retreated and dropped her hand. "I know I sound nuts. But you're wrong."

"Wrong about what?"

He looked at her. How could he make her understand? How could he explain that the OSS agent haunting him was a friend who needed his help? How could he explain his kinship to the apparition standing across the room from them?

"What happened to Trick McCall does matter. He was no more a traitor than I am. What happened to him in 1944 happened to me two weeks ago. Maybe by the same people. Maybe not. I'm going to find out who did this to us, and when I do, the Grey Coat Inn might claim another body."

Chapter 35

W e need to visit Quinton Properties." Jeremy Levin looked over the chest-high reception counter at the young Indian woman dressed in a security uniform and bearing the nametag, *Sonja*.

"What floor?" Finch added. "We'll show ourselves up."

Sonja looked confused. "Quinton Properties? I'm sorry, gentlemen, but there's no one in the building under that name."

Jeremy flipped his badge case open. "BCI. Let's try that again, Sonja. Check your files, will you?"

"Of course, sir. But I've been here for more than a year and I've never heard of them." Sonja tapped on her computer keyboard and ended with a shrug. "Oh, there's a note here. Please wait, I'll get my manager."

Finch smiled. "No thanks, just tell us what floor and suite, okay?"

"Well, it says fourth floor, suite 423. But I tell you, I've never heard—"

"Thanks," Jeremy said, heading for the elevator.

Finch gave Sonja a wink and ducked into the elevator just as the door closed.

On the fourth floor, they wondered the halls for ten minutes. Several businesses with door placards identified them as real estate moguls and financial analysts. Other doors had no name placards and only secure access card readers affixed. The halls led them on a tour of suite 400 to suite 430, skipping 423.

"No four-twenty-three?" Jeremy said. "There's no four-twenty-three?"

Finch retraced their path down a long corridor and found an unmarked door with a digital security access lock. "This one has no number. Maybe it's four-twenty-three."

"There is no four-twenty-three," a voice boomed from the hallway behind them. "Never has been."

Finch turned and saw a bald, round man walking toward them. "What does that mean? And who are you?"

"I'm Hubert Concord, the property manager. I understand you're inquiring about the Quinton Property people? May I help?"

"Yes, you can." Jeremy flashed his badge and credentials again. "What did you mean, 'never has been'?"

"They never physically occupied the suite. We provide a service for them."

Finch exchanged glances with Jeremy. "A service?"

"Yes, but may I ask what this is in reference to?" Hubert stopped beside Finch. "We don't provide client information to just anyone."

"No, you can't ask," Jeremy said. "Was this their office?"

"Yes, they paid for its use so I haven't filled it." Hubert glanced between the two BCI men. "And they haven't occupied it."

Finch tapped the access lock. "We want to check inside."

"Then you have a warrant?"

"No," Jeremy said. "We don't have a warrant. Not *yet*. But we can go floor to floor, customer office to customer office and see if any of the tenants in this building know the Quinton folks and why the property management is stonewalling us."

"We'll bring in a couple uniforms to help. I'm thinking four or five." Finch grinned. "It could take all day."

Hubert rolled his eyes and took a ring of keys off his belt, fingering through them until he found the right one for the door lock. "Fine. Have it your way."

Finch pushed open the door and led Jeremy inside.

The effort was wasted. The suite was composed of two large offices and a small reception area facing the door. The offices had barren, empty desks and office chairs. No plaques or motivational posters hung on the wall. There were no golf trophies or autographed baseballs on the desks. No pencils, pens, tablets, or other wares were left behind. The reception desk had the only telephone they could find and it was void of names or speed dial numbers.

The office had never been used.

"What the hell?" Finch said, opening the desk drawers and looking for any sign of business. "Did you ever see anyone here, Hubert?"

"No, I did not. I came after they signed their lease and it was empty then. That was two years ago. They renewed last year via courier and I haven't seen nor heard from them in this building since."

Jeremy sat at the receptionist desk and yanked drawers out, turning them over and dropping them on the floor. He probed beneath the desk looking for any wires or indications of computer terminals or access devices. There were none.

"A courier?" Jeremy asked, slamming one of the drawers closed. "Do you have the address it came from?"

"Yes."

"Good." Finch slapped him on the back and nudged him toward the suite door. "Let's go get it."

"Well, yes, all right."

Hubert led them back to the elevator and down to his office on the first floor. There, he opened one of his desk drawers, thumbed several files, and pulled one from the drawer. He jotted down several lines of information on a notepad and handed the page to Finch.

"I have their forwarding address, too, I believe. I'm supposed to forward all mail to them if and when we get it. It's all for naught, though. We get nothing."

Jeremy snatched the envelope from Finch's hands. "Thanks, Hubert. Anything else you can tell us?"

"No, no I don't think there is." Hubert sat down at his desk and folded his arms. "Anything more you'll need a warrant, gentlemen."

Finch smiled. "You bet, Bert. And, hey, you had this information pretty handy. How come?"

"Well..." Hubert shrugged. "You're not the first asking. An older gentleman came here asking for them. I looked up the information then and still had it on file."

Finch leaned across the desk. "What older gentleman and when was he here?"

"Two weeks ago but he didn't leave a name." Hubert's face whitened until he found the scribbled note on his calendar. "He refused to sign in and our security man had to see him out. Security did get this license plate number just in case. The man seemed very agitated."

Chapter 36

After Christie left, Trick reappeared stretched out on the sofa. "You know, that Christie reminds me of a gal I knew back in DC. Spunky, easy on the eyes, and bright. She's like that. She's also devious. She's up to something, sport, you mark my words."

"Are you trying to tell me something?"

"Nope, I told you, I'm not a gypsy with a crystal ball. I can't see the future. I'm just saying she lit out of here like her skirt was on fire. And, she's not telling you the whole truth."

"Maybe she thinks I'm nuts or that I'm holding back on her, too."

"Oh, she does."

"She does which?"

"Both."

Jax turned away. "Did you think Abrielle was always up to something? She was dangerous and tricky, right?"

"You got that right." Trick looked up from beneath his hat. "My Socks, she was something else. Tricky, smart, drop-dead gorgeous, and a killer. And I mean a killer, Ricky. Those Underground gals were as lethal as they come. That's why they were so good. The Krauts didn't see them coming."

"True love, right?"

Trick's eyes looked sad. "No, not for her anyway. I

asked lots of times, but she wouldn't marry me. She just kept saying 'maybe.' I always had bad luck with broads."

"Sorry, Trick. I know how that is." Jax retrieved his jacket and car keys. "I've got an idea. I'll be back later."

Trick sat up. "Didn't you hear Christie? You're supposed to stay put. Where we going?"

"We?"

"Sure, if you leave and get into trouble, who'll find my killer?"

"I have to talk to Lydia before I see Antonio Cavallo. She and her family should lay low until this is over."

Trick followed him to the Jeep. "I think playing Sam Spade on your own is a bad idea. You're not a cop anymore and I'm already dead."

"I'll be careful. Stay close and warn me if you hear anything from the other side that can help."

Trick played with the radio trying to find a station he liked. "I told you, Ricky. I can't see the future."

Chapter 37

In the daylight, Casa de Amigos was even more daunting than when Jax and Christie visited Lydia the night before. The building was stone and stucco built to look like an Old West hacienda. Instead of horses tied out front, a dozen motorcycles were parked side-by-side facing the road. An army of Latinos—gruff and unsavory gangbangers—stood amid decked-out pickups and street rods parked around the lot.

Trick stood watching the gang members staring at Jax's arrival. "Holy mackerel look at all the fancy cars. Is this some kind of show lot?"

"No, Trick," Jax said, watching twenty pairs of eyes locked onto him. "It's a gang hangout. Most of these cars are customized with stolen parts."

"You don't say? Well, they might be gangsters, but they're pretty talented."

"I'll be sure to tell them you said so."

It was after one-thirty pm and the restaurant was half-empty. The empty-half side of the room had checkered tablecloths covering six tables and four booths void of patrons. The not-so-empty half was full of tattoos and swagger from a dozen *Salvadorian Muchacho* gang members.

The moment Jax walked in, the room sucked air and the temperature rose ten degrees.

Trick stopped in the doorway and surveyed the groups of

gangbangers. "I gotta hand it to you, Ricky. I've dropped behind the Kraut lines a few times with nothing but my Sten and some chocolate bars. You got guts."

"Relax. They can't do anything to you now. Can they?"

Jax took a table nearest the front door where a hasty retreat was possible if his plan went sour. It didn't take long for Lydia to come to his table. "Senor Jax, *por favor*, you come back later?"

"No, tell your papa it's okay." He lowered his voice and feigned interest in the menu. "Antonio called me. Are you all right?"

She nodded. "Hector is here. *Por favor,* Senor Jax, go."

Three bulky Latinos parted a sea of gang art and testosterone and ambled across the room to Jax's table. Two of the men wore baggy jeans and over-sized tee-shirts with pounds of gold and silver around their necks. They were young but the ink and battle scars put years on them that overcame any youth they once may have had. The third wore cargo pants and a heavy denim shirt that hung over his waist. His sleeves were buttoned but didn't hide the ripple of muscle and power in his arms. The man's face was clean-shaven and his neck adorned with more gang art. His shaved head was large and menacing like a pit-bull.

Hector Lupino.

"*Buenos dios*, Jax," Lupino said with a wide, forced smile. "I haven't seen you for a long time. A very long time. I hear you got lit-up."

"*Hola*, Hector." Jax tried to keep his voice steady and calm. Every time he was in Hector's presence, he fought the urge to smash him in the face. "Hear anything good on the street?"

"*Si, si*, lots. I hear you popped your pal, Carraba. How come you pop one of you own and you still walkin' around?"

"You know I didn't kill Leo."

"*¿Qué?*" The gangster leaned back in his chair and threw

a chin at his two friends sitting behind Jax. "You hear that boys? Jax thinks I know 'bout Carraba."

The two thugs grunted amusement. The bigger of the two chuckled. "Was it cold layin' in the gravel, Jax?"

"*Cierra la boca,*" Hector growled. "Enough, *Oso.*"

"*Oso?*" Jax turned to him. "Hey, I heard of you. You're famous."

"Restaurant here is closed," Hector said. "Get out."

Nerves balled up in Jax's stomach. Coming to the restaurant had been a bad idea. A very bad idea. Still, he was committed now and had to see it through. "Hey, Hector, who played Muggs in the 1940s movie, *East Side Kids*? I'll give you a hint. It's about a bunch of street punks who do lots of funny stuff. You remind me of Muggs, in a Latin gangbanger-sort-a-way."

Hector leaned forward and grabbed hold of Jax's right arm, twisting it until the pain eked out of Jax's lips. "I said go."

"Leo Gorcey." Jax pulled his arm free and winced doing it. "How about another? This one I think you'll get right away. Ready? Who owns a dark van that might have blood-stains in the back?"

"No."

"'No,' you don't know, or 'no' there aren't bloodstains in the back? How about the thug with the dagger tattoo?"

"Tattoo?" Hector waved a hand and his gang closed around Jax. "My *muchachos* here don't have no dagger tattoos. See for you-self."

Like a chorus line, the gang members rolled up shirt-sleeves and slipped off jackets, displaying bulging muscle and ink. Several of them leaned in and pressed powerful arms into Jax's face and laughed as he slid back from the table and stood.

"Okay, Hector, I get it. Dagger-tattoo isn't here."

"Time to go, Jax." Hector threw a chin and the gang stepped back from the table. "Say hello to Antonio."

Jax stood. "What about the van, Hector?"

"Dunno nothin' 'bout no cargo van, Jax." Hector yanked a stubby automatic from beneath his shirt and jammed it into Jax's throat. "You outta nine lives, man."

Jax held Hector's eyes and backed toward the doorway. "Did I say it was a cargo van? But okay, you win, Hector."

"This was your plan?" Trick was at the front door.

Before they reached Jax's Jeep, Christie drove up from behind the restaurant. "What are you doing here?"

"Lunch. How about you?"

"I saw your car and knew you were in trouble." She shook her head. "I thought you were staying put at home?"

"I never agreed to that."

"Jesus, Jax." Christie got out and went to the trunk of her cruiser. She retrieved a heavy, black nylon case that she handed to Jax. "Take this. If anything happened to you, I'd feel responsible."

Jax unzipped the bag and withdrew a Glock .40-caliber automatic identical to his that Captain Martinez seized. "Thanks, Christie."

She patted his back. "What did Hector Lupino tell you?"

Jax slipped the gun into his waistband behind his back. "He was either at the inn when Leo was killed or he knows something about it."

"How do you know that?"

"No kidding." Trick nudged an elbow into Jax. "How do we know that?"

"He knew things. Like that I was looking for a cargo van. And that big lug, Oso, asked how I liked lying in the gravel. I don't think that was in the news, do you?"

"No, I don't think it was," Christie said, watching Lupino in the doorway. "Oso? Like the code we found?"

"Just like."

She turned her back on Hector's gaze. "And you didn't put the van in a statement yet. So nobody, including any of our folks, knows everything you remembered. What else?"

"He's gunning for Antonio Cavallo."

Chapter 38

Jax pulled up to the curb in front of his home and stopped beside his mailbox. Sitting in his driveway was a sleek, black Cadillac Escalade with dark tinted windows. The engine was running. A broad-shouldered man in a dark suit stood outside the front passenger's door with his arms folded watching the street. When Jax stopped on the street, the man tapped on the rear passenger's window and nodded. Then, getting some signal from within, he walked to the rear of the Escalade and stopped there, watching Jax.

Jax watched the man watching him. Twice the man—a security man for certain—touched his right ear and spoke.

As Jax got out of his Jeep and walked up to the Escalade, he glared at the security man. "Can I help you?"

The security man gestured to the driver's side rear door. "Mr. Singleton would like a word, Agent Jax."

"John Singleton?"

Another brooding security man in a dark, bulging suit climbed out of the driver's seat and opened the rear door. "Are you armed?"

Jax nodded. "Of course. I'm a cop. Are you armed?"

The second man stepped toward Jax when the passenger's window rolled down. The voice inside said, "Marcus, it is all right."

"Yes, sir," Marcus said. He motioned Jax into the vehicle. "Please get in, sir."

John Singleton sat in the passenger's side rear seat and gestured for Jax to join him inside. He was thinner than he looked in his internet photographs, but he was still distinguished. He had a full head of gray hair, strong features, and piercing blue eyes. He wore an expensive dark blue suit and a bold, fall-orange tie. Age had been kind to a man closing on ninety years old.

As Jax slid into the rear seat beside him, Singleton offered his hand and his eyes held Jax's.

"Agent Jax, it is an honor to meet you. Do you know who I am?"

"I do, Mr. Singleton." Jax shook his hand as the driver closed his door, remaining outside on guard. "What's this about?"

Singleton gestured toward a small panel affixed to the rear of the front seat. "May I offer you something? Bourbon?"

"No, thank you. It's early for me. What can I do for you?"

"Patrick McCall was more than my comrade, Agent Jax," Singleton said in a sad, low voice. "He was my friend. Many men go to war and find friendship. Few go to war and learn kinship."

Jax nodded. "I understand."

"No, you do not. But that is perhaps as it should be." Singleton coughed into a handkerchief. "I may be a powerful man, but I'm an old man, Agent Jax. I'm older than most today and older than my very few remaining comrades. I've accomplished much in my life but it was you who accomplished my one true goal."

"What was that, sir?"

His voice faltered. "You've returned my friend." Singleton reached over and touched Jax's knee. "Thank you. You have done me a great service."

"Yes, I found Trick. And I'm going to find out who killed him, too." Jax watched the old man smile. "I think whoever is behind his murder might be behind my partner's murder, too."

"Oh?" Singleton's eyes widened. "I've read about the other agent. Carraba, was it? You were injured as well."

"I was, but I'm better." Jax watched the old kingmaker. Singleton seemed approachable for such a powerful man and he decided to press him. "Sir, I found your business card in Agent Carraba's personal things. And we found some kind of a code being used on a website. The code resemble the OSS codes during the war."

"Codes? How interesting." Singleton looked down for a moment and seemed lost in the past. When he looked up, his piercing blue eyes bore into Jax. "As for the business card, I assure you, I had no dealings with him. But, as you might know, I have many colleagues. Perhaps one of them had contact. I'll inquire."

"Thank you. But, sir, would they give *your* business card to him?"

"Perhaps. Perhaps he visited my offices. I have to say, Agent Jax, that I cannot answer for this because I simply don't know." Singleton looked Jax over before his eyes cast down again. "And you think Agent Carraba's murder is connected to Captain McCall? Incredible. Tell me, how did you find Trick? We've been looking for him since 1944."

Jax started to answer when Trick turned around in the front passenger's seat looking back at them. "Johnny looks good for an old codger. Doesn't he?"

Jax ignored him and repeated the lie he'd given Martinez and Finch. "You see, sir, I was in and out of consciousness the night I was ambushed. I heard someone talking about a body. I thought it was the man I shot. As it turns out, it was Captain McCall."

"Extraordinary, Agent Jax. But that is preposterous."

"He's calling your bluff, Ricky," Trick said,

"Agent Jax," Singleton said, looking out his window. "We both know there is something more here, don't we? No matter. Keep your secrets. We all have them. But Trick was more than my friend, and I'm sad to know he died that way."

"Thanks, Johnny. I wasn't Harriet, pal. I hope you know that."

"Harriet must have killed him," Jax said.

Singleton considered Jax for a long time. "You know about Harriet?"

"I do. Finding Trick's body proves he wasn't the traitor."

"Not to everyone." Singleton's voice choked a little. "But I can see you know a little about him. Good. His life was cut far, far too short. He, like most of the OSS I served with, were all heroes in some way. Trick and I had many adventures together. We fought, bloodied, killed, and even loved along the way together. Even though it might mean he was a traitor, I always hoped he'd lived his life."

Trick slipped his fedora onto the back of his head. "That's great of you, Johnny. You were always a good friend. But what about Harriet? Any clues you can share?"

"Harriet, yes, yes." Singleton lifted his finger into the air. "That traitor was responsible for smuggling many poor souls out of France at enormous profit. Despicable. He has eluded us for many years. Decades. I always knew Trick wasn't he. I fought with the Outfit and later the Agency over that very fact. Now, they'll have to reckon with me again. And soon."

"Sir, are there any clues? Anything that you can tell me to figure all this out?"

"Agent Jax, did they find anything with him?"

"He means the diamonds," Trick said.

"I know, I know." When Singleton cocked his head and narrowed his eyes on him, Jax recovered with, "Yes, I know that was a question. No sir, we didn't. No diamonds and no evidence. Nothing. He was shot in the back of the head and dumped in the old root cellar. He never left the inn that night."

"I see that now. If I had any clues or evidence to share, I

would. The advice I give you is to take care. Take great care. Harriet could very well still be about."

Trick looked at Jax and winked. "He's got a point, Ricky. The way things are going to hell around you, Harriet might still be in town. Old maybe, but still a killer and a traitor."

"Sir," Jax said, considering Trick's warning. "Schiller escaped that night as well. He sneaked away from the inn before Trick was shot. Did you ever find him?"

Singleton leaned back in the seat. His face paled. "What did you say?"

"Did you ever find Schiller?" Jax pressed him. "Perhaps he had some information that might help find Harriet."

Singleton stared at Jax, unblinking. "I see you've done some research. Tell me, Agent Jax, what do you know of the night McCall was killed?"

"Now you've done it, Ricky," Trick said, pushing his hat onto the back of his head. "He knows you know a little too much."

Jax hesitated and stayed close to what Christie had told him earlier. "I know that Harriet was an OSS agent smuggling Germans out of Germany during the war for profit. Trick set up an operation at the Inn to catch him, and he was killed there. The official record says Trick was the traitor. I think we just proved them wrong."

"Not yet, but you're close to proving it." Singleton raised his chin and allowed a broad smile. He pointed a crooked, aged finger at Jax. "I would be interested in how you came by your research. Much of that is still classified today."

Jax waved a hand in the air. "A source. It doesn't matter. But, Mr. Singleton, you never said if you ever found Schiller?"

"We often thought Trick helped him escape. Some believed Trick killed him and disposed of his body before taking his diamonds and money and going into hiding."

"But did you find him, sir?"

"No, I never did." Singleton looked away. "I'd like to

ask you a personal favor, Agent Jax. I'd like you to work with someone on this Harriet matter. A Dr. Alex Vouros." Singleton motioned for his driver to prepare to leave. "Alex is a historian with the Washington OSS Historical Foundation. It's a cause I support with much funding. Perhaps the two of you can solve this together. Collaborate. No one knows about Harriet more than Alex Vouros, except perhaps, myself."

"All right," Jax said. "But, Captain Martinez might not agree."

"I've made arrangements." Singleton slipped something out of his suit coat pocket and handed it to Jax. "My private number. I am at your disposal."

Jax's door opened and the driver waved him out. Jax slid out and turned to face Singleton. "Thank you."

Trick looked back at Singleton. "Johnny, you're a good man. You stood by me all these years, pal. I appreciate it. Jax and I will sort this out. You have my word."

"Thank you, that means a great deal." Singleton glanced toward the front seat. Then, as Jax started to close the door, Singleton said, "Trick McCall was a good man. He stood by me all those years ago. My resources are yours as you need."

As the Escalade backed out of his driveway, Jax turned to Trick standing beside him. "What was that last part all about? I'd swear he heard you? Did you share him like you do me or something?"

"No." Trick watched John Singleton drive away. "I just connect with some people, Ricky. Mostly with people I've shared life and death with I guess. Like you. Johnny and me, we did it all together—life and death. That's what this is all about."

Chapter 39

Jax hadn't even reached his front door when his cell phone rang. "Jax." The voice on the phone was frantic and twice Jax had to calm the caller to understand what he was saying. After another barrage of information, Jax said, "Give me an hour." He hung up the call.

"That dish, Christie?" Trick asked, tripping his hat back on his head. "Have her come over. I'd like to share her, too."

"No, it was Antonio Cavallo." Jax's face tightened noticeably and his subconsciously rubbed his neck scar. He headed for his car. "I'm going to meet him."

"You sure he's on the level?" Trick said, slipping to the Jeep seat beside Jax. "This could be a double-cross."

"Do I have a choice? Cavallo was very specific. He wants to meet at the old farm. It's where Leo and I used to meet our informants. Leo must have met him there, too."

"What if it's an ambush?"

"Ambush?" Jax shot a sour look at Trick. "This isn't France, Trick. And he says he's got evidence about Leo's murder."

"Sure, sure. This isn't France." Trick leaned his head against the window and dropped his fedora over his eyes. "Ambushes *never* happen around here."

⌘⌘⌘

Jax rolled his Jeep to a stop three miles northwest of Leesburg along Route 9. The road made a sharp bend and the farm entrance was on the far side of the turn just ahead. A quarter of a mile down the dirt roadway was a dilapidated, two-story barn that hadn't seen a farmer or upkeep in ten years. Farther down were a rundown farmhouse and three other outbuildings that shared the neglect.

"Trick?"

Nothing.

"Trick?"

The seat was empty. "Damn you, Trick. Either stay or go but at least tell me when you do."

He tugged his automatic out of his waistband and checked to make sure there was a round in the chamber. He inched the Jeep forward down the farm's drive and rolled to a stop in front of the old barn.

Silence. There was no one around.

The farm was more than abandoned, it was *dead*. Years of weather and neglect had taken their toll and left the carcass of a once thriving business. The skeleton of a large corral was little more than rotting rails and a rusting tractor's corpse lay broken in overgrown weeds. The only thing that wasn't aged and decrepit was a new moped scooter toppled on its side behind a rusted, tireless tractor.

"Antonio?" he called. "It's me. I'm Agent Jax. I'm alone."

"He won't answer." Trick walked out of the barn and gestured to the scooter. "He isn't here."

Jax knelt down beside the scooter and found a small, black backpack lying beneath it. The pack was empty and each of its side pockets cut open. Its main cavity was shredded. Scattered around beyond it were several bits of dirty clothing. There were at least two shirts and what was once a pair of denim jeans. They too, were shredded into pieces. A pair of sneakers survived the knife blade. They were tossed aside but were still tied together by the laces and hanging from a branch of a wild raspberry bush.

"Someone was looking for something," Jax said.

Trick knelt beside him and pointing to the backpack. "They played hardball to find it, too. Look."

Jax examined the left shoulder strap and found sticky, red ooze. "Blood."

"Your stool pigeon isn't around, Ricky. You think this pack is his?"

"Yeah, and it looks like whoever found him got what they wanted. The pack's empty."

Trick walked a few steps toward the barn and turned back around. "No, I don't think they did."

"Why's that?"

Trick waved his hand in a circle. "There's no body."

"Maybe." Jax tossed the backpack onto the scooter. "I'll look around."

"No need, Ricky. I've done that. Cavallo isn't here."

"Why does that mean that whoever was here didn't get the evidence?"

"What kind of a cop are you?" Trick winked. "If they got what they came for, then Cavallo would be in the bushes with this backpack. He didn't have the evidence or whatever it was with him."

Jax looked around him and finally settled back on the backpack. "You're, right. They took him somewhere to get it out of him. Cavallo is alive."

"For now."

Chapter 40

Jax sat at his home office desk, ignoring his buzzing cell phone. He often found a quiet, comfortable refuge to sit and think. No noise. No interruptions. No phones. Just silence.

That silence was broken by Trick calling him from across the room.

"Ricky? What are we going to do now?"

Jax shook himself and stood. "I have to run some computer checks on the codes we found on-line."

"Come on, we need to hit the bricks." Trick folded his arms. "Bad guys are caught with footwork and sweat. Well, maybe a few tricks here and there, but you get what I mean. You don't find evidence on a computer."

"This computer can help us find some leads. Besides, Martinez won't let me close enough to the case to run any of the team's real leads. So we have to find our own. We'll start with the jargon codes Cavallo led us to earlier. The ones on the website."

"And you think your computer is going to help?"

"Sure. I'm thinking we can figure out what the codes mean without the decoded plain text."

"No you won't." Trick shook his head. "That type of code system can't be broken without the decoded clear text. That's the whole point, Ricky. One phrase means only one thing to one OSS team. Each had a designation. That's what the numbers before the phrases are I'm sure. The phrase is pre-set. You know, 'the chair is against the door' means 'we bomb the Jerries at noon.' If you don't know that, you won't be able to figure it out."

"Maybe someone made it easier to remember. Using the web is brilliant. You can access it with a smart phone and there's no telephones calls linking people together."

"It's just like using the radio back in France," Trick said. "The bad guys can't figure out who is receiving and sending the signals very easy."

"Or in this case, the good guys can't trace you either." Jax pulled out the list of codes he and Christie copied from the website earlier. "It can't hurt to try, right?"

"It's a waste of time, Ricky. But okay."

Jax began running the code phrases through the online search engine. The first one he tried was *2-The pine trees are stacked into firewood for the winter*. The computer found no matches to the phrase. He tried another two and the same results came back. *No Result Found.*

"Don't say I didn't warn you." Trick stood behind him, grousing at each failed attempt. "You need the decoded clear text."

"Let's try another way." Jax found the first code phrase—*Alice chases the rabbit from hole to hole on Friday nights.* He typed in, "Alice," "rabbit," and "hole."

A second later, the search results returned a page of Lewis Carroll's *Alice in Wonderland* references and assorted storybook passages. The last reference on the page was different.

"Alice's Crossing Golf Course, Eighteen Holes of Golf," Jax read aloud, clicking on the hyperlink to read the article. "It's a few miles out of town south of the Grey Coat Inn. It's been closed for years. Some developer bought it for a housing project."

Trick tipped his hat onto the back of his head. "So? You think this is a lead?"

"Maybe. The Inn is an old abandoned property, too, like

the golf course. Let's go see if they have anything else in common."

Trick followed him out the front door. "What about Antonio Cavallo?"

"I'll call Christie on the way. She can put out an alert and re-search the scene. But so far, the bad guys seem to be one step ahead of us."

Chapter 41

Jax wheeled his Jeep into a crumbling parking lot ten miles south of Leesburg and headed down the mile-long lane from the highway. "This place hasn't been used in years, Trick. Let's hope we get lucky."

"You take me to all the nicest places."

The golf course was a shambles. Grass, weeds, and neglect had overtaken the property years ago. The few fairways in view looked more like narrow farm pastures now. The clubhouse was a two-story wood structure with its front windows boarded over. The sign above the main entrance still read, "Alice's Crossing" but the paint was badly peeled and the words sun-bleached out making it difficult to read.

There were no vehicles or signs of life anywhere.

Trick stood in front of the clubhouse and tried peeking through a crack in the window coverings. "I don't see anything, Ricky. Maybe this was a wild goose chase and your computer isn't as smart as you think."

"We just got here, Trick."

Jax went around back and wound his way between stacks of debris and rows of broken, stripped golf carts long ago abandoned. At the rear clubhouse entrance, he found a severed piece of chain cut away from the double-door where a sign announced the pro shop and club rentals.

"Someone's been here recently." He tugged his Glock out with one hand and lifted the chain with the other. The

chain was rusty but its ends were snipped straight and revealed clean, un-rusted metal. "Someone used bolt cutters
on this."

"Ricky, I was wrong. I'm getting something inside."
Trick disappeared at the entrance, calling in his wake, "Follow me. The young girl who saved you was here. I'm sure
of it."

Jax slipped inside and pulled out his penlight, resting his
gun-hand across his wrist to track the muzzle along the narrow beam of light.

"Trick, what makes you think that girl was here?"

He was gone.

"Jesus, first I can't shut you up. Now I can't get you to
answer."

Jax worked his way from the pro shop reception counter
around three large rooms, left empty but for display coun-
ters and various shelves and racks left where golf equipment
and sports attire had once lived. Around the side of the reception area was a grand staircase that led to the banquet
room above. He tried the lights but there was no power, so
he decided to finish the first floor before tackling the darkness above. He worked his way around the first floor section by section.

First, he cleared the sales area and then a small snack bar
where a fountain drink machine still sat behind the counter
and four tables were stacked against one wall. In the lounge,
nothing remained but empty packing materials and the remnants of cardboard boxes and twine. It took only a few moments to finish the first floor after clearing the men's and
ladies' locker rooms. He found nothing but old metal lock-
ers and empty shower stalls.

Jax was leaving the men's locker room when he heard it.

Footsteps over head on the second floor.

Dead OSS agents didn't make noise with their footsteps
so Jax flipped off his penlight and picked his way toward
the staircase.

When he looked up, a figure scurried past the upper landing and Jax flipped on his light again, aiming his Glock into its path and calling, "Police, come down."

The figure froze just beside the landing, standing back from the beam of light.

As Jax passed the light back and forth across the top of the stairs, the figure's shadow moved with it, just out of the cone of light.

"Come down. This is the BCI. I'm armed. Come down now."

No movement. No sound. Nothing.

The figure disappeared.

"Dammit." Jax started up the stairs, keeping his light and gun tracking across the top landing. "Identify yourself."

Nothing.

At the top of the stairs landing, Jax began a slow, careful pivot shining his light into the cavernous banquet room. Halfway through his turn, something moved behind him and he whirled.

The blow came through the darkness and knocked him backward against the landing railing. The second struck his outstretched arm and his gun tumbled to the wood floor and skidded away into the darkness.

Jax anticipated the third strike and sprang to his right, feeling the whoosh of air as something swung past him and struck the railing hard. He jumped forward to grab his attacker. He found clothing and arms and he tried to swing the attacker around and drive him to the floor.

Someone cried out and flailed back, kicking and slamming a hard, bony head against him.

His grip lessened with each kick to his legs. When the attacker found his aim, a strong, hard head-butt sent Jax reeling backward and down on the floor. It took him valuable seconds to rebound, find his Glock, and get to his feet.

Clambering footfalls were already halfway down the stairs.

"Freeze, BCI!" He took the stairs two at a time, leaping

the last three onto the figure's back as he headed for the door.

For a second, Jax tasted bile. The pain in his shoulder exploded so he lay heavily on the figure's back, clutching an outstretched arm and bending it behind for control. The needles in his arm subsided and he slid off the figure, got to his feet, and kept his Glock ready.

"On your feet. Who are you?"

The figure rolled over but stayed prone. He was a shaggy, raggedy-dressed man with a stubble beard and uncombed hair. He was a homeless man who looked to be in his fifties. Living out of abandoned houses and makeshift shelters had aged him well beyond his years.

"Leave me alone, man. I ain't doing nothing but livin'."

Jax stepped back and motioned with his gun for the man to stand. "Easy."

The man stood. "What you want, man? They said I could come back today. What's your problem?"

"Who said you could come back?" Jax stepped forward and patted the man down. In one of his pants pockets, he found a roll of twenty-dollar bills. "Where'd you get this, pal? Must be two hundred here. What's your name?"

"Charlie," he said, wiping his face with a dirty sleeve. "I ain't botherin' nobody. And it's my money. I earned it."

Trick was at the bottom of the stairs now. "Leave him alone, Ricky. He's just a hobo."

"Homeless. We don't use hobo these days," Jax said. But when Charlie cocked his head and looked around, Jax added, "How did you earn so much?"

Charlie snatched the money back. "Security."

"Security?" Jax returned the money to him. "Come on, Charlie, tell me or you're going in for trespass."

Charlie considered that as he counted the bills as though Jax had somehow stolen some through sleight of hand. "This big guy watchin' the others, he tell me get out of my spot for a couple days. He told me he'd give me two-hundred if I stayed out in the workshop 'round the side and watched for anyone coming. You know, like security."

"Who was this guy and what others are you talking about?"

Charlie shook his head and backed up a couple steps. "Nope. He said he'd be watchin' and would get me if I talked. He was a mean one, too. He treated the others bad, 'specially the girl and her daddy. Mean one, man. But the girl was nice."

Trick walked and looked Charlie over. "Ricky, look at his wrist."

On Charlie's right wrist was a string of amber beads. When Jax reached for them, Charlie pulled back. "They're mine, man. The girl gave 'em to me. She brought me some tea and these beads."

They were the same worry beads the young girl had given him the night he was shot.

"That's her, Ricky," Trick said. "And that's your evidence. She was here."

"Charlie, did you hear them say where they were going or anything that will help us find them?" Jax watched the vagrant stuff the beads back in his pocket. "We have to find the girl before the man hurts her."

Charlie shook his head. "No, sir. The mean one wouldn't let me in here. The girl came and brought me some tea and these beads one day. She didn't say much. Don't think she spoke English good."

"Ricky, he doesn't know anything. Let him go."

"Okay, Charlie." Jax slid his Glock back into his waistband. "Can you be here if I need to talk to you again?"

"Sure, yup. Bring me some coffee if you come back."

"You got it."

Charlie eased away and headed out the front door, turned the corner, and disappeared.

Jax watched after him. "What do you think of my computer now, Trick?"

"Computer?" Trick returned to the stairs. "Your computer didn't find the beads and the girl, Ricky. Charlie did."

Chapter 42

K haled, come here," Ameera said, waving for the nine-year old to drop his soccer ball. "Khaled, come."

She pulled Khaled's sweatshirt hood over his head to warm him against the late October breeze. Both were accustomed to the cold. Their village northeast of Kabul knew harsh winters and their home had little heat from the stoves. As she pushed Khaled away to play, she noticed Manuel and Lobo working in the rear of the old shed. They were moving provisions from the big American van into the house that her family had called home for a few scattered days.

Khaled's ball rolled to her and she returned it with a kick, past a pile of pine logs ranked for the winter fires, sending him running farther each time for his turn.

Since arriving in America three weeks ago, Ameera had not thought of home. It was violent and scary and, for a young girl, it was without hope. A future for her was worse now than her mother had ever known. At least her mother had been lucky. She came from Kabul and married her father when she was perhaps a year older than she. Her father was a doctor with a promising future. For her mother, there had been hope of change.

The Taliban ended that hope.

After three clashes with hooded thugs sent in their name,

her father took her away to the mountains and started over. He spent years caring for the old and sick, many who had never healed from other wars not long in their past. For as long as she could remember, they had driven the mountain roads village to village so her father could tend to his patients. Neither the Taliban, nor winter's cold and snowy passes, had deterred him.

Ameera had only been a baby when the Americans arrived. For her father, they brought a sliver of new hope for something better for his children. Her memories had flashes of village gatherings where the elders met to pray and share those dreams. When the Americans had come, they brought safety and food and medicine. Everyone believed they would not leave and let the Taliban return.

It had all been a lie.

For ten years using his medical skills and tribal contacts to aid the American soldier's work, Ameera's father had saved all their payments for one chance to leave it all behind. But time had been running out. The elders said the Americans would be leaving, and everyone feared what would happen in their wake. Village would turn on village. Some would retaliate against her father for his collaboration with the Americans. Retaliation even if that help had rooted out the Taliban and stopped the violence.

It was time to leave.

One late night her parents whisked Khaled and her away to Kabul. Days later and many roads travelled, they emerged at a dusty, rundown airstrip east of the capital.

Just two days and three weeks ago, they finally arrived in America.

Ameera watched Manuel carrying an armload of supplies from the shed and he smiled at her. He was much like the young men who secreted them from Kabul a month ago. He was young, strong, and kind. She knew nothing of his Salvadorian roots. Manuel was just another foreigner to her. Now though, in America, she was the foreigner.

"Ameera," Khaled called. "*Min Fadlak.*"

"*Na'am*—yes."

She kicked Khaled's soccer ball deep into the pine trees and he ran after it. A few seconds later, he called for her. It was lost and he was scared to be in the woods alone. She ventured through the brush and scrub trees, but after several minutes lost sight of him.

"Khaled?"

"*Hola*, 'Meera," a harsh, deep voice whispered behind her. "Lose this?"

She spun around and saw Lobo standing beside a fallen pine. He held Khaled's ball out. "Come here, 'Meera. I show you to play."

"*La, la, la.*" She backed away and concentrated on English words. "No, no. Lobo, throw ball. *Min Fadlak*—please."

Lobo grinned and bounced the ball once on the ground, caught it, and held it out for her. "I don't hurt you, 'Meera. Come on. Come on and play."

"No, no." She looked around the woods. "Khaled? Khaled, come to me. Khaled?"

She felt Lobo's hands grip her shoulders and she tensed. "No—*La, la, min fadlak.*"

"Come on, 'Meera, come."

Ameera twisted away as Lobo jerked sideways and crashed onto the ground beside her. She looked past him, saw Manuel wave her away, and she ran. As she emerged from the woods, she paused and looked back, listening. Manuel launched into an angry tirade and Lobo responded as their voices raged in Spanish. Manuel saved her. From what, she could only fear. There had been men like Lobo in the mountain villages, too. It was part of her young life and she had learned that fear. Learned what she could to avoid and survive. Those villages were in the past. But that wasn't her worry now. Now, though, her worry was not that Manuel had to save her. Her worry was would he be there to save her again?

Chapter 43

Jax walked into the BCI office and was stopped at the reception counter by Mrs. Leweski. "Sorry, Jax, Captain Martinez said you can't be here."

"It's all right, Mrs. Leweski," Christie called, walking around the corner. "Let him through. I'll handle the captain."

"You do that, missy." Mrs. Leweski returned to a cup of tea beside a stack of papers on her desk. "The captain will chew me out for letting him in."

Jax followed Christie back toward the agent bullpen. "Thanks, Christie, the captain is cutting me off—"

"Chief Rogers was murdered."

"What?" Jax froze. "Dammit, I knew his death wasn't right."

Christie stopped in front of her desk, looked across the bullpen at Jeremy and Finch talking, and lowered her voice. "Autopsy report just came in. Someone murdered him."

"Why would anyone want to kill Chief Rogers?" Jax asked.

Before Christie could respond, Finch and Jeremy walked over.

"Funny, I was going to ask you that, Jax," Jeremy said.

"What does that mean?" Jax faced Jeremy, taking a step closer than Jeremy liked. "You got something to say, rookie? Out with it."

"You were missing for three hours that night, Jax." Jeremy stepped back. "Right about the time Rogers was killed."

Jax looked at Christie. "What time is that?"

"Around five or five-thirty," she said glaring at Jeremy.

Jax sighed and grinned sarcastically at Jeremy. "I was at the library. I told you that already."

"No one saw you," Jeremy snorted. "No one."

"Check my books, dumbass. Even if no one saw me, I still signed them out."

"Were you checking out books to conjure up some more dead spies and ghosts?"

Jax reached for Jeremy but Finch stepped between them, patting the air. "Everyone relax. The chief makes two homicides."

"Two homicides that Jax is involved with," Jeremy quipped. "And counting."

"You stupid bastard." Jax shook his head. "I'm no more involved in Rogers' homicide than any of you."

Christie pulled Jax's arm until he eased back toward her. "Easy, no one is saying you killed him."

"Yet," Jeremy sneered. "Your alibis are wearing thin."

Jax face reddened. "And where were you last night at five, Levin?"

"Out looking for you." Jeremy forced a laugh that sounded asthmatic. "Captain's orders."

Jax pressed. "Anyone to corroborate your story?"

"Enough," Martinez yelled from across the bullpen. He strode from his office up to them and stabbed the air toward Jax. "What the hell are you doing here?"

"My job, Captain." When Martinez' face tightened, Jax softened his voice and added, "I came by to see if there was any news. That's all."

Martinez looked from Christie to Finch and then to Jeremy. After a long moment, he returned his attention to Jax. "Good. I just got off the phone with the colonel in Richmond. He got heat from the governor's office."

"About me?"

"No." Martinez let a thin, taunting smile crack his lips. "It seems a John Singleton has a lot of clout down in Richmond."

"Patrick McCall's partner in OSS," Jax said. "He's also a pretty powerful guy around DC. I met him earlier today."

"Interesting," Martinez said, waving in the air. "Mr. Singleton has requested from the governor, who has directed the colonel, who just now kicked my ass, to have one of Singleton's OSS historians review McCall's remains and any files we have."

Jax gave Martinez a wry smile. "Yeah, I think he mentioned that."

"You're meeting Alex Vouros in thirty minutes at the Inn. Don't be late."

"Who's this Vouros character?" Finch asked.

"Some PhD-something-or-other working for the OSS Historical Foundation in DC," Jax answered. "He's interested in our discovery of Trick—Captain McCall's—remains."

"Finch shrugged. "What's some historian-PhD got to do with this? I thought it was a national security matter?"

"It is," Martinez said. "But John Singleton has major clout. Vouros is coming out to document everything about the McCall discovery. So play nice, Jax."

Christie laughed. "Yeah, some old geezer following you around for a while. That'll be fun."

"It should keep you out of my hair, Vouros included, for the rest of the day," Martinez said, walking away. "See that it does."

Chapter 44

Before Vouros gets here, let's take a private tour," Jax said, looking over the grounds of the Grey Coat Inn. Trick sat in the front seat as Jax stopped the Jeep in front of the new yellow crime scene tape stretched across the Inn's entrance. A placard posted on a pole in the center of the drive warned the area was restricted as a crime scene by the Federal Bureau of Investigations and all persons were forbidden from proceeding.

"Does that mean us?" Trick asked.

Jax jumped out and ducked under the tape, knocking the wood pole and placard down onto the gravel drive. "Sure does."

Trick followed. "I think you just committed a federal crime."

"We'll add it to the list."

They went to the main Inn's front door and found it double-locked with a heavy security padlock and hasp the FBI had installed.

"Great," Jax said, peering through one of the windows. "I'm no good with locks."

"I am." Trick cracked a wry smile. "Get something like a piece of wire or a paperclip. You know the stuff."

Jax eyed him. "Okay, but if you're going to do what I think, then warn me first."

"Would I share you without permission?"

"Yes."

Jax returned from his Jeep with two paperclips, a stiff, narrow stick of wire, and a thin screwdriver. "Okay, now what?"

"Consider yourself warned." Trick held Jax's shoulder and stepped into him. The rush was instantaneous and the wave of euphoria and exhilaration were less foreign to him. Still, Jax nearly fainted.

"Watch and learn, Ricky."

When Jax's body steadied, it took only a minute for the FBI's locks to fall away. Thirty seconds later, the door lock succumbed, too. As soon as the door opened, Trick released his hold on Jax.

"Damn you, Trick." Jax shook off the dizziness, gasped a couple times, and steadied himself against the doorframe. "I told you to give me some warning."

"I did."

"Before you do it." Jax looked at the locks and open door. "Just don't plan on doing that too often, okay? It's unsettling."

"It's a little unsettling being dead, too." Trick walked inside the Inn. "But you don't hear me complaining all the time. Maybe if we shared a cup of joe and some doughnuts once in a while, I'd feel welcome."

"Okay, okay."

Inside, there was very little light from the few windows and Jax shined his flashlight around the hallway. "I'm not sure what to look for."

Trick shrugged. "Something your people missed?"

"My people don't miss things at a crime scene, Trick. Neither does the FBI."

"Sure they do. If they didn't, they wouldn't think you killed Leo. And they would have found me before you did, right?"

"Point taken." Jax shrugged and moved on.

After more than an hour searching room to room—often

on his hands and knees—Jax gave up. "They didn't miss anything, Trick. There's nothing here."

Trick was looking out the kitchen window. "Someone's been digging in back."

Jax walked over and joined him, looking out at a three-foot circle of missing gravel and earth. "Christie said Chief Rogers was working on something around the grounds. But, I didn't see anything in Martinez's report that would account for this."

"The same Chief Rogers who was murdered?"

Jax nodded. "Another point taken."

"You're cop-pals all act like they're hiding something. People who hide things are up to no good."

"You were a spy, Trick. You hid things all the time."

"True. I was a sneaky bastard. Why do you think they called me Trick? Now, your pal Martinez, he's a different kind of sneaky bastard."

"He's not my pal."

"My point exactly."

Jax considered what Trick was suggesting. Martinez had become increasingly unfriendly since Leo's murder. While Jax didn't blame him, it struck him that trust was a commodity he couldn't buy from him. Maybe Trick was onto something without knowing it. Maybe Martinez was a problem.

He shook it off and began searching the kitchen for the third time. He stopped at the antique gas stove and opened the lower oven door. He took three long, deep breaths before he reached in and dug around the oven base. He stood up and examined several bits of dried matter he'd scraped from the oven's under-panel.

"Do you smell, Trick?"

"I beg your pardon. I don't smell. I may be dead, but I don't smell that way."

"Not that." Jax showed him the small bits of dried material in his hand. "I mean can you smell. It looks like some kind of cooked meat and rice. And not too long ago, either."

"What if it is old meat and rice? It's an inn and that is an oven."

Jax knelt down and examined the rest of the stove. "You said it earlier. It's an old inn. Except, this place hasn't been used in years. This spilled food and grease is recent. Maybe a couple weeks at best." He looked out the window above the sink. "There's a small propane bottle out there. Why?"

"Someone has been staying here. At least overnight."

Jax nodded.

"See, I could be a detective," Trick said. "We should go into business together. You know, like 'McCall and Jax, Private Dics.'"

"Oh, brother. Remind me to explain what's wrong with that later."

Outside, a car pulled up and Trick went to the rear kitchen door. "Hey, Ricky, what's Alex Vouros all about? Some kind of doctor or something?"

"A PhD, Trick. Some old guy from the DC History Foundation. Why?"

Trick whistled a cat-call. "Because Alex Vouros isn't some old guy. In fact, *she* isn't anything you're expecting."

Chapter 45

Alex Vouros wasn't just an intellectual connected to powerful people like John Singleton, she was beautiful. She was in her late-thirties with a full, strong figure that demanded a second and third review. Her complexion was soft and tanned and her eyes dark with an intelligence that penetrated Jax like X-rays. She wore khakis, a white, button-down cotton shirt, leather jacket, and hiking boots. She looked like an archeologist on her way to the great pyramids.

"Doctor Vouros?" Jax asked, walking up to her Mercedes. "I'm Agent Jax, BCI. Captain Martinez told me to meet you."

"Yes, but call me Alex." She met Jax in front of her car and shook his hand. She studied him for a long time before smiling. "Agent Jax? You found Captain McCall's remains. Thank you for agreeing to help me."

"Mr. Singleton didn't make this optional, I'm afraid."

Alex rolled her eyes. "No, I guess he wouldn't. He is our largest contributor to the OSS Historical Foundation. And, as you may know, he's a very powerful man. He's been supporting my research for years."

"What research do you do?"

"I'm a historian, Agent Jax."

"Just Jax."

"Jax, then." Her smile had him for the second time. "I've

been working with the foundation for many years. I investigate and validate OSS stories or discoveries of historical significance. Patrick McCall has been one of the remaining mysteries with the foundation since the beginning. I've been interested in this case for years. I'll be documenting the conclusion to his case and advising on any historical correction that is necessary."

Trick ran his thumb over the brim of his hat. "Did you hear that, Ricky, she's been interested in me for years? She's a keeper. She'll know things about my case I wasn't around for. Finding them out would take you too long on your computer. So, don't make a mess of this, okay?"

Jax snorted. "One missing OSS agent has kept the government busy for almost seventy years?"

"OSS having a rogue agent was very unusual. And it's also about a lot of corruption smuggling illegal German scientists and industrialists into this country."

Jax's nodded. "Like Schiller. How much money?"

"You know about Schiller?" Alex's eyes sparked like a child offered a treat. "Of course, John told me you spoke. You're also familiar with Harriet's misadventures?"

"I've had some schooling on this, yes. But let's get to business. What would you like to do first?"

"Show me where you found him, please? I'd like to see for myself."

Jax pointed toward the carriage house across the drive. "There's a hidden room off the cellar."

"Interesting." She reached back into her Mercedes and retrieved a canvas duffle from the rear seat. "The Inn was part of the Underground Railroad. Local lore says it was used to hide Colonel Mosby's men during the Civil War, too."

Trick fell in behind them as they headed across the drive. "See, Ricky, she's a keeper. She's easy on the eyes and smart, too. She'll be running our new detective business in no time."

Chapter 46

You found him here?" Alex asked, taking a heavy four-cell flashlight from her duffle. "Extraordinary."

"Yes, right in the far corner." Jax pushed back the crime scene tape and shined his flashlight into the cellar's antechamber. "He was wrapped in an old tarpaulin. Not much left of him, I'm afraid."

"Did you find anything with him? Any evidence? Clues?" Alex waved her flashlight around the empty stone floor. "Anything?"

"No, nothing." Jax waited in the entrance. "He was still in a suit and his stupid fedora."

"Hey, my favorite hat isn't stupid," Trick said from the entrance. "It makes me look dapper. You might think about getting one. No one wears hats anymore. Just those punks at the restaurant. And they wear them backward and sideways. I don't get that."

"It's about attitude," Jax said, but when Alex looked over at him, he added, "dealing with all this takes the right attitude."

"Right." Alex looked around very carefully. "I've seen photographs of Captain McCall. He was a very handsome man."

"I'm going to like working with her. Ricky."

Jax led her out of the antechamber and realized she had stopped when he reached the cellar stairs. "Alex?"

Alex was looking back and her voice was low and strained. "That's no way to die, is it? No one deserves to lie alone and to be abandoned for so many years. Will you help me find out who was responsible for this?"

"Absolutely." He waited for her to reach the stairs. "What's the story with the diamonds? They keep coming up."

"They were part of Harriet's payment," she said. "Some Swiss Francs, diamonds, sometimes jewels or gold. Each escapee had to pay thousands to Harriet. We think as much as five-thousand or more each."

"Schiller had at least that much," Trick said,

Jax repeated him and added, "And the others?"

"They were desperate men trying to flee Europe. Some were in hiding and would pay anything to get out. Others were those that OSS rejected for Operation Paperclip. Harriet set up a network to sneak them out on his own. For money."

Jax cocked his head. "Operation Paperclip?"

"Yes, that was the code name of the OSS program to relocate scientists and engineers out of Germany back to the United States during the war. Most of them came of their own free will. Others had to be persuaded. In the end, it was a tug of war with Russia for the last of the hardcore Nazi scientists at the end of the war."

Trick leaned back against the wall eyeing Jax. "It wasn't as simple as it sounds."

"Harriet used OSS channels and transports to move two or three extra people out of Europe with each group of legitimate Operation Paperclip people," Alex went on. "Once they got into the States, he got them into his own underground network. They wouldn't pay until they arrived in the States, and he wouldn't release them until they did. If they balked, he killed them."

"Great customer service."

Jax led the way back upstairs and outside to the parking lot. He thought about his vision of Trick's murder and meeting Professor Schiller. Once back at her car, he stopped and looked at the carriage house.

"Alex, tell me about John Singleton."

"He is amazing." Alex looked star struck and her voice went soft and familiar when she spoke. "John was a junior operative when he worked with McCall. They were part of a cell that worked in France bringing in support and helping move scientists and others out. Singleton was here—right here—the night McCall disappeared. As a matter of fact, John was almost killed, too."

Trick was surprised. "Johnny was shot?"

"Something went wrong?" Jax said.

Alex nodded. "Very wrong. They walked into a trap and John was shot in the leg. He lost consciousness and never knew what happened. When he came to, it was over. Two of the other OSS agents with them were killed. So were Kirkman and Fuchs, the other two scientists Harriet was transporting. Both Schiller and Trick vanished."

"And all the money."

"Gone, too."

"How much money were they taking in?"

Alex leaned against her Mercedes coupe. "As I said, each paid a fortune for their passage. It all disappeared. That trip alone was about fifteen thousand or more. That would be almost two-hundred thousand today. That was each trip. John believes Harriet made more than a half-dozen trips a year. The money has never been recovered or accounted for. Some in the OSS believed Trick was Harriet and used it to go into hiding."

"Jeez," Jax said, leaning on his Jeep hood watching her. "Back in '44, fifteen thousand was a lot of money."

"Yes, a small fortune."

Trick stood beside Alex now. He stuffed his hands into his pockets and stared at the ground. "Well, that's one lie that can be laid to rest. I never took the money, and I didn't kill any of them. It's all lies."

Alex watched Jax staring at nothing beside her. "Jax? What is it?"

He looked up. "Oh, sorry. I was just thinking, you know, that since OSS branded Trick the traitor, finding his remains proves them wrong. No gold, no diamonds, nothing. He was shot in the back of the head and that old root cellar was closed up so no one would find him."

"Yes, unless he had accomplices who turned on him."

"She doesn't sound convinced," Trick said.

Jax slid away from the Jeep. "Trick didn't kill those men, Alex. Harriet did. And Harriet took the money."

"I agree." Alex folded her arms. "I'm here to learn who Harriet was. To find the truth."

Jax studied her face for a long time. Her eyes wouldn't hold his. She was hiding something. "I'm here to find the truth, too, Alex. Starting with who killed my partner, Leo. And the truth about Trick's murder."

Alex had a faraway haze in her eyes and a stare at him that sizzled the air between them. "Maybe it's the same truth."

Chapter 47

Another dead end." Finch slammed his car door and laid the file he carried on the dashboard. He looked out the window at the three-story office building where Hubert Concord had sent them.

"A mail drop, just like the last one. Oh, and our mystery-man was here two weeks ago asking about the Quinton Properties, too. Same general description and bad attitude Hubert gave us."

Jeremy frowned. "I called Richmond. Quinton Properties is owned by another company called the Pettington Corporation. It's located in Tysons Corner."

"Probably another mail drop. Hubert told us they got a check every year from here. The manager inside said the money was drawn on a general fund bank account. They pay any bills that come in for Quinton."

"Anything else?" Jeremy asked.

"Nada. Let's go to Tysons Corner. It's a waste of time, but we might as well close the loop."

"You know, Finch," Jeremy said, starting the unmarked cruiser. "I'm the BCI agent and you're the deputy sheriff. How about I give the orders?"

"Sure, whatever, Jeremy."

"You old guys just don't know when to retire, do you?"

"Sure, we do. After we've trained all you young punks." Finch looked out his passenger window. "But first we need to teach you some manners. Starting with who your betters are."

Jeremy said nothing.

Thirty minutes later, they sat in their cruiser staring at a construction site off the Capital Beltway where a rundown office building was being demolished. Both their GPS and a construction worker confirmed they were at the address of the former Pettington Corporation. Now, it was nothing more than a massive pile of debris.

"Maybe it's a glitch," Finch said but he knew better. "Could be they haven't updated their business records with the Secretary of State's office."

"Maybe." Jeremy dumped his half-full coffee out the window. "And maybe it's a mistake all these companies have empty offices and mail dead-drops, but I doubt it."

✇✇✇

At the BCI office, Finch hung up his desk phone and turned to Jeremy who was hunched over his desktop banging on its keys. "That was my postal inspector pal. He gave me two more addresses and a third company name, Wellington International. All the addresses are mailbox rental companies around northern Virginia. Except Wellington International. It has a Washington DC address and active phone number."

"I got you beat." Jeremy pulled a stack of papers off his printer and handed them to Finch. "Those are corporate records identifying their corporate officers like president and vice presidents. They're Todd Berringer and Davis P. Valence for Quinton Properties, and Maria Marconi and Michael Santiago for Pettington."

Finch didn't bother to read them and dropped the papers on Jeremy's desk. "Okay, let's find these bozos."

"They're all dead."

"Dead?"

"Dead. The last one died over a year ago. All the mail-boxes were rented by the names I gave you. And get this, all the mailboxes were closed after Carraba's murder. The *day* after his murder."

Finch sat at his desk gazing at Jeremy. "So, Carraba is killed at an inn owned by Quinton Properties, which is owned by the Pettington Corporation. Pettington is owned by Wellington International. Both Quinton and Pettington have bogus company offices and dead-drop mailboxes. And, they're run by dead people."

Jeremy rolled his shoulders. "That's about right. The Grey Coat Inn is owned by a family of shell companies run by dead guys. Let's hope there's someone left alive at Wellington tomorrow."

"Oh, one more thing. I ran that license plate Hubert gave us." Finch said, looking at his notes. "Who the hell is Roman Clay?"

Chapter 48

My steak was delicious." Alex swallowed a less-than-petite mouthful before taking a long drink of wine. "You're a great cook."

"Thank you. I try," Jax said. "It's therapeutic."

Alex finished her wine and watched him over the rim of her glass. "I know. You've had a rough few weeks."

"Yes, I have. And I'm seeing ghosts, too." Jax poured more wine and sat watching Alex devour her T-bone as if she was a recent parolee. He'd spent the past hour giving her a complete rendition of events surrounding the discovery of Trick's remains. He left any mention of the fedora-wearing OSS agent sitting across the dining room table. Between Trick's objections, he backtracked a few times and twice veered into painful stories surrounding Kathleen and Leo.

Dinner together had become evident by the time they'd finished searching the inn for the second time. In the hours they'd spent at the Grey Coat, they'd bridged the gap from polite strangers to friends. After safe conversations about profession, they eased into more personal matters of living single, failed romances, and future dreams. Although Alex's one-year marriage to a Greek immigrant fell shy of Jax's disaster with Kathleen, they quickly found themselves kindred spirits that neither could quite understand and both were unwilling to admit out loud. Yet, it took no time at all for their polite chatter to morph into laughter and reminiscence of life gone by. Alex had been raised by her grandmother after losing her parents before she could remember. She'd traveled most of her young life all over the world. Jax grew up in foster care moving from home to home. At eighteen, he joined the army and followed his tour with college. Alex spent seven years at universities around the country completing her doctorate in American History. Both loved forties' swing music, old film noir movies, and good wine. On both their minds was how their meeting was the product of murder and intrigue like some '40s noir. An almost impossible coincidence. By the time Jax insisted on cooking them dinner, they were flirting with more than just the idea of working together.

"Ghosts?"

Trick rolled his eyes watching Jax across the table. "Enough with the wine before you start spilling the beans about me. She's a great lady and we don't want her running out screaming about a crazy man. Do we?"

"No ghosts. Just kidding." Jax laughed and patted the air. "Honest."

"I hope so." Alex changed the topic. "Your investigation is very scary. There's two people dead and two missing." She slid her empty plate away toward the center of the table. "Do you think your Leo was onto something that got him killed?"

"If he was, he didn't tell me. I didn't even know why I was at the inn that night. And when I got home from the hospital, someone had broken in here. Maybe someone thinks Leo gave me something or told me something."

"Tell her about the young girl that night, sport," Trick said. "The one who saved you. But go easy. A little finesse goes a long way."

Jax did and then added the incident at the abandoned golf course earlier.

Alex listened to his story—the lie of a sudden memory instead of a ghostly visitation—and then followed Jax into his living room with their second bottle of wine. "Do you think the young girl can help you? Might she be part of that gang you told me about? You know, Lupino's men?"

"Perhaps. " He motioning her into a leather chair. "Hector Lupino's gang moves drugs, guns, even people. He's very diversified. Someone has been at that inn and staying there for a time. Maybe Hector's behind that."

"Unless it's another homeless man."

She had a point. It wouldn't be unusual for some homeless people to stay in an abandoned structure. It would be a good place to camp. He nodded, filed the thought away for later, and changed topics. "Alex, how did you get involved with John Singleton?"

"As I said, he's an amazing man." Her face lit up a bit and she raised a finger in the air. "But wait here, I can show you better."

She went outside to her car and returned with an old, worn leather briefcase. She opened it on the dining room table and withdrew a six-inch thick, brown courier pouch. Inside that was a plethora of documents, grainy photographs, and handwritten notes.

"Here's part of the reason," she said fanning the contents out. "Take a look for yourself."

Jax grabbed the bottle of wine and glasses and slid into a chair beside her. After a swallow of wine, he picked up a stack of black and white photographs. The paper was odd to the touch and the images scratched and fading from decades of handling. The first photograph was of two bodies lying face down on the ground with two sets of car lights illuminating them. The cars were dark colored Fords with military markings—World War II military markings.

He examined the bodies—OSS agents McKinney and Thoreau, and two pasty-faced older men he presumed were the German scientists Fuchs and Kirkman. He knew neither was Schiller whom he met that night in his vision. Both men had gunshot wounds to their heads. He swallowed hard as his fingers shuffled through the remaining prints slower and slower until he couldn't take any more.

"Damn, the inn has seen its share of murder, hasn't it?"

Alex nodded. "Yes, it has." She sorted through the photographs and found one of a young, thin man being carried on a military stretcher by two uniformed soldiers. The man was gaunt and his eyes closed. Someone was tightening a field dressing on his left leg just below his hip where his pants were torn away and left dangling. Even in the old black and white photograph, it was evident blood had soaked through the fabric and the man was in immense pain.

"That's John Singleton," she said, handing the print to him. "They found him shot outside the inn."

Jax stared at the print. "My God, he looks so different."

"Sure, he's almost ninety today but still looks and acts fifty. He and Trick were a real team back then. It was this file that got me interested in the Harriet operation."

Jax found another photograph that showed different angles of McKinney and Thoreau. Both men had been shot in the head. Executed. "I don't understand."

"They were good men, Ricky," Trick said, standing back from the table. "I don't want to see those."

Jax placed the photographs face down on the table and gave him a faint nod.

Alex fingered the photographs. "My doctorate is on the impact of refugees on the home front during World War Two. I began working with the OSS Foundation when I met John. He told me he discovered Harriet's smuggling operation during a mission in France in late 1943."

Trick cleared his throat. "That's a bunch of malarkey. I discovered it. Singleton always did like to steal the glory. Most often from me, too."

Jax tried hard not to stare at Trick across the table from them. "The traitor was named 'Harriet'?"

"After Harriet Tubman and the Underground Railroad. When they found out Harriet was using old inns and locations like the Grey Coat, the name stuck. I think John named him that."

Trick laughed. "Okay, I'll give him that one."

"Don't be fooled by the name, though. Harriet was a dangerous, ruthless man." Alex dug through the stack of papers and found an inch-thick, dog-eared stack of photocopied documents. She handed it to Jax. "This says it all."

The documents were a copy of what appeared to be the original OSS after-action report on the Grey Coat Inn investigation. The fuzzy, irregular type had blotches of ink and misaligned letters from a manual war-time typewriter. Affixed to the report were a series of intelligence memos on Harriet's activities beginning in 1943. The reports were sparse and filled with speculation and conjecture, but as Jax read the pages, the events seemed to match his trips with Trick into the past.

Jax returned to his wineglass, leaving one of the memos open in the report "They almost caught Harriet once flying a plane from England to Maine. But he downed the aircraft out to sea to hide his trail when they got too close. He killed everyone but himself. What a bastard."

"Harriet was making a fortune and was guilty of treason," Alex said, taking up her wineglass for a long pull. "If caught, he might have been hanged."

"Did Singleton ever say what went wrong at the inn?" Jax asked. "How the OSS team was discovered?"

"There was a second traitor on the team." Alex tapped the photographs of McKinney and Thoreau. "He believed one or both were with Harriet. Clay and Vetner were also assigned to the team. They received a signal right before the raid to stay back and wait for orders."

"They were called off?"

"Yes. They received a radio signal from Trick. That's part of the reason OSS believed he was Harriet. The rest of the team was killed and only John survived the ambush."

"Lies," Trick said and walked away from the table

mumbling something Jax couldn't hear.

Jax flipped through the photographs and found Fuchs and Kirkman. Both men were sprawled on the ground, their arms and legs bent in awkward angles. Their clothing was strewn about—pockets pulled out, jackets yanked away from the bodies.

Jax shook his head. "No money, gold, or jewels were found. Trick and Schiller disappeared. They believed Trick killed them all and ran with the money. What about Schiller?"

"He was never found." Alex cocked her head. "It's hard to believe, I imagine, but it all points to Captain McCall."

Jax saw Trick standing across the room. His face was sad and his eyes angry. It must be difficult to hear the case against you. To hear you're a traitor to friends and country. A painful epitaph for a man murdered to hide the real traitor.

"That's not right. None of it." Jax shook his head. "Trick's radio was in a rucksack he left at the carriage house. And Trick was shot twice in the back and once in the back of the head while lying face down on the ground. He was executed."

Alex sat forward. "How do you know that?"

"A—ah—" Jax stammered a second before the lie came to him. "I'm a good cop. Crime scenes are my thing. There's a photo of his rucksack beside the carriage house foundation in the file. One plus one is two. Even in 1944."

She eyed him suspiciously. "How'd you know about the radio?"

"I'm right, aren't I?"

"Yes, you are." Alex refilled her wine glass and stared at him over the rim. "OSS thinks his co-conspirators double-crossed him, killed him, and ran with the money. Harriet had accomplices to handle the logistics from Europe to around the States. He had an entire network. Finding his remains doesn't prove him innocent."

"What about Singleton?"

"Vetner found him on the far side of the inn's grounds, wounded. He passed a full investigation. Besides, he's the one who planned the raid to capture Harriet in the first place."

Jax shrugged.

Alex frowned. "He thinks that Harriet sent that radio message to Clay and Vetner to trick them into thinking it was from McCall. He fought the government for decades over McCall's innocence. And, he's been helping me and the OSS Foundation for years."

Jax sat back swirling his wine. "Why? Loyalty? Guilt?"

"Both. To this day, John Singleton is convinced Harriet ambushed the others with McKinney and Thoreau, took the money, and ran."

"I don't know what's worse," Trick growled from across the room. "Getting murdered or being labeled a traitor."

"It must have been Harriet who hid Trick's body in the root cellar so OSS wouldn't know he was dead," Jax said. "The longer he was missing, the longer he was guilty."

"That's what I think, too," Alex said, packing up her file. "It worked."

"You know, Trick ran into Schiller at the carriage house before the shooting started."

Alex's face froze. "What?"

"Here we go, Ricky. She'll be running for the hills any minute."

She stared at the file in her hands. "I don't believe there's anything in here that—"

"Schiller tried to bribe him to help him escape," Jax said. "In fact, Schiller gave him a gold watch just before Trick sent him into the woods to meet a confederate he'd brought along for 'just in case.'"

"A gold watch? A confederate?" Alex forced a smile. "Now you're making things up."

Jax crossed his heart. "No, I'm not."

Alex pushed away from the table and stood up, walked

to the window and looked out. "It's not possible that you know that."

"You have to trust me, Alex. I know what I'm talking about."

"How?" She spun around and her face was tight and angry. "Do you have a source at the Historical Foundation? Did John tell you something?" Alex looked at the thick courier pouch on the table. "This is important to me, Jax. There's no way you can know all that. I'm not even sure John Singleton knew about the watch or Trick bringing an ally along. How do you know?"

Jax stood up and patted the air. "Please, Alex, wait. I can't explain now. You have to trust me."

"I want to, Jax, I do." She returned to the table and picked up the courier pouch. "I'm here to find the truth about Patrick McCall. You claim to know more than anyone else alive. So, you're either lying or you've found something. A file, a witness. Give me something."

"You have to trust me. Please."

"As much as I want to, I won't until you level with me. Or give me some evidence."

Trick whispered to Jax and he repeated it. "Trick's confederate in the woods that night was with the French Resistance."

Alex's eyes exploded. "You cannot possibly know that. You just can't—no one knew that."

"The confederate was *Abrielle Chanoux*." Jax was as surprised as she. "Trick called her *Socks*."

Chapter 49

Who told you about 'Socks?'" Alex stood across the table from Jax holding the courier pouch with white knuckles. Her face was tight and her eyes moved between the pouch and Jax's face searching for some explanation. "Who?"

"Alex, it's difficult to explain."

"Try. Try, dammit. I came to dinner believing you were my ally. You've been telling me things no one could possibly know. Tell me the truth. Tell me how you know all this or I'm leaving."

"Don't let her go, Ricky." Trick moved beside her. "Tell her you found some notes or something on my body. Tell her anything. Lie for Christ's sake."

Jax took a long breath and plunged. "Look, the night I was shot—lying there—something...well, strange...happened to me."

Trick snorted. "Oh, boyo. Not what I had in mind, Ricky."

"Strange?" Alex locked her eyes on his. "Talk fast, Jax, or I'm leaving."

Jax swallowed hard, grabbed his wine, and finished the half-glass in one gulp. "I had some kind of vision or something. I died. Four times, the doc says, I died. The first time was right in the spot where Trick died. I know. I know because I saw it all. Trick was there."

Alex stared at him and her eyes hardened. "Stop it, Jax. You're either lying or crazy. Did you get into my files? My research? How? Are you investigating me or something? There's no way you know all this. There's almost no one who knows. Who is helping you?"

"Will you just listen? How else would I know Abrielle's nickname? How would I know about Schiller? At the hospital and the inn, something happened when I died. Ever since, I see things. Please, I'm not lying."

"You have to be. You're saying you saw a ghost? Captain Trick McCall's ghost?" Alex closed her eyes. "I suppose that's who you've been talking to when you think I'm not looking? To him? To McCall?"

Jax didn't answer. He didn't have to.

"Great," she said and headed for the door. "I find someone after all these years, and he talks to ghosts." She reached the front door and turned around. "Okay, Jax. One more chance. Tomorrow. I want to go over every detail of what you know, or claim to know, about the night Patrick McCall disappeared. But I want the truth. All of it. I want to know how you came by all these little secrets."

Jax folded his arms. "Will you believe me? Or at least be willing to have an open mind?"

She turned, opened the front door. "Not if you tell me Patrick McCall whispered in your ear."

Chapter 50

So, Finch," Jax said, closing the door behind him. "What's wrong now? Did I assassinate the governor or something?"

Finch arrived just as Alex backed out of Jax's driveway and hurtled toward town. When he asked about his visitor, Jax just waved him into the house.

"No, but I wanted to come straight here and talk to you. Before, that is, the captain puts the kibosh on things. Better to ask forgiveness than permission."

"So true," Trick said from the kitchen. "I've said that myself on many occasions. Once, I sneaked someone into the States that I wasn't supposed to. She was—"

"Later, okay?" Jax threw Trick a "not now" look and motioned for Finch into the living room.

"Later?" Finch looked around the room. "Me?"

"Forget it. What do you have?"

"Nothing and that's the problem." Finch picked up Alex's empty wine glass, scooped up the newly opened bottle from the table, and poured himself a rim-tight glassful. "I don't know what you and Leo stumbled into, but it's bad."

"Bad enough to kill for." Jax waited for Finch to drain his glass and another glass. "Have another while you tell me."

Finch took fifteen minutes explaining his investigation through Northern Virginia looking for the various owners and shell companies tied to the Grey Coat Inn. He finished his tale with the morbid connection between the company's four corporate executives. "None of the corporate executives are alive today. They're all dead."

"That's not so bad, look at me," Trick said,

Finch refiled his glass. "We wore out a set of tires and all Jeremy and I got were dead ends. Pardon the pun. I'll know tomorrow if that's the case with Wellington International."

Jax took it all in while he made a pot of coffee. Leo had said that Antonio Cavallo was onto something big. What "big" was he never said. But it was big enough to hide behind a string of shell companies, closed mailboxes, and dead executives. It was also big enough to kill a cop and a forensic examiner. That was pretty damn big.

He told Finch just that. "I've no idea what's going on, Finch. But let me tell you some more." He launched into a brief description about Antonio Cavallo's disappearance and the website he and Christie discovered. After a few questions, he finished with his foray at the old golf course and the homeless man's story.

Finch sat back taking it all in. "We've both been busy. You know, some guy named Roman Clay showed up asking questions about Quinton Properties and the Pettington Corporation right after Leo's murder."

"Clay? Alex Vouros just told me—"

Trick interrupted him. "Ricky, that's one of the OSS agents with me at the inn."

"Told you what?" Finch asked.

"That Roman Clay was one of the survivors from the inn the night Patrick McCall disappeared."

"Clay would be what?" Finch cocked his head and narrowed an eye on Jax. "A hundred years old or something?"

Jax did the math in his head. "Okay, ninety. That's odd."

Finch watched Jax and gulped at his wine. "I'll check with DC Metro PD about Clay and Wellington. I got lots of pals down there. What about Cavallo?"

"Put out a BOLO and have some uniforms dig around

for him," Jax said. He had to hold back emotions when he said, "Anything on Kathleen?"

"Sorry, no." Finch shook his head. "The blood on the carpet is her type. We assume it's hers. It looks bad. I won't lie to you. It looks bad, but you already knew that. That security guard is sticking to his story that you were the last one at her place. He's got the captain and Jeremy all fired up."

"He's a liar."

Finch shrugged. "I'm going to have another chat with him."

Trick was positioned on the couch again with his feet up and his fedora over his eyes. "A set up, just like me, Ricky. Someone wants all the hounds chasing you. Just like they did with me. The longer they chase you, the farther they get from the real killer."

Jax repeated Trick's analysis and Finch nodded all through. Then Jax retrieved the coffee, filled two mugs from the kitchen, and returned to the table where he handed one to Finch. "What about the crime scene results?"

"Well, maybe something. But you're not going to like it."

"I don't like any of this. Tell me."

Finch sipped his coffee, looking everywhere but at Jax. "I gotta be careful with what I'm saying here. I'm an outsider. The sheriff likes it that way. But sometimes, well, sometimes it's damn uncomfortable. You guys aren't a real warm bunch, you know? And Martinez all but threatened me the other day."

"Just tell me, Finchy," Jax said. "Everyone thinks I'm a murderer. How bad can it be?"

Finch shrugged. "I don't know."

Jax smiled and ran his finger in an "X" across his chest. "Mum's the word."

"Me too," Trick said. "And hope to die."

"That morning at your crime scene, some weird stuff

happened," Finch said, leaning back with his coffee. "I was working the main house and watched the goings-on from the second floor window. Jeremy was watching the captain close. *Real* close. He acted strange about it, too. Anyway, the captain took something out of an old wood pile beside the carriage house. He pocketed it and whatever it was, he never logged it into evidence. And the hell of it is, Jeremy watched him do it, too. I spent all day with him today working this case. He never mentioned it. When I asked him if he thought the captain was acting weird, he went out of his way to say no. On top of all that, Jeremy is spinning that security guard's statement like its gospel. Me, I say it's bullshit."

"If the captain found something, maybe it wasn't worth logging into evidence."

"Rule of thumb is if you aren't sure, take it into evidence and let the lab sort it out. Right? And later, Chief Rogers sent a lab report to the captain that never made it into the casefile."

Trick snapped his fingers and sat up. "Ricky, get rid of this guy so we can talk. It's hot, pal. Smokin' hot."

Jax ignored him. "Finch, are you saying Captain Martinez and Jeremy are manufacturing this case against me?"

Finch held up his hands. "If I were saying that, I'd be saying it to the commonwealth's attorney. Whatever they're doing, they sure are trying hard to ignore any evidence in your favor. Whatever he found at the scene, I think he gave to Rogers. Then he hid the lab report on it."

"Rogers was murdered." Jax stood up. "Do you know what you're saying?"

Finch's mouth tightened.

Trick looked at him. "He doesn't know if he can trust you, Ricky. I'm not sure you should trust him, either. Not that you have a choice."

"Finch?"

"Okay, Jax, okay." Finch dropped his head into his hands. "Look, you been good to me on the squad, and I appreciate that. But, hey, I don't know whose side I'm on right now."

"What's that supposed to mean?"

Finch stood up as his face darkened. "You're kidding, right? Your gun killed Leo. No witnesses. Then it turns out he was involved with your fiancée."

"Finch, I had nothing to do with Leo's murder."

"Yeah, yeah." Finch patted the air. "You claim someone broke into your house and stole a gun there's no record of you owning and no signs of a break in. While you're nowhere we can verify, Chief Rogers is whacked and Kathleen Cullen disappears. Then you find a World War II skeleton that everyone has been looking for since 1944. You found it right where all this started."

"I know this looks bad," Jax said. He looked around the room stalling until he could find something calming, something credible to say in his defense. He found nothing. "I—"

"Ricky!" Trick was on his feet running toward the front door. "You gotta get to Alex. She's in danger. Something is about to happen to her."

"Alex? What's happening? Where is she?" Jax looked at Trick and noticed Finch staring at him above his coffee cup halfway to his lips. His cell phone rang and saved him. "Yes, right...where are you? Okay, stay put. I'm there in ten."

Trick was already at the door. "She's at the Great Hall Hotel. Hurry, she's in danger. It's happening right now."

Chapter 51

Two rapid shots splayed Finch's front windshield. The third set him careening off the road where he sideswiped a tree beside the hotel parking entrance. His body slammed sideways into his driver's window. A contusion erupted above his ear and blood sprayed his face as he slumped against the steering wheel.

"Finch!" Jax dived sideways on the front seat, dodging any more bullets that might invade the cruiser. "You okay?"

Finch groaned and Jax laid him low on the seat, checked his pulse, and grabbed the radio microphone hanging off the rearview mirror. He checked the channel and put out an emergency call for assistance.

"Hang tough, Finchy." Jax dove from the passenger's door and hit the grass on his hands and knees. The jolt sent pain ricocheting through his shoulder until it stole some of his wind.

He cried out but got to his feet and stumbled ahead toward a row of parked cars. There, he caught his breath before sprinting another few yards to a pickup truck. The nausea and pain grabbed him and he wretched bile and tried to get his feet steady. He drew his automatic and peered around the truck fender looking for the shooter.

Another shot cracked the darkness and struck the truck's hood just above his head.

"Ricky, focus." Trick knelt down beside him. "Alex is

across the lot hiding behind her car. You have to get to her. You have to move now."

"Alex, right." Jax straightened himself against the truck fender as his shoulder sent pain stabbing him. A wave of nausea fermented and he wavered. Twice he readied himself for the sprint across the lot but the pain was intense and the lightheadedness held him back. He waited for it to pass.

Trick stood beside him. "Ricky, you have to get to Alex."

"I can't. I'm trying. I landed on my shoulder—I—"

Another gunshot. Somewhere across the lot, Alex called, "Jax, is that you? I can't see who's shooting. I can't move."

"Hold on and stay low." Jax tried to rise but couldn't. He tried focusing but the pain in his shoulder was too much. He pressed his back against the truck and closed his eyes. "Well, here's another nice mess you've gotten me into." When he opened his eyes, he was calm. "Oliver Hardy, *Sons of the Desert*, 1933."

"There's no time for that, sport. It's time to share." Trick bent down and gripped Jax's shoulder, melting himself into him like steam through a vent.

A surge of adrenalin careened through Jax's body. His heart pumped and strengthened his legs. The nausea abated and the pain eased its assault. The relief calmed him and he allowed Trick to take control. Dizziness yielded to strength. He stood, moved to a crouch, and skirted the rear of the truck.

He snapped the Glock from his right to his left hand—his weak hand—and took a quick step from behind the truck's cover but retracted before his foot hit the ground.

A shot whistled inches past him.

He pinpointed the muzzle flash and snapped two shots toward the corner of the woods behind the hotel. The second he squeezed the first shot off, he bolted from the truck and fired the second as he sprinted to a four-by-four one row behind Alex's Mercedes.

"Alex," he called. "Stay low. I'm coming."

Jax fired a third shot into woods and dashed to the next row of cars where he found Alex kneeling beside her coupe. Her passenger side window was shot out and one of her tires flattened. Glass covered the ground.

He looked her over and gently held her hand. "Are you okay?"

She nodded. "Thank God, you are, too. When the car crashed, I thought the worst."

"It's Finch. He's one of my guys. He'll be okay. Are you sure you're not hit?"

She took his hand. Hers was shaking. "I got hit with a lot of glass but it's just scrapes and cuts. I'm okay. I pulled in and, as soon as I parked, someone started shooting."

In the distance, two wailing sirens approached from Leesburg to the west. Someone at the hotel yelled toward them but the words were indistinguishable when another siren blared close by.

"It's all right now. Backup is almost here."

A shot shattered glass on Finch's cruiser. The instant it did, Finch returned fire with two shots from behind his vehicle. A second later, he fired a third as he made his move. He maneuvered from car-to-car heading for them. He fired twice more as he zigzagged his approach. When he reached the minivan to their right, he threw Jax the OK sign and dropped to a seated position, winded.

"You guys okay?" Finch called.

"Yes, we're three cars down, "Jax said. "I'm with Alex Vouros. You okay?"

"I'll live."

The vigor drained from Jax's body, taking Trick with it. It took a moment but the exhilaration faded and Jax regained control. His heart slowed from its rampant rhythm and steadied, his breath followed. He gasped twice and shuddered. Trick was gone.

"Finch, don't move," Jax called. "The shooter's in the trees."

"I know, but I haven't seen him."

A rush of lights and sirens flooded the hotel grounds. Two sheriff's patrold screeched to positions inside the parking lot. Searchlights roamed the lot and hotel walls. Two more cars arrived and four deputies jumped from their cars, flanked one another, and leapfrogged across the lot until they were positioned around them.

"Stay put, Jax." Finch ordered, taking control. He waved to the deputies, identified himself, and barked orders. He called two by name and led them into the woods. Two other two deputies braced themselves over car hoods with readied shotguns to protect their advance.

Alex leaned back against her car and took long, deep breaths. Her body quivered. She stared straight ahead and squeezed Jax's hand. "Oh, my God. I cannot believe this."

Trick knelt beside her. "Sorry about the short notice, Ricky. You know, sharing you like that? You were pretty out of it. I figured I better take charge."

"Thanks, you did good." When Alex looked at him, he just winked.

"I did?" Alex leaned in close to him. "I was terrified."

Jax put an arm around her. "Who would try to kill you, Alex? And why?"

She shook her head. "I don't know. Maybe he wasn't trying to kill me."

"Really?" Jax moved around in front of her and checked her arms and face. He found a few scratches and cuts from the car glass. "If he tried any harder, you'd be dead."

"If I were," she said, trying to laugh but failing, "you'd be talking to me now not Trick McCall."

Chapter 52

You'll be sore again for a while. Luckily, I don't think you tore anything open," the emergency medical technician told Jax. "You're very lucky. Your shoulder is healing much faster than I would have imagined. Take it easy on it and it'll be okay."

Jax buttoned his shirt and gave his shoulder a couple slow rolls to test the tenderness. He winced when he got the answer. "Thanks. I'll try not to leap out of cars for a while."

"That'll help."

The second EMT gave Alex the thumbs up and made some notes on a pad. "You're fine, Ms. Vouros. Nerves spiked your blood pressure a bit and I cleaned and tended to the cuts, but all is well."

Alex thanked him and joined Jax at the rear of the ambulance. "How's the shoulder?"

"Complaining, but it'll be fine." Jax touched her arm and noted the cuts and scrapes. "I'm sorry about this."

"Why would you say that? It wasn't your fault."

Jax brushed some dirt from her hair. As he did, her eyes softened and closed. He withdrew. "Sorry."

"No." She smiled. "It's all right. And I owe you an apology for earlier. You scared me. You scared me a lot. But that's behind us. Let's talk later."

Christie appeared from around the side of the ambulance. "What the hell happened here, Jax?" She waved the EMTs away. "I missed Finch's radio call but I picked up the chatter from the deputies an hour ago and just arrived. Jeremy and I finished searching the woods."

Jax looked around. "Where's Finch?"

"He hit his head pretty good, but he's okay. He's interviewing the hotel people."

"Good."

"What happened? I got the official story from the deputies." Christie folded her arms. "I'd love to hear the unofficial one."

Jax looked from Christie to Alex, who gave him a tin, tight smile. He introduced them.

"*You're* Alex Vouros?" Christie's lips tightened as her eyes fixed on Jax. "The old crinkled college professor?"

"Excuse me?" Alex's eyes flashed a bit. "What—"

"What started this, Ms. Vouros?"

"I have no idea. We had dinner and when I got back here someone started shooting at me. I called nine-one-one"

"Dinner?" Christie glanced at Jax again. "Late night research, Jax?"

"Whoa, Christie," Jax said, holding up a hand. "The OSS Historical Foundation sent her here to follow up on Trick McCall's remains. Captain's orders."

"And that is best done over dinner?"

Alex framed a counterfeit smile that fooled no one. "Yes, we didn't want to wait on breakfast. And in case you didn't notice, Agent Krein, someone tried to kill me. I called the police, then called Jax. He arrived first."

"Why'd you call Jax?"

"Because he's the only one I know in town. And, if you must know, I assumed it was connected to what's been going on."

"Oh? Why do you say that?"

"Time out." Jax shot Christie a stern look. "Jeez, Christie, will you relax? Why else would someone try to kill her?"

"I don't know, Jax. I just met her, and I don't like her much."

"Now you listen, Krein," Alex snapped, leaning forward. "I think you need to take a step back. Way back."

"Okay, okay, everyone calm down." Jax put a hand on Alex's arm and stared at Christie. "Come on, it's been a tough night."

Christie looked away. "No, I get it. Sorry. Finch told me about Cavallo and the tramp. Finch and I will get on that."

Jax cursed and his face softened. "I should have called you but I got busy."

"I can see that." Christie looked at Alex with an exaggerated smile. "If you don't mind, I need to speak with Agent Jax."

"Sure," Alex said. "But have him back soon. Breakfast is the most important meal, after all."

Jax rolled his eyes and followed Christie to her cruiser parked several cars away. From there, she watched Alex and fired a barrage of questions at Jax. Her eyes hit the high-points.

"For a grieving, gunshot-recovering fiancé, you don't waste time."

Jax allowed a grin. "Why, Agent Krein, if I didn't know any better—"

"You don't." She stepped close to him, looking around the parking lot. "Do you know what you're doing? Do you know what this looks like?"

"Yes, like someone tried to kill her."

"Maybe they did and maybe they didn't." Christie peered over Jax's shoulder at Alex. "Don't you think it's kind of coincidental that she shows up all mysterious and such in the middle of this?"

"There's nothing mysterious about her. That foundation sent her. Where's Captain Martinez? Ask him."

"He's enroute. He lives way out along the Potomac and it's a few miles out. You can bet he's anxious to talk to you."

"Great."

"So, about Vouros. You checked her out? Her credentials, I mean? I'm sure breakfast will fill in the gaps."

Jax's face tightened. "No, I didn't. Why would she lie? What's her motive?"

"Motive? Did those bullets in you make you naive? How about motive to get close to you and this investigation? Maybe someone is trying to keep tabs on you."

Jax thought about that. Any other time, it would have made sense to him. Still, he wasn't sure. "For what, Christie? I'm under investigation for murder and maybe kidnapping and who knows what else. Keep tabs on me? You guys are doing that well enough."

"Listen." She touched his arm. "Did you ever think that maybe she's not who she says she is? This Singleton guy is pretty powerful. He's connected everywhere. *Everywhere*, Jax."

"What's that supposed to mean?"

"That McCall guy was a spook, right? OSS. Today, it's the CIA?"

"And?"

"*And* maybe she's not a historian." Christie glanced over at Alex and faked another smile. "Who the hell cares about a 67-year old pile of bones, anyway?"

"She does," Jax snorted. "And the FBI and me. It seems like a lot of people do."

"Listen, you better watch yourself with your friend there. Her timing is too convenient for me. I don't like it, or her."

"I'll be fine. A day or so and she'll be gone."

Christie looked away. "Good."

Jax changed the subject. "Did you follow up on those addresses from Leo's black box?"

"Yes." She looked at him and shrugged. "Nothing. A couple residences he was at. No one remembers him being around and no one will admit to talking with him. They're a dead end."

"A dead end? A BCI agent is digging around and no one remembers?"

"Dead end, Jax. It happens." She turned to leave and then stopped, looking back to him. Her voice lost its edge. "You're not yourself. I'm worried about you. A lot worried. If you need to talk, come see me. And for Christ's sake, be careful with Vouros."

And with that, Christie walked off toward the hotel bellowing orders at a cluster of crime scene technicians, sending them scattering.

Jax watched her leave. Christie surprised him. She showed a side he'd not seen before and not one he wished to see again. As she walked away, she glanced back twice and Jax waved on the second time. Then he shook his head and rejoined Alex just as Finch walked up.

"Are you all right, Dr. Vouros?" Finch asked. "You got a lot of cuts and scrapes."

"Yes, fine. Please call me Alex. You look a little worse, yourself."

Finch shrugged it off and took out his cell phone, snapping a couple photographs of her face and arms where the medic had treated her. "For the casefile."

"Finch, did you find anything new?" Jax asked. "Anything that'll help?"

"As a matter of fact, yes," he said. "We found a car abandoned in a housing development a mile behind these woods."

"Did you find any fingerprints or anything?" Alex asked.

"There's a gunshot hole in the side fender and it's got a flat. We think the perp parked the car on the access road behind the hotel and walked in here. One of us must have hit the car in the shooting. The perp drove it clear but ditched it when the tire got too bad."

"Good," Jax said, "maybe we'll get lucky and find some prints."

"CSI is on it now." Finch was rubbed his head. "We ran the plate and it's a fleet vehicle registered to a DC firm."

"What company?" Alex asked.

"You won't believe it." He looked from Alex to Jax. "Wellington International."

Chapter 53

The next morning, Jax sat at his breakfast table sipping coffee. He'd been looking around all morning for Trick until he appeared across from him. "Where have you been? You disappeared after the shooting stopped last night."

Trick winked. "I got you through it okay. Didn't I, Ricky?"

"Well, I think I did okay, too."

"Sure, sure. But when your pals all started showing up, I had something else to do."

Jax sipped his coffee. "Did you have to find Amelia Earhart or something?"

"Amelia? Why, is someone looking for her? I can get her if you want. I know just where she is."

Jax laughed. "Yeah, right." When Trick shrugged, he said, "Really? No, what were you doing that was so important?"

"Investigating."

"Now you're a detective?"

Trick shot a gun-finger at him. "Sure. After you showed me that computer, I got curious. You know, you can find almost anything. Like where people live and all sorts of stuff."

"You're telling me you were on the computer all night?"

"Believe it, pal-o." Trick leaned back in his chair. "Yesterday, Finch told you about the companies that were all strung together hiding each other, right?"

Jax nodded. "They're called shell companies. Quinton Properties, Pettington Corporation, and ..."

"Wellington International." Trick nodded. "So I did some spy work on the computer. Boy, the pictures of pin-up girls alone made me blush. And all I was doing was snooping."

"It's called surfing."

"Whatever." Trick waved in the air. "Anyway, I found Wellington. All the other companies are from my past, Ricky. Quinton was the name of the first OSS agent killed in France. He jumped in one night on a mission and landed right in a Kraut camp. Pettington was the codename of our command headquarters in England. You remember, Ricky."

"Right, yes, from my dream. What of it?"

Trick tapped the table. "None of this is by chance. Wellington stumped me at first, your computer kept giving me all kinds of trash about the Duke of Wellington, Beef Wellington, all hogwash."

"Spam."

"Huh? I love Spam. Especially with eggs and potatoes. Overseas, we'd trade all kinds of stuff for a few more rations of Spam. The boys loved it. Real meat was hard to come back then."

Jax rolled his eyes. "Wellington?"

"Right. Wellington was a joint campaign with the British SOE. That's the Special Operations Executive. I never met a more uppity bunch of palookas in my life. I bet you couldn't get a matchstick up their—"

"I get it. You think all the companies are named after OSS operations?"

"Well, not operations alone, but somebody connected them. The computer said so."

Jax took his coffee cup and stood up. He began pacing

the breakfast nook. "That confirms what we've said all along. Your murder and Leo's are connected."

"Your murder?" a voice asked from the hall.

Jax spun around.

Alex stood in the kitchen entrance wearing an oversized, button-down nightshirt and socks. The shirt was long and while Jax's imagination connected the dots, none of those dots were showing.

"Good morning." Jax tried hard not to notice the window light silhouetting the contours of her body. Those contours had tantalized him since he met her, but the sunlight removed some of his imagination. He headed for another coffee mug and took his time filling it. "I was just...um...want coffee?"

"Yes, coffee would be great." She sat at the table and watched him drop her spoon on the floor. "You were just what?"

"Nothing."

Last night, the deputies finished taking their statements well after midnight. Jax brought Alex home for the night. Reporters were camped at the hotel and neither of them wanted to face them.

Christie and Jeremy had been handling the scene until Captain Martinez responded, and Jax wanted to be gone before he arrived. Martinez would be on a rant once he found him involved in another shooting.

"And thanks for the spare room. I didn't sleep much, but it was more than I would have at the hotel."

"Any time." Jax handed her the cup of coffee. "Alex, someone tried to kill you after getting involved with me. I think you should go back home and forget this case."

She sipped her coffee and looked at him over the cup. "No. I'm staying. Someone must think you told me something important. Maybe something Leo told you."

"I don't know anything to even tell you. We've been over that."

Alex cocked her head. "Then I have no other idea why

anyone would want me dead." She glanced around. "Did I hear you mention Wellington International?"

"Yes." Jax refilled his coffee and followed her eyes searching the kitchen. How much had she heard him talking to Trick? "Finch came by last night after dinner. After you left."

"So rudely left, that is. I'm very sorry about that."

He shrugged. "No, it's all right. Anyway, Finch has been investigating the inn's ownership." He gave her the details of everything he knew about Quinton, Pettington, and Wellington International. He finished with, "And last night, the shooter was driving a fleet car from Wellington."

"What does it all mean?"

"It means Wellington is up to their necks in this." He watched Alex sit and stare out the window. She was avoiding his eyes and he knew it. "What is it, Alex?"

She hesitated for a long moment, then turned to face him. "Jax, how did you know that McCall called Abrielle 'Socks'?"

Bam. Direct hit.

Jax just stared back at her. Now what?

"Please, Jax. I have to know."

Trick suddenly landed in a kitchen chair beside Alex. "This ought to be a humdinger, sport."

Jax's eyes widened a little. His voice was light and mirthful. "Well, what do I have to lose? I died and was revived. I've lost my fiancée. I'm under investigated for murder, and the ghost of an OSS agent is haunting me."

"You think Patrick McCall is haunting you?"

"Oh, lady, let me tell you what." Jax leaned forward in his chair. He began with first seeing Trick lying on the cold gravel driveway while he lay feet away bleeding out. He told her about Trick's visits in the hospital and his dreams of parachuting into France where he met the beautiful and deadly Abrielle Chanoux. He agonized over witnessing Trick's murder. He told her every detail, including how it felt to be an OSS agent in 1944 France. He ended his tale with Trick leading him to his own remains at the Grey Coat Inn.

"There you have it. Love me or hate me. It's the truth." He sat back in his chair and folded his hands on the table. "Oh, one last thing. The BCI thinks the blood loss and trauma left me whacko."

Alex put her cup down and looked down at the table in front of her. Her fingers began a slow, steady drum on the tabletop. "I've researched Captain Patrick McCall and Abrielle Chanoux for more than a decade. You've seen the file I've created. I've even accessed the classified files on both sides of the Atlantic. No one, nowhere, mentioned the name *Socks*."

"Alex, trust me."

"No. I can't." She sipped at her cup and let the hot coffee warm her to her core. Then she looked right into Jax's eyes. "Okay, Jax, let's see how much you really know."

Trick leaned against the window frame across the room. "Oh, I think she's going to be clever, Jax."

Alex watched him carefully. "McCall first went into France months before he met Abrielle. He told her the story of his first drop—he'd never parachuted before and ..."

Trick laughed with a roar and startled Jax. "She's good, sport. I crapped my pants on the way down. They just about pushed me out of that C-47—I went halfway to the ground with my eyes closed."

Jax repeated his story and watched as Alex's face burst with surprise. "Amazing, but—I guess—not hard to guess. Okay, McCall and the others used to bring her gifts from England like silk stockings and chocolate."

Trick told Jax a different story.

"No, Alex," Jax said, smiling. "Singleton brought her stockings. Clay and Vetner would bring chocolate and candy. Trick brought her Spam. We were just talking about that. And when they were hiding from the Krauts—sorry, German patrols—she'd make them Spam with eggs at the farms they hid at. Trick would pass the time telling her about the movies in the States."

Alex was stunned. She closed her eyes and laughed, at first, then slowly quieted as she digested the story. "Yes, like Bing Crosby and Bob Hope."

"Abbott and Costello, doll-face. Those were her favorites." Trick walked over and sat beside her. "Socks loved those guys. Some of the jokes were hard to explain to a Frenchy, but I did my best."

"She didn't understand some of the gags and thought they were silly," Alex said, gazing out the window. "But she laughed and played along just to make him feel better. He never knew."

Jax set his coffee cup down and asked what Trick was wondering, too. "Alex, how is it that you know so much about Abrielle Chanoux? I doubt those intelligence reports talked about Abbott and Costello or Bob Hope. I know you said you've been investigating Trick's case for years, but how do *you* know these personal things about her and Trick?"

"Yeah, sport," Trick said, leaning close to Alex. "You took the words right out of my mouth."

"I cannot say." Alex stood up and went to the window. She stayed there for a long time looking out at nothing. "I gave my word."

"Your word?" Jax glanced at Trick who threw a chin toward her, sending him from the table to her side where he took one of her hands. "You gave your word to whom?"

She tried to speak but the words choked her and she stood looking into his eyes. They silently pleaded with him to let her go.

"Alex?"

"No one can know those things you know." She lowered her head. "No one."

"You've spoken with Abrielle Chanoux?" Jax asked in whisper. "How?"

"No, first tell me how you knew about Socks."

Jax listened to Trick and then he repeated it to Alex. "The first time Trick dropped in to meet the Resistance, he was crazy about her. He asked if she'd want some nylons when he returned, but she said no. She was a country girl and preferred socks."

Alex's eyes rained tears. "Oh my God, I'm the only one. No one else knows all this. No one. Please tell me how? How do you know these things? If anyone finds out it would be so dangerous. They will kill her."

"Come on, sister." Trick's face was soft and his eyes showed tears of their own. "You knew my Socks?"

Alex threw herself into Jax's arms and wept. She clung to him. Her body shuddered and drained itself of emotions perhaps pent up for too long. Something was fighting to come out. A secret. She struggled to keep it in. When she leaned away from Jax, she surrendered.

"The night McCall died, Abrielle ran away." Her voice was a whisper—distant and afraid. "She's been in hiding since 1944. Abrielle Chanoux is alive."

Chapter 54

Alive?"

Jax looked over at Trick. He had tears drifting down his cheeks as he watched her. "I want to see her," Trick said. "Where is she?"

Jax sat across the table from Alex and reached over, taking her hands. He sat quietly there, watching her, giving her time to consider all he'd told her. She trembled and held his eyes, waiting for him to say anything—anything that would restore her faith that she had made the right decision to reveal her secret.

He didn't fail her. "Alex, you're safe with me. I won't tell a soul, I promise. Where is Abrielle?"

"No, I cannot tell you that." She wiped away the fear draining down her cheeks. "The truth is, I don't know where she is. She doesn't tell me. I found her accidentally years ago when I was right out of college. That's how I first got interested in this story."

"Is she all right?" Trick asked. "How can we contact her?"

Jax repeated the questions.

"She uses aliases and moves around. If she is ever found, it might be dangerous for her."

"Explain that to me, Alex. Why is she in hiding? It's been so long."

"A lifetime." Alex squeezed Jax's hand. "Trick McCall

fell in love with her during the war. It was against all the rules and all common sense, but he did. He wanted to marry her but it was too complicated. It was too dangerous. And in France, there was someone else, too."

"She's right, sport. It was crazy."

"During a mission, Abrielle was shot and was dying. There wasn't the right medical help available with the Underground. McCall used his team to fly her out of France to England. It took months but she recovered. By then, McCall refused to send her back and she disappeared."

Jax looked at Trick. "Disappeared?"

"Yeah, Ricky. I told you, I once sneaked someone out of France without permission. What would you have done? Johnny Singleton and Roman Clay helped me. Roman helped juggle all the paperwork. And by juggle I mean, well, you get it, sport."

Alex squeezed Jax's hand. "When she got better, they moved her here to the States."

"But why stay in hiding all this time?" Jax asked.

"She was there the night McCall was killed as you know," Alex said, straightening herself up. "She found Schiller in the woods and she hid him out of the way. By the time she returned to the Inn, Vetner and Clay were charging in. She knew it went bad and fled. Schiller and she made it out."

Trick was in tears now, slouched back in his chair playing with his fedora. "Did she see who did it? Did she see Harriet?"

Jax repeated him and added, "What happened to Schiller?"

"By the time she secured Schiller, it was over and too late for her to help."

"Why didn't she ever come forward?" Jax asked.

"She couldn't," Alex said, looking at the empty chair Trick was in. "Later, she learned that the OSS thought Trick had disappeared with all the money, jewels, and diamonds. OSS was convinced he was Harriet and began a manhunt."

Jax started putting it all together. "Abrielle was terrified the real Harriet would find her and kill her to keep her from revealing what really happened."

"Yes," she said. "If OSS got to her or Schiller, Harriet might yet find her. They went into hiding."

"For nearly seventy years?" Jax found it fantastic. "Wouldn't Harriet have given up?"

"Schiller was the only witness who knew Harriet," Alex said. "Abrielle knew where Schiller was. Harriet needed them both dead to protect himself."

Jax took it all in. "Okay, that's Trick's situation. There has to be a connection back to Leo and the others."

"I don't know," she blurted softly. "I just don't know."

"Can we speak with Abrielle?" Jax asked. "She may be able to help us."

"Maybe." Alex gave him a faint smile. "I'll get word to her. Give me some time. It takes a couple days. If she is willing, she'll set up a meeting with us. But I can't promise anything. Remember, she's old, but she's still afraid."

Jax thought a moment. "Let's find Clay and Vetner if they're still alive. If McCall's and Leo's killing are connected, maybe they know something."

Trick tapped the table again. "Ricky, one of them might be Harriet. We have to be careful for Alex's sake. You don't have to be young to kill."

"We'll be careful."

Alex narrowed her eyes at Jax. "Roman Clay is dead, Jax. He died more than a year ago. And don't you think finding Cavallo or the girl who saved you is more important? Can't they clear you?"

"You're right." Jax touched her hand. "But I can't do much on Cavallo. I have to rely on Finch and Christie to find him. Captain Martinez won't let me anywhere near that case."

She shrugged. "Then how do we find the girl?"

"Only one way I know." Jax led Alex to his computer.

"We have to crack more of these codes on the website. If we found the golf course, maybe we can find their next hiding spot."

"Yes, of course. Then what?"

"We put her into protective custody." Jax banged away on the computer keyboard but each time he hit "enter" all he found was an error message that the website was not found. He tried again and again without success.

"The website is gone. They took it down."

Alex leaned over his shoulder and tried twice with the same results. "How could they know you found it? Who have you told?"

"Just my BCI team."

"No, Ricky," Trick said slowly, carefully drawing out his words as though they were bitter. "You told Johnny Singleton, too."

"Damn, I told John Singleton, too, Alex."

Alex shook her head. "John's on our side. You can trust him. I am sure there are ways of knowing who's logging onto their site."

"Alex, we have to be very, very careful from now on." Jax stood. "Too many people have been hurt."

Trick tipped his fedora onto the back of his head. "You're tellin' me."

Chapter 55

Sheriff's department. Open the door," Finch commanded. He stood beside the second floor apartment door and pounded again. "Open up, Koontz. Now."

Footsteps inside the apartment grew louder and someone jiggled a security chain. The door opened a few inches. "What do you want? I'm sleeping."

"I want to ask you a few more questions about Kathleen Cullen."

Koontz rubbed his eyes. "Come back later. I already gave a statement. I got nothing to add. Talk with Agent Levin."

"Open up, Koontz, or you'll be unemployed by sunset."

Koontz cursed loudly and opened the door, blocking the doorway in his underwear and a dirty, ripped tee-shirt. "Come on, man, I worked all night. I'm tired."

"Thanks," Finch said, pushing him back out of the way and walking in, "I'd love to come in."

He looked around the kitchen and adjoining living room. The trash container beside the refrigerator overflowed onto the floor and empty pizza and takeout boxes littered the counter. There were at least two empty six-packs of beer strewn about and it had been weeks since anyone washed the mountain of dishes in the sink. The dull scent of stale beer and dirty clothes hung in the air.

"Nice place, Koontz." In the living room Finch found a

plastic bag of green herbs in an open glass bowl on the coffee table. Beside it were an ashtray and a grungy pipe. "Glaucoma? Got a prescription?"

"Whatever." Koontz stood beside the front door watching him. "You can't force your way in here, Officer."

"Detective to you, Koontz. "

"Whatever. The weed ain't mine. What do you want?"

Finch turned and closed on Koontz, jamming an iron finger into his chest. "Listen, dipshit, I don't care about the weed or anything else in here. But you should care that one call to the Virginia private security office where your guard-card gets issued and you're done."

"Okay, okay." Koontz waved toward a chair but Finch held his ground. Koontz shrugged and said, "What do you want, Detective?"

Finch smiled. "Let's go back over the night Richard Jax saw Kathleen Cullen, shall we?"

Koontz nodded.

"I read the statement you gave Agent Levin. I'm not as impressed as he was. I'm not as gullible, either."

"Ah, look." Koontz slid around Finch and found a rickety, wooden straight chair across the room to slink into "I wrote what he told me to write and I signed it. Leave me alone."

"Oh?" Finch grinned and walked over to him. "What Levin told you to write?"

Koontz looked down and shrugged.

Finch leaned down within inches of Koontz's face. "Who did you let in to see Cullen that night? It wasn't Agent Jax, was it?"

"Yes, I told you it was him."

"No, your statement said the guy *said* it was Jax. Then your statement says you saw him before you let him in. The problem is Jax wasn't anywhere near Cullen's place that night."

"I told Levin—"

Finch tapped a finger into Koontz's head like a jackhammer. "You're lying, Koontz. Or do I smell burning meth lab in the bedroom? I may have to call in my squad to tear this place apart."

"You can't do that. I know my rights. Agent Levin said he'd make sure I was okay."

"Screw Levin." Finch pulled out his cell phone and feigned a call. His finger never touched the keypad. "This is Finch. Officer Koontz is growing marijuana in his apartment. He may have a lab inside, too. I'm outside his door right now and can smell it. Send over some units and a drug canine team."

Koontz slid his chair abruptly away from Finch. "Stop. Okay, okay."

Finch grinned again. "Hold on, Sheriff, something's come up. Sit tight, I'll call right back." He glared at Koontz. "Who visited Cullen's that night?"

"Jesus, I knew this would happen." Koontz's face blanched and his eyes found the ceiling. "The guy said he was Agent Jax to see Ms. Cullen."

"He said that? He said, 'Agent Jax?' "

Koontz nodded.

Finch flipped his phone. "Did he always call himself 'Agent Jax' when he went to see Cullen?"

"Come to think of it, he always just said 'Jax for Ms. Cullen.' He was sort of informal. Not like her. They didn't want the neighbors knowing he was a cop."

"Why?"

Koontz shrugged. "Rich people are weird like that. They have parties all the time, you know, they smoke a little, do some crack or something. We're supposed to look the other way."

"But that night, he said he was, 'Agent Jax?'"

Another nod. "Yeah."

"Didn't you recognize him?"

"Well, no." Koontz leaned forward on his elbows and cradled his head in his hands. "Shit."

"You never looked, did you?"

"No, sir."

"What, you were watching porn or something?"

Another nod. "Something like that."

Finch's face lightened. "And you heard a voice over the intercom say it was Agent Jax and you buzzed him in without looking at the CCTV cameras, right?"

"Yes, sir."

Finch pounced on him and dragged him to his feet. "And you signed a sworn statement saying it was Agent Richard Jax who last saw Kathleen Cullen."

Koontz dangled in Finch's grasp and nodded. His face was pale and his eyes awash as he sniffed back his guilt. "No, it's not like that, sir. I tried to tell Agent Levin, but he just kept sayin' 'Don't worry about it. You know it was him. Forget it.' Am I going to jail?"

"No, you little twerp," Finch shoved the pudgy security guard back onto the chair. "You're gonna quit your job tonight pal. Security work isn't for you."

"Yes, sir."

"And this afternoon, you're gonna come to my office and tell Agent Krein everything you just told me. And you won't mention our little visit or I'll put your ass in jail for selling dope, perjury, and obstructing justice. *After* you get out of the hospital."

"Yes, sir." Koontz slumped in the chair as sweat beaded on his forehead. When he found his voice, he stopped Finch at the front door. "Detective Finch, did Agent Jax kill Ms. Cullen? Do you think he did that?"

Finch closed the door behind him without answering. It wasn't that it was a bad question, he just didn't know the answer.

Chapter 56

Finch left Koontz's apartment and headed straight to the BCI office. He had to tell Christie what he'd learned, especially Jeremy's manipulation of Koontz's statement. Martinez was hiding evidence and Jeremy was intimidating witnesses. The question was why.

Christie was his last confidant. His only one. He trusted her and her alone.

When he entered the office, Ms. Leweski bellowed at him. "It's about time one of you got here. I'm late for lunch. Janice hasn't got back to reception but I'm leavin' anyway. You answer the phones."

Finch waved in the air. He knew better than to argue with the self-anointed bitcher-in-chief. If he showed his annoyance, it might result in all manner of lost mail, dropped calls, or receiving every crank call in the office on his private cell phone.

"I'd be happy to, Ms. Leweski. Have a nice lunch."

She grumbled and fled—running into a deliveryman in the doorway and barking a less-than-polite "give it to him" on her way passed.

The deliveryman looked after her as she left then turned to Finch. "I'm glad I don't come here often. I got a courier package for Captain Martinez."

"He's out. I'll sign."

"Can't. Him only. He has to sign."

Finch threw a thumb at the front door. "Then sit outside or come back."

The courier checked his watch and handed the clipboard to Finch. "Sign."

After the courier left, Finch went to drop the manila shipping envelope on Martinez's desk when the return label caught his eye. It was from Chief Rogers's office and it was marked, "Forwarded Under Special Courier."

Finch looked around to ensure the office was empty. Then he went to his desk, envelope in hand. There, he took out a small razor knife and took great care slicing open the bottom seam of the envelope.

Inside was a second, folded manila shipping envelope. On it was the Pennsylvania State seal and the address of the Bethlehem Regional Office of the Pennsylvania State Police Bureau of Forensic Services. The inner envelope had been opened and resealed with packing tape. Finch sliced it open and pulled out a sheet of letterhead from the Forensic Services Office, signed by Chief Forensic Examiner, Dr. Arun Tomar.

He read it twice before realizing what it could mean. On the third time, his stomach churned.

The letter was a forensic summary report detailing a ballistic examination and a blood sample comparison conducted two days after Leo Carraba's murder. The document did not reference any investigation number or incident location. It didn't need to. Clipped to the letter was a less formal, handwritten note that made it all clear.

> *Reggie: I'm afraid this won't help you much. The ballistic data and the physical bullet were compared with the FBI and regional databases with no matching results. I am holding the bullet in evidence in my lab should you wish other examinations or comparisons at a later date. The blood analyses were not much help either. We attempted a comparison between your baseline sample*

against Carraba and Jax. Neither is a match. I still do not understand why your own lab facilities didn't assist you, but I'm happy to trade my services for my Penn State wagers. I believe they are now paid in full. See you for the holidays. A.T.

"I'll be damned—*again*." Finch rechecked the office. It was still empty. Then, he made a quick photocopy of the document. He stuffed the copies in his pocket and repacked the courier envelopes, taking care to replace the packing tape with fresh tape from the mail counter. Then he dripped a few drops of superglue over the sliced end of the outer envelope and pressed a new seal. He dropped the package on Ms. Leweski's desk and locked the office on his way out. He speed-dialed his cell and got a voicemail. "It's Finch. We need to talk and soon and not at the office. Let me know when and where. And, Christie, don't tell anyone I called. And I mean *anyone*."

Chapter 57

Detective Finch made his way into the eastern side of Spotsylvania County where rural Virginia sprawled without towns for miles. Despite his GPS, he missed the turnoff and had to double back twice to find it. As he rolled up to the road, he called Levin for the third time and left another message.

"Levin, I'm down at Clay's place. I'll call you when I'm done. And for Christ's sake, answer your phone once in a while."

Hubert Concord's security man had given him the license plate number of the mysterious man digging around for information on the Quinton Properties. The plate was registered to a steel-gray, 2005 sedan belonging to Roman Clay at this rural Spotsylvania County address. Jax had told him that Clay was one of the OSS agents involved in Patrick McCall's last mission. The mission that ended in McCall's murder. A quick computer search told him Roman Clay was deceased.

That took coincidence right off the table.

Whoever was driving Clay's vehicle was tracing Quinton Properties' business roots and the Grey Coat Inn just as Finch was doing. Finch was moments from finding out just who that was. He drove a half-mile farther to a rundown trailer and detached garage. The lot was surrounded by cars and trucks of various ages lined up outside. Beside the double-door garage was a late model Lexus and a monster-truck. On the garage door read a sign, "Clay Motors" and promised cheap repairs and honest work.

Finch wondered who would venture this far into the Virginia countryside to read the sign.

"Homey," he said to no one. "And nice Lexus."

Finch didn't make it ten feet from his unmarked cruiser when the trailer door banged open and an older man wearing jeans and an oil-stained sweatshirt appeared. He was in his late sixties and had a dirty beard and a puffy face. He had little hair beneath his ball cap and his hands were grease-covered.

Despite his age, he was sturdy—tall and wide-shouldered and he walked with a powerful gate as he started toward Finch. "You lookin' for car work?" the man asked in a casual, easy manner. "Or just lost?"

Finch flipped his badge case open and didn't wait for the man to read it. "Detective Finch, Loudoun County Sheriff. I'm looking for Roman Clay's family."

"A cop?" The man eyed him. "Loudoun's a long way from here, detective."

"I'm attached to BCI. You Clay's family?"

The man's mood darkened. "I'm Andrew. Roman was my dad. What you want?"

"Nice car." Finch threw a chin toward the Lexus. "Is it yours?"

"Do I look like a Lexus man? A friend of Dad's wants me to look it over. I'm a mechanic, ain't I?"

Finch took a step toward Andrew and slid his sunglasses off, leaning forward and getting to the point quickly. "Andrew, now don't go pissing me off, okay? Your dad's '05 sedan was seen at two businesses up in Loudoun a couple weeks ago. I want to know what it was doing up there."

Andrew shook his head. "No it wasn't. That car's been here and gone nowhere for months."

"Bullshit, Andrew. Do I have to bring in the local sheriff or can we do this the easy way?"

Andrew Clay pulled out a rag from his pocket and wiped grease from his hands. He looked around as though unsure of what to do or say next. Then he turned and headed for the garage door, saying over his shoulder, "Come on in, Detective. I'll get some iced tea. No need for being that way with me. It's you cops always screwin' with my family that's got me riled."

Inside, Finch waited in a crude office in the side of the garage while Andrew went into the trailer to get tea. Normally, he never would have allowed him out of sight without backup nearby, but once Andrew disappeared out the side door, Finch went to work. He started with the rickety metal desk and searched it drawer by drawer for anything—notes, files, or a weapon. Anything that might shed light on Andrew Clay. In the top left drawer, he found a stainless steel .45 semiautomatic pistol. He slid it out and checked the chamber. It was loaded.

"I don't need a permit for my own gun in my own office in my own house," Andrew said from the doorway where he was holding two iced tea glasses. "Do I?"

"No, you don't." Finch dropped the weapon's magazine onto the desk and jacked the slide to extract the round in the chamber. But I get nervous around folks with guns when I'm talking to them."

"I've had three break-ins this year. All redneck kids looking for cash and booze. I ain't having a fourth."

Finch sat the gun onto the desk and moved around to the filing cabinet. "I don't blame you."

"BCI, huh?" Andrew handed him a tall glass of tea and sat behind the desk watching him. "You the one who found that McCall guy?"

"You know about that?" Finch had his segue. "Is that why you were in Loudoun two weeks ago?"

"Sort of," Andrew said, nodding slightly. "Paper didn't say much about things."

"McCall was murdered at the inn back in '44. The same place your dad and the other OSS guys tried to capture that traitor, Harriet. Or maybe you knew that."

"Yeah, I know." Andrew laughed and snorted all at once. "I don't give a damn about all that, mister."

"Then why were you up looking into Quinton Properties?"

"Money." Andrew went to the filing cabinet, pulled open the top drawer, and withdrew a stack of envelopes. He handed them to Finch. "I found these in dad's stuff. They're old invoices. He was getting paid for work with Quinton and they still owed him near as I can figure."

Finch read through the top invoice. It was for a little more than two-thousand dollars. "He's been dead a while. It's a little late to be collecting debts."

"Yeah, I know that. But then I read about that company in the paper, you know, sayin' they owned the inn, I got curious. I tried callin' up there, but all I got was the run around from this uppity jerk."

"Hubert Concord."

"Yeah, that's him." Andrew sat back behind his desk. "So I went up there to talk to them. Dad did a lot of odd jobs for small businesses; mostly engine repair and maintenance. I didn't have any record of them so I went askin'. I got my hands slapped for it, too."

Finch cocked his head. "What's that mean?"

"Nothing," Andrew took long swallow of tea and looked at Finch as though in deep thought. "So they caught up with old Dirty-Trick McCall? Murdered? Good, I'm damn glad he's dead. Looks like he got what he deserved."

"What does that mean, Andrew?"

"Government hounded dad his entire life," Andrew snapped. "They never gave him a break. First, they said he screwed up that mission, and when they had no one else to blame, they called him a traitor. Sons-a-bitches dogged him his whole life. No more. No more I tell you."

Finch let Andrew go silent for a moment. He nursed his tea and watched the big mechanic smoldering. "I'm real sorry about that, Andrew. But, it wasn't me. Now, what happened with Quinton? Cut the bullshit and help me out."

Andrew lifted his chin and looked Finch over again. He stood and just as Finch prepared for a punch, he dropped his head and wiped his brow with the rag.

"Don't know that I can. It's all this bullshit the government put him through." Andrew looked away. "He wasn't a traitor and he didn't fail that mission. I've heard it thousands of times and he did what he was told."

"Andrew, what about Quinton Properties?"

"About two weeks ago, just after I saw that story in the paper about the dead cop, I went up there. Then somebody kept calling, asking for dad. When I told them he was dead, they called me a liar and told me to stay away. They kept calling and sayin' shit like that."

"Who was it?" Finch asked.

Andrew shrugged. "Don't know and don't care. If I find out, I'll have more than words for them. I'm sure it was one of them from the old days."

Finch held up the invoices. "Andrew, did your dad ever mention Wellington International?"

"Sure. Why?"

"You don't seem surprised I'm asking."

He shrugged. "No, it's not like no one else is asking about Dad, you know. Couple fellas were here the other day asking the same questions. Funny, though, they never said McCall was found."

"Who were they?"

"Couple FBI men. Least that's what they said. They never showed me no badge or nothing."

"What did they want?"

"Same thing. I told you. They wanted to know about Wellington and Quinton."

"And what did you tell them?"

"Can't say. Them feds told me to keep my mouth shut.

They asked same things as you and told me if I repeated anything I said, they'd lock me up. Same old thing. They can do and say whatever they want and I get locked up if I defend myself. Just like Dad."

Finch sat in the chair across from Andrew and leaned forward on the desk. "Andrew, this is real important. Cut the games and tell me what you can about Wellington."

"Look, I don't know anything. Dad said he worked for Wellington decades ago. That's it. Now, I got work to do, okay? So if you don't have a warrant, I'll be wantin' my invoices back."

Finch leaned back. "Is that all you told the FBI?"

"Warrant, Detective. You bring me that and I'll spill what I told them feds."

"Okay," Finch dropped the invoices on the desk and played his last card. "How about John Singleton, Andrew? Your dad ever mention him?"

"Another bastard," Andrew snorted. "He's all mighty and powerful. He did everything but blame Dad himself. Until he started fighting back, then Singleton left him alone."

"One last question," Finch said, watching the big man's eyes for a lie. "Did you have any contact with Agent Leo Carraba?"

Andrew cocked his head. "That cop who was killed? No, sir, never spoke to him and never met him. If someone is sayin' I have something to do with that cop, they're lying."

"Thanks, Andrew," Finch said, standing. "And I'm sorry about your dad."

"Too late, detective. Ol' Harriet killed him sixty-seven years ago. He just took longer to die."

Chapter 58

Andrew stood wiping his hands with a rag as he watched Finch disappear down the dirt road. His gaze was indifferent until Finch was gone from sight. Then he spit on the ground and stuffed the rag into his pocket, cursing in his wake.

"Well now, maybe you can help me after all, detective." A dirty smile slipped through the oil and dirt on his face. "Bastards."

He went inside the trailer and returned to his garage office with a beer. Then he pulled open his center desk drawer, filing through its contents. After three files, he tossed the last onto the desk. Then he began a search of the clutter in the old metal filing cabinet and the bulletin board that hung crooked above it.

"Damn." He kicked the bottom filing cabinet drawer closed and sent the bulletin board crashing down.

He stopped to retrieve the papers and old notes pinned to the cork board when his eye caught an old black and white photograph that had fluttered onto the floor. He picked it up and examined it. The photograph was tattered and torn in half, but he recognized what was left of the print in an instant.

It was a late Saturday night in 1942 and his father had just finished training at a makeshift camp south of Washington DC. He and his OSS team were celebrating at the first of several bars on F-Street in DC. By the end of the night, the military police would be pouring them into a jeep and escorting them home to their rooming house. Andrew knew the story well. He'd heard it over and over when he was younger and Dad had been willing to share the good times he'd had during the war.

When Andrew looked around the garage, he forced a bitter laugh. The acre of rusting engines and piled car frames was not a product of Dad's good times.

Not at all.

The photograph was young Red Vetner's idea after he'd cajoled a passing waitress into taking a group picture at one of the bars. Red was one of the youngest on the team, except for John Singleton who was no more than six months his senior. John had just turned twenty. Sitting around the table was John, Red, and Patrick McCall. They'd been recruited across different east coast military units and universities within days of each other and assigned to the same OSS unit a month later. John aspired to be an engineer on his way to some Ivy League university, Red handpicked from a Ranger unit in North Carolina, and McCall from a successful law firm in D.C. where he studied for the bar.

Dad had been a mechanic found in the motor pool in North Carolina but he was missing from the photograph and Andrew knew why. Anger and cheap whiskey threw him into a rage and he tore the photograph in half decades ago. What became of the other piece Andrew didn't know. The photograph was torn top to bottom across the left side of the table, cutting part of Red's arm off. What remained were three of the four drinking buddies with a table full of beer glasses. Andrew tried to remember what vanished on the missing half of the picture, but he couldn't.

That photograph gave Andrew an idea.

He cursed and found what he was looking for still tacked to the bulletin board and tore the crumpled business card away. He dropped into his desk chair, lifted his feet onto the desk, and chugged a beer. Then he picked up his desk phone.

"This is Andrew Clay." The voice knew exactly who he was and what he wanted. "I don't give a damn, put him on. He'll want to talk to me."

A few seconds later Andrew's face tightened. "Yeah it's me. I don't give a damn about what you said. Some people have been here asking about the good ol' days again." The response angered him and he chugged on his beer. "Oh? Well, you should care. First it was the FBI and now some snooping Loudoun detective says he works for the State BCI."

Silence. Then a long rebuttal. "Just a bunch of old men and still they're chasing him. That's the way it's always been. Yeah, yeah, you'll be hearing from them. I guarantee it."

More rebuttals.

"Same as before. When?"

Silence. Then angry words.

"No. By tomorrow. If I don't hear from you by then, I'll pick one of their names out of a hat and call."

Silence.

"I thought so."

Andrew slammed his phone down and contemplated his feet over the rim of his beer can.

"Bastards, you'll never let it go."

Chapter 59

Christie made the turn down Jax's narrow street and slowed. The street was lined with cars and she had to pass his drive and make a U-turn at the next block to find a parking spot. The inconvenience turned lucky or she would have walked into Jeremy Levin relocking Jax's front door with a lock pick. Instead, she watched from a half-block away as Jeremy jogged across the street tucking something into his jacket. He climbed into his a steel-gray foreign coupe and sped away in the opposite direction from Christie's unmarked cruiser.

What the hell are you doing, Jeremy?

She knew the best way to get her answer. She followed him.

Jeremy cut through side streets and maneuvered around the center of Leesburg until he caught Route 7 and headed east. He didn't seem concerned about being followed. He gave ample turn-signal warnings and kept within the speed limit. His driving was void of the sudden turns and varying speeds intended to flush out anyone following. All the while Jeremy meandered through town as he talked on his cell phone.

Once outside downtown Leesburg, he drove straight to the Great Hall Hotel. There, he parked in the valet lane, flashed his badge at the attendant, and walked inside.

Christie parked in the side lot where she observed him

without fear he could get a clear view of her. She dialed her office and waited for Ms. Leweski to pick up.

"Christie here, I can't reach Agent Levin. Do you know where he is, Ms. Leweski?"

"He left with Captain Martinez." Ms. Leweski ruffled some papers and sighed twice. "They didn't say where to and I didn't ask. Try his cell." Ms. Leweski abruptly hung up.

Next, Christie hit speed-dial four and reached Martinez on the second ring. "Hey, Cap, Christie here. I'm heading out to see someone about Lupino. I'm hoping to get a lead on Leo's missing snitch. Can you spare Jeremy to ride shotgun with me? The office said he was with you."

Silence. Then a grunt. "He is with me and we're on our way to see the Bureau. We can't be disturbed. Call Finch."

"But—"

"Christie, we're in the middle of something. We'll be out of touch for a few hours. Call Finch. Gotta go. Check with me later."

He hung up.

You fucking liar.

Christie dialed four-one-one and had information connect her to the Great Hall Hotel. "How can I direct your call?"

"This is Deputy Rollins from the sheriff's office," she lied. "Agent Levin should be at your hotel. I need to speak with him and he's not answering his cell. Can you tell me if he's in your dining room?"

"Agent Levin just arrived. One moment. Yes, Agent Levin was shown to a guest's room, a Ms. Vouros's room. Room 221. Shall I ring that room?"

"No, I'm almost there. I'll catch up. Thank you."

Before she climbed out of her car, Jeremy emerged from the hotel and jumped into his coup. Traffic was light and he pulled right onto Route 7 heading back west toward town. Christie followed several cars behind.

After twenty minutes, he entered a conclave of rundown

townhouses, parked in front of a shabby, brown unit that showed no sign of home improvement or repair in years, and went inside.

She pulled to the curb and looked the neighborhood over. Parked two cars down from Jeremey's coup was Captain Martinez's car.

Christie passed the parking lot entrance and made a long loop around the neighborhood. She didn't know the area well but knew Leesburg and the BCI operations enough to know they had no safehouses nearby.

What Martinez and Jeremy were doing baffled her. She hit another speed dial on her cell. "Finchy, where are you? Okay, good. Can you meet me at the Grey Coat Inn? Twenty minutes. Don't tell anyone where you're going."

৫৲৩৫৲৩

"What do you think he took?" Finch sat behind the steering wheel of his unmarked cruiser, sipping a cup of coffee. They'd been sitting for a half hour in front of the FBI's crime scene tape that surrounded the Grey Coat Inn. "Martinez has been acting odd, but this is off the charts."

Christie frowned. "Maybe it's the heat from the FBI."

"That doesn't explain Jeremy sneaking into Jax's place. Our search warrant has expired and I haven't heard of any new ones. Besides, as far as I'm concerned, Martinez and Jeremy have been weird since way before the FBI showed up."

Christie stopped sipping her coffee. "Oh? What does that mean?"

"I didn't want to say anything. But, hey, you're good with Jax, right?"

She nodded.

"That morning at Leo's crime scene, I saw Martinez pull something out of this old wood pile. Jeremy saw him, too, but hasn't said boo about it."

"Maybe it wasn't important."

Finch laughed. "You sound like Jax. If it wasn't, why not share it? He never logged it into evidence and there's no lab report on it. In fact, lab reports are missing from the file, too."

Christie returned to her coffee. Her eyes wandered around the inn's grounds, looking at nothing. Finch was right and she knew it. How right might be the difference between good cops and corrupt cops.

"Finchy, you might be onto something. You ever wonder about Jeremy? He speaks three languages, has a big-time Princeton degree, too. For what? To be a state cop? Why not a fed or the CIA or state department?"

"Yeah, I asked him about that one day. He gave me some line about wanting to work his way up and all that. Total crap."

"Then Alexandra Vouros shows up. Right on the heels of us finding that pile of bones at the Inn. And the FBI declares a sixty-seven-year-old homicide a case of national security? Is it me or has the planet started spinning wrong?"

Finch shrugged. "Weird, all of it. Jax said Vouros is with some historical bunch in DC. So maybe that makes sense."

"She has no history. It's like she just appeared one day in DC."

"Huh?"

Christie turned in the seat. "Alexandra Vouros doesn't exist before DC. I started wondering about her. A lot."

"Yeah, I'll bet you did." Finch laughed. "She's hot and smart. Not that you're not but she's what you don't want hanging around Jax these days, huh?"

"Stuff it, Finchy Are you going to listen or what?"

"Sorry."

"Anyway, I did a quick background search on her. I can't find anything at all. Nothing. She has a DC driver's license but the address is old. Her social has no credit history or other history that I can find."

"Maybe she's rich and doesn't use credit cards." Finch

waited for Christie to shrug. "Are you saying she's lying about everything? Jesus, Christie, someone down at BCI headquarters in Richmond told Captain Martinez Vouros was approved. And you go investigating her background?"

"I ran down her connection to this OSS historical group. She's been working around them for five years. She's some kind of stringer like the newspapers use. She runs down stories for them. Get this. Some anonymous goodie-two-shoes pays her salary and expenses. One of the old OSS geezers sent me her resume. She got a fancy private grant to go to George Washington for a master's in history and then on to her PhD. She drives a Mercedes, for God's sake."

"Ah, Christie, she's a PhD for crying out loud. What do you expect?"

She frowned. "She doesn't have a PhD from GW and she doesn't have any work record that checks out. And get this, she's adopted and no one knows anything about her. Nothing. Where she's from or who her parents are. She's a flippin' ghost, Finchy. And she appears on Jax's doorstep like his fairy godmother?"

"You think she's trouble?" Finch's eyes twinkled and he cracked a smile. "Or is this you being protective? Could it be she's hot, rich, and private, and you don't like that?"

"No, it's me wondering who the hell she is and what she wants. It sure can't be about some pile of bones. She's hiding something."

"Maybe she is. Christie, you just ranted about Martinez and Jeremy and now Vouros. You sound as nuts as Jax."

"Maybe I am." She crumpled her coffee cup up and tossed it into Finch's back seat. "I don't know. It's you, me, and Jax on one side, and everyone else on the other. I don't trust any of them. And I don't think you should either."

"Sorry, Christie, but I don't trust any of you staties. I just pretend." When Christie flipped him off, he added, "Well, maybe you. What's the plan?"

"We work off the record. We have to find out what's going on before Martinez catches us. That's the first thing. The second thing is we gotta make sure Jax doesn't get himself into more trouble."

"More? Jesus, he's built a better case against himself for two murders than we could. Is there a third thing?"

She opened her car door and stepped out, shut the door, and peeked back through the open window. "We find out what Little Miss Smarty-Pants is up to because it can't be good. I'm not going to let her screw things up for me."

Chapter 60

I still don't think he'll be able to help us," Alex said. "Red's a dying man. And besides, I've already interviewed him. What do you think we can learn?"

Jax and Alex had driven through a small town some seventy-five miles southwest of Washington into the foothills of the Shenandoah Mountains. They followed the highway north and then traversed several secondary roads that climbed toward Wolf Mountain. The roads wound the mountains until they reached the grand, two-story log home secluded in a range of pines hidden from the road. Red Vetner's home was surrounded by a tall, brooding iron fence. At the front gate, a sign warned visitors that solicitors, reporters, or anyone else were unwelcome.

Two oversized Rottweilers reinforced that warning.

"I don't know. Maybe nothing," Jax said. "Finch went to see the Clay family today."

"Why? Roman Clay died over a year ago. I'm not sure there's anyone left."

"We'll soon find out."

Alex sighed. "I phoned earlier so he's expecting us." Then she gestured to the intercom beside Jax's driver's side window. "I'll buzz the house."

She leaned across the seat to reach the intercom, brushing against him behind the wheel. She rested there, leaning against his chest, waiting for the voice on the other end to confirm their appointment. It took just a moment, but Alex played it much longer.

"Will this take long?" Jax said, holding his breath. "Not that I mind."

She let her hair brush his face as her body glided across him to her seat. "There, all ready."

"We sure are."

A moment later, Jax parked the car.

Red Vetner didn't look like a crack OSS operative any longer. His frame slumped in his wheel chair like a pile of half-filled clothes. His wheelchair sat across the room near the living room's French doors where the mountain's view was pleasing. An oxygen tube ran from the rear of his chair around and up to his face. His breathing was loud and irregular and with each breath, his body shuddered as though it might be his last.

A nurse waved them into the room. "Please don't be long. He's very ill."

Alex and Jax waited until she left the room before they approached Red and woke him from a nap. "Red? It's Alex Vouros."

Red slowly opened his eyes and took several deep breaths. After several moments, a smile cracked his leathery face when he focused on Alex.

"Ah, Alexandra, you look wonderful." He took a deep, slow breath of oxygen. "I remember you well, my dear. How are you?"

"I'm well, Red. I'm sorry to see you feeling so ill."

Red patted the air. "No, no, my dear. Not to worry. I've had a long life but my bad habits are about to catch up to me." Another breath of oxygen. "My nurse said you were coming by. What can I do for you?"

Jax followed Alex to the sofa near Red where they sat down. "Hello, Mr. Vetner. I'm Richard Jax."

"This is my friend, Red. He's a state BCI agent working on a homicide case."

"Oh?" Red looked him over with a sour eye and attempted a half-hearted wink at Alex. "I'm innocent, copper."

"Of course. But I could use some help, sir. My partner was murdered at the Grey Coat Inn. I'm investigating his case."

Red's eyes went wide and he gasped another deep breath of oxygen. "I see. That damn inn again. Tell me."

Jax gave him a quick accounting of Leo's murder and the events afterward. "Two days ago, we discovered Patrick McCall's remains hidden on the property. He was murdered, sir. He never left the inn back in '44."

"I'll be damned." Red started nodding. "John was right after all. Trick was not Harriet."

"No, he was not," Alex said. "You never thought so either."

Red glanced at her and his eyes got far away. "You know, Roman and I were devastated that night. We never believed for a moment it was Trick who sent that radio message. No, sir."

"You heard it too, sir?" Jax asked. "The message I mean."

Red nodded. "We all did. Roman and I each had a radio. The message was coded and sent by Morse. But never once did we believe Trick sent it."

"Mr. Vetner," Jax said. "We believe there may be some connection between what happened to Trick all those years ago and my partner's murder."

"Of course there's a connection, my boy." Red sucked in oxygen and smiled. "The Harriet fiasco, you're partner's murder, then finding Trick. Unless, you believe in coincidences."

"No, sir, I don't."

Alex reached out and touched Red's hand. He smiled and looked at her like a grandfather admiring a child. She smiled back. "You see, the inn has been traced to three companies—Quinton Properties, the Pettington Corporation, and—"

"Wellington International." Red's face paled and he adjusted his oxygen line for a few deep breaths. His eyes left Alex's and fell to the floor in front of him. He sat there, breathing in heavy rasps. "Dear God, not again. After all these years. I can't hide from it even now."

Trick appeared at the French doors and walked over to Red, knelt down beside him, and touched his hand. "Hey, Red, it's all right. It's me. It's Trick. It's all right. Tell them everything you can."

"Trick?" Red looked up at Trick's face. His eyes went wide again and for a moment he tried to find a memory. Then he smiled, nodded, and turned to Alex. "All right, yes. Of course."

Jax exchanged glances with Alex. "Sir," he said. "What can you tell us about Wellington?"

"Oh, that's easy." Red inhaled a long pull of oxygen. "Years ago, I worked for that outfit. Maybe forty years ago. I remember it well enough. As soon as you mentioned Quinton and Pettington, I knew Wellington was involved."

"Why?" Alex asked. "Did you know they owned the inn?"

"No, no, of course not." Red shook his head and leaned forward in his chair. "But I knew Wellington propped up Quinton and Pettington for overseas work. They fronted companies so it was harder to know what they were up to. That's part of why I resigned. I never did trust them."

"What was Wellington involved with that they needed to hide?"

Red looked up at Trick again and nodded. One more time. "Old OSS shenanigans. Except back then, that was war. But Wellington was all about profit. See, a lot of the old outfit went CIA after the war. Not me, though, and not Roman." He took several breaths before continuing. "Roman and I were blackballed after Harriet's mess. If it hadn't been that we all heard that radio signal, we would never have been cleared. Some of the outfit never did believe us."

"But you got through it?" Alex asked. "You did all right for yourself."

Red drew on his oxygen. "Roman and I went to work for Wellington. They were the only ones who would touch us after Harriet. We didn't last long."

"Because they were doing OSS work?" Jax asked.

"In a way, yes. After the big war, there were Korea, Vietnam, and the Russians. Wellington contracted with the CIA and did some of their dirty work."

Alex looked over at Jax. "Wellington International is part of the CIA?"

"If the government needed something nasty done, they turned to the CIA. If the CIA needed something nasty done, they turned to Wellington."

Jax stood up, went to the French doors, and looked out. Trick joined him and touched his shoulder. Sparks began igniting inside him.

"They smuggled people into this country," Trick said.

Red turned in his wheelchair and looked at Jax. "For the agency, sure. But that's not smuggling, is it?"

"Did Wellington smuggle people for profit?" Jax asked. "Like Harriet did?"

"Yes, they did." Red frowned. "That is why I quit."

"Tell us, Red. Tell us what's going on." Alex squeezed his hand again. "How could that involve the inn and why would that get people killed?"

"It's very simple, isn't it?" Red fed on the oxygen for a few moments. "Wellington relocated special clients for the CIA. A Korean general here, a Russian industrialist there." More oxygen. "Sometimes, they did it for the agency. Sometimes, for profit. Not always good people, either."

"What about Roman?" Alex asked. "Where did he go?"

"He'd been working abroad when I left and I heard he quit later. Haven't spoken to him since. Mad as hell at me. Never knew why."

Jax looked at Red. "Mr. Vetner, we found evidence of a

code being used on an internet site." He repeated a sample of the code phrases off the website from memory. "Does this mean anything to you?"

Red closed his eyes and took in oxygen. When he opened them again, he pointed toward his desk across the room. "Bottom drawer, my boy. There's a small black notebook."

Jax went over and retrieved it. "I've got it."

"We used those during the war to communicate with the Underground." Red's head leaned back for a short time. "I jotted many notes about my exploits. Those I could recall years later. I fancied writing a book. Never did, though."

Jax flipped through the small, black notebook. There were number codes and letter substitution codes all penned with handwritten notations explaining where and how Red had used them in the war. Toward the end of the notebook were two pages of similar sayings and phases he'd seen on the website. Below each code phrase was its clear text meaning. Some of them made perfect sense. *The moon is highest when Jack walks home*, meant, *Rendezvous at midnight for extraction to base*. A following set of numbers and letters translated to the date of the pickup.

"This will help us, Red. Thank you." He slipped the book into his pocket.

Red could only cough and nod.

"Easy, Red," Trick said, returning to his side. "Take your time."

"How can your notebook help now?" Alex asked.

"Don't know. We often made easy codes, things we might remember—not supposed to. Take the book. Perhaps you can decode others."

"Sir," Jax said, returning to the couch, "what about the Grey Coat Inn?"

"It was a safehouse back then." Red took a long breath and held up his hand. A moment later, his eyes brightened and he went on. "Wellington used—same MO."

"And still does." Trick put a hand on Red's shoulder and

gave him a squeeze. "I think we get it all now, Red. Harriet's still in business. Or someone is."

Red lowered his eyes and coughed. He coughed again and again trying to catch his breath. When he settled, he looked up at Alex. "There are some things you should know."

"Yes," Alex said, taking his hand. "When you're better."

He nodded. "The night—Trick was killed has haunted me my entire life. If Roman and I hadn't—received that message—we'd have been killed, too. By the time—it was over."

"Red, who do you think Harriet was?" Trick asked.

Red coughed repeatedly and his body quaked, gasping for breaths in between coughs. The episode worsened and he pressed a button on the wristband of his sleeve. A second later, his nurse came in with steaming tea and several containers of medication.

"I'm sorry," she said abruptly, sorting out pills into Red's hand. "You'll have to go. You've stayed too long and he has to rest."

Alex leaned down and kissed Red on his cheek. It made the old man glow. Jax thanked him but the nurse waved off a handshake while she checked his oxygen.

"Wait." Red lifted a bony, shaking hand and pointed toward a wall of photographs and mementos behind his desk. "There—the wall—"

Trick crossed the room to the photographs. He knew the photo Red meant. It was off to the right side near several black and white prints from World War II. The photograph was taken that late Saturday night on F-Street in 1942. Trick recalled the night through foggy memories born of too much beer. He called Jax over and tapped on the frame's glass. "There's something about this photo, Ricky," he said, standing beside him. "I know it was at the Café of All Nations, at the Warner Theater, but there's something about it I just can't remember. And this fella in the background, at the table a couple behind ours, looks real familiar but I just can't place him."

Jax stared at the photo.

Red coughed violently and took a long, heavy draw of oxygen. "Yes, Agent Jax. That's Trick in the photograph. It was one of our watering holes before we shipped out." He coughed and waited to catch his breath. "That's me, Trick, John Singleton, Roman Clay. I will tell you more but—next time. I'm sorry—"

Jax slipped the frame off the wall and carried it to Red, laying it in his lap. "Red, do you know any of these three men sitting at that back table?"

"Tall one—on left—Peter—Trappe." Red's breath was getting shorter and shorter. He gasped and waved his hand. "See me tomorrow. Trappe—he started—Wellington—he started it all."

Chapter 61

Jax and Alex finished their lunch at the tiny country store three miles from Red Vetner's house. They'd been sitting at the wrought iron table facing the road for an hour. There was one other car in the narrow parking area beside the store and little traffic had passed by but for an occasional fall-foliage hunter.

"I want to get back and see if Red's code book can help us with those codes from the internet," Jax said as he returned with two fresh coffees. "They may help finding a lead on the young girl."

"I agree." Alex took a coffee. "Red's faltering since I saw him last and he seemed to have more to tell us. We should go back tomorrow."

"Didn't he ever tell you about Clay and him working for Wellington before?"

She shook her head. "We didn't discuss much about his career after the war. He mentioned working overseas, but he was adamant he stopped working for the government and left it at that. Clay, too. Neither wanted to talk much about life after OSS."

"I wonder why he told us now."

"It's McCall. Finding his remains is going to conjure up a lot of things."

Jax sipped his coffee. "These OSS guys are something. You must have learned a lot from them in your research."

"I did. The OSS recruited amazing people—thinkers, schemers, and daredevils. They dreamed up daredevil plans to harass and sabotage the Germans and just went out and did them. Anything went. No rules per se. And the best of them went on to the CIA. They were amazing people."

Jax grinned. "You sound romantic about it all."

She blushed. "Well, what they did was heroic and most of them got nothing to show for it but stories. I've sat with many of the surviving OSS agents and listened to them for hours. You can't help but share their nostalgia, I guess."

Jax watched her look away and wondered about what she learned about Trick McCall and the OSS. What stories and secrets did they share with her? What other secrets was *she* keeping?

"Will you call Red's nurse tomorrow and get us another appointment? I'd like to hear what he wanted to tell us at the end."

"I'll call first thing."

Jax sat his coffee down. "We should go. It's a long drive back."

"I know there's a lot to do," Alex said, taking a deep, slow breath. "But let's take our time. I love the fall leaves."

Jax touched her hand. "Fall leaves, slow, country drives. You *are* a romantic."

"I can be."

Two miles farther down the mountain road, Alex leaned across the seat and kissed Jax's cheek. She lingered there, nuzzling him, then took his hand before pulling away.

He squeezed her hand. "What's this for? If it's the free coffee, I'll buy champagne later."

"Thank you for doing all this." She leaned back into her seat. "I've been trying to prove McCall's innocence from the beginning. Very few cared. Everyone has been willing to let him be a traitor. Almost everyone."

Jax squeezed her hand and rested their hands on her leg. "I'm not Lancelot, but I am on your side. I'm doing this as much for my own motives as yours. Martinez won't let me get close enough to Leo's case to clear myself, so the only chance I have is if there's a link to Trick. Then there's Kathleen and Cavallo, too."

"Yes, but—"

A gunshot! The rear window shattered. The second shot slammed into the radio console on the dash between them.

"Get down." Jax floored the accelerator and veered the Jeep hard left then right, swerving to keep the shooter from finding his target. "Get as low as you can."

Behind them, two motorcycles rode parallel. Both bikes had passengers leaning out, taking aim on them with handguns. Another shot whistled above the vehicle and scraped the roof as it passed.

Jax tried but couldn't get a good look at either bike or riders. They were large, heavy touring bikes and their fairings gave the drivers concealment. Both riders and passengers were dressed in black leather with full-faced helmets; no distinguishing features were left to identify.

"Who are these guys?" Jax yelled. "They're pissing me off."

One of the bikes veered into the on-coming lane and tried taking a position alongside the Jeep. At the last second, Jax veered left and blocked the bike. The second bike swerved right and back left, looking for an opening to move up and take another shot broadside to them.

Jax continued serpentine down the mountain road, accelerating as fast as he dared, weary of the unfamiliar ground. He gained distance on the curves. Lost distance to the bikes on the straights. He pulled his Glock from its holster and handed it to Alex. "Get ready to shoot back. If they get alongside, don't wait. Shoot before they do."

"Okay." She was low in the seat with her knees sideways leaving as little of her torso as possible above the window line. "I can't see well. Tell me when."

One of the bikes made another move along the right side of the Jeep.

"Now," Jax yelled.

Alex popped up off the seat but hesitated too long. The bike skidded the moment her gun rose and both her shots missed.

The other motorcycle passenger fired a shot that punched through rear quarter panel into the back of the Jeep. This time, Jax veered sharply, cut his move short, and hit the brakes, and forced the bike behind them to lock his brakes and dive around them to avoid a collision. The seconds gave Jax the advantage and he floored the accelerator to gain precious distance.

Two more shots strafed across the Jeep's roof and side panels but injured nothing but paint and trim. The motorcycles quickly regained position behind them, but stayed far enough back to avoid being rammed off the road. One of the riders fired at their left front tire but missed.

Jax had enough. "Screw this. Hold on."

He jumped on the brakes and put the Jeep into a hard skid. Both motorcycles roared by one on each side. As soon as they cleared his front fender, he accelerated again, and took his Glock from Alex.

"Help me with the wheel."

Alex leaned over and gripped the right side of the wheel, holding the Jeep steady. Her face was pale and tight as she readied for the strike.

Jax maneuvered toward the motorcycles but they were ready and began their own evasive maneuvers. They hurtled down the mountain road, shifting and swerving in a death-dance. Ahead, less than a half-mile, was the state highway intersection where tractor-trailers lined the road around a busy truck stop.

The lead motorcycle's passenger turned and fired twice. One round struck the right front headlight and the second whistled by Jax's open window.

Jax gripped his Glock left handed and leaned out the window, firing back—once, twice, three times.

The motorcycle swerved and its passenger shot again

and hit center in their grill. Steam began pouring from beneath the hood.

"Dammit, we have to make the truck stop." Jax veered left to draw the motorcycle right. As soon as the bike reached the center of the road and slowed its drift, Jax veered back hard right and caused the motorcycle to drift left into his line of fire.

He fired three rapid shots.

The second found its mark.

The rider's arm flailed up and his body pitched forward against the driver. He slipped sideways on the rear of the bike but the second motorcycle closed the distance between them and his rider pushed the body back center. As soon they were secured, they accelerated and moved ahead.

The Jeep spewed steam and before Jax could give chase, he began losing power. The distance from the bikes grew second by second. The motorcycles quickly gained and disappeared beyond the highway overpass and were gone.

"Dammit," Jax cursed as they limped into the truck stop entrance. He found an empty space behind the garage and stopped. He spun in the seat and quickly checked Alex over. "Are you all right?"

"Yes, are you?" Her face was white and her hands trembled. "What happened?"

"I don't know, Alex."

"This is the second time someone has tried to kill me."

"Us, Alex. *Us.*" Jax frowned. "It's the second time for both of us."

She took his hand. "Let's hope there is no third time."

Jax took a deep breath and got out to survey the vehicle damage. Of the six holes in the vehicle, only one found its intended mark. The radiator continued to pour steam and water onto the gravel lot.

"Alex, call Red Vetner's nurse and warn her. Those guys might have been at his place before getting to us. I'll call the state police and get someone over here."

"All right." She pulled out her cell phone and began dialing as she walked away from the Jeep.

As she walked off, Trick appeared in front of the Jeep. "Holy smokes, Ricky, you've been busy." He examined the bullet holes and slipped his suit coat over his shoulder. "They won't bother Red, Ricky, so don't worry."

"Where have you been, Trick?" Jax tried to open the hood but the steam was too much still. "We were being shot full of holes. You missed it all."

"No I didn't." Trick looked after Alex and nodded. "You lined those thugs up like a dogfight over the channel. You were great, Ricky. And Alex gave them what-for, too. She's a gutsy dame, I tell you. She never flinched."

"Alex is calling Red's nurse to warn them in case they go there."

Trick turned and looked at Jax with sad, dark eyes. "No need. I stayed behind with Red. Those thugs never showed."

"Is that why you stayed behind?" Jax asked with a touch of irritation in his voice. "Did you know it was going to happen?"

"Not them. No." A painful, sad darkness covered Trick's face as he looked away. "I stayed behind so Red wouldn't die alone."

Chapter 62

MacTavish stepped out of the townhouse and waited for the door to be double-locked from the inside before he left the stoop. He took his time, scanning the parking lot for any nosey neighbors, neighbor watch, or a random police patrol.

He was alone.

As he walked the distance to his car parked one street away, he speed-dialed number two. It rang once. "We're getting close."

The voice on the cell wasn't pleased. "Close isn't good enough. You have to break him."

"We'll get it. You have to give this time. He's untrained, unaccustomed to this process. He's just hours away from giving us everything he knows."

"I still do not understand why you didn't use more conventional methods."

MacTavish looked around again and moved to the opposite sidewalk. "Our new friend already tried those means. He resisted all of them. We moved him here, and I'm taking over."

The voice erupted. "If your decision to bring him into this goes bad, it's your ass. I gave you no such authority."

"Relax," MacTavish said. "It was unavoidable. He approached me. Somehow, he figured out what we had. Let's just say he was more interested in what we could do for him than in getting in our way."

"So you made an arrangement?"

"We did."

Hesitation. "And you're confident you can control them? With all safety in mind?"

"Of course. He has no idea what he's gotten into. If he gets too close, I'll change the deal."

Silence.

MacTavish reached his car and slid his oversized frame behind the wheel. "Trust me, sir, he's in my pocket. Give me until tomorrow morning, and I'll have Antonio Cavallo in the other."

"Nine o'clock, Mr. MacTavish," the voice said. "At nine-oh-one, if you don't have that film and those who have seen it, I'll send someone to do things my way."

"Nine o'clock."

The call went dead.

∾∾

Finch lay back in his car seat as the big FBI man drove away. He'd watched him leave the townhouse and walk to his car. Caution kept him from following MacTavish out of the neighborhood. If he were caught, there would be no recovery from such a mistake. Instead, he waited an extra five minutes before pulling from the curb and heading back into Leesburg.

Just as he cleared the neighborhood, his phone rang and the screen displayed Christie's name. "Finch."

"I just heard from a friend. A well-placed friend and we should meet."

"Yes we should. I left Martinez's secret safehouse you found. Someone else was there, too."

"Was it Jeremy Levin again?"

"MacTavish."

"This is getting weirder and weirder," Christie said. "My friend never heard of FBI Agent MacTavish but he's checking with another source in DC."

"Martinez said MacTavish was from the WFO. No one ever checked, did they? Then Martinez ordered us not to chase any leads without his permission. No one is even allowed to talk with MacTavish."

"And?"

"Now they're sharing a safehouse."

"Who do you think they're hiding in there?"

Finch thought a moment. "I'm not sure. There are two people who might clear Jax. Both of them are missing."

"Antonio Cavallo and Kathleen Cullen." Christie's voice was thin. "But don't you think they're both dead?"

"No." Finch pulled his car into the Casa de Amigos parking lot a few blocks east of the BCI office. "I think at least one of them is still alive. Maybe both. My bet is they're in this safehouse."

"You think Martinez is hiding Cavallo and Kathleen? Why not just prove Jax's innocence and let everyone know what you got?"

"That's what he should do, unless MacTavish isn't an FBI agent and Martinez is on the take, helping him."

"Jesus, Finchy. Are you nuts? Helping him do what?"

He circled the parking lot full of pickups and motorcycles until he found Christie's sedan. He nosed in beside her and rolled down the window.

"To finish whatever got Leo Carraba and Chief Rogers killed."

Chapter 63

I didn't get champagne."

Jax looked up from his plate of eggs and pancakes at Alex across the kitchen table. Her hair was disheveled and his blue dress shirt-turned-nightgown was too large and hung off her tanned shoulders. She'd left the top buttons undone to reveal a tantalizing eyeful of a body maintained with great care and crafted to sultry perfection through her thirty-eight years.

"Huh? What?"

Alex flipped a forkful of pancake and hit him on the chin. "Champagne. I thought you promised me champagne for another kiss."

"Well, I'm fresh out. I guess I owe you a case."

"Two." She slid her chair around the table beside him. Then she leaned over and kissed him full and long until he dropped his fork and attempted an embrace. She giggled and withdrew. "Champagne first."

Jax shrugged. "Alas, no champagne." Then he turned serious. "Alex, let's work on those codes and see if Red's code book can help."

"All right, I guess we didn't get to that last night, did we?"

"Ah, no. We got a little sidetracked with those bikers." Jax winked. "But we have time now."

Alex frowned and pulled his shirt closer around her

shoulders. "It all scared me to death. I'm glad you forced me to stay the night. For my safety of course."

"Of course."

"I'll get the file." Alex disappeared into the back bedroom. She was gone several minutes when she called out, "Jax, it's gone." She returned to the kitchen pale and angry.

Jax stood when she walked into the kitchen. "What's wrong, Alex?"

"My briefcase and file are missing. So is my computer. Your notes with all the codes are gone, too." She sat at the table. "My OSS archive notes were all in there. I set the briefcase on your desk with your notes before we left for Red's yesterday. Someone took them all."

"Are you sure?" Jax headed to the rear office. "Maybe you left your briefcase at the hotel and just forgot."

Alex followed him. "No, I know I left it here. Years of my research is gone."

Jax furiously searched the room and dropped down behind the computer. "You're right; my notes are gone, too" A few moments later and dozens of keystrokes beneath his fingers and his mouth tightened. "The website is still gone. We've got nothing to go on."

"This can't be happening." Alex's face tightened and she fought back tears. "Why would someone take everything? Unless there's something in there I don't know about. Something I didn't know was important."

"I'll call Christie. Maybe—"

"Maybe nothing, Jax," Alex's eyes rained. "Everything I've done—thousands of hours—gone."

"We'll check you out of your hotel. I don't want you staying there." Jax put his arm around her and kissed her cheek. "Can we rebuild your files somehow?"

She closed her eyes. "No. My original notes and OSS archived copies were all there in my case. My hardcopy files were backed up on my computer. Both are gone. God, I never thought I'd lose everything."

"We'll get it all back."

"We have to, Jax. The answers we need might be in those pages. We have to find my files."

"May John Singleton can help. We'll go straight to see him."

"Why not go straight to Wellington? It had to be them."

"John Singleton has clout. A lot of clout. Trappe is behind Wellington and he was in the photograph with Singleton and the others. I want to hear what John has to say about Red's story before we confront anyone at Wellington."

"What about Cavallo and the girl?" Alex took his hand. "Want me to go see John and you find them? We can cover more ground that way."

"No, Alex. Twice someone tried to kill us. I don't want you alone."

She shrugged. "All right. John has been good to me over the years. If he can help, he will. He's the reason I met you, after all."

"I like John more and more," Jax said, grinning. They returned to the kitchen where he cleaned breakfast plates, stealing glances at Alex. She stood at the kitchen window, staring out at nothing. Her arms were folded and her face tight and angry. She'd been attacked twice and her life's work was gone—stolen. Both the reason and those responsible escaped them.

"We'll find the files, Alex. I promise." His words fell away to silence.

She continued gazing out the window. Something churned in her thoughts that kept her silent and removed.

Jax could not recall the last time he had company all night. Especially female company. Kathleen had been peculiar about their relationship. It was rare she stayed late into the evening. She never stayed all night. The nights they spent at her home were short and irregular. She blamed it on her five a.m. fifty-mile commute to her DuPont Circle Washington office. She worked long hours every day, so their time together was rushed and limited.

He often wondered why she bothered with him at all, wondered aloud many evenings as he kissed her goodnight. Her answer never came.

As he watched Alex, two thoughts consumed him. Was one night enough to move past Kathleen and start fresh? Would Alex Vouros one day feel the same as Kathleen— bored with a cop in a small town?

Alex jerked him from his thoughts. "Jax, are you going to tell me how you know so much about Trick and the inn?"

"I've already told you, Alex."

"Ghosts?" She shook her head. "Okay, we both have secrets."

"Secrets. I told you mine." He tried a smile to chip away at her mood. "What are yours?"

"You already know most of mine. You know, about Abrielle." She brightened and returned to the table. "Did you learn any more about Red?"

Trick popped into a seat at the breakfast table. "Ah, she's still here for breakfast. "Things are looking up, Ricky."

Jax ignored him. "More about Vetner?"

"Red went quiet and happy." Trick patted Alex's hand but got no response. "As for afterward, I got bored listening to you explaining to the police about the bikers and went out on my own. I found something important."

Jax repeated him, ignoring her glances around the room. Then he added, "Martinez will have a fit when he hears about yesterday."

"Later, Ricky, trouble's coming." Trick jumped up and went to the front window. "Martinez is on his way. They found Kathleen. I'm sorry, Ricky, she's dead. There's more, too."

"Jesus, no. Dead? Are you sure?" A sudden ache erupted in Jax's stomach. "How? Where?"

"Who's dead?" Alex asked, taking his arm. "What's happened? What's wrong with you?"

Jax swallowed bile before he told her what Trick had

said. Then he turned from her to Trick, "How did it happen?"

"I don't know, but you have to get out of here. And Ricky, I have to talk to you in private later, but get out of here first. It may help you solve this caper."

Alex sat there staring at him.

Four loud bangs on the front door interrupted them. "Open up, Jax. It's Captain Martinez."

Jax went to the front door and opened it. Two uniformed deputies brushed past him into his living room. One held up his hand and stopped Alex at the kitchen archway. The other stood beside Jax and put a hand on his arm holding him there.

Captain Martinez strode in with Jeremy close behind. Christie arrived next. She walked up to Jax and touched his arm with a light, sympathetic hand. "We've found Kathleen. She's dead," she whispered. "I'm sorry, Jax. I just found out."

"Thanks." Jax followed Christie's eyes to Alex standing across the room in his dress shirt. "Christie, I—"

"Unbelievable." She looked from Alex to Jax as her face hardened. "Kathleen's murder hasn't slowed you down. Maybe I'm not so sorry after all."

"You should be." Alex buttoned her top buttons. "You, more than anyone, know he's innocent. Don't let jealousy get in the way of common sense."

"Stuff it, lady," Christie snapped. "And stay quiet or you're going with him."

Jeremy stepped behind Jax and slipped handcuffs onto his wrists. "Nothing personal, Jax." Then he tightened the cuffs one ratchet too far. "Not much."

Martinez looked at Alex and walked up to Jax. "I'm sorry. I have no choice."

"Where did you find her, Cap? I want to know it all."

Christie stared bullets at him. "She was shot point blank, Jax, in an abandoned trailer down along the Potomac."

Jax had to turn his head. "Jesus, no."

"She had your engagement ring clutched in her hand," Martinez said, giving Jeremy a chin. "It was a forty-five, Jax. I'm betting yours."

"You thought the forty-five was my imagination," Jax said, but Jeremy jerked the cuffs and sent pain stabbing his shoulder.

"Richard Jax," Jeremy said, pushing him toward the door. "You're under arrest for the murders of Leo Carraba and Kathleen Cullen."

Chapter 64

So what's the worst that can happen, Ricky?"
Jax sat on a steel bench against the wall of his holding cell with his feet propped up on the small table in front of him. The cell was dim and cold but Martinez had relented and let him sit without handcuffs or other restraints. At least for now, some professional courtesy remained.

Across the room was a steel cot affixed to the wall and a small toilet and sink. Of the many times he'd put prisoners in the room, he never thought about the stark, intimidating veil the room wore. Courtesy or not, he felt less a cop and more a criminal with each passing moment.

"I don't know, but murder is on the table. No one is saying anything about any deals yet. Not that I need a deal."

"No deals, Ricky. Only the guilty need deals." Trick stood in the corner of the cell. He slipped his fedora onto the back of his head and whistled. "Then again, murder can get you hanged."

"No, Trick," Jax said, finding it odd to laugh. "They don't hang people any more. At least not in Virginia."

"Well, that's good. So what's the worst?"

"In Virginia, you have a choice on death row."

"A choice?" Trick smiled. "Like your last meal?"

"No, lethal injection or the electric chair." Jax dropped his feet on the floor and sat forward. "But I'm innocent, remember? I don't plan on having to make that decision."

"Good, 'cause if I get to have a roommate, she won't look like you."

"Thanks, pal." Jax changed the subject. "Look, you said you had something to tell me. I have time to listen."

"Oh, yeah, right." Trick sat down on the bunk across from him. "Last night, after I left Red's house, I got thinking about the night Leo was killed. It reminded me of this film I saw."

"Get to the point."

"I found Ameera."

"Ameera?"

Trick winked. "The girl who saved you."

Jax looked at him with a sideways glance. "How do you know her name all of a sudden?"

"It's complicated. Let's just say those beads she gave you sort of worked like that new-fangled radar stuff, ESP or whatever."

"GPS."

"Yeah, that. Anyway, last night, late, I found her and her family. Her pop is some fella named Khalid Al something-or-other. You know, a good Irish name."

"Middle Eastern. They'll be hanging me before you make your point."

"I found Ameera, her brother, and her mom and dad at another safehouse. It's just like Red said. Someone is using other places like the inn. At this one, these thugs moved them in and dropped off enough groceries for a couple days. There are two guards with them."

"That's great. Where? Ameera and her family can prove I didn't kill Leo. If I can make that case, maybe Martinez will see I didn't kill Kathleen, too. At least it would be a start."

"I don't know."

"You don't know what?"

"I don't know where Ameera is." Trick looked down. "Those beads aren't a postcard with a return address, you know. It ain't like Western Union, either. But I have a plan."

Jax leaned back and folded his arms. "Terrific."

"We share. This time, you do the detective work and look around while we're watching Ameera. You're the sleuth, not me. Maybe you can find something I missed. You're Holmes, I'm Watson."

"You know, Trick," Jax said, standing up and walking to the cell door. "You're not half bad for a sixty-seven-year-old corpse. It might just work."

"Yeah? You think so?"

"Can't hurt."

Trick gestured to the bunk. "Lie down. I wouldn't want you falling onto the floor."

Jax did.

Trick stood over him and took hold of his shoulder. The sizzle and static began crossing from his fingers into Jax's arm. A second before he melted into him, he said, "And don't scare the little girl, sport. She's terrified enough already."

"She can see us?"

"I'm not sure." Trick squeezed his shoulder and began the slow descent into him. "Some can, Ricky. Some can. And they don't always admit it."

Chapter 65

Jax landed in a barren room where dust and mildew hung in the air. The walls were blemished with dirty, peeling wallpaper. The floor was cold and litter-strewn and its vinyl tiles looked like they'd had been laid in the fifties. There was one window he could see and it was closed with shutters or boards that blocked out the daylight.

There were no sounds. No sign of life. No Ameera.

"Trick, what the hell?" He knew Trick could not answer, or perhaps couldn't even hear him. Jax was alone here, in some bizarre reality he would never understand.

He found the same conditions in two rooms across and down a dark hallway. He found a staircase leading down and heard the faint flutter of voices from below. He went searching for them below, in what had been a living room or parlor beside the landing. Inside were tattered pieces of old furniture, two chairs, a ripped green couch, and a long, hardwood dining table that, with work, might be a beautiful piece of antique furniture. In an adjoining room were six fold-up cots. Four of them held suitcases and duffels that were open and spilling clothes and personal items.

The voices were gone but other faint sounds led Jax down a narrow hall where he came to a grungy kitchen. Inside, he found a girl making tea in a half-dozen cups. She was a small, thin teenager he guessed was no more than fourteen, with black hair that escaped the side of her *hijab*.

She wore a long, dark skirt that hung to her feet and a dark top not traditional Muslim garb but still intended to provide a combination of youth and modesty.

A teapot of water began to boil on a gas camp stove, and when she turned to fill the cups, Jax recognized her dark, pretty eyes. She was the girl who saved his life at the Grey Coat Inn.

He remembered what Trick had said and stepped into the kitchen doorway.

"Ameera?" he said. "Can you hear me?"

The girl stopped pouring the tea and looked around wearily. "*Salam*? 'ello?"

"Ameera, I'm Jax. You saved my life at the old inn. Can you understand me?"

She looked past him, through him, and then turned toward the rear door, expecting someone to enter at any moment. "Shush. Go away, s*habah*. You frighten me. Go away, please."

"Don't be afraid, Ameera. I won't hurt you."

Her head nodded in slow, uncertain movements. Her pretty, young face lightened and a touch of her fear vanished. "*Shabah*, go, please. I told you before I cannot help you."

"I need to know where this is. Where you are."

Her face suddenly twisted. "The men come. Go. They come."

Two beefy Latinos strode into the kitchen through the rear door. They were dressed in jeans and baggy shirts. Both wore coats that failed to conceal the weapons tucked into their belts. They looked familiar but Jax was not sure where he had seen them.

The first Latino was stout and strong, like a football player still in his prime. He was young—no older than thirty—with tight-cut hair and a dark complexion marred by the irregular healing of scars across his neck and jaw.

The second man was not as muscular and leaner. His black hair was longer and pulled back in a short ponytail.

His features were sharp and chiseled, and he projected the confidence of a very dangerous man.

The stout Latino scooped up a cup of tea and pointed to Ameera's *hijab*. "Take that off, Ameera. You no wear that stuff while you with us, *si*? Maybe when you go away again. *Si*?"

She smiled but it faded when the second man stepped forward.

"Don't baby dis brat, Manuel," he snapped, grabbing a cup of tea. He took a sip and spat it back into the cup, dumping it into the sink. "Tastes like shit. Get you papa,'Meera."

Ameera ran from the room.

"Lobo, you an ass." Manuel shook his head in disgust. "Don't do that to the kid. I don't like it."

"Tough." Lobo turned and opened a short, bar-sized refrigerator. He withdrew a longneck bottle of beer, snapped the top off against the countertop, and drained half of it in one long gulp.

"You not up to this, Manuel. You never was." As he raised his hand with the beer again, Jax saw the dark dagger scar across his forearm and wrist. This was the man he'd seen at the inn. This man was there at the beginning.

"Don't push the kid around." Manuel lifted his chin. "You hear me?"

Lobo laughed a guttural laugh. "Oh, yeah? Wait till tomorrow morning."

Manuel sat his tea on the counter. "Tomorrow morning? We movin'?"

"Oh, yeah. We movin'." Lobo emptied the beer with his second gulp. "But not how you think. We gonna cut and run."

"No. I not do that. I ain't killin' no kid. Not dis one."

"Jesus, no." Jax felt panic churn in his stomach. "Dammit, Trick, where are you? We can't let this happen."

Lobo threw his beer bottle into the sink where it shattered into pieces. "You do what you told. The man pay us good."

Anger gripped Jax and he knew he had to learn where this house was if he were to save Ameera. He left the two Latinos arguing and searched the house room-to-room. He found nothing. The windows were shuttered and when he peered through the thin openings, his heart sank. All he saw was a long dirt road. Overgrown weeds and trees surrounded the house. Near the road were three fallen pines blocking any view of the area. Nothing gave him the slightest clue where he was.

"Come on, give me something."

Manuel and Lobo were upstairs arguing with someone, now. Ameera was back in the kitchen and he sought her out. Her *hijab* was gone and her long, black hair flowed across her back. Her face was sullen and sad as she picked Lobo's broken glass from the sink. She tensed each time Lobo's voice got louder. When she'd accumulated the broken glass into a pile, she took a large, square piece of cardboard from the trash bin and folded it to use as a dustpan. She began piling the glass pieces onto the box.

Jax noticed the underside of the cardboard. It was crusted with dried food. "Ameera, is that a pizza box?"

She shifted the cardboard and stacked more broken glass onto it. "Please, *shabah*, do not make me more afraid. Go."

Jax went to the trash and found the remains of another pizza box. "Where did you get this? Please, Ameera, it's important. Try to hear me, try *hard*."

Someone called out in what Jax guessed was Arabic. It was a woman's voice and Ameera looked nervously around before running from the kitchen.

Jax looked after her. "I'm gonna fix this, Ameera, I promise."

His heart fluttered and something pulled at him inside. His time was ending. A strange, swirling darkness enveloped him and he tried to fight it. "No, Trick. I'm not done. I haven't found out where she is."

The flutter swelled inside as his legs weakened. His breath grew shallow. A second before he left the room, he looked back at the pizza box Ameera had dropped into the trash bin. On the edge of the flap, obscured in tomato sauce and dried cheese, was a telephone number.

"Ameera, I'll save you. I will."

He slipped from the room and was gone.

Chapter 66

"Calm down, Alex," Finch said into his cell phone. "Give me fifteen minutes and get over here. I'll take care of everything."

Finch hung up, picked up a file from his desk, scribbled a note on a yellow legal pad, ripped it off, and barged into Captain Martinez's office.

Martinez was on his telephone and waved him out. "Later, Detective. I'm busy."

"Not later. Now, Captain." Finch dropped the yellow legal page in front of him. "You don't have much time."

"What?" Martinez glanced down at the note. He looked up and his face reddened. He slammed his phone down. "What do you think you're doing?"

"Giving you notice," Finch said matter-of-factly. "If Jax isn't out of the holding cell in five minutes, you'll be on the evening news in fifteen."

"How dare you?" Martinez jumped to his feet and attempted to throw the yellow note back at him but it fluttered in the air and fell back onto his desk. "What are you talking about, Finch? Who do you think—"

"That's the address of your *illegal* safehouse."

"Fuck you. I don't report BCI operations to you or the sheriff."

Finch grinned. "You don't report all your evidence to the commonwealth's attorney, either."

"What does that mean?"

Finch opened his file and handed him the copies of Dr. Arun Tomar's lab results along with several more documents. "Four minutes left."

Martinez riffled through the pages. With each one his face reddened more. By the time he reached Officer Koontz's revised statement his temples were exploding. "You've done it, Finch. You're fired. You've interfered in my investigation and are derelict in your responsibilities to this office."

"Release him, Martinez. Levin coerced a half-true statement from Koontz. Read it. Oh, you'll like the part where Koontz says he tried to correct it but Levin wouldn't let him. Then you concealed evidence from a crime scene, failed to provide exculpatory evidence to the commonwealth's attorney, falsified information for your arrest warrant, and, as far as I can see, should face charges of corruption and witness tampering."

"You bastard." Martinez lunged across the desk but missed Finch's collar by a foot. He retracted and crumpled the copied documents into a ball. "Screw you, Finch. You don't know what you're talking about. You can't prove anything."

"Yes, I can," Finch said just as Martinez's phone rang. "You might want to take that call. It might be Judge Dyre."

Martinez looked down at his phone. In a slow, unsteady move, he lifted the receiver. "Captain Martinez."

The voice was stern and coarse.

"Yes, Judge, but this is not as it appears. The FBI—"

Judge Dyre's voice grew louder.

"No sir, but there is other evidence." A pause. "No sir, the FBI is...Yes, sir." Martinez hung up and glared at Finch. "You bastard. You have no idea what you've done. This is bigger than you and me. Bigger than your sheriff, and bigger than that two-bit judge."

"No problem." Finch gathered his copies and stuffed

them back into his file. "I'll clear my desk tomorrow, Cap. It's been fun. I hope we can work together again. *Not*."

"Finch, when I get through—" Martinez's cell phone buzzed on his desk. The number made his eyes flash wide, and he grabbed the cell up. He never spoke but, as he listened, he glared bullets through Finch. When he hung up, he leaned on his desk with both hands and dropped his head.

"Jesus, Finch. You've gone too far. Way too far."

"What now, Cap? Does the judge want to see you in chambers? He was pretty pissed when the sheriff spoke with him. Two-bit and all."

"You stupid bastard." Martinez looked up as his angst and anger collided. He pounded his fist on the desk. "Where's Cavallo?"

Finch eyed him suspiciously. "What are you talking about?"

"Cavallo, you asshole. You took him from the safehouse. Do you have any idea who you're dealing with?"

Finch stepped back. "Antonio Cavallo was in your safehouse? Thanks, he was my first guess. But I don't have him."

"Don't screw with me, Finch." Martinez stabbed a finger at him. "Someone just busted in and took him. There's a man down and Cavallo is gone. Where is he? Where did you take him?"

Finch's face twisted. "I don't have him. I wasn't even sure he was in there. But that just adds to the list. I'm taking Jax out, and we're leaving. I got Judge Dyre on speed dial, so don't screw with me."

"Don't lie to me. Where's Cavallo? I can't stop these people, Finch. Where is he?"

"Sorry, I don't have him." Finch shot him a sarcastic wink. "Wow, you kidnapped *and* lost a material witness, all in one week? Judge Dyre is gonna be pissed."

"You don't get it, do you?" Martinez whirled around and stared out his window. "If you didn't take him, who did?"

Chapter 67

Okay, sport, I got one." Trick leaned against the cell wall. "Who played Topper in the '41 picture, *Topper Returns*?"

Jax was still lying on the steel holding cell bunk. "Roland Young."

"Too easy. Who played Asta in *The Thin Man* movies?"

"Jax?" Alex asked as Finch opened the cell door. "Is everything all right?"

"Come on, buddy, time to go." Finch motioned to the cell door. "You're cracking up. I guess we sprang you just in time."

Trick was gone.

"How did you get me out?" Jax looked out the cell door, wondering if it were a trap. "It can't be bail. I haven't had a hearing yet."

"There won't be any hearing." Finch shoved him out the door. "I'm not sure you were heading for one, anyway."

In the hall, Alex crushed into Jax. "I was so scared. Finch thinks something awful was going to happen. Let's get out of here."

"It's okay, Alex." Jax turned and offered his hand to Finch. "Thanks. I owe you."

"No kidding. Let's go. Neither of us works here anymore."

Outside, Finch followed Alex and Jax to her Mercedes.

There, he handed Jax a small nylon shoulder bag. "Here's your personal stuff. I grabbed it off Martinez's desk. And I put a piece in there. One of my spares. You and Alex get going. Keep your head low. I gotta find out about Cavallo."

Jax took the bag. "Cavallo?"

Finch related his meeting with Captain Martinez and filled Jax in on the scant details of Kathleen Cullen's crime scene. He finished with, "Now for the weird parts. Cullen's scene was seized by MacTavish's people. Then MacTavish arranged for Martinez to take you into state custody. It doesn't make sense. Any other time when the FBI swoops in for the glory, they also claim the prize. Seems like they don't want their hands dirty with you, Jax."

"It's nice to be wanted."

"Why is this happening?" Alex slid her arm around Jax and rested her head on his shoulder. She was scared and worried, and her eyes were filled with emotion. "There can't be evidence against Jax. He didn't do anything. Are we getting too close to someone else?"

Finch shrugged. "There's something about Cavallo, too. I stumbled onto a safehouse Martinez and Levin were using. It ain't on our books, either. Christie and I were watching it last night. When I confronted Martinez, he wet himself. Then he got this call from Levin saying somebody busted into the safehouse and took Cavallo. He suspects me."

Jax thought about that for a long moment and none of his thoughts were good. "We have to find Cavallo. It's almost noon. Where's Christie?"

"On her way." Finch looked around. "She was out all morning after they arrested you. She's at Martinez's safehouse."

Jax looked at the ground. "Jesus, in all this, I'd almost forgotten about Kathleen. Cavallo might be next. Or he already is."

"What's the plan?" Finch asked.

Trick appeared beside Finch. "Ricky, what about Ameera?"

"Right. Ameera."

Finch looked at him and then at Alex. "Ameera?"

"I don't know how to explain this, Finch, so you'll have to go on faith." Jax squeezed Alex's arm. "The night I was shot, a young Arab girl—Ameera—and her family were being moved out of the inn. It was being used as a safehouse to move illegal refugees into the country. Wellington International is behind it all."

Finch frowned. "Wellington. Of course. And this Ameera and her family are involved?"

"They were there, Finch. Ameera saved my life. Now, her family is being held at another safehouse, and they're in danger."

Finch took a step back, eyeing first Jax, then Alex. "Where'd you get all this?"

Jax took a deep breath and told him about Red Vetner, ending with, "He told us about Wellington's using safehouses, paid protection. It fit into the Grey Coat. Think about the shooter the other night. He had a Wellington car. Everything points to them."

"Okay," Finch cocked his head. "How do you know about Ameera and her family?"

"Because I know," Jax said abruptly. "Call it a dream. Call it a vision. Hell, call it ghosts. Just help me save her, Finch. I'll never ask anything else of you. If we don't find Ameera by tonight, she and her family are dead."

"Vision? Ah, shit." Finch stared at Jax. "At first, I thought it was all bad coincidences—Leo getting killed and you shot up. Rogers and Kathleen killed when you were missing with no alibi. When you found McCall's body, I thought maybe you figured it all out from all those books you have on World War II and the town. But this is different, Jax. Very different."

"I know," Jax said, watching him, trying to see how far Finch would let him go. "You've come this far, right?"

"What are my choices? Crazed killer or nut-job seeing

ghosts and having visions?" Finch looked from Alex to Jax. "I just stuck my head into the noose with Martinez. Give me all you have."

Jax reached into Finch's suit coat pocket and took his pen and notepad. He jotted some numbers down and handed it back. "The house they're in sits by itself outside town. This telephone number is a pizza place. Maybe they delivered there last night. Maybe not. Find this place, Finch. Fast. Ameera is there."

"All you got is a pizza shop number?"

"You're looking for a remote, run down old house. There's a bunch of fallen pine trees around one side." Jax tried to picture the house. "There are at least two Latino guards—Lobo and Manuel. Lobo has a scar on his forearm that looks like a dagger. He was there the night I was shot. I think they're Hector Lupino's men."

"Jeez, Jax," Finch shook his head and looked away. "Now you know their names and one has a dagger scar?"

"Trust me." Jax smiled. "We're going after a guy named Peter Trappe at—"

Finch held up a hand. "Wellington International. I came across him while I was doing background on Wellington after Alex's shooting. He's big. Very big. Metro PD says Trappe is untouchable. He's connected all the way to Pennsylvania Avenue."

"No one is untouchable, Finch," Jax said. "Your Metro pals didn't mention anything about MacTavish, did they?"

"Yeah, they sure did. No one ever heard of him; not even at the FBI. Another ghost."

Chapter 68

Tell me the truth about Ameera," Alex said from the passenger seat of her Mercedes on the drive east to John Singleton's Great Falls estate. "You never told me what you just told Finch."

"I just figured it all out, Alex." He told her about his vision to see Ameera. All the while, he wondered if she'd make him stop the car and get out. She didn't.

Alex bit her lip. "A dream? In your cell?"

"It wasn't a dream. It was more a vision or some kind of connection to her. Trick helped me. They're in danger."

"And you think it's all real? Trick and the vision?"

"It's real. I know you're having a hard time with this, Alex. But trust me, please. I thought you believed in Trick?"

"I want to, Jax because I know you do. The things you know and all that's happened...I want to."

Jax drove on. "How could I have learned all this from anyone other than Trick?"

Alex laughed a nervous laugh. "Why hasn't he figured everything out by now?"

Trick appeared in the rear seat. "Just give me time. I was a spy, not a detective. But still, I think I'm doing okay."

Jax rolled his eyes and turned north off Route 7 into Great Falls. After weaving through town, they entered a prestigious neighborhood of grand homes and rolling estates. Congressmen, diplomats, and powerful business ty-coons called this home.

They made a wide turn around a wooded area and approached an estate sitting a quarter-mile away from the other sprawling properties. The estate sat back from the road and was surrounded by a brick and steel fence that appeared more decorative then secure. The home resembled a nine-teenth-century courthouse with brick walls, a tall, two-story front portico, and brooding columns. The grounds were immaculate and could have been on any cover of any land-scaping magazine in the country. They rolled to a stop in front of a tall, iron security gate where a muscular security guard wearing gray slacks and a bulging blue blazer waited.

Alex spoke with the guard who waved them through the gate as it opened.

"Ricky, there's something you should know," Trick said, leaning forward over the seat.

Jax listened then turned to Alex. "So, you work for John Singleton, not the foundation? Singleton hired you to solve the Harriet mystery? Does he know Abrielle is alive?"

Alex spun in the seat with her mouth agape. Then she glanced into the back seat, turned forward, and folded her arms. "No, he doesn't. But apparently your sources do. There are people still trying to hurt her, Jax. They came very close several times and even captured her once."

"What happened?"

Alex's face tightened. "Abrielle was in hiding. One night in Charlotte, two men found her. The captured her at her apartment."

Jax took her hand and squeezed. "And?"

"She killed them both before they could kill her." Alex looked down. "They had notes indicating they'd tracked her for a year. She buried them in the woods and ran from Char-lotte."

"Sounds like my Socks, Ricky." Trick leaned forward in his seat again. "She was an amazing woman."

"Yes, amazing," Jax said, pulling up in front of the main

house. "Alex, no one will get hurt when this is over. I promise you that."

A starched, pressed security guard appeared from inside the house and opened Alex's door. Another appeared, greeted them, and showed them inside. There, another security man escorted them into a great room in the rear of the house.

"Mr. Singleton is on his way," the guard said as a maid appeared with a pitcher of iced tea and glasses. The guard followed her out and closed the doors behind them.

Trick dropped himself onto a long, wide leather sofa and propped his feet on an expensive French Hollandaise table. "Wow, Johnny's done okay for himself, eh, Ricky?"

"Yeah, he's done well." Jax admired a collection of books and photographs lining a stone fireplace mantel at one end of the room. "Very well."

Alex took his arm. "Are you going to ask John to help find Ameera? He has far more resources than we can muster."

"No." Jax frowned. "How am I supposed to explain her to him? It's one thing telling you, and it was hard enough lying to Finch. If we're going to get his help with Peter Trappe, better he doesn't think I'm a loony."

"You're not loony, Jax." She giggled lightly. "A little eccentric, perhaps. But not loony."

"Thanks."

The great room doors opened and John Singleton walked in. The security man, Marcus, whom Jax recognized, followed close behind, posted himself beside the doors, and looked on.

Singleton gave Alex a warm, long embrace with the ritual pleasantries. To Jax, he offered his hand and asked about his injuries. Then he bade them to the sofa and stood for a moment hovering over Jax.

"Agent Jax, I'm glad to see you again. As we don't know one another well, I'll ask your understanding of my directness. Alexandra tells me there has been much danger."

"Well—"

"John," Alex broke in. "I have to admit we've had some trouble, serious trouble. I know you're busy so I'll get to the point. We need your help."

"Please, tell me what I can do."

Jax gave him a summary of events since his leaving the hospital and leading up to his arrest. Alex explained what she and Jax had learned from Red Vetner and their trouble on the mountain road. Singleton took it all in.

"So you see, John," Alex said. "We cannot rely on the police. They're building a case against Jax and they're ignoring any other suspects. Without Cavallo or Ameera, we're afraid they'll arrest him again."

Singleton sat across from them and, when they were done telling their stories, he took a few moments to consider it all. "I'm sure you'll agree Agent Jax's situation is not unlike my own, and Trick McCall's, years ago."

Alex nodded. "Yes, it is."

"How can I help?" Singleton turned to Jax. "I owe you a debt for finding my friend and I wish to repay it. It appears now is the time."

"Red Vetner mentioned Peter Trappe."

"Peter?" Singleton folded his arms. "How interesting. Tell me more."

"Red believed he might be Harriet. If he is, then he's still smuggling refugees into this country. Ameera and her family may be the proof we need. If we can find her and Antonio Cavallo, they can clear Jax and perhaps point to the real killer."

"I see. And that leaves just three of us from that night."

Trick sat up from the couch. "Three? There are just two. Red and Roman Clay are dead."

"What three are you referring to?" Jax asked.

A smile crept across Singleton's face and his eyes sparkled like a fox eyeing prey. "Ah, I'm certain you know of at least two. But I can tell you there are still three of us alive from that inn in 1944. There were four, but Red died."

Alex looked straight at him. "Then you know Abrielle was at the inn that night?"

"Yes, of course." He laughed. "I helped her escape from England at Trick's request. I knew Trick arranged for her to be present that night. And yes, I know she is still alive, my dear."

Alex looked down and nodded.

"Is the third Peter Trappe?" Jax asked. When Singleton nodded, Jax continued. "How was he involved?"

Singleton stood up and went to a tall bookshelf beside the stone fireplace. He took down a framed photograph and returned to the sofa. He handed the picture to Jax.

"He's right here."

The black and white photograph was taken during the war. It showed several men standing in front of a C-4 cargo plane with parachutes and weapons. Alex and Jax recognized three of the men in the photograph. They were the same men from Red Vetner's photograph taken on F-Street—John Singleton, Red Vetner, and Roman Clay. Standing behind them, half-in the aircraft hatch, was a fourth man whose face now made perfect sense. He wore a leather bomber jacket, a parachute harness, and a sidearm holstered beneath his flying harness.

"Do you understand now? The night we went to Leesburg to capture Harriet, the man in the background was our pilot. That's Peter Trappe."

Chapter 69

Finch tapped away on his computer keyboard and waited for the results. Two hours of searching online state and county land records revealed that hundreds of companies were behind on their taxes. It took him another thirty minutes and two telephone calls to the county tax office before he found the records he was looking for.

"Gotcha," he said to no one in his small condo. "Let's see how much real estate you own."

He tapped in "Wellington" into the Loudoun County site and hit on twenty-five property listings. He eliminated more than half of them as Williames, Marthas, Thomases, and other names. He also found company listings. Two were for "Wellington Real Estate" and the remaining eight were Wellington International. A map search hit a dead end. All the properties were industrial parks or commercial buildings in the Dulles industrial corridor. None of them fit Jax's description.

Finch was about to give up when he got an idea. Going back through the property records, he searched all the real estate transfers over the past six months involving Wellington International, Quinton Properties, and the Pettington Corporation. It took another hour but, when he compiled his list, he hit pay dirt again. Sixteen properties had been sold. Ten were transferred between the three companies, and five more were sold to a fourth entity, Mosby International Enterprises. The last one was a private sale that listed Wellington as the seller. It was an estate valued at more than a million and a half dollars. When Finch checked real property record, he saw the name of the owner.

"Son of a bitch." He returned to the five Mosby International properties and duplicated his map-searches using those addresses. All were located in rural county areas, including two in nearby Fauquier County. He pulled out his notepad and found the pizza telephone number Jax gave him. It was a Loudoun County exchange. He used a reverse look-up and obtained the street address. Then he plotted the address on the internet search map with the other five addresses. After calling the pizza shop, he learned there were no deliveries to any of the addresses he had. Only one of the addresses was within the same telephone exchange as the shop.

That address was on Fallen Pines Road.

Chapter 70

Sir, you have no idea who Harriet was?" Jax had been sitting beside Alex on the leather sofa sipping tea for more than an hour. In that time, John Singleton had lamented about fighting Nazis with Trick and the French Underground. At every turn, he charmed Alex with his stories of the "old days," stories Jax was sure she'd heard many times.

"If I had proof, Agent Jax," Singleton said in a low, dry voice, "I'd have put him in jail decades ago." He looked away past Jax to his wall of photographs. "No, that's a lie. If I had proof, I would have killed Harriet myself."

Alex put a hand on his arm. "John, is there anything that you can tell us that will help when we go see Peter Trappe?"

The old OSS man's wry smile sent a chill down Jax's spine.

"There's too much to explain and that's why I'm going with you," John said. "And perhaps while Agent Jax and I are interrogating him, Alex, you can have a look around his office."

Jax glanced over at Alex. "I'm not sure about that, Mr. Singleton—"

"He's right," Alex said. "Maybe I can find something helpful. He'll be less focused on me while you talk to him."

Singleton nodded. "I've had contact with him over the years, of course, and even done a little business here and there. I want to hear what he has to say now that McCall's remains have been found at *his* inn. And one of his cars was used by whoever tried to kill Alexandra, correct?"

"Yes, all right. It might work," Jax said. Then he looked at Singleton and caught his eyes. "Mr. Singleton, you investigated everyone associated with the inn and Harriet. Did you also investigate Peter Trappe?"

A smile crept across the old man's face. "Yes, I did. As did OSS. You see, of all of us, Peter was the least noteworthy. He was, after all, the pilot. He flew us here and there but never participated on the ground. He had no knowledge of our operations other than destinations and timetables."

"And at the inn?" Jax said.

"He flew us there. He had no knowledge of our mission to find Harriet and did not participate in any planning. He could not have known what we were up to. In fact, we didn't give him our destination until we were airborne. So, you see, Peter was cleared very early in the investigation."

"Then why do you now think Red Vetner could be right?" Alex asked. "After all these years?"

Singleton looked far-away for a long time before answering. When he did, his voice was edgy. "Because I'm getting old, my dear. I've done all I could do on this matter. I'm willing to consider anything—anything at all—to let Trick McCall rest."

Trick listened from across the room. He'd been quiet, wandering Singleton's home and losing himself in the photographs and memories displayed everywhere. Singleton's house was more museum than a home, but for Singleton, and perhaps Trick, it was a comfort borne of nostalgic adventure. "Thanks, Johnny. That means a lot." Trick joined them by the sofa. "Ricky, I have an idea. Can you get Johnny-boy to let me share him?"

"What?" Jax's eyes flashed wide. He caught Alex staring. "I don't see we can say no to Mr. Singleton's offer. What he knows could be valuable."

"Come on, Ricky," Trick said. "Get him to sit on the couch. Tell him anything. Just get him to relax a little."

Jax looked around, trying to form a plan. "Mr. Singleton, you said you never saw who shot you at the inn. Is that right?"

"Yes, that's true. Trick and I had a signal. I sent it to him but he never responded. When I moved in on the inn, all hell broke loose. I was searching the grounds and someone wounded me. I tried to fight back but I lost consciousness and never saw the bastard who did it."

"Sir, can you walk me through everything you can remember?"

"I don't see how this will help."

"You might remember something about Trappe," Jax said. "Something you forgot or blocked out. It might help us find Harriet."

Singleton looked at him for a long time. Then he crossed the floor and sat down beside Alex. "Well, yes. Let me see, we flew into Leesburg in a storm as I recall."

Trick moved behind the sofa and stood behind Singleton. "Okay, Ricky, here we go." He took hold of Singleton's shoulders. A second later, he eased himself down into his comrade and evaporated into him. Singleton's head bobbed and fell back against the sofa.

John Singleton was gone. So was 2011.

⌒⌒

October, 1944:

Trick opened his eyes. He was standing on the cold October ground beside the Grey Coat Inn's front veranda. His breath billowed around him as night sounds chanted in the darkness everywhere. Beside him was a young, thin, John Singleton holding a .45 semiautomatic.

Trick turned in a circle, trying to find the rest of the team secreted in the darkness. "Ah, Johnny, where are the others?"

Two gunshots erupted somewhere behind them.

Singleton spun around and retreated back against the inn. He knelt and strained to see through the darkness. His face was red from cold and angst. Voices inside the inn murmured through a window beside him, and he glanced in to find the source. He took out a small flashlight from his pocket and aimed it at the trees north of the inn, snapping it on and off several times in code. Seconds later, the same code flashed back. A figured emerged, trotted from the trees, and angled toward him.

Trick watched John Singleton raise his gun. He fired two rapid shots, downing the man mid-way from the trees. Singleton sprang forward, crouching low with his .45 at the ready.

A voice called out in German through the inn's window, "*Stopp, bitte stoppen.*"

Three more shots rang from the trees where the downed man had emerged seconds before.

"Ah!" Singleton was hit. "You bastards. You bastards." He fired twice at the muzzle flashes. "I see you, you bastards."

Trick ran into the darkness and the trees beyond. Someone sprinted ahead of him and he gave chase. Twice he lost the figure. Each time he stopped, listened, and started out again. After circling the rear of the inn, he caught up with the shooter.

The man was crouched beside a fallen tree, watching the inn as he slipped a fresh magazine into his handgun.

Trick moved closer trying to see the face in the dark. John Singleton's assailant knelt just feet from him. As the man stood, the night lit up with gunfire. Men yelled and barked orders. Shots rang out. Somewhere at the inn, glass shattered and more shots.

As Singleton's assailant turned, a second form revealed himself. Trick shuddered and the sky lit up.

A moment later, Singleton forced Trick from his thoughts.

෴

Singleton shuddered and awoke. He mumbled to himself for a long time. Jax went to him, leaned down, and listened.

Marcus rushed forward but Singleton opened his eyes and waved him back. "No, Marcus, I'm all right. Just give me a moment, please."

"It's all right, John. Relax." Jax retrieved a glass of iced tea from the pitcher and handed it to him. "You fainted, sir."

Jax turned to Trick who fell back from the sofa. He was hazy like a cirrus cloud fluttering in the winds. He was shaken and off balance. "Jesus, Ricky."

"Yes, yes, I did." Singleton took a long sip of tea. "Extraordinary. I'd swear that McCall was there with me. I was talking about that night at the inn and something grabbed me. I'd swear it was Trick in my dream."

"But you're all right?" Alex asked. "John?"

"Yes, yes, fine now." Singleton shuddered again. His face was white and drawn; his hands trembling. "It was amazing, my dear, amazing. I was recalling that night. It was so vivid and real. I hadn't recalled that event with such clarity in years. By damned, I even felt the bullet."

Alex glanced at Jax and back to Singleton. "John, did you recall anything new?"

Jax cut her off. "Sir, did you see who shot you? You said you felt the bullet.'"

He frowned. "I don't know, my dear."

"Yes, he did." Trick came around the front of the sofa. "Johnny shot a guy right before all hell broke loose." Trick told Jax what he saw.

Singleton stood and got his balance. "Yes, I did recall

some things. I remember now. I gave the signal to McKinney and Thoreau in the woods. At least, it should have been them. Someone gave me the wrong counter-sign. Then they charged me. I shot one of them. Dear God, I never saw who it was."

"More importantly, sir," Jax said, looking at Trick. "Whoever signaled was working with Harriet."

"Yes, of course. Harriet brought his own team. He knew he was through and came prepared for a fight." Singleton went to an arm chair, sat, and took a long, slow drink of his tea. "Agent Jax, Alex, tell me. Tell me if I said anything else to help."

Alex looked to Jax for the answer.

"No, sir, you didn't. We still don't know who Harriet is."

Chapter 71

Finch leaned over the hood of his cruiser with his automatic aimed at the man pointing a shotgun toward him. "Sheriff's Department! Drop the weapon. We have a warrant to search the house. Come out with your hands in the air. Walk toward me. Do it now."

"Go to hell," the Latino yelled from the doorway of the rundown country house.

"Drop the weapon." Finch surveyed the deputies posted on both sides of the house. A SWAT team was positioned behind two sheriff's cruisers to his right and left. "You can't win this one, pal. Just put your gun down."

The Latino fired his shotgun.

One of the deputies to Finch's left cried out, "I'm hit!"

A rifle loud crack from behind Finch startled everyone and the Latino in the doorway fell. The SWAT sniper hastily positioned atop their tactical assault vehicle had taken no chances on a second officer being hit.

"Go! Go!" Finch yelled and charged toward the house behind the SWAT team.

Inside, a systematic search found locked door at the end of a hall.

"Sheriff's office. Drop your weapons and come out," Finch ordered. "Now."

"*Si, si,*" a man called back. "I coming. Please do not shoot."

When the door opened, a young Arab girl stepped out in front of a powerful Latino with his hands raised high. Her face was red and wet from tears. Her eyes begged for understanding. She stopped in the doorway, blocking the deputies' red laser sites from fixing on the Latino.

"No, please. He is our friend. Manuel help us. He save me. Please, no shoot."

"Everyone hold." Finch half-lowered his semiautomatic. "You're Manuel?"

"*Si*, I am Manuel. I go with you."

Two SWAT deputies swooped in. One yanked Manuel from behind the young girl and drove him to the floor. The other secured the open door.

Finch stepped forward, took the girl's hand, and guided her safely from the doorway. "You must be Ameera," he said, putting a gentle hand on her shoulder. "Jax said to tell you hello."

"Jax?" Ameera's eyes flashed wide. "Oh, yes. *Shabah*."

"*Sha*-what? Never mind. Are you okay?"

"Yes. Manuel protect us."

Two more SWAT deputies had entered the hall, barked commands at the open doorway, and slithered inside. Seconds later, Ameera's family emerged, shaken but unharmed. In a line, the deputies ushered the family outside.

Finch sat Ameera in his cruiser with the family standing nearby being questioned. "I'll be right back, honey. You're safe now."

Ameera just nodded.

Finch returned to the front porch where Manuel was being held. Beside him, lying dead on the porch, was the Latino the sniper killed. Finch knelt down and examined the body, noting the dark scar on his forearm. "I'll be damned, Jax. This must be Lobo."

Manuel nodded and spat on the corpse. "*Si, he* Lobo. I dunno his real name. Get you pen, Detective. I got lots to say. I didn't want none of this."

"None of what?"

Manuel jerked a chin at Lobo. "No killin' kids and their mamas. They pay me to watch them and to move them here and there. No one said killin' kids. I ain't doin' that."

Finch took notes for twenty minutes as Manuel sealed Hector Lupino's fate. When he was done, Finch moved Manuel to his cruiser's rear seat where Manuel brightened when he saw Ameera.

"You safe now," Manuel said. "I no let anyone hurt you. I swear dat."

Ameera smiled. "I know, Manuel."

"I'll want a full statement at the office, Manuel," Finch said.

"*Si*. I help what I can."

As Finch closed the door, one of the deputies called out from the ramshackle garage behind the house. "Detective Finch, we found someone in here. EMTs are enroute."

Inside the garage was a white cargo van. The van's rear doors were open and a deputy was untying a short, gaunt Latino who'd been bound hand and foot.

The man wore dirty jeans and a torn sweatshirt. His face was puffy with purple and black welts. Dark red globs had dried around his lips and cheeks.

Raw welts circled his wrists where he rubbed his fingers to regain circulation.

As Finch walked over, the man looked up through two blackening eyes. "Deal man. I want deal or I not talkin'."

Finch held up a hand. "Are you Antonio Cavallo?"

"Yes, sir."

"We finally got you." Finch watched Cavallo's face blanch and quickly added, "Relax. Leo Carraba was a friend of mine. So is Agent Jax. He sent me to help you."

The EMTs arrived and began examining Cavallo. They helped him out of the van and toward a wheeled gurney. Cavallo leaned against it and twice wavered but one of the EMTs held him firmly.

Cavallo turned to Finch. "They tried to make me tell. I

not tell. I have the proof, though, and I did not tell. I want a deal."

"Who did this to you?"

Cavallo winced when an EMT dabbed antiseptic on his cheek. "If Jax send you, you okay with me." He took a deep breath. "It started three weeks ago, back at the inn."

Thirty minutes later, Cavallo was bandaged and lying on the gurney, waiting to be loaded into the ambulance. "And I got proof, Detective. But I not gonna give it without no deal."

"If your story holds water, you'll get more than a deal," Finch said in a low voice. "So, you were supposed to meet Jax at the old farm but the feds got there first and took you?"

"Yeah, man. They wouldn't let me go. The big one, he scare me. He kept threatening me. He wanted everythin' I see and know. But he not dealing with me, man. He said he was gonna send me back to El Salvador. If he did, I dead. But then dis happen. The others bust in and take me from the feds. It all so crazy, man."

"Was it those two gang-bangers who brought you here?" Finch threw a chin toward Manuel sitting in his cruiser thirty feet away. "Him maybe?"

Cavallo shook his head. "No, it was others. One of them feds went out of da house. All of a sudden-like two guys came bustin' in. One of them shot the fed. The other guy, an old dude, grabbed me. They put a hood on me and then I was here. I dunno what the hell is happening."

"You took cell phone pictures at the inn, Antonio?"

"*Si*, Hector and da others. They all the big shots. They had dis meetin' one night. I was there, and snuck some pictures. Carraba want them. But I never see him again. The feds and these guys here, they wanted my pictures. I not give 'em. I not givin' anyone until I got a deal. Pictures got Hector Lupino, his boys, and some other big shots. Maybe a cop, I dunno."

"What was so important about this meeting that it got Leo Carraba killed?"

"Don't you know, man?" Cavallo leaned over as his voice lowered to a whisper. "They *coyotajes*."

"Coyotes?"

"*Si, si.* They bringin' people here from everywhere, even Arabs and like dat. They sneak them on they planes and Hector hide them and move them around where the bosses say. Lots too. Families even. They pay lots for comin' here. Just like my family did. But we pay Mexican coyotajes. These not Mexicans."

Finch waved the EMTs and his deputies out of earshot and waited for them to leave. "Who, Antonio? Who's behind this?"

Cavallo shrugged. "I dunno names."

"You said there was a cop at this meeting?" Finch pulled out his cell phone and flipped through his folder of pictures until he came to several from last year's sheriff's Labor Day barbecue. Everyone from the BCI office and their families were there. The photos were followed by several he'd taken of crime scenes the Grey Coat Inn and the Great Hall Hotel. He showed the photographs to Cavallo. "Do you see anyone in these photographs who was at that meeting?"

Cavallo looked through dozens of pictures. He went through Finch's phone twice, then stopped on one and his eyes darkened. "*Si,* Detective. Dat one." He tapped the screen. "Dat one was at the meeting and go to the inn the night Carraba was killed."

Finch's stomach knotted and he tapped the phone off. He tasted bile as he called the EMTs and his men back. "Antonio, I'm sending two of my deputies with you to the hospital. They will not leave you. It's going to be okay."

"What 'bout my deal?"

"Oh, hell yes, Antonio, you got a deal. You got whatever you want."

Chapter 72

Finch sat in his cruiser and watched the SWAT team mopping up around the old house. Cavallo had made a positive identification of a key figure in Leo Carraba's murder—maybe even his murderer. That identification burned a hole in Finch's gut. Cavallo had attended a clandestine meeting of "scary bad people," including Hector Lupino and his gang, who were involved in human trafficking. Finch's words, not Cavallo's. Cavallo had called them *coyotajes*—people who sneaked refugees and others into the US from Middle Eastern countries. All for a hefty price. All illegal. The entire voyage dangerous. At that clandestine meeting, Cavallo had secretly taken photos, and, after being discovered, he'd sent them to his sister in Richmond; deputies should be finding her within the hour. Still, whoever the circle of "scary bad people" were, they had hunted Cavallo until they'd found him. Then, they'd killed an FBI agent to retrieve him. Their hunt had also led them to Leo Carraba.

Finch had no proof who murdered Leo Carraba, Chief Rogers, or Kathleen Cullen. Cavallo had no idea, either. All Finch did have was speculation surrounding witness tampering, obstruction of justice, and murder. But he had Antonio Cavallo and a cell phone snapshot of a face. He needed a link. More evidence. He needed the coup de grâce.

He dialed the BCI office and waited for Ms. Leweski to pick up. "This is Finch."

"Finch? Where have you been? I haven't seen you all day."

"I've been out chasing leads and can't get back into the office. Ms. Leweski, I need you to check something for me."

"I'm leaving soon."

"Of course." Finch threw down the one thing he knew would get Ms. Leweski's attention. She had adored Leo Carraba. "This might solve Leo's murder."

"What do you need me to do?"

Finch explained, ending with, "I guess you better check all the phone records with Rogers, Carraba, and check them against Kathleen Cullen. Wait, check them against Christie's, and mine, too. Just to be thorough. Call me back as soon as you can."

Ms. Leweski shuffled papers. "I'll get started right away."

Finch hung up and called Christie. "Listen fast. I found Cavallo. He's in pretty bad shape but he'll be okay. There's another witness, too. Be ready on a moment's notice. I may need backup and will text you a location when I find it."

"What are you talking about, Finchy?" Christie's voice was anxious. "What location? What other witness?"

"Just be ready." He tapped off the call.

Next, Finch called Sheriff Michaels to make sure a full security team was headed to the hospital to watch over Cavallo and Ameera's family. It took him twenty minutes to explain. Michaels listened in total silence and when Finch was done, he groused through a dozen questions. Finch had few answers.

"Finch, if you're wrong, you're done. You know that, right? In fact, we're both done. You're playing games with the wrong people. This has disaster written all over it."

"I'm not wrong."

"Don't be." When Sheriff Michaels hung up, Finch knew he was smiling.

It took more than an hour, but Ms. Leweski finally called

back. Between complaints and shuffling papers, she gave him her results. Next, Finch dialed Jax's phone three times, and each time, it went straight to voicemail. What he now knew wasn't a message to leave on a cell phone. What he now knew wasn't something he wanted to know at all.

Chapter 73

Peter Trappe was a rich, powerful man. His estate grounds adorned acres of cherry, oak, and other hardwoods, painting a brilliant fall canvas inside the eight feet high stone walls. His home was stone and timber, fashioned as an English manor house. Manicured gardens accompanied a stone drive that passed through the gates and up to a portico entrance. What wealth wasn't built into its structure hung framed on the interior walls or was molded into bronze and porcelain.

"You think I am Harriet?"

Jax stood across from Peter Trappe, his back to the solarium windows overlooking the Chevy Chase estate. Alex was beside him and John Singleton sat at a round glass table in front of them. Trick was there, too, standing in the archway leading into the main house.

"Peter," Singleton said, waving his hand in the air like a magician about to pull a rabbit from his hat. "We've been through a lot, you and I."

"The hell with you." Trappe's face darkened and he thrust an angry finger toward him. "You waltz in here and accuse me of being a traitor?"

"Mr. Trappe," Jax said, patting the air, "we believe your company has been smuggling refugees into this country for money. That's exactly what Harriet had done during the war. You own the safehouses used to hide them. "

"That's absurd."

"People are dead—murdered—surrounding this scheme. You had everything to lose if it were known." Jax's eyes bore holes through him. "My partner, Leo Carraba, and others paid the price."

"What are you talking about?" Trappe's face reddened and he turned to Singleton again. "You're part of this?"

Singleton said nothing.

Alex cleared her throat. "One of your company cars was used by whoever tried to kill me. John told us—"

Singleton held up his hand. "Peter, it's over. I don't want to believe any of this, but Agent Jax appears to have put it all together."

"Ah, Johnny-boy," Trick said, moving closer to Trappe. "Truth be told, I helped out a lot, too."

Trappe swatted at his ear like a fly was buzzing him. "Oh, he's figured it all out, has he? So he knows my company leases properties all over the world? He knows Wellington is a subcontractor to a hundred classified programs? He knows I have tens of thousands of employees and contractors? Does he know I can no more be accountable for rental properties or fleet cars than you can?"

Jax caught Alex's eye and tipped his head toward the patio doors leading inside Trappe's home. She feigned a confident smile. While Singleton parried Trappe's verbal assault, she slipped away.

"I don't care about all that," Jax said, closing on Trappe to cover Alex's disappearance. "I care about murder. About three murders. Maybe more. You were there the night Trick McCall was murdered. It all started then."

"McCall?" Trappe's face was on fire. "Of course I was there. I was part of the team. But, I was at my aircraft."

"Peter, you could have sent that signal on the aircraft radio, couldn't you? Then, you could have gone to the inn." Singleton held up a hand. "It's over. It's time to end this charade."

Trappe glared at him. "You bastard. First you went after Red and Roman. You tried to destroy them. It took you sixty-seven years to finally come after me?"

Jax inched his hand around his waist until it was just inches from his semiautomatic. "You were there, Trappe. You had a radio and sent that signal. You killed Trick."

"I *was* there but you weren't, sonny-boy. You don't know anything."

"Ah, but I do, Petey-old-boy." Trick leaned close to Trappe. "Remember me?" He grasped Trappe's shoulder and squeezed. "Did you miss me, Petey?" Trick tried to melt into him, see what he'd seen, and learn the secrets hid inside. Trappe refused and slammed the door the instant Trick had peeked inside.

"No!" Trappe jerked sideways and stumbled back against the cocktail bar in the corner of the sunroom. He stood shaking as though he'd grabbed a bare electric wire. "What? No. It can't be—"

"Ricky, back off," Trick said. "Something's wrong here."

Alex emerged through the patio doors just as Trappe leaned over the bar and pulled out a stainless steel revolver.

Trappe pointed the gun at Alex. "Okay, everyone, stand very still."

"Really, Trappe?" Jax eased his arm around Alex and slid her behind him. "You just proved us right. Innocent people don't pull guns. You won't—"

"Get far? How cliché. I only need to escape from here."

"Listen to me," Jax said but the gun pivoted toward his face. "Easy, Peter. There's no need for more violence."

"Don't 'easy' me. I have to defend myself. I know what these people are capable of. John's a powerful man. More so than even me. If he points his finger, people fall. Not me. Not this time." Trappe waved his gun. "I know you're armed. Take out your weapons and slide them to me."

Jax hesitated, but realized he had no play so he slid his Glock from behind his back and tossed it on a nearby lounge chair. Singleton just stood there watching Trappe, unmoving.

"Now your cell phones. Take them out. Toss them onto the floor at my feet." Trappe jutted the gun at each of them one after the other until they complied. Then, he smashed the phones into broken bits of circuitry and plastic with his heel. "No one move."

"Enough." Singleton held up his hands. "Peter, think. You're ninety years old. You can't run far. And there are things you don't know. Abrielle was there that night. She knows you were there, too."

Trappe's face flared. "Abrielle?"

"Yes, Peter, she's alive. Alex knows where she is. It's time to end this."

"Yes, it is." Trappe turned the gun on Alex. "Let's go see Abrielle."

"No, Peter." Jax eased forward but Trappe's gun stopped him. "She's not going anywhere."

"Let him go, Ricky," Trick said. "It's okay."

"You fools. You have no idea, do you?" Trappe cracked in a wide grin. He strode up to Jax and struck him on the side of the head with the revolver. Jax went down. As he hit the floor, Trappe thrust the gun against Alex's cheek. "Take me to Abrielle."

"I'm not going anywhere with you." Alex knelt and helped Jax back to his feet. "You'll have to kill me."

Trick touched her arm. "Doll, it's okay." He pulled back and looked solemnly at Jax. "I should have known, sport. I'm sorry."

"Shut up." Trappe aimed his revolver at Alex's head and looked at Singleton. "Maybe I need to tell these two a few things about you, John? Would you like that?"

Jax sprang toward Trappe but the gunshot surprised him and stopped him in his tracks.

The shot surprised Peter Trappe. His eyes bulged and his mouth exploded open without words. He turned around as his left hand reached up to his chest and touched the dark spot growing across his shirt.

Peter Trappe dropped to the floor.

John Singleton wasn't surprised at all. When Marcus entered the solarium behind everyone like a cat, Singleton knew what was coming. He stepped back the moment Marcus drew his gun and shot Trappe without hesitation.

Trick dropped down beside Trappe and took hold of his shoulder. It took only a second. "Sorry, sport. I can't get anything from him."

"Is it over?" Alex's voice was a whisper as she clung to Jax. "Harriet is dead?"

Jax checked Trappe's pulse. "No, he's alive."

"Marcus, call an ambulance," Singleton ordered. "Then do what you can for him."

Marcus pulled out his cell phone and went to Trappe, holstering his handgun.

Singleton turned to Alex. "Did you find anything inside, my dear?"

"No, I didn't have time," she said. "But there's one locked drawer at this desk. I couldn't open it."

"Let me try," Singleton said, and he disappeared into the house.

"It'll be okay now," Jax said.

"I hope so. I—"

A loud crack came from inside the house and, a moment later, John Singleton emerged. He carried a thin, black leather notebook in one hand and a small semiautomatic handgun in the other. He handed the notebook to Jax.

"It's a code book, Agent Jax, identical to those we'd used in OSS. I found the book and this gun in that locked drawer. Peter had weapons hidden everywhere."

Alex looked down at Marcus still tending to Trappe. "I guess we know why."

Jax flipped through the notebook to several paperclipped pages toward the end of the book. On one of the pages was a list of a dozen phrases preceded by numbers. He showed them to Alex. "These are the same ones on the website Cavallo led us to."

Singleton took the book and scanned through it. "I cannot believe Peter has been behind all this." He flipped the book closed. "Dear God, you have to get to Abrielle, Alex."

"What's wrong, John?" She wiped nervous tears off her cheeks. "Trappe was Harriet. It's over."

"Perhaps." Singleton's looked down at Trappe. "Peter couldn't have worked alone."

"What are you saying?" Jax asked.

"It isn't over, sport," Trick said, putting a hand on Jax's back. "Sorry, pal. But Harriet wouldn't be working alone. There are others out there."

"I need to check around here. You go to Abrielle to ensure she's safe. Trappe has people. Dangerous people." Singleton lifted the book. "They could be hunting Abrielle."

Chapter 74

"What the hell is going on here?" Captain Martinez barked as he walked into the BCI bullpen with Jeremy on his heels. He waved a hand toward the empty desks. "Ms. Leweski?"

"Well, you fired Finch," Jeremy said, snorting a laugh. "And you let Jax out."

"Shut up, Jeremy."

Ms. Leweski emerged from the hall. "Are you looking for me?"

"Where the hell is Agent Krein?"

"*Well.*" Ms. Leweski stopped, glared icebergs at Martinez, and retreated to her desk with a *Humph.* "I don't care for that tone or language."

Martinez closed his eyes. "Yes, of course. I'm sorry. Where's Christie?"

"My guess would be with Detective Finch."

"Finch?" Jeremy thrust his hands onto his hips. "Finch was fired."

"Fired?" Ms. Leweski raised her eyebrows. "No one informed me. I just spoke with him a short while ago."

Martinez went to her desk. "All right, Ms. Leweski, if you don't want to join him on the unemployment line, tell me what's going on."

She looked up at him. "You never informed me he was fired. I had no idea or I wouldn't have provided information to him."

"What information?"

She looked away. "He asked for some phone records and other information."

"Oh, he did?" Martinez leaned on her desk with both hands and forced her to look up at him. "What information?"

"Well, as long as it's clear I didn't know he was no longer working here." She explained Finch's request. When she was done, she found the manila file in her out-basket and handed it to him. "It's all in there. Everything I told him. He wanted all the calls with Agent Carraba, Chief Rogers, and Ms. Cullen cross-referenced with everyone involved in the case."

Martinez snatched the folder from her and flipped it open. "All of them?"

"Just for the past three weeks." Ms. Leweski sat back. "It wasn't easy."

Martinez flipped through the pages of cell phone records until he found the notes Ms. Leweski made on the pages. He checked each of the accounts and handed the file to Jeremy.

"Jesus, look what he found." He looked at Ms. Leweski. "Where is Finch now?"

She shrugged. "I have no idea. No one tells me anything around here."

Chapter 75

P eter Trappe was Harriet?" Abrielle Chanoux sat in an overstuffed chair, facing the others with a quilt draped over her aged legs. At eighty-six years old, she still had a full head of hair, albeit gone gray, and a strong, sturdy physique. "Amazing, after all these years, finally finding Harriet."

Abrielle's two-story log home was hidden miles deep into the Shenandoah Mountains along Virginia's northwestern border with West Virginia. It was already dark when Jax and Alex arrived. Trick was already waiting inside. In a near panic, Alex had explained everything to Abrielle the moment they sat down inside her cabin. Abrielle didn't seem surprised by any of it, despite the revelations of Peter Trappe, nor was she surprised by Jax's involvement. She greeted him by name as though a longtime family friend. During the entire discussion, Trick stood nearby, mesmerized by her every word.

"Isn't she something, Ricky," Trick said, standing near the fireplace gazing at Abrielle. "I'd know her anywhere."

"Yeah, amazing," Jax said, as much to Trick as in response to Abrielle. He wondered if Trick saw the old woman staying warm beneath the quilt or the young nineteen-year-old French Resistance fighter he'd fallen in love with decades before. "But I'm not as sure as John Singleton is that Trappe was Harriet."

"Why?" Alex asked. "He had he code book and he pulled a gun on us."

"People do strange things when they're cornered," Jax said matter-of-factly. "I can't explain the code book. In fact, I'm surprised by it. But think of it. Trappe was an OSS pilot. How could he have been Harriet?"

"What do you mean, Agent Jax?" Abrielle pulled her quilt higher on her legs. "He was involved in many of the OSS missions moving refugees out of Europe, wasn't he?"

"Yes, I suppose he was. But he was a flyer. How did he make the deals and find the refugees to begin with? He wasn't on the ground in France."

"Does that matter?" Alex asked from a chair beside Abrielle. "Couldn't he run the smuggling network from anywhere?"

"That's unlikely." Jax stood up and wandered to the large bay window. "Someone had to be on the ground in France, recruiting the people who wanted to escape. Someone had to make the deals. You can't do that from a cockpit."

Alex looked at Abrielle and the two exchanged shrugs.

"I think you're right, Ricky," Trick said. "Peter isn't Harriet. He can't be."

"And the night Trick and the others were killed, Trappe was at the airplane. Vetner and Clay were posted a mile from the inn." Jax turned around. "If they got a signal to stay back, then someone else sent it."

"Yes, yes, I see," Abrielle said, nodding. "Unless someone is lying. Or, perhaps, there was no signal at all."

"But there *was* a signal. Even if one of them lied, the others still heard it."

"Could McKinney or Thoreau have been working for Harriet?" Alex asked.

"Maybe. But then who killed them?" Jax shook his head. "Abrielle, tell me what you remember about that night."

She frowned and her eyes glistened as sadness washed

over her. "I was trying to save Patrick. I was in the woods behind the carriage house. When he and John made the plan to capture Harriet there, Patrick didn't trust anyone and sent me ahead to be his backup."

"Did he tell Singleton the details of the raid?" Jax asked. "Anyone else?"

"No," Trick said. "We kept the raid hush-hush. Trappe didn't even know until we were airborne."

"No, I don't think so." Abrielle had a far-off look in her eyes. "Patrick found Schiller and sent him back to me. I hid him in the woods. Then I started back to help Patrick. I'd been gone thirty minutes or so. By the time I returned, it was over."

Jax finished her story. "John was wounded and the others were dead. Did you see Trick? Did you see Harriet kill him?"

"No." Her eyes softened and went to her lap as she wiped her cheeks. "I never got close enough. I found Kirkman and Fuchs dead at the carriage house and didn't see Patrick anywhere. I suspected he was dead. We had a plan to meet up if things went bad. He never arrived and never would have left me behind. He was such a sweet man. I knew something drastic happened."

"Sweet man? After all these years the best she remembers is I was a sweet man?" Trick walked over behind Abrielle's chair and stood there. He reached down and touched her hand, his face saddened and his eyes softened into tears. "I guess my memories are a little frayed around the edges, too, Ricky"

Abrielle shivered, as if a chill ran through her at Trick's touch. "I took the money Fuchs and Kirkman had that was meant for Harriet and returned to Schiller. We made our escape and I've been hiding ever since."

"So, Jax," Alex said, narrowing her eyes. "There was Clay and Vetner, John, and Trappe. Clay and Vetner were ordered to stay back. Trappe was alone at the plane and could have gotten to the inn that night. There was no one to stop him."

"Ricky, that goes for the rest, too," Trick said. "Any of them could have gone to the inn unseen."

Jax repeated him. "Someone was recruiting the refugees who could pay their passage to the States. Someone had to arrange the OSS flights out, too. They piggybacked them on the Operation Paperclip flights I guess."

"That makes sense," Alex said. "But if not Peter, then who?"

Trick suddenly jumped forward. "Down!"

The bullet shattered the bay window and struck the wall beside the fireplace—but not before scoring a furrow across the shoulder of Jax's coat.

"Alex, get the lights." Jax yelled, pulling his Glock and flattening himself beside the window. "I don't see anyone. Stay here."

As Alex plunged the room into darkness, Jax ran into the hallway and out the front door.

The second shot seared the room into silence.

Chapter 76

Do you see anything, Trick?" Jax whispered, kneeling beside a chest-high stack of firewood on the front porch. "It's too dark and I can't see beyond the car."

Trick stood beside Alex's Mercedes twenty feet in front of him. "Nothing. I'll look around."

"No, go back inside. Stay close to Alex and Abrielle. If anything happens, get me fast."

"Right." Trick disappeared.

Jax remained still, listening for any telltale sound or misstep—a broken twig, the rustle of branches, or a heavy step. Twice he raised his Glock and readied for a shot but the target transformed into the phantom shadows of tree limbs moving in the breeze. Staying low, he circled the woodpile and crept across the driveway to Alex's car.

No shots. No sounds. No shooter.

When he turned toward the house, movement caught his eye and someone rose beyond the corner of the cabin, silhouetted in the moonlight. He tried an old night-surveillance trick by looking at the figure from an oblique angle, not straight on. It worked.

It was a man. He was tall and dark, and standing just beside the corner of the cabin facing him.

"Freeze." Jax raised his Glock. "BCI. Don't move.."

The man fired two rapid shots and disappeared around the corner.

The first shot screeched across Alex's car hood. Jax was already prone and fired back. The second shot went high and he returned fire again, rolled to the rear of the car, and got to his feet ready for another assault.

Trick's voice reached him. "Ricky, someone is at the back door. Hurry."

Jax bolted for the front porch, traversed around the woodpile, and moved to the corner of the house. Adrenalin quivered his hands and sweat pooled beneath his eyes. Rolling out around the corner of the house, he kept his Glock out in front, searching for a target, poised to shoot.

Nothing.

"Ricky, hurry."

He pressed himself against the house and eased forward, placing each footfall as though walking on broken glass and trying to avoid the shards. He inched to the far corner and stopped.

Silence.

He pivoted around the corner and saw him again.

Kneeling on one knee beside the rear cabin door was the shooter.

"Don't move. BCI.. Drop your weapon and raise your hands. Now."

The man's hands rose in steady movement. "Don't shoot, Agent Jax. You have this all wrong."

Jax moved in, keeping his gun trained on the man's chest. The moonlight was obscured by the trees but he didn't need any more light to see the automatic lying at the man's feet and the familiarity of his eyes.

"Stand up, slow and careful."

John Singleton rose to his feet.

Chapter 77

He damn near killed me," Jax said, shoving Singleton into the living room. "Everyone okay in here?"

"Yes, we are," Abrielle said and then her eyes narrowed on Jax's prisoner. "John? You? What is this about?"

Jax pushed Singleton down into a living room chair, quickly searched him, and went to the fireplace. He kept his gun trained on him and sat Singleton's automatic on the mantel.

"That's not my gun, Agent Jax," Singleton said with a huff. "Whoever shot at you took mine and left that one behind."

"Really? Wild coincidence, huh?" Jax turned to Alex and Abrielle. "I didn't see this coming."

Alex turned on the remaining room lights and went to Jax, crushing into him. "Are you all right?" She ran her finger along the bullet crease in his coat. "That's awful close."

"Johnny, how could you do this?" Trick stood beside Singleton, glaring down at him. "And here I was on your side the whole time."

Jax stabbed a finger at Singleton. "Okay, Singleton, start explaining."

"I did not shoot at you, Agent Jax." Singleton raised his chin and stared at him with an intensity that made Jax be quiet and listen. "I was rounding the other side of the house when the man shot at you. He ran into me in the dark and we both went down. He must have dropped his gun and picked up mine instead. The weapon you found at my feet is his."

"Agent Jax," Abrielle said, pulling her quilt higher on her old legs. "Did you see anyone else?"

Jax shook his head.

"Did you hear anyone else?"

"No."

Abrielle's mouth tightened and she lifted her chin. "I thought not. As much as I don't want to believe John a killer, we cannot afford a mistake. Didn't you say it was John who found the code book in Peter Trappe's office?"

"Yes, it was," Jax said, realizing where she was going. "And no one was with him."

Singleton patted the air. "Now, listen to me. I don't know anything about that book."

Abrielle's eyes lowered for a second and when she lifted them, they were stone. "And it was John's man who shot Trappe."

"John, what have you done?" Alex asked in a meek voice. "Not you?"

"Listen to me," Singleton snapped. "I'm not an assassin. You must believe that. I came up here to help you. I know who Harriet is."

"We thought we did, too, John," Alex said. "But now I'm not sure."

Trick put a hand on Singleton's shoulder and faded. He was gone for an instant. Not long enough to steal the old man's breath, but long enough. When he returned, Trick stood beside Jax.

"He's a good guy, Ricky. He's innocent." Next, Trick put his hand on Jax's shoulder and what he had seen in the brief seconds in John Singleton rushed into Jax like a tsunami. "John's one of us."

Jax faltered and caught himself on the mantel. For a long moment, he stood there, trying to sort through Trick's thoughts and regain his own. When he settled himself, he lowered his gun from Singleton. "I believe you, Mr. Singleton. Something isn't as it should be. I'm sorry."

"So am I," a voice said from the hall.

A tall, strong, bald man emerged from the dark hallway. He had a puffy face with a neat, trimmed beard, and powerful features. Gone were his greasy, dirty work clothes. In their place were an expensive suit jacket, gray slacks, and a pistol.

Andrew Clay leveled his pistol on Jax. "Drop the gun, Jax. You know how this goes."

"Clay, put *your* gun down." Jax held his gun at his side and readied to use it. "There's no need for this."

"Of course there's a need." Andrew looked at Abrielle and Alex and moved two steps aside to the side of Singleton where he could watch everyone more easily. "I can't worry if you'll let Singleton go. He hounded my dad until he died. Enough of this."

"Yes, Andrew," Singleton said, facing him. "I agree. Enough of this charade. The trail to Harriet ends now. It ends with you."

"Shut up, Singleton. Are you going to frame everyone as Harriet?" Andrew said, stepping into Singleton and prodding him with his gun. "You bastard. You have a lot to answer for."

"Andrew, your father was Harriet." Singleton received another jab from Andrew's gun. "Who was his compatriot? McKinney or Thoreau? Both?"

"Shut up. I'm here to finish old scores."

Singleton didn't quiet. "Which one shot me that night? Or did your dad to do the treachery himself?"

Andrew grabbed Singleton's arm and spun him around to shove him down. But Singleton was ready. When Andrew turned him sideways, Singleton grabbed his gun and twisted him off balance. They collided. Andrew was younger and far more powerful, but Singleton was fighting for his life. As Andrew tried to break free, Singleton refused to let go and tangled himself around the gun with both hands.

Jax started forward but Trick called him off. "Ricky, no—wait."

Singleton's old frame danced like a marionette beneath Clay's powerful grip, but he held onto the gun. Just as Andrew loosened him, Singleton drove a hard knee into his groin and yanked the gun away. Then, he stepped back and lifted the gun. "Now, let's all—"

A shot rang out and the bullet struck him.

Everyone turned and stared at Abrielle.

She had fired her pistol from beneath her quilt. The bullet struck Singleton in the chest. He staggered back as she flung away the smoldering quilt and stood. She fired two more times. The second round hit him in the chest an inch from the first, the third shot was in the center of his forehead.

"Abrielle, stop," Jax called.

She stood in front of her chair, glaring down at John Singleton's lifeless body. Then she closed her eyes, whispered something, and fell back down, wrapping herself in the quilt again as though nothing happened.

Jax stared. "Abrielle, what have you done?"

She raised her eyes to him and her voice was shaky and faint. "He—He would have killed us all. I—Oh, my God."

"What's happening?" Alex cried. She spun and stared at Andrew. "Do something. Help him."

"Johnny's dead, Ricky," Trick said. "Andrew—"

"I know." Jax looked from Andrew to Abrielle and then down at Singleton's body. The truth stung him. He leaned down and took the gun from Singleton's grasp.

"Andrew," Jax said slowly, lifting his gun and turning toward him. "You took over for your dad. He was Harriet. You're behind all the killings."

"Go to hell." Andrew's face darkened. "I came here to even things with Singleton. That's all. He tried to destroy Dad and it's over now."

"No more lies, Andrew." Jax backed toward the fire-place, keeping the gun on him. "You *were* checking on the Quinton and Pettington. They didn't owe you money, you were making sure your Dad's tracks were covered. You lied to Finch."

"Go to hell," Andrew repeated coldly. "You can't prove anything."

Jax nodded. "Maybe I can. It all started with Trick McCall. Anyone at the inn could have gotten to his radio and sent that signal. Roman's confederate sent that signal to give him an alibi. That confederate could have been any of them. McKinney, Thoreau, any of them."

"Yes, Agent Jax," Abrielle said. "You're right. Anyone of us could have sent that signal."

Jax turned and looked at Abrielle.

She was standing again. In one hand, she dangled a gold pocket watch and in the other, she held the gun she'd used to kill John Singleton. Now, that gun was aimed at Jax's head.

Chapter 78

Ricky," Trick said walking over to Abrielle. He slid his fedora onto the back of his head and whistled, looking over the watch in her hand. "That's Schiller's watch. He gave it to me that night."

"Roman Clay was not Harriet, Agent Jax," Abrielle said, watching him over her gun barrel. "I am. This enterprise was mine from the start. It was my ticket to America and a better life. Roman Clay was my partner."

"Abrielle, no." Trick's voice was low and somber and his eyes showed a mixture of confusion and betrayal. "The watch—*you* murdered me."

"Please, stop. Both of you," Alex cried. "For me, please. Stop this. Stop all of this."

Abrielle motioned for Jax to lower his gun. "Alex, my dear, I'm so sorry. Move over next to him. Now, dear. Don't make this something it doesn't have to be."

"But—"

"You won't hurt her," Jax said, eyeing her and then Andrew. "Let her go. I'll stay. There's no one to stop you."

"Oh, we know." Andrew took Jax's gun and looked at Abrielle. "*Mère*, why didn't you just stay quiet? There was no need for this. I will take care of it all."

"I know you will, my son." She smiled a thin, tight smile. "Your father would be proud of you. Proud as I am.

But there is no need for anyone to take responsibility but me. Do you all understand? Me alone."

Trick looked from Andrew to Abrielle and back. Each time he did, his face grew darker and his eyes filled more with sadness. He went to Abrielle. "You and Roman? I loved you. You betrayed me. You betrayed all of us."

"Abrielle," Jax said, "how could you betray Trick like that?"

"Trick?" Abrielle's tone was strong and defiant. "This wasn't about Patrick. It was about Marguerite."

Andrew prodded his gun at Jax. "*Mére* was pregnant when she arrived in this country. Pregnant with Marguerite, my older sister. Dad had to protect them and Trick would never have gone along with the plan. They needed a fresh start and lots of money."

"Ricky, I'm sorry." Trick looked down, embarrassed. "I missed it all. All those years ago and I never would have believed Abrielle was—"

Jax stepped toward Abrielle. "Trick loved you."

"Yes, he did," Abrielle said with a voice that seemed sad. "But Marguerite wasn't his child. She was Roman's. We wanted a life here. It would have been impossible in France."

Jax was sorting the pieces. "You ran things from the Underground and Roman planned the escapes. The Underground never learned you betrayed them."

"I didn't betray them. We just had different objectives. The Underground wouldn't have understood."

"Jax, tell them it's over," Alex pleaded. "Please, tell them it's over. For me."

Jax started forward but Andrew's gun stopped him. "Trappe wasn't a part of any of it, was he?" Jax asked. "Did he even know?"

Andrew laughed. "He didn't want to know. We made the deals, he supplied the logistics. Dad and I were making him tons of money. He looked the other way."

"Peter's alive," Jax said, dryly. "He'll nail you."

"Don't be a fool, Jax," Andrew said. "I'll pay him a visit and then the company will be mine. You see, Dad was making him so much money Peter made him a silent partner. When Peter goes, Wellington passes to his partner's heirs. *Me*."

"You bastard," Trick yelled. "You'll kill Peter just like the rest of us. You're as much a traitor as your father."

"What about Leo and Chief Rogers and Kathleen Cullen?"

"Success is all that matters." Andrew glanced at Alex. "Now, you two move across the room. Slow."

"No." Alex took Jax's arm. "Jax, tell them it's over. Tell them you'll walk away. Let them go. Please."

Jax turned to her. "It's not over, Alex. It didn't stop in 1944. It won't stop now."

"Shut up," Andrew barked. "Move back."

Jax didn't move. He wasn't through yet. If he was going to die, he wanted answers. "Abrielle, you sent the radio signal and killed Trick. And the others?"

"McKinney shot John." Her voice was reminiscent. "He and Thoreau were with Roman and me. They took care of the others and helped me hide Trick's body. Then—"

"You killed them."

"I have many regrets." Abrielle wiped her eyes. "And Patrick McCall was not the last."

"Schiller?"

Andrew forced a laugh. "Stupid Kraut ran off. It took Dad three days to find him. He should have run farther."

"Why not just leave?" Trick yelled. "Why did you have to kill me? Dammit, Abrielle, I loved you."

"Why not just walk away once you got into this country?" Jax asked.

"As I said, Agent Jax, you were not there. I had to remove any trace to me. If I were caught, they would have sent me to prison or worse."

"Worse?" Jax asked.

"I had Marguerite. If caught, I would have been sent back to France to stand trial after the war. Do you know what the French did to traitors? To the *Vichy*? That would have been horrible. But, nothing compared to what the Underground would have done to me. Done to us." She stared at Jax. "It was the most painful thing I did during the war—killing Patrick. He deserved better from me."

"Yes, I did." Trick watched Abrielle and his tears turned into something odd—understanding. "She's right, Ricky. They would have killed her. Maybe killed Marguerite, too. My God, I was stupid. Blind and stupid. Betrayed by the people I trusted the most." Then he turned and took Jax's shoulder. "Sorry, pal. There's no time."

The journey was over before Jax knew it began.

Trick took control of Jax and quickly shed the dizziness. Then he winked at Alex and stepped toward Abrielle with a broad smile.

"Hi, ya, Socks, it's me. It's Trick." The voice from Jax's lips hadn't been heard since 1944. "Socks, put down your gun. Andrew too."

Abrielle's mouth went agape and she stared at Jax, her eyes wavering around his face, trying to understand, searching. Then something inside fell into place and she paled. "No, no, it cannot be."

"Sure it can, Socks. It's me. It's Patrick, doll."

Abrielle gasped, "No. Stop this."

Trick smiled and took a step closer. "*Je m'appelle Patrick. Il fait trop sombre pour faire la promenade.*"

"No, no. It cannot be."

"Don't you remember the code, Socks?" Trick took another step closer. "*Oui, mais on peut voir au clair de la belle lune.*" Another step closer. "Yes, but the moonlight is enough to see. It is beautiful."

"No—no, no, Patrick. How?" A tiny, thin smile cracked the corners of her mouth. "Patrick? Can this be you?"

Andrew raised his gun. "No, *mère*, it's a trick."

Her eyes flashed to Andrew. "It is him. It *is* Patrick. He's back."

Trick leapt on Abrielle's gun and yanked it free. He shoved her down on the couch, spun around, and fired a quick, ill-aimed shot.

Andrew grunted and fell to the floor. A red blossom grew across his waist. Another inch to the right and the bullet would have missed him; another to the left and he might be dying.

"Stay down, Socks," Trick ordered, kicking Andrew's gun out of reach. "I'm sorry. You left me no choice."

Vehicle lights flooded the bay windows. Doors slammed. Voices grew louder. Feet crossed the gravel just before the front door crashed open.

Dylan Finch burst down the hall and took a position in the archway, peering inside the room. His gun stretched out in front of him, searching. "Everyone stay still. No one move. Jax, are you and Alex all right?"

"Ah, Detective Finch, how good of you to ask," Trick said still with his 1944 voice. "For a copper, your timing ain't bad."

Finch inched into the living room, studying Jax through narrowed eyes. "Jax? Your voice?"

"Yes, Detective, he's here and doing well." He gave Finch a quick salute. "I, however, am Captain Patrick McCall of the Office of Strategic Services. And I am at your service."

Chapter 79

L et's start with evidence tampering," Jax said to Martinez and MacTavish. "And obstruction of justice. For starters."

"Kidnapping, too," Finch added, aiming a gunfinger at MacTavish. "Cavallo was an informant and a good kid. He was witness, not a bad guy. Now he's *our* witness."

MacTavish and Captain Martinez had arrived with the ambulances and local county sheriff, five minutes behind Finch. After giving them a briefing on the case, Jax pulled them out into the parking lot for a private discussion and to give the crime scene team room to work Abrielle's cabin. What he and Finch had to say was better without an audience.

"We had Cavallo in protective custody, deputy," MacTavish snapped, tight-jawed. "If you hadn't been snooping around, Andrew Clay never would have found him."

"Snooping around? I get paid to snoop around, jackass," Finch said. "And according to Cavallo, you kidnapped him."

"He is a material witness. It's legal."

"Legal?" Finch shook his head. "Unbelievable."

"Look, I get you're pissed off." MacTavish raised his chin. "I would be, too. But this is national security."

"More bullshit." Jax jutted a steel finger into MacTavish's chest. "You two tried to frame me for *three* murders. How's that national security?"

Martinez stepped forward, nudging Jax away from the FBI man. "Agent Jax, I regret we had you swinging in the breeze like that. MacTavish had to have Clay believe he was in the clear. He had to get him to relax so we could get the case sewed up. It bought MacTavish time."

"That's right," MacTavish said. "I've been after him for years. Killing Carraba and the others finished him. We didn't know about Abrielle Chanoux and this other mess. As I've said, we're dealing with national security."

"Bullshit." Finch snorted a laugh. "And you're not FBI, MacTavish. NSA? CIA?"

"Doesn't matter," he said. "What does is I've been trying to nail Clay for ten years. He's through. After the trials—"

"Trials?" Jax looked at Finch and his face darkened. "Andrew is worth millions and Abrielle is almost ninety. She'll die before their money runs out fighting you. Good luck getting either of them into a courtroom."

Martinez looked from Finch to Jax. "You're right. Even more reason we'll need all you have on Leo, Rogers, and Cullen's, murders. Everything."

"Yeah, yeah," Jax said. "What do you think, Finch?"

Finch grinned. "Well, we're still working the details on those murders. Maybe tomorrow."

"Tomorrow?" Martinez narrowed an eye on Finch. "What the hell are you not telling me?"

"I'll handle this, boys," a voice said from behind them. "You've had a full day." Sheriff Michaels walked up and threw a thumb toward the cruisers where two deputies were helping Abrielle into a rear seat. "The three suspects are mine. Witnesses, too. When I'm through, you can have what's left, Martinez."

Martinez threw up a hand. "Hold on, Sheriff, listen to me."

"No, sir, you listen." Sheriff Michaels had a broad, counterfeit smile blossoming. "Sheriff Towe from this county is gonna hold them until we get things sorted out. Then they're coming back to Loudoun with me. State's attorney agrees. It's a done deal."

"Sheriff, Agent MacTavish and I are here to help."

"Too late," Finch said, patting his shoulder. "We got all the help we need."

Martinez looked at Jax. "This was all out of my hands. I cannot go into any of it, but I was under orders. I owe you an apology. But it *was* business."

Sheriff Michaels eyed MacTavish. "You boys need to move on. *Now*."

"That's not going to happen, Sheriff," MacTavish said, jutting out his chin. "I'm taking Cavallo and I want that Arab family, too. Ameera somebody and her folks. I want—"

"You want? The commonwealth's attorney disagrees." Sheriff Michaels waved to two bulky deputies standing by his car. They walked toward him. "She gave me orders to use all means necessary to keep jurisdiction."

"Easy, Sheriff." MacTavish glanced at the approaching deputies. "Let's not be stupid."

"Oh, now I'm stupid?" Sheriff Michaels laughed as the two deputies stopped beside him. "Who has the witnesses and suspects and who has his head up his ass, MacTavish? Now, get the hell out of my crime scene."

"It's not over." MacTavish turned and headed to his car.

Captain Martinez watched him go. "Jax, we had to make them think you were our prime suspect. It worked. Between them grabbing Cavallo and Ameera's family, we've got a solid case. We had to play rough."

"You didn't have to do any such thing, Captain," Sheriff Michaels said gruffly. "I put a call into your BCI commander in Richmond. He's anxious to have a talk with you first thing in the morning. In *his* office."

"I understand." Martinez looked from Finch to Jax. "I'm sorry. I truly am. Things got out of hand." And with that, Captain Martinez followed MacTavish away.

Sheriff Michaels slapped Finch on the back and shook Jax's hand. "You let me know if they give you any more trouble, gentlemen. I enjoyed kicking federal ass. Finch, see me in the morning."

As the sheriff walked off, headlights rolled into the drive behind a waiting ambulance and Christie jumped from her cruiser. Finch's face fell. "Jax, it ain't over, pal. We gotta talk about Leo."

"Yeah, we do." Jax waved for Christie to join them. "You know something. Give."

"Ricky," Trick said, appearing beside him. "It gets harder from here."

Chapter 80

Cavallo identified Leo's killer," Finch said, looking at Jax and Alex across Abrielle's dining room table. "It wasn't Andrew Clay."

"Who?" Christie said, whirling toward him. "You didn't tell me that earlier."

"Me either," Jax said. "We just told Martinez—"

"I said we were still working that out." Finch took them through Ameera's rescue and explained finding Antonio Cavallo. "I used my phone to take photos like I did at the sheriff's barbecue last summer and of crime scenes. Cavallo identified the killer in one of them."

"Show us," Christie said.

Finch took out his cell phone and flipped to the photographs. He held the cell up to her. "Cavallo recognized someone from my photos who was at a secret meeting at the inn with Lupino and all the players. Cavallo took pictures with his own cell phone that night. That's why they were trying to kill him. One of the people in those photos killed Leo, thinking Cavallo told him everything."

"Cavallo was a sneaky bastard," Christie said. Then she stepped away from Finch and drew her semiautomatic. She aimed it at Jax. "I'm sorry, pal. I'm real sorry."

Jax pulled Alex closer to him and wrapped his arm around her. "What are you doing, Christie?"

Finch turned the cell phone around and held it up for Jax.

It was a photograph he'd taken at the Great Hall Hotel shooting scene he'd responded to with Jax.

It was a photograph of Alex Vouros.

Jax face twisted and he shook his head in slow, painful movements. "Alex?"

"She was at the meeting, Jax. She and Andrew Clay." Finch came around the table and peeled Alex from beneath Jax's arm. "Cavallo didn't know their names, but he sure picked her out of my photos. I'm sorry, pal."

"Ricky," Trick said. "I guess we both have lousy taste in broads, huh? And there's more you need to know." He took Jax's shoulder and melted their thoughts together.

The secret froze Jax into ice.

"...I checked the phone records back at the office," Finch was saying. "She called Chief Rogers the day after Leo's murder. She made an appointment with him."

"Rogers told me he had to meet with some doctor the night he was killed," Christie said slowly, piecing it together. "I never made the connection. She's a doctor. A PhD, that is."

"Two days before Leo's murder," Finch added, "Leo got a call from the OSS Foundation, too."

Jax lowered his eyes and his voice was a near whisper. "John Singleton's card. The appointment on Leo's calendar: 'AC one-thirty.' We thought it was Antonio Cavallo." He turned and looked at Alex. "But it wasn't."

Alex's lips tightened and she looked away.

"AC. Alexandra Chanoux. Your maiden name." Jax leaned in close to capture her eyes. "Abrielle was Andrew and Marguerite's mother. Marguerite was your mother. Andrew's your uncle. You're Abrielle's granddaughter."

"Oh God, yes." Alex tried to return to Jax but he pushed her away. Her face paled and her head dropped when Finch snapped the handcuffs on her. The tears flowed. "I'm sorry, Jax. You won't believe me, but I am. I never imagined it getting this far."

Finch read her rights to her, but she waved him away. When he was through, he turned back to Jax. "She went to the inn that night Lupino's men shot you, Jax. And you shot one of them."

"I hope I killed the bastard."

"You did." Finch gave Alex a push toward Christie. "Manuel, one of the guards on Ameera's family, is taking us to where Lupino dumped the body. Between Manuel and Cavallo, we know most of it now. Alex found you bleeding out and waited for Leo to show. She killed Leo with your gun."

"Why, Alex?" Jax asked, fighting the urge to grab her and shake her. "For some money?"

"*Some* money?" Alex looked at them and a strange, cutting smile crept onto her lips. "You don't call a hundred million '*some money*.' Roman owned half of Wellington International. *Half*. With Trappe gone, Andrew and I own it all. Leo was onto us—me. He would have stopped our plan. Besides, I couldn't let my family go to jail. They'd be ruined, humiliated. They'd be—"

"Traitors." Jax walked over and leaned in close. "You've been lying from the start. No one ever stalked Abrielle. She's been with Clay since France. The two of them kept the Harriet enterprise alive."

"They built an empire and Harriet's legacy was just one part of it." Alex looked away. "She raised me after my mother died. That wasn't a lie."

"It's all been a lie, Alex."

"No, but I owed them everything. Don't you see? All I had to do was protect them."

"And kill for them."

Alex eyes turned sad. "I never thought I'd fall for you, Jax."

"Shove it, lady." Christie grabbed Alex's shirt and lifted her onto her toes. "You killed three people. And I bet it was you who clobbered me at Leo's place the night Jax and I searched it."

Alex shrugged and said nothing.

"Bitch." Christie shoved her backward onto the dining table. "Manipulative bitch."

"Alex, so many lives." Jax turned away from her. "You killed Leo because Cavallo told him about the human trafficking operation. Why Kathleen? What, you were worried about pillow talk?"

Alex clenched her jaw and stared at him.

"You took Leo's key and alarm code for my house. You stole my forty-five to kill Kathleen and framed me. Or was that Andrew?"

Alex turned away but Jax moved in front of her and forced her to listen.

"Rogers was too smart. He was following the evidence to you. I'd be next, right? I'm just a sap."

"No," Alex said in a whisper. "I didn't play you. I protected you. Andrew was going to kill you, Jax. I stopped him."

"Gee, thanks," Jax sneered. "I guess the hotel shooting and the motorcycle thugs at Red Vetner's were all show-and-tell? Everything was an act. Who helped you with Kathleen that night? Andrew?"

Alex face blanched and she closed her eyes. "I'm not saying anything else."

Finch had been taking mental notes and finally stepped forward. "By the way, I found Clay's other house. Get this, it's worth about a million-five. That dump I found him at down south was all for show."

"She planted the codebook in Trappe's office for Singleton to find," Trick said. "But don't feel bad, Ricky. I bought her malarkey, too. I bought Abrielle's even longer."

Jax nodded. "You never believed me about Trick, did you?"

"Are you serious? No one believed you. You see ghosts, Jax..." Her voice trailed off for a moment. "Not until I heard what you—what he—said to grand-*mére*. I'm sorry for us both, Jax. I am."

"Get her out of here, Finch." Jax watched Finch pass Alex to one of his deputies in the hall and then turned to Christie. "I don't know what to say to you, Christie. I've been stupid and foolish."

"Yep, you have," she said, patting him on the back. "Typical man."

Trick laughed. "Like I said, we're lousy at picking skirts, Ricky."

"Yeah, lousy luck with women."

Christie smiled. "That can change."

"Jax," Finch said with a strange look on his face. "You know that thing you did earlier, in the weird, 'I am Captain Patrick McCall' voice?"

"Took you long enough to ask."

Finch shook his head. "No, forget it. In fact, don't ever explain any of this again."

Chapter 81

Jax watched the deputies drive away with Alex and Abrielle. He turned and looked for something in the darkness that wouldn't make his hands quiver or his stomach churn. He didn't find anything. He stood there for a long time with his hands in his pockets and his thoughts circling, waiting to land with something better to look forward to.

Christie put a hand on his arm. "Are you okay?"

"I'll live. Thanks to you and Finch."

"No, I mean are you *okay*?"

"I'll make it." He looked down the mountain road as the line of sheriff's cruisers began their trek home. He turned to Finch who was leaning on his cruiser watching him. "Hey, Finchy, how did you find us up here? I didn't tell anyone where I was going."

"A ghost told me," Finch said.

"Are you saying—"

"Oh, hell no." Finch laughed loudly and slapped Jax on the back. "Remember that bag of personal stuff I gave you today? The one at the office? I slipped a GPS vehicle tracker in there. It's tucked into a pair of your old running shoes from under your desk."

"Damn, for a minute I thought—never mind." Jax looked around for Trick. "Good thinking."

Finch winked at Christie. "Hey, Jax, what about that dog?"

"What dog?"

"Asta? Some dog? I heard you asking yourself that when I sprang you from jail."

"Asta the dog?" Christie laughed. "From the *Thin Man* movies? His real name was Skippy."

"Uh, oh, sport," Trick said, walking out of the darkness to them. He jerked a chin toward Christie. "You didn't see her coming. She's something."

Jax cocked his head. "Christie, you like old movies?"

"Are you kidding me? Trivia, old movies. Especially Hope and Crosby. They're my favorites. Oh, and swing music, too. I was born in the wrong era."

"I didn't know that."

"You didn't ask." She tapped the side of her head. "And just so you know, Leo used to text me for the answers when you two were playing trivia."

"He cheated me?"

Finch slapped Jax on the back again. "I'll call you in the morning, Jax. But not too early." He walked off.

"Maybe you're right, Christie," Jax said. "Maybe things are about to change."

"Here we go again." Trick faded. "I'll be at home waiting for a couple good bourbons and pizza. I think you owe me some sharing later, pal."

"Sure, and doughnuts."

"Doughnuts?" Christie asked then shrugged and followed his gaze at the caravan of police cars disappear into the night. As they stood there, she began telling him about her collection of film noir and Glen Miller records.

Jax nodded but didn't hear a word. He was thinking about Roman Clay and Abrielle.

They were the worst kind of killers. They believed themselves untouchable. But they weren't. No one was. Some were just harder to reach and often ensnared others in their webs. Many innocent and many not. Did that explain Alex?

Was she once innocent before becoming entangled in her family's web? Might he have saved her?

None of it was certain. Almost none of it.

One thing was certain. He and Captain Patrick McCall were bound. Not just by life and death. By something else. Something greater than a paranormal magnet hidden beneath the Grey Coat Inn. Trick McCall saved his life, even knowing his own was lost. In return, Jax helped him stop the killing and return his honor. Perhaps what brought them together was as simple as history repeating itself until someone intervened. Or perhaps, it was something else, something deeper.

In the end, murder was like history. With both, there were consequences.

End

About the Author

Tj O'Connor first fell in love with writing while in grade school and, over the years, continued to dabble with characters and stories whenever life allowed. Recently, he has focused his energy on pursuing this dream—interrupted only by life as a security consultant and the demands of his Labrador retrievers.

He's completed nine novels and is working on another—a thriller surrounding a rogue terrorism consultant and a mind-blowing plot to attack America. Today, his alter ego is as an independent security consultant in Northern Virginia. His practice works with government agencies and private businesses, providing anti-terrorism consulting, security programs, and all types of investigations. He counts his blessings for great clients and the best professional team he could ask for.

Prior to working independently, he was a senior executive of a global risk mitigation firm that specialized in security consulting and investigations. They served clients all over the world, providing consultation in major criminal and civil investigations, risk assessments, anti-terrorism, surveillance, kidnap and ransom services, and management consulting.

During the 1980s and early 1990s, O'Connor was a government agent and had the fortune to work with some of the finest, most dedicated people he's ever known. During those years, he lived and worked around the world, conducting investigations and anti-terrorism operations. Uncle Sam sent him to places like Athens, Rome, Venice, London, Istanbul, Madrid, Frankfurt, and many others, which shall remain nameless. He will be forever thankful to the friends and colleagues he met along the way and the opportunity to have had a tiny share of the history made back then.

O'Connor was born in Worcester, Massachusetts, and was raised in New York's Hudson Valley. His loves include writing, reading, cooking, Harley Davidson motorcycles, and hanging with his lab companions, Toby and Annie Rose—and of course, his wife! They have raised five children in northern Virginia where they continue to live.

CPSIA information can be obtained
at www.ICGtesting.com
Printed in the USA
LVHW082035091122
732578LV00005B/101